Magic By Any Other Name

MAGIC
BY ANY
OTHER NAME

The Witch's Odyssey

Book One

ALISON LEVY

Published by SparkPress, a BookSparks imprint,
A division of SparkPoint Studio, LLC
Phoenix, Arizona, USA, 85007
www.gosparkpress.com

Published 2023
Printed in the United States of America
Print ISBN: 978-1-68463-224-4
E-ISBN: 978-1-68463-225-1
Library of Congress Control Number: 2023906891

Interior design by Stacey Aaronson

For everyone who has experienced generational abuse and said,

"This cycle ends with me."

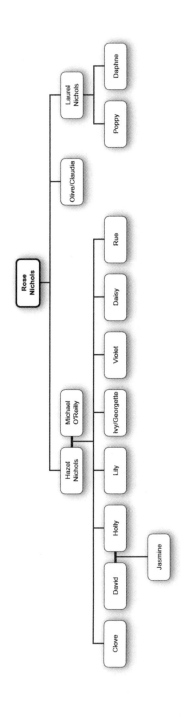

Prologue

Olive/ Claudia

RIDING THE MELODY PLAYING ON THE TURNTABLE, CLAUDIA SET aside the stress of her deadlines, her ever-growing to-do list . . . and the other thing. Over the course of thirty years, she had learned how to set that thing down—but she could never forget it, and like the ache of an old injury, it could only be ignored for so long. Eventually, it would demand her acknowledgment, if only for the moment it took to shove it back into the darkest corner of her mind. There it crouched and lurked until the ache of it crept up on her again.

A knock at the door interrupted the music. Thinking that Lulu had forgotten her keys again, Claudia opened the door without bothering to look through the window first. Her smile vanished. It wasn't Lulu. It was a young woman with a purse tucked under one arm and a potted marijuana plant in the other. Through thick-lensed glasses, the girl stared at her, a look of weary desperation etched into her face.

"Olive Nichols?" she asked.

The aching thing sprang from the darkness and clawed its way through her brain matter, tossing up memories from a life long ago discarded. Claudia felt a sickening twist in her chest, accompanied by a nauseating rush of adrenaline.

She straightened up, jaw tight. "You have the wrong address. There's no one by that name here."

A flash of confusion crossed the girl's face but then she shook her head.

"No," she said. "No, this is the right place. Are you Olive Nichols?"

Claudia's heart thundered painfully. She had hidden from this moment for thirty years, and now she felt as exposed as a fresh wound. Her trembling hand gripped the edge of the door, and she began swinging it shut. "No," she said firmly. "You need to leave."

The girl gasped in panic as the door came between them. In a split second, she shoved her purse in the path of the door, blocking it. Claudia, now panting, shoved at the bag, but the girl threw her weight against it and refused to move.

Terrified, Claudia cast her eyes about the room for a weapon. Before she could find one, the girl's voice squeaked and let out a tiny sob. "Please," she pleaded. "Please, it's you, isn't it? Aren't you my Aunt Olive?"

"Aunt?"

The word stirred an unexpected reaction in her. This was not the reckoning she had expected. Wary, she cracked the door back open and glanced around at the dry brush and dusty ground that served as her front lawn. The arid heat of the day reflected off the asphalt road in mirage-like waves, slightly distorting her view of the neighboring ranch houses. Seeing no witnesses, she turned her attention back to the stranger standing on her doorstep and gave her a closer look.

The girl was short and thin, one missed meal away from scrawny. Every disheveled piece of clothing she wore looked like it belonged to someone else. Over her shoulder, parked in the driveway, Claudia saw a rust-splattered car with a cracked windshield. The empty booster seat in the back suggested the car was probably not hers; she was no more than twenty, a bit young to be the mother of a grade-schooler.

Claudia's eyes flitted to the potted plant in the girl's arms. She sensed something from it, something faint but undeniable. She tried forcing her vision to penetrate the veneer of reality, but it was like trying to flex an atrophied muscle; her disused othersight could give her only the fuzziest glimpse of the truth.

Claudia stepped over the threshold, moving into the blazing sunlight, and examined the girl's face in detail. Though there was no obvious resemblance, there was something familiar about the slope of her cheeks and arch of her brows. But that frizzy blonde hair and freckled, flour-white skin couldn't offer a bigger contrast to the sisters she remembered.

The girl's anxious blue eyes awaited judgment, hugging the plant like a child holding a teddy bear.

"You're Laurel's daughter?" Claudia whispered as she glanced around the yard, looking for prying eyes.

"No," the girl said. "Hazel's."

"Hazel?" Startled, she spoke before she could censor her words: "My God, she must hate the sight of you."

The girl showed no sign of hurt or offense. She simply nodded, her expression flat. "I left."

Claudia gave a sharp nod and said the two things that came immediately to mind. "Don't go back. You can't stay with me."

3

"That's not why I came. I just . . . I need some help."

It was on the tip of Claudia's tongue to refuse, but her thought was interrupted by a passing car. She felt a surge of panic that the driver might see her with this fugitive from her past and frantically waved the girl inside.

Whether in response to Claudia dropping her resistance or the blast of air conditioning from inside, the girl's face flooded with relief as she stepped over the threshold and closed the door behind her.

"Thank you," she said.

"I'm not offering to help you," Claudia said, leading her into the living room. "I escaped decades ago, and I've stayed hidden ever since. I need to know how you found me so I can make sure Hazel doesn't find me the same way." She pointed to the sofa. "Sit."

The girl obeyed, dropping her purse to the floor and gently setting the plant on the end table.

"Wait here." Claudia went into the kitchen just long enough to pour three glasses of lemonade and return with them on a tray. She put the tray on the coffee table and took a seat on a chair across from the girl.

"What's your name?"

"Ivy O'Reilly," the girl said.

Ivy. Hazel was sticking with their foremothers' flora-based naming scheme. That made sense. The easiest way to continue the unbroken line of authority was to uphold old traditions. But O'Reilly? Hazel must have married.

The last time Claudia had seen her sisters was by their mother's death bed in southern England. Had Hazel met her husband overseas—Ireland?—or had she come to America first?

4

She quashed her curiosity. She couldn't afford to get bogged down in these pointless thoughts. Instead, she turned her attention to the plant. "And who's that?" she asked, nodding in its direction.

Ivy turned to the plant and said something in a foreign language. The marijuana rustled, shimmered, and jolted—and a petite feminine form emerged, leaving the plant behind. In the first instant, Claudia saw the being as she was: a brownish-green thing, vaguely human-shaped and covered in moss, grass, and sprouts. With one blink, however, her long-neglected other-sight surrendered to the glamour that coated the plant-person, so that she saw only what the magic instructed her to see: an ordinary young woman.

The Nymph smiled nervously and nodded at Claudia. "Mei-Xing Ma," she said.

Without acknowledging the girl's introduction, Claudia looked at Ivy again.

"Is she your familiar?"

Ivy shook her head. "She's my friend."

This raised a lot of questions, but Claudia was set on only one train of thought. "Is there a crack in the spell I cast to hide from Hazel?" she demanded.

The Nymph took a seat next to Ivy and reached for the third glass of lemonade as the young woman shook her head again.

"Not that I know of."

"Then how did you find me?"

Ivy took a swig of lemonade before responding, "Your web page."

"I don't have a web page."

"But you're on your friend's web page," Ivy said. "Your artist friend? The one who makes stuff out of wood?"

"Lulu," Claudia said. "She's my wife."

"I saw you in the background of one of her photos."

Olive shook her head. That didn't sound right. "Explain."

"There are some old photos of you in Aunt Laurel's house. I scanned one and used it to run a search for your face on the internet."

"You found me online from a photo taken thirty years ago?" she asked skeptically.

"I attached a spell to the search."

Claudia stared at her.

Ivy shrugged, seeming to shrink behind the glass she held to her lips. "I'm a computer science major. It wasn't hard."

Claudia drew a deep breath and exhaled slowly. She didn't know much about technology, but Ivy's explanation sounded honest. It eased her mind. Thirty years ago there had been no internet, so her spell had not accounted for such a thing—but that meant any spell Hazel had used to track her would have the same shortcoming. Claudia would be willing to bet that Hazel hadn't updated her spells to keep up with the times either—and thirty years gone, she would be far from Hazel's top priority at this point anyway. Still, she would have Lulu remove that photo from her website and make sure to close that gap in her spell, just in case.

A tad more relaxed now, she drank some lemonade before returning her focus to the girl.

"What do you want from me?"

Ivy downed the rest of her lemonade and set the glass on the tray under Claudia's unblinking eyes. Despite restlessly shifting her weight, the girl was obviously tired; she carried her lack of sleep in shadows under her eyes. In those eyes, Claudia saw a maelstrom of fear, desperation, and misery—though deep in the swirl of it, very nearly consumed by its madness, there was also a faint glimmer of hope.

In Ivy, Claudia saw herself thirty years ago. Just like Claudia when she ran, Ivy had probably burned through every last reserve of strength just to leave Hazel's house, and now she lived from one moment to the next in abject terror that the matriarch was on her heels. Every thought of Hazel made her heart race and her stomach twist. And yet, the temptation to go back home, even though doing so would mean a lifetime of unhappiness, must be overwhelming. In the first flush of freedom, the familiarity of pain seemed less frightening than the unknown life ahead. Claudia knew that feeling well.

Clenching her fists, Ivy leveled her shaky gaze at her hostess. "Can you give me the spell you used?"

Claudia flexed her fingers and ran her tongue over her teeth. Her impulse was to refuse. With every person who learned a secret, the less power it had, and she had kept this secret to herself for thirty years. But if Hazel snatched Ivy back, it would put Claudia in jeopardy. For their mutual safety, Ivy needed to disappear.

She closed her eyes, drew a breath, and unlocked her vault.

"The spells aren't special," she said. "Any concealment spell will work. You've probably been using them since you left."

Ivy's eyes narrowed behind her glasses. After exchanging glances with Mei-Xing, she looked at Claudia askance.

"It's true," said Claudia.

7

"But that can't be it," the girl pressed. "Mom can break through any concealment I cast. I know my craft is the weakest in the family, but no way yours is stronger than Mom's."

Even in her desperation, Ivy still had the presence of mind to be critical of her aunt's suspiciously simple advice. Claudia liked her. It was a rare witch who had the strength to run from a powerful family, and a rarer one still who had the strength to run from Hazel. She would need that strength in the years to come. And she would need the secret. Claudia let go of her lingering reluctance and opened a sliver of her heart.

"There is one more element," she said. "You need to change your name."

Claudia saw her niece's blue eyes light up with surprise, then doubt. Claudia nodded reassuringly.

Clearly unconvinced, Ivy glanced at Mei-Xing again. The Nymph shrugged.

"Change my name?" Ivy said. "That's all I have to do? But that's so easy."

"No," Claudia said, her tone one of a parent scolding a child. "It's not easy."

Ivy immediately shut down, her face overtaken by a well-worn glaze of neutrality. Claudia saw the hand of her sister at work in the girl's reaction. Taking a reprimand without question or argument was exactly the sort of response most likely to keep Hazel's temper in check.

"You need to *become* your new name," Claudia said. "O'Reilly or not, you are a Nichols. That name has been branded into you. Figuratively and"—she flicked a mystic spark onto Ivy's face—"literally."

The astral glow of the Fae letters—their clan mark—illuminated Ivy's cheek, casting spectral shadows over her freckles. The Nymph gasped and muttered something in her language. Ivy brushed the offending patch of skin with two fingers and frowned. Claudia remembered that feeling. She still had the mark burned into her aura by her late mother, the mark she only learned of on the day she saw her mother apply it to newborn Laurel's face.

"That mark came from Hazel," Claudia told Ivy. "As the matriarch, she can sense every Nichols mark. That's how she'll find you."

A visible jolt went through Ivy. Her lip trembled and she looked around the room as if expecting Hazel to jump out at her. She swallowed hard, pulled her knees up to her chest, and hugged them tight.

"How do I hide?" she asked in a voice that had shriveled into a childlike version of itself.

Ivy gently rocked forward and backward in her seat. Mei-Xing stroked her messy curls and cooed in her strange tongue. A swell of pity mingled with annoyance in Claudia's anxious mind. She clasped her hands together, rested them in her lap, and locked her gaze on her niece.

"You have to absorb the new name into yourself," she explained. "Create a new person and step into her life. Invent a past as rich and detailed as you can and live the lie so convincingly that you really become that woman." She leaned forward. "You have to distance yourself from the Nichols identity to such an extent that it no longer feels like it belongs to you. You must become an outside observer of Ivy and see her as a person apart

9

from you." She sighed. "It's easier said than done. It took me years."

"Years?" Ivy said, looking alarmed. "How did you hide until then?"

"A lot of spellcraft and moving around. A lot of living in diffi-cult, unsavory places that your mother wouldn't search. I felt my Nichols mark burning on my cheek every day like a beacon, like it was screaming for her attention. I made up a new name, invented a fictional past, and dove into both until I was submerged. I . . . drowned my old self. About three years into my escape, I was at a grocery store and picked up a bottle of olive oil, and it gave me déjà vu. It wasn't until an hour later that I remembered that Olive used to be my name. That's when I felt ready to put down roots. I came to this town, I met Lulu, and I made a new life. I only need a mini-mum of spellcraft these days—although," she added with a huff, "I'll need more now that you've brought the past back to me."

An apology in her eyes, Ivy opened her mouth—but Claudia held up a hand to stop her. "What's done is done," she said. "If you want to make it up to me, don't let Hazel find you."

"She hate her name," the Nymph said, her voice choppy from her thick accent. "Since I meet her, she hate it."

Ivy nodded assent. "It's never felt like mine. It feels like the name of the daughter Mom wanted, not me."

Knowing Hazel, Claudia thought that was more than a little likely. "Good," she said. "That'll make it easier. Let it fall into the dust and make yourself someone new."

"Was it hard?" Ivy whispered into her knees. "Getting away from Mom? Was it hard?"

Sitting there, consumed by fear, the girl was a pitiful sight. Though technically an adult, she seemed very small.

"It was scary," Claudia admitted. "I never knew if Hazel was right around the corner, or if she had just cast me off like my mother used to cast off men once she had their money. I knew tracking me down and securing my loyalty by threats would be a lot harder for her than just having children she could control right from the start. But I still worried."

Ivy stayed quiet, seeming to turn this over in her mind. It occurred to Claudia that she had just admitted to sacrificing her hypothetical nieces to secure her own escape. Thirty years ago, she had thought of it only in passing. Those nieces hadn't been real at the time, so they'd been easy to ignore. She had not thought of it again, in fact, until today, when an actual niece appeared on her doorstep.

With a quiet sigh, she let the guilt slide into her past. It had been a necessary cost to build her new life, and she wasn't tempted to apologize. Whether Ivy realized it or not, she was now sacrificing those she'd left behind for the same reason.

After a moment, the girl's grip on her knees loosened. "She has my sisters," she said. "She has my cousins. She likes all of them more than me. Maybe she'll let me go."

"Hope for the best, plan for the worst," Claudia said. "Go from place to place, change your appearance, and commit yourself to being a new person. Do not make friends. Do not fall in love. Do not use more magic than necessary. Do not sleep deeply until you can safely say that you are no longer Ivy O'Reilly. Turn your thoughts away from the Nichols family as often as necessary and only look forward."

Ivy slowly nodded as she let her legs slide down until her feet were on the floor. She closed her eyes for several breaths. Then she opened them, looked directly into Claudia's eyes, and asked, "Was it worth it?"

For the first time since opening the door, Claudia smiled. "Yes," she said. "Living a life I chose for myself, instead of the one my mother or sister chose, was absolutely worth the struggle. Never doubt it."

The sound of a lumbering vehicle gradually rose from underneath the constant hum of semis on the highway and grew louder as it approached. A shock of recognition went through Claudia; she jumped to her feet, snatched up the tray of glasses, dashed into the kitchen, dumped the glasses in the sink, and ran back to the living room.

"That's Lulu!" she said. She grabbed the purse off the floor and shoved it into the Nymph's lap. "You need to go!"

The girls stood and headed to the door without argument. Though they moved quickly, it wasn't fast enough for Claudia's liking. Through the front window, she saw Lulu coming up the walk with a new chunk of wood cradled in her arms and artistic inspiration dancing in her eyes. Claudia saw her wife's gaze flit over the unfamiliar car in their driveway as the girls arrived at the door, bag and plant in hand.

Ivy smiled at her with weary but genuine gratitude. "Thank you."

"Forget you were here," Claudia said—and as she opened the door, she hissed, "My name is Claudia."

Mei-Xing moved onto the front steps, the purse slung over her shoulder. Just as Ivy, plant in her arms, stepped forward to follow, Claudia, on impulse, put a hand on her shoulder and leaned close to her ear.

"You said you're the weakest," she whispered, "but you're wrong. It takes strength to walk away from Hazel. If you're the only one of your sisters who's run away, that makes you the strongest. Believe in your strength. You're going to need it."

Before Ivy could reply, Claudia pushed her forward, and the girl continued moving out the door without complaint—the automatic action of someone who was used to taking orders.

As they crossed paths with Lulu on the front walk, the girls smiled politely at her. Ivy flicked two fingers in Lulu's direction and a subtle shimmer went through the air. Claudia blinked and the marijuana plant in Ivy's arms suddenly became a shoulder bag. She smirked a little. The girl was good with glamours.

The two young women waved goodbye with calls of "Thanks, Claudia!" before ducking into the car and driving off, soon disappearing around the corner.

Lulu watched them go, then turned a quizzical eye to her wife. "Who was that, Claude?"

"Another bunch looking for the pharmacy," she said lightly. "They saw me out front and stopped to ask for directions."

"Oh," Lulu said with an eye roll. "Apple Maps strikes again." She glanced in the direction the girls' car had gone and cocked an eyebrow at her wife. "What was their story?"

With Ivy gone, Claudia's past retreated back into the shaded places of her mind. She smiled at the love of her life as she wrapped herself in the familiarity of her chosen identity.

"You know," she said with a smile, "I can't remember."

1 Ivy

NOSE INCHES FROM THE DIRT, IVY STARED AT THE FOREST GROUND as her glasses slipped down her face. She drew wild, ragged breaths, all thick with earthy smells. Rocks dug into her knees, and both of her hands gripped fistfuls of grass as she tried to steady herself. She sweated heavily, but her skin felt ice cold.

A mossy hand snaked its way between her face and the ground. A tiny stem sprouted from the palm and a little bud formed on its tip. Within seconds, a white flower bloomed and released a fragrant aroma that sent a shock through Ivy's senses and made her yank her head up and sneeze. The vertigo vanished, and the clammy feeling in her skin began to subside.

Ivy pushed her glasses back into place just in time to see Mei-Xing standing over her, reabsorbing the flower into her hand. Without her glamour, she blended seamlessly into the trees and shrubs that surrounded them. The last light of the setting sun coated her inhuman body in an orange glow.

"You okay?" Mei-Xing asked in Mandarin.

Ivy saw in the Nymph's iridescent eyes that Mei-Xing knew she was not okay. Ever since they had left Olive's home, Ivy's anxiety, already at manic levels, had reached new heights. It was as if her body's adrenaline valve was broken; it turned on at the slightest provocation and then wouldn't turn off. A large part of her anxiety stemmed from having learned about the spectral Nichols mark. Now that she knew it was there, she felt it burning on her cheek—a sensation that kept her tense and dizzy all day and night. Though she told herself that the feeling was all in her head, it felt real. She was afraid—and she hated herself for being afraid.

"Yeah," she lied. "I'm fine."

Mei-Xing pulled Ivy to her feet and held her by the arm until she could stand without swaying. Once steady, Ivy plucked off her glasses and wiped the tears from her eyes. She didn't remember starting to cry. It felt more like her body was leaking excess fear. She looked at the tears on the back of her hand, smeared across a patch of freckled skin. The freckles began at her knuckles and ran in thick clusters all the way up her arm, over her chest, and across her face. Every time she saw them, she was reminded of her mother's smirk whenever her sister Lily called her "Dalmatian girl."

Ivy inhaled deeply. The air in the National Forest was crisp, clean, and pleasantly cool. Camping in places like this was dirty and uncomfortable, but since Ivy knew her mother wouldn't be caught dead in anything less than a four-star resort, it made her feel safe. Mei-Xing, meanwhile, was revitalized by their environment; the moss and sprouts that covered her body were becoming greener and fuller by the hour, and her potted plant was perking up with her. After weeks of sweltering heat, during which the Nymph had by necessity stayed in the shade as much as possible, she was now openly walking around in the noon sun. If not for having to deal with Ivy's anxiety attacks, she would be in great spirits.

Knowing that made Ivy feel guilty.

"I'm sorry," she said. "I just . . . I saw that car pass us, and it looked like my sister Holly's. All I could think was that Mom was looking for me." She glanced around at the forest. "Where's our car?"

"That way," Mei-Xing said, pointing. "When you pulled over, you jumped out and ran into the woods."

"Oh," Ivy whispered. "I didn't realize."

The Nymph made a familiar face that Ivy was never sure how to interpret. The petals of her lips wrinkled and fluttered as the bark-like structures of her cheeks swelled. Sometimes she made that face when annoyed, and sometimes when she was sad. In the current context, Ivy wasn't sure which emotion she might be expressing.

"Your mother's in Boston," Mei-Xing said. "She probably hasn't even realized yet that you didn't go back to college. And even if she has, she doesn't know where you are."

Eyes closed, Ivy took deep breaths. "She could have reported me missing."

"The police aren't going to—"

"Not the police," Ivy said. "She would go to the kobold network and post a reward for any witch who finds me."

Mei-Xing's moss rippled and her grass shoots waved as if caught in a breeze. "I doubt it," she said. "She doesn't like spending money on you. She might even be glad you left."

"I hope so," Ivy replied. Her blue eyes swept around the twilit forest, searching for her mother's spies. "If she finds me, she'll bring me home." The pitch of her voice rose. "I can't fight her. Even if I was as strong with magic as Lily or Clove, I'd never be able to use it against her. I can't." A new wave of vertigo seized her. She heaved a breath and sobbed. "I should just go home."

Ivy felt strong hands grip her by the shoulders. Startled, her face snapped up toward her friend's and the two locked gazes. In the ever-shifting colors of the Nymph's eyes, Ivy saw a cool resolve that she desperately envied.

"When we met," Mei-Xing said, "I thought there was no way your mother could be as terrible as you described. Then I traveled to America with you. Your mother hadn't seen you in weeks, but she waited two days before showing up unannounced at your aunt's house to check on you. She brushed past me, then barely hugged you before going straight for your suitcase. She dug through your things like a customs agent searching for contraband. She confiscated almost everything that you had bought for yourself overseas. I kept waiting for you to speak up, but you just watched it happen, like you'd been expecting it. Your mother took your things and left. Two days later, I saw your cousin Daphne wearing a skirt you'd bought."

Ivy's tears dried up. She was surprised that incident had made such an impact on Mei-Xing. In her memory, it was just one of a thousand similar events. Hell, the skirt was nothing; her mother had given Daphne her bedroom six years ago, forcing Ivy to move into her Aunt Laurel's house. From a very young age, Ivy had learned that if she really treasured something, she had to keep it hidden. By the time her mother came to see her after her return home from China, she'd long since removed the new items she most valued and hidden them in her room. Then, she'd intentionally left her suitcase out, still packed, for her mother to rummage through so she wouldn't dig around anywhere else. To Ivy, this was as natural as putting on a coat in cold weather. It took someone like Mei-Xing, someone normal, to remind her that her upbringing wasn't ordinary.

"If you go home," Mei-Xing continued, "it will never stop. Your mother will steal from you all your life. Worse, she'll make you marry that man, have children, and then steal them from you."

Ivy's heart thundered, and she gasped for breath, the world spinning around her in a tilting blur. She didn't want to marry Zachary. That was what her mother wanted. Running away was terrifying—but not half as terrifying as the thought of spending the rest of her life living out her mother's plan. With great effort, Ivy took deep breaths until she felt her pulse slow.

"I'm ready to go now," she finally said. "Thanks."

Mei-Xing nodded. The swell in her cheeks deflated and her lips plumped. Her multicolored eyes drifted to the darkening horizon. "It's late," she said. "I'll be unconscious soon."

"I'm wired," Ivy said. "I'll keep driving."

Side by side, they walked through the forest toward the car. Mei-Xing resumed the glamour Ivy had devised for her as they neared the road, but even cloaked in a human guise, Mei-Xing was still subject to her Nymph biology. As the sky dimmed, she drooped and swayed.

The spell that connected them was a *Hathiya*, the spell a witch used to bind a familiar, but it was unlike the one Ivy had learned from her mother and aunt. A traditional *Hathiya* was a one-way street, allowing the witch to draw a steady flow of power from her familiars. The *Hathiya* Ivy had invented was a loop, binding her and Mei-Xing together in a way that allowed them to draw on each other's power. As such, Mei-Xing could draw on Ivy's power to stay awake at night if she wanted to—but both Mei-Xing and Ivy made a point of using the loop as little as possible. They adhered to this standard as if it was part of an agreement, when in fact they had never actually discussed it.

By the time they spotted their car, Mei-Xing was staggering, her eyes barely open, and Ivy was struggling to keep her upright. She was glad her friend was so small; supporting her was a lot easier than lugging her aunt to bed after too much wine. Even so, when the Nymph's legs gave out several yards short of the car and Ivy was forced to drag her, it was no easy task.

When Ivy had her almost to the back bumper, Mei-Xing opened her eyes and flopped her head to the side.

"S'bear?" she mumbled.

Confused, Ivy glanced over her shoulder and gasped.

A huge, furry mass hunched by the driver's door of her car. The creature shifted its weight and grunted, giving no sign that it had heard them approach.

Heart pounding in her ears, Ivy slowly lowered Mei-Xing to the ground with one arm and lifted her free hand. Trembling, she managed to work her craft, casting a glamour around them to make them both invisible.

A glamour was the first thing she could think of, but she wasn't sure it would work. Ivy was a city girl, and her magic lessons reflected her upbringing. A glamour would fool human eyes, but a bear's? She didn't know. And even if the bear couldn't see them, it might still smell them. Crouched next to her prone friend, she put one hand on Mei-Xing's arm, tried to think of a better spell, and waited.

Suddenly, the bear rose up and lowered one front paw into the driver's window, which Ivy now realized was smashed. It fished around the inside of the car before withdrawing its paw, Ivy's purse hooked in its claws. Squinting through the darkness, she watched in astonishment as the animal pried open the bag, dumped the contents on the ground, and inspected the items carefully before picking up her wallet.

Ivy gaped. There was a half-eaten granola bar in her purse that this "bear" had completely ignored.

She was still considering her next action when the animal reached into the car again, this time stretching its arm toward the backseat—toward Mei-Xing's potted plant.

In a flush of protective anger, memories of offensive spells rushed into Ivy's mind. She stepped through the glamour, leaving Mei-Xing safely hidden, and moved toward the thief with her fists balled.

"Hey!" she yelled.

She instantly regretted shouting when the animal snorted, reared up—a full five feet taller than her—and turned around with shocking fluidity.

Though it had bear-like qualities, this was definitely not a bear; its head was too narrow, its snout was too broad, its ears were too large—and its coat, which in the dark had looked brown, was actually spotted throughout the torso and striped on the legs. The thief seemed to smile at her, showing off a mouth full of pointed teeth, as it leaned toward her, its eyes afire with an unnatural glow. It emitted a wild, jittering sound like the crazed giggling of a madman.

Though frightened to her core, Ivy remained staunch. She wasn't such a novice that she couldn't tell the difference between someone with real power (like her mother) versus someone wearing a veil of power. This giant hyena might look like a monstrous animal, but that furry hide was just a disguise.

Hardening her expression, she threw out her arms to her sides, summoned a spark of power, swung her fingers to eye level, and spat an incantation.

The grass under the hyena's feet crackled and burst into white flame. The hyena yelped and jumped back but the fire followed, abandoning the lightly singed grass and gripping the creature's paws like flaming socks. Shrieking, the hyena bolted, taking the blaze with it, into the forest, the eerie white lights on its feet blinking through the shadows as it ran.

Ivy heaved a ragged sigh, both relieved and alarmed. This couldn't be a coincidence. Had her mother sent this creature? Was it one of her familiars? If so, it was now on its way to report her whereabouts.

She quickly gathered up the contents of her shredded purse. They needed to keep moving.

She brushed the broken glass out of the driver's seat, tossed her wallet into the glove box, and put her torn bag on the floor before retrieving Mei-Xing from behind the car. As she clumsily loaded the Nymph's limp form into the passenger seat, she heard a sound echoing in the distance. A painful, laugh-like howl. A prickling sensation went up her spine. She hastily buckled Mei-Xing in and darted around the car to the driver's side.

21

Ivy jumped behind the wheel and fired up the engine. If she drove all night, they could be in Las Vegas by tomorrow. If the hyena followed them, she would keep driving. If it kept following them, she would keep going. If she had to go to California, or Mexico, or Russia, she would. Just like Olive told her, she would keep moving forward and never look back.

2 Ishak

ISHAK'S FEET CONTINUED BURNING LONG AFTER THE WHITE flames extinguished. The return through the forest was excruciating, like walking on lava, yet he smiled all the way. He had never expected to meet another witch. It was the opportunity he'd been praying for.

Just before midnight, Kivuli Panon met him in the motel parking lot. The gold bangles on the witch's wrists and ankles tinkled as she walked, and her colorful coat waved in the wind. She thrust her hand, palm up, into his inhuman face, filling his nose with her scent: the faint odor of smoke, old leather, and dead roses.

"What have you brought me?" she demanded.

"I was injured," he said, his voice dull and mechanical.

She narrowed her eyes, her hand slowly dropping. "You have nothing?"

"I was injured."

Her lips drew into a tight line. Ishak waited, silently praying that she would not ask him to explain his wounds. If she asked, he would be compelled by her magic to answer and tell her about the blonde witch—and keeping this secret was his best chance of escape.

Kivuli Panon glared, her eyes twin cauldrons brewing shadow and sin. She yanked back her arm, then slapped him hard across the snout. The blow stung for only a moment. She was so small that even if she had thrown all her weight into it, it would not have left a bruise. A less intimidating woman Ishak had never met.

His instinct was to snarl and lunge at her—but although his brain sent the command to his muscles, his body did not obey. The brand on his back that marked him as her familiar intercepted the order and silenced it, once again bending him to her will.

"I can barely afford another night in this shithole motel!" she yelled. "Bring me money!"

With a snarl, she turned on her heel and made a beeline for the motel.

Watching her retreating form, Ishak remembered the first time he saw her. It was months ago, across the ocean in his village of Kabultiloa. He'd been enjoying a meal with his wife, Kalilah.

Fighting against the restraints of the brand, he growled. He had not seen his wife since this bitch abducted them both and branded them as her familiars.

Repressing the burning pain in his feet, he took off at a run back the way he had come. If he hurried, he might catch up to that blonde witch by sunrise.

3  Mei-Xing

THE RISING SUN BROUGHT MEI-XING TO CONSCIOUSNESS IN THE
passenger seat. They were parked at a rest stop just off a highway.
Theirs was the only car in the lot, though on the opposite side of
the restroom building she saw several eighteen-wheelers.

Ivy had fallen asleep with her forehead pressed to the steering
wheel. A cool morning breeze blew through the smashed driver's
window, carrying the warring scents of diesel fumes and pine and
rustling Ivy's limp curls.

Wanting to let her friend get the rest she needed, Mei-Xing
quietly slipped out of the car and walked across the parking lot
toward the tree line. The light of the dawn warmed her skin,
feeding her chloroplasts. As her hunger slowly abated, her slug-
gish body livened. She felt the nearby trees and shrubs enjoying
the light alongside her, though none of them housed Nymphs.

Mei-Xing had sensed other Nymphs at various times since
arriving in America, but she had not interacted with them. Even
half a world away from her birth grove, she still feared word of
her whereabouts would reach her family.

She turned her back on the forest and returned to the car. Her
grove thought she was dead, and that was the way she wanted it.

She spent the next couple of hours sitting on the hood of the car, soaking up the sun and listening to the gradual increase in traffic, letting Ivy sleep so she'd be able to drive when she woke. Mei-Xing disliked driving. She was a plant, and a plant had no business working a machine—though Ivy had taught her how a few months earlier in preparation for this escape.

She and Ivy had tried keeping the lessons a secret; Ivy was afraid her family would see them and deduce their plan to escape. Mei-Xing didn't tell her but all of Ivy's six sisters and two cousins had at some point noticed that the lessons were happening. Most had rolled their eyes and muttered darkly about Ivy wasting so much effort on a "servant." Underneath her glamour, Mei-Xing had felt the bark of her chest tighten with irritation. *Servant* was the least offensive word they used.

Of all the Nichols clan, the only one kind enough to treat her as an equal and perceptive enough to correctly deduce their intention was Rue, the youngest.

As they loaded up Ivy's car with luggage, Rue came to say goodbye. The rest of the family assumed Ivy was going back to college for the fall semester and didn't bother to acknowledge her departure. But Rue sprinted out the front door, threw her arms around her big sister, and whispered, "You're not coming back, are you?"

"No," Ivy whispered back.

"I wanna go too."

Not a surprising request. Mei-Xing had noticed that Rue was frequently mistreated by big sisters Clove and Lily, always under their mother's willfully blind eye.

"You can't," said Ivy.

"Please," Rue pleaded. "Don't leave me here."

Mei-Xing saw Ivy's resolution waver. She put a hand on her shoulder, and Ivy lifted her face and gave her a little smile of reassurance. It eased Mei-Xing's concern, but not by much.

She'd known from the moment they agreed to run that she would have to be Ivy's support, just like Ivy had been hers when they left China. Abandoning everything you had ever known, no matter how unpleasant it might be, was wildly disorienting. Having a hand to hold made all the difference.

The two Nichols girls looked so unlike each other that it was hard to believe they were related. Sunny curls versus midnight waves, blueberry eyes versus chocolate, speckled milk skin versus olive cream. Only the haze of deeply rooted fear that surrounded them was identical.

"You can come find me when you're eighteen," Ivy told Rue. "Just," she added quietly, "don't tell them where you're going."

Rue pinched her eyes tight, tears leaking out the sides. After a moment of clinging to Ivy, she nodded.

"Mom has OnStar in all the cars," she said. "You should ditch yours soon and get another one."

Ivy squeezed her baby sister hard before disentangling herself from her embrace. Once separated, the sisters quickly moved apart and went about their respective business, as if worried that someone would be suspicious to see them together. Their mutual paranoia spread to Mei-Xing, and she cast her gaze around to search for spies.

"Can you really trust her?" she asked Ivy in Mandarin. "It's a big secret for a thirteen-year-old."

"If I'm caught," said Ivy, "it'll be harder for her to escape in five years. She won't risk that."

It was as convincing an argument as Mei-Xing could imagine.

She slid off the hood and stepped around to the side of the car. The sun was warm, the highway humming. It was high time for them to get back on the road. She reached through the glassless window, intent on giving Ivy a shake, but stopped, her hand inches from her friend, when her eyes fell upon a distinctive mark in the dirt at her feet: a huge pawprint. A hazy image crawled out of her memory. A bear. Was that where the print had come from? *But that was in the forest. This is a rest stop.* Concerned, she nudged Ivy awake.

Ivy yawned, swiped at her blurry eyes, and rubbed at the imprint left on her forehead by the steering wheel. She looked at Mei-Xing—and immediately saw that something was wrong. "What is it?" she asked anxiously.

Mei-Xing pointed down at her feet. Ivy leaned out the window to look, and the sleep left her face immediately.

"*Aah!*" she cried, throwing open the car door so suddenly that Mei-Xing had to jump backward to avoid being clipped. "*Aah!* It followed us! It followed us!"

Mei-Xing frowned. "What followed us? The bear?"

"Not a bear!" Ivy cried as she exited the car and began to pace in circles. "*Aah!* Not a bear! It was a . . . it was a . . . Were-hyena!"

Through the babble and desperate gasps of Ivy's anxiety attack, Mei-Xing slowly gleaned the full story. Ivy was convinced her mother had sent the hyena-man, but Mei-Xing suspected otherwise. If Hazel had bothered to spend the time and magic to send a familiar after her unloved daughter, she would have been ruthless about it; she wouldn't sanction one of her servants quietly watching the runaway instead of snatching her up. Still, Mei-Xing understood Ivy's fear. The first few months after leaving China, she'd jumped at the slightest rustle of leaves, convinced that someone from her grove had come to fetch her. Ivy had spent a lot of time talking with her, listening to her, and crafting spells to keep her hidden. It was just what Mei-Xing had needed, and she wanted to return the favor now.

Whether connected to the Nichols clan or not, the Werehyena was clearly following them. Step one of dealing with a threat was to work Ivy through her anxiety—the quicker the better.

Distraction usually worked. "You still haven't picked a new name," she said.

"W-what?" Ivy panted, wide-eyed.

Mei-Xing hooked her arm through Ivy's elbow and led her to the passenger side of the car. "A new name," she repeated. "Like your aunt told you. Have you thought of a name yet?"

The sudden change of subject stalled Ivy's panic attack. She blinked rapidly behind her glasses and looked at her friend in bewilderment.

Mei-Xing smiled, opened the car door, and eased Ivy down onto the passenger seat. "You've never liked your name. Is there another one you do like?"

The tension gradually melted from Ivy's face as she sank into thought. Mei-Xing got behind the wheel and fired up the engine. As she steered the car onto the highway—trying to hold back a grimace at the unnatural feeling—she saw Ivy shift in her seat out of the corner of her eye.

"How did you choose your name?" Ivy asked.

Mei-Xing smiled. It sounded like her friend's mind was officially diverted. They would get back to the problem of the Were-hyena soon, but for now this was best.

"It was the name of the stewardess on our flight out of Shanghai," Mei-Xing said. "I didn't know anything about human names, so I just picked the first one that sounded nice to me."

"Maybe I should do that," Ivy said. "Just pick something."

"No," Mei-Xing said. "You're not me. You've hated your name for a long time; you must have thought about what names you like better."

Ivy fell silent for a long beat.

"My sister Holly," she finally said, drumming her fingers on the armrest, "had this friend who would come to the house sometimes when I was seven or eight, and the friend had a big sister who always came to pick her up. She had curly hair—kind of like mine, except *her* mother didn't make her get straightening treatments. She was curvy, too, definitely heavier than Mom would have let me or my sisters get. And she always wore mini-skirts and V-necks and form-fitting dresses, all the stuff I wasn't allowed to wear. She was so cool." Ivy, smiling like she was nursing a juicy secret, leaned toward Mei-Xing. "Every time she came by to get her sister, my mother would look her up and down like she was made of slime; sometimes she even made snide remarks about her clothes. But this girl, who was maybe seventeen, would roll her eyes at Mom and walk right past her, just . . . fearless. Sometimes she even snapped bubblegum in Mom's face. I wanted to be her."

The happy memory of a disrespectful teenage girl had lifted Ivy clear of her anxiety. Mei-Xing smiled and nodded encouragingly. "What was her name?"

"Georgette," said Ivy. "That's pretty, don't you think?"

"Georgette," repeated Mei-Xing, feeling out the word. She didn't know much about names, but this one had a friendly sound to it. And saying it made Ivy happy. That made it special. "I like it. Should I start calling you Georgette?"

"*Hmm.*" Ivy exhaled. "Maybe we could try it out for a few days and see if it takes."

"Okay." Mei-Xing drew a deep breath and flexed her fingers around the steering wheel. "Well, Georgette, I think we need to deal with the hyena-man."

She braced for another panic attack but was pleasantly surprised not to hear any gasps from her friend.

"You're right," Ivy said in a surprisingly calm voice, tapping her foot against the floor mat. "Let's work something out."

4   Ishak

AFTER PICKING UP THE SCENT TRAIL, ISHAK FOLLOWED IT FOR miles. At his fastest, he couldn't match the speed of the car—particularly on burned feet—but after a couple of hours of constant running, he found the vehicle parked off the highway.

In the hazy glow of the rest stop's lights, he stood next to the car and watched the two occupants sleeping.

Seeing the witch up close, his optimism dimmed. The girl was young, probably in her early twenties. And she was short and skinny. Despite the magic she'd used to chase him off, she didn't look like a formidable opponent. The other one, meanwhile, confused his senses. She looked normal—thin, delicate, young like her companion—but her scent was contradictory. She smelled like grass and dirt. *Not human*, he soon concluded. That boosted his hopes. There was a glamour on the plant creature that was strong enough to fool his eyes. The witch, young and small though she was, must have some skill.

Ishak stared at the girls, fighting against the *Hathiya* brand on his back. Kivuli Panon's orders to him were very clear—steal and don't be seen. Try as he might, he couldn't knowingly violate those commands. Instead, he waited—trembling and silently praying.

Wake up, little witch. I have to find Kalilah. I have spent months suspended in nothingness, feeling only pain as Kivuli Panon drains me of power. But Kalilah was with me; I felt her as clearly as I feel the wind in my fur tonight. Kivuli Panon abducted us together, branded us together, and transported us here together. So where is she now? Kivuli Panon tells me nothing and forbids me from asking.

I have known Kalilah all my life, little witch. We were children together, and we grew up learning Bultungin ways side by side. She was a better pupil than I; while I struggled with transformation, she took to it with ease. I caught up eventually, but she never let me forget that she was first, even after we married. How I love her. And yet I am yoked by a spell and can do nothing to help her. Wake up, little witch. I need you. I must find my wife.

But hours passed, and still the girls slept. Dawn approached. Kivuli Panon would be expecting him.

Brokenhearted, he left the girls' car and ran off. He had passed a small town on the way. He would find something there to steal and take it to Kivuli Panon, and she would return him to the darkness until she summoned him again.

5   Nicolás

SOMETHING'S OFF.

Dropping packets of herbs into a bag, Nicolás felt as if his hands were on automatic pilot. He smelled the Botanica's usual mélange of herbs, oils, and candles, but today the aromatic haze filled not only the shop but also his head, wrapping his brain in a fog.

As he completed the order and folded over the top of the bag, he took a moment to self-assess. He didn't feel sick, just off. He knew this feeling and knew what it signified, but he couldn't imagine why it was happening now.

"Nico!" his *tía* hissed, snapping her fingers at him. "Get your head out of your ass!"

Jolting to attention, Nicolás immediately shifted into his customer service persona.

"Here, *Tía*," he said, handing her the bag. "It's ready."

Aunt Mariana snatched the bag and shot him one last disapproving look before turning back to face her customer. She tossed her head, bouncing her black hair about her lightly lined face, and smiled winningly as she purred, "Here you are, Ms. Kazimiera. We are always grateful for your business. Come again soon."

The customer smiled as she accepted the bag with one gloved hand. As she turned to leave, she glanced back at Nicolás over the tops of her sunglasses.

Nico tried to smile, but, as usual, Ms. Kazimiera's eyes made him shudder. There was something uncomfortably eager in those amber eyes, something . . . hungry.

Seeing him shiver, she grinned. Then she pulled her wide-brimmed hat lower, draping her face in shadow, and walked away. The door chimed as she exited. She opened a parasol over her head and sauntered out of sight.

Mariana grabbed him by the arm, pinching his bicep. She jabbed a finger an inch from his nose.

"Stay away from that woman," she said. "*El diablo conoce su sonrisa.*"

"*Sí, Tía,*" he agreed. "I think she'd eat me alive."

Nodding, she started to turn away but then paused. As often happened, something passed between them—an empathic understanding. She grasped his chin in her hand and pulled his face closer to hers.

"You feel strange," she said, peering deep into his eyes. "When did the feeling begin?"

"This morning. I woke up with it."

"*Hmm.*" She tapped her front teeth with a long fingernail before smacking her lips. "Do you remember your dreams last night?"

He had already given his dreams some thought but hadn't reached any conclusions. Maybe Mariana could provide him with some insight.

"I dreamt of a desert," he said. "I was driving on a road that ran through it. Something was chasing me. I felt like it was behind me every step of the way, but every time I looked back, nothing was there. Then I was surrounded by . . . lights, like a huge cloud of fireflies but humming with music. They crowded me until I couldn't see or hear anything else. When they cleared, I saw myself at home, looking out the window, but the Botanica stood where the deli should have been." He scratched a spot on his cheek, feeling some stubble that had escaped the razor that morning. "What does it mean?"

Hands knitted together before her chin, two fingers over her lips, Mariana stood still and closed her eyes. Nico recognized this as her interpretive stance, the pose she adopted while her spirit allies helped her find truth. He waited patiently until she opened her eyes and lowered her hands.

"What was the music?" she asked.

The question surprised him. He hadn't considered the music. Returning to the dream as best he could, he tried replaying the moment. The song was familiar, but it took a lot of concentration for him to place it. "You know," he said slowly, "I think it was Neil's ringtone."

She cocked her head, squinting.

"Neil," he repeated. "My roommate."

Snapping her eyes closed, she smiled and nodded. "Neil!" She chuckled. "Of course."

"What does it mean, *Tia?*"

"What do *you* think it means?"

He had to fight the urge to roll his eyes. Mariana was never one to pass up a teachable moment.

With a sigh, he scanned his memory of the dream one more time. "Maybe I'll go on a trip and learn something important to my training?" he ventured.

Mariana stared at him for such an uncomfortably long time that he knew he must be wrong. Eventually, she pursed her lips and puffed a breath through her nose.

"I've taught you better than that," she said. "Think what you told me, *mijo*. You didn't see yourself on the road but then you did see yourself at home. What does that tell you?"

With the illumination of her words, he saw his mistake clearly. "I wasn't seeing through my own eyes," he said. "I was experiencing someone else's desert journey."

"*Eso es.*" Mariana nodded briskly, satisfied.

"Someone," Nico added, "who's coming to me."

She smiled at him, her eyes full of pride.

Energized by her silent praise, he asked, "But what about the lights? And the music?"

The pride evaporated, replaced by aggravation. She threw up her hands and launched into a rapid string of Spanish, only half of which Nico caught. What he did understand was that she was disappointed.

"Clients will come to you with their dreams, and they will expect answers!" she finally said in English. "*Dios mío*, I've spent ten years nurturing your natural *curandero* gifts! Is this as far as you've come?"

She relapsed into Spanish, rambling about taking him back to basics: relearning the tarot cards, quizzing on the purpose of different herbs, and guided meditations. Inwardly, he groaned.

"I'm taking three psychology classes today, *Tía*," he said, interrupting her tirade, "and then I'm scheduled at the therapy clinic until closing."

"Then I'll see you here *after* closing, Nico," she told him, pointing a finger between his eyes.

"*Sí, Tía,*" he said with a sigh.

The door chimed and Mariana immediately turned to greet the customer.

Taking advantage of the distraction, Nico slipped into the back room, where he closed the textbooks and notes he'd been studying earlier and shoved them all into his bag. He slung the bag over his shoulder, peeked around the corner at Mariana—she was engrossed in conversation with the customer—and made a break for the door.

He pushed outward—and at the chime, he saw Mariana's head swivel in his direction.

"Nico!"

He flinched—but much to his relief, she smiled.

"You bring us dinner tonight after your internship, you hear me?"

He returned her smile and nodded. "*Sí, Tía.*"

6  Ishak

WHEN ISHAK NEXT EMERGED FROM THE NOTHINGNESS, HE felt ill. He quickly realized he was seated in the back of a moving vehicle, unfamiliar scenery passed by in the twilight.

He felt a wave of fear and anger. There was no way to know how much time had passed since the night he'd watched the blonde witch sleep, nor how far from her he was now.

From the passenger seat, Kivuli Panon adjusted the rearview mirror and fixed her gaze on him through the reflection. The evil in her eyes squirmed and twisted like eels in baskets.

"It's almost sundown," she said. "When we pull over, get out and go find me more money."

Coming back from the rest area that night, compelled by the brand in his skin, he had ripped open an ATM and returned to Kivuli Panon with a stack of bills in his jaws. It should have taken her weeks to burn through that much cash. If she was broke, then surely the blonde witch had long since left his reach. He had lost his chance. Grief washed over him, as powerful as if he had seen Kalilah die in his arms.

"When you have something valuable," Kivuli Panon said, "bring it to me at the Waldorf Astoria. I have a suite there."

Ishak blinked. A suite. Waldorf Astoria. That sounded expensive. Was that how she was spending the ATM money? He looked out the window again, this time with greater interest. They were in a suburban area filled with nearly identical houses, small patches of green lawn, and backyard swimming pools peeking through the fences. Though there weren't many cars on the road with them, Ishak heard a busy highway not far away.

"Where are we?" he asked.

Her gaze sharpened, and she pushed the mirror back toward the driver. "Don't ask questions."

The command shot through him, starting in the brand on his back and jolting through every nerve.

Jaw clenched, he shifted his eyes to the driver as she readjusted the mirror. It was one of the witch's other familiars. He had seen her before, but due to the spell that held them both captive, they had never spoken to one another. They locked gazes in the rearview mirror, but she quickly looked away. She drove the car with dull resignation in her eyes, her feathered arms mostly hidden beneath the sleeves of her coat and her talon-feet concealed by the shadow of the dashboard.

With a gesture from their captor, the bird-woman turned the steering wheel and brought the car to a stop by the curb. As the last light of day faded, Kivuli Panon turned and fixed Ishak with her slithery eyes.

"Get out," she commanded. "There's plenty of money in this city. Go out there, stay out of sight, and bring me money."

He leaped from the car, happy to obey an order that took him away from her. As soon as he closed the door, the bird-woman drove off, chauffeuring Kivuli Panon to the expensive hotel she would likely run him ragged to afford. He only had until dawn to find out if the blonde witch was close enough to reach and steal enough valuables to keep Kivuli Panon appeased.

With a full-body flex, his human form folded in, and the hyena emerged, transforming him. Now four-legged, he broke into a sprint. The pads of his feet still ached, and he was pleased to feel it. If he still hadn't healed from his encounter with the two travelers, then he had not been removed from the world for long. He put his nose to the wind and inhaled deeply, frantically sorting through the barrage of scents that came to him. So many humans! He would make a sweep of this city and take in all the smells he could. If he didn't find the girls—

He smelled them.

Ishak stopped dead, throwing all his focus into his nose. The blonde witch's scent was shockingly strong, as if she had passed through the area only minutes before. The scent trail tugged at him, pulling him toward its source with an insistency he had never experienced, as though the smell of the two young women actively overrode every other smell in the city. The strangeness of it would have been unnerving under any other circumstances, but given his desperation, Ishak felt nothing but relief.

His prayer had been answered. Following the smell, he darted off.

The scent led him to a motel in the orbit of an airport. The stink of narcotics and sex was thick in the air, as was the sound of rodents and cockroaches scurrying through the walls. Though Kivuli Panon stayed in cheap places when necessary, she would

41

never stay in a place like this. These were rooms for the secretive, the desperate, and the hopeless.

The blonde must be a very different sort of witch, thought Ishak. *Thank God.*

Their room was at the far end of the building in an area unlit by the sparse streetlamps. The smell of them was undeniable, but when he pressed an ear to their door he heard no one within.

Their absence meant that entering was within the scope of his orders. He half-shifted so that he was bipedal, giving him the use of his clawed hands. He ripped the door from its hinges and peered into the dark room.

The magnetic pull of the scent drew him in. He crossed the threshold.

The room suddenly grew bright. Startled, Ishak dropped to all fours, fur bristling, and lips curled back from his teeth. The floor, walls, and ceiling were coated with magic, a pattern of spells woven into a cage that, when he stepped inside, lit up all around. The magic sealed the room from the rest of the world, isolating him. Ishak's eyes darted around the motel room and landed upon the blonde witch as she emerged from a cloaking spell in the corner, one trembling hand outstretched to maintain the magic that imprisoned him. Behind her stood her inhuman friend, her glamour of humanity gone. She clutched a potted plant in her arms and watched him through iridescent, bark-framed eyes. *I was correct*, he realized. *She is not human; she is a Nymph.*

Encased in another witch's spell, Ishak felt Kivuli Panon's hold over him weaken. The tether of the brand on his skin slackened; it was as if his captor had dropped the leash that connected them. Feeling as if he was breathing fresh air for the first time in months, Ishak flexed and pulled his patterned fur into his pores. He shook his head and retracted his snout and upright ears. He rose onto two legs and straightened his skeleton into an upright posture. Fully human, he drew a deep breath of air as a free man.

Well, almost free.

The witch stepped forward, her hand held before her, and spoke. It sounded like gibberish. Ishak shook his head. She was likely speaking English, but with the link between him and Kivuli Panon temporarily severed, he could no longer understand the language. The Nymph said something in another language, also incomprehensible to him. The women looked at each other, muttered a few words between them, and then returned their focus to him.

"You speak Fae?" asked the witch.

Ishak sighed in relief. He nodded.

The witch drew herself up tall and swallowed heavily. "Who sent you?" she asked, her voice quaking. "Was it my mother?"

"Your mother?" Ishak was amazed to hear himself speak to someone other than Kivuli Panon with only the slightest pain from the brand. "What do you mean?"

"My mother!" she shouted. "Hazel Nichols O'Reilly! Did she send you after me?"

"I know no one by that name. I was sent by a witch named Kivuli Panon."

The witch glanced at the Nymph, who shrugged and shook her head.

"Did my mother send *her*?" the witch asked.

"I do not believe the evil bitch takes orders from anyone," he said.

"Then what does she want with us?"

"Nothing. She sends me out at night to steal."

"Then why have you been following us?" the Nymph demanded. "You must have realized by now that we have nothing worth taking."

Ishak steeled himself. This was the moment of truth.

"I need your help," he said, meeting the witch's gaze. "I need you to free me from Kivuli Panon."

She squinted as if she didn't understand. "What?"

"You are a witch," he said. "One witch can counter another's spell." He charged to the edge of the cage, startling the two girls. "Look!" He whirled around and lifted his shirt, exposing the witch's brand on his back. "See this?"

"You're her familiar," the Nymph said. "How long?"

"Months, I think. I am not sure."

The witch wore a look of sympathy, which gave him hope.

"Please," he said. "Break the spell that binds me to her."

"I can't," she said. "I'm sorry."

The Nymph said something to her in another language and the witch nodded. While they spoke, Ishak looked closer at the Nymph. A suspicion crept into his mind. He scanned her and spotted what he was looking for: a mark on her wrist.

"This Nymph is your familiar?" he asked the witch.

"I don't have a familiar," she replied.

His gaze darted to the Nymph for conformation. The inhuman girl nodded. But he didn't believe it. She was covered in moss, grass, and bark—clearly flora-based. Ishak didn't know a lot about flora Nymphs, but he did know that they lived by the sun, and it was well after sunset; she should be asleep.

As if reading his mind, the Nymph—potted plant still cradled in her arms—stepped toward the witch, pinched the sleeve of her outstretched arm, and gently pulled it back from her wrist.

Ishak's eyes widened at the sight of another brand, identical to the Nymph's, on the witch's skin.

"See this?" said the Nymph. "The mark doesn't drain my power; it lets us share our power with each other. It's allowing me to stay awake."

A witch who shares power? It was unheard of. He asked the only question he could. "Why?"

"Do you really have to ask?" the witch said. "Anything else would be wrong."

This scrawny slip of a thing could be a godsend.

"If you believe so," he said, "then free me."

"I can't," she repeated.

"Please," he pleaded. "Please help me. I have to find—"

"You don't understand," she interrupted. "It's not that I won't. I really can't. To do what you're asking, I would need whatever vessel she's using to hold you when you're noncorporeal; without it, the spell can't be broken."

"Noncorporeal?"

"The darkness," the Nymph explained. "The lost time. Witches dematerialize their familiars and store them in small containers for ease of transport."

Though he hadn't known this, it made sense. He considered it for a moment and then locked eyes with the witch. "If I can get that vessel for you, could you free me?"

A shiver rippled through the witch's body, releasing a powerful whiff of fear that flooded Ishak's nostrils. "Witches don't collect familiars for the hell of it. Familiars give them power. A witch who collects power will fight to keep it. I'm not combat-trained. She might kill me. And even if I got away, she'd probably sell me out to my mother."

Ishak believed Kivuli Panon would sell her own soul for an enticing enough price. But what the witch was saying was both devastating and infuriating. Was she so fearful of her own mother that she wouldn't lift a finger to help him?

He should not have expected help from a witch. Still, against his better judgment, he persisted. "My wife," he said. "Kivuli Panon abducted us both, but my wife has disappeared. While the witch controls me, I cannot demand an explanation or go in search of Kalilah."

The witch licked her lips, her brow furrowed. "Was your wife also . . . what you are?"

"Bultungin, yes."

"Most witches wouldn't bother to keep two of the same kind," she said. "There's no benefit to having familiars with redundant abilities and keeping them under control is a strain on a witch's power."

"Then where is Kalilah?" Ishak's fury melted into horror. "My God, did she kill her?"

"No!" the girl said. "No! Don't think that way! If Kivu . . . Kivu . . . what's-her-name is anything like my mom, I bet she sold or traded your wife."

"Sold or traded?" No two words had ever wounded him so deeply.

"Yeah. There's an entire brokerage market built around famil-iars for witches." A strange expression came over her—something like disgust. "I was engaged to a broker, so I know a thing or two about it. A witch would never just throw away a familiar when she could go to a broker. And someone like you or your wife, a creature that most witches don't ever see . . . that's gotta be worth something."

Ishak sank to his knees and fought through his grief and panic to digest her words. At least there was hope that Kalilah was alive somewhere. But the thought of his beloved being sold like a piece of furniture nauseated him. He could think of nothing but finding her and taking her back to Kabultiloa, no matter what.

The witch's hand shook, and she drew ragged breaths. Ishak had seen enough of Kivuli Panon to know that when a witch grew tired, her magic faded. At any moment, this girl might drop her spell, and when she did, the cage of his momentary freedom would collapse.

"Help me," he repeated. "I must find Kalilah."

The witch's eyes grew blurry, and she teetered a bit. "I'm sorry," she said.

Her eyes rolled back as she fainted, and the magic rained down around him like a shattered rainbow. Ishak felt the authority of Kivuli Panon's brand reassert itself and lock his tongue behind his teeth. His impulse to obey orders and flee from these witnesses racked his body with pain.

Turning away from where the witch lay in the Nymph's mossy arms, he trudged toward the door; with every step, the sting of his disobedience eased a bit more. He had one foot over the threshold when he thought of Kalilah and stopped. *Sold or traded.* Bultungins must be valuable. Perhaps valuable enough to retrieve if lost.

The pain coursed through him like an electric current, but he would not leave the motel. Teeth clenched, he stepped back inside the room and planted his feet. It was a gamble, but it was a bet he felt was in his favor. She would feel the defiance, the refusal, and it would enrage her.

Afire with pain, he stood and waited for Kivuli Panon to come for what was hers.

7  Mei-Xing

CROUCHED NEXT TO HER UNCONSCIOUS FRIEND, MEI-XING
lifted her shimmery eyes to the Bultungin. In human form, he
was tall and fit, with a thick beard, and looked about ten years
older than Ivy—*No, Georgette*, she reminded herself. She needed
to get used to her friend's new name.

Since coming to America, Mei-Xing had seen a greater range
of skin colors than she ever had in China, and this man was one
of the darkest. He also spoke the Fae language with an accent she
didn't recognize and referenced places and species she had never
heard of. It made her realize what a sheltered life she had led.

The Bultungin remained just inside the door, still as a boulder. As time ticked by, Mei-Xing became increasingly nervous.
She knew enough of witches by now to understand that once
Kivuli Panon sensed that her familiar was rebelling, she would
either send another familiar to fetch him or, more likely, come
herself to reassert control.

Mei-Xing tried dragging Georgette to the car, but she wasn't
strong enough, and she didn't want to hinder her friend's recu-
peration by drawing on more of the power they shared. But she

did not want Kivuli Panon to find them there, defenseless, either.

Her fear grew, gnawing at her like an insect infestation.

Will Kivuli Panon sell Georgette to back to her mother? Will she keep me like she's kept the hyena-man? She looked at the underside of her wrist, at the intricate interlocking curves of the *Hathiya* mark that looped her power with Georgette's. She imagined that mark replaced by a duplicate of the one on the Bultungin's back and shuddered. *I won't go. I've already been sold by my family and misused by my husband. I didn't fake my death just to go through it again.*

But she would have little say in the matter. She could fight, she could run, but she might be caught. And it would all be because of this man.

She tried pushing the Bultungin out the door, even punched him several times as hard as she could, but he was steadfast. When her fists proved ineffective, she grabbed him by the shirt, shook him, and pleaded with him to go.

"Please," she begged. "You can't imagine what we have left behind. I know my friend; I know her heart. She would help you if she could. But look at her!" She pointed to Georgette, out cold on the carpet. "And what can I do? I can grow a bouquet of flowers. I can grow a batch of pot. Would Kivuli Panon be persuaded by that? Please, leave!"

For all the response she got, he might as well have been a statue. His dark eyes looked through her without seeing. His face, his entire body, was like one huge, tightly coiled spring.

Mei-Xing watched him a moment, sighed, and turned aside. She would have to find another way.

8 Ivy/ Georgette

SEVEN-YEAR-OLD IVY PLAYED IN THE LIVING ROOM. THERE was a playroom at the opposite end of the house, but her sisters were there, and she avoided them whenever possible.

Poppy—her cousin, just five months older—played with her. They took turns tossing a stuffed rabbit onto the armchair from across the room. Keeping score, they competed for who could land the bunny onto the cushion the most times in a row.

Excited for her turn, Ivy took the rabbit and got ready to throw.

"What are you girls doing?"

It was her mother. Ivy saw diamonds in her ears, on her fingers, and around her neck, all of them glittering in the afternoon sun. A designer dress of purple silk draped over her body, only partially succeeding in disguising her pregnant belly. Her straight russet hair cascaded about her face and shoulders, accenting her bronze skin, and framing the spotless artistry of her makeup. The long magenta nails of one hand tapped the side of her belly, while those of the other wrapped around a wineglass containing cranberry juice.

"What are you doing?" she asked again.

"I'm tossing the bunny into the chair," said Ivy.

"Why?"

"It's a game, Aunt Hazel," Poppy said.

Hazel's eyes glossed over Poppy and drifted back to Ivy. The Nichols matriarch calmly set her glass on a nearby shelf.

"If you miss," she said, "I'll spank you."

Ivy blinked and gave her mother a bemused look. Spank? Her mother didn't spank. And Ivy wasn't doing anything wrong. Was she? If she was misbehaving, her mother would have told her to stop. Absolutely nothing about it rang true.

Ivy took the stuffed rabbit and threw it toward the chair. It struck the arm, flopped, and landed on the floor. Before Ivy could react, Hazel took her by the arm, yanked her close, and spanked her.

It was her only memory of ever being spanked.

Her body went numb as it happened, her mind too startled to register the sting of the blows. She looked at Poppy with a slack-jawed question on her face. *What's happening?*

Poppy stared back at her, still and silent. Ivy recognized the look. Poppy would never acknowledge that this had happened; if pressed, she would insist that Ivy had imagined the whole thing.

As Hazel left the room, her glass in hand, she glanced back at her daughter with a smirk on her lips. It was an expression her child-self memorized, though she couldn't process it at the time. That image remained, a frozen moment in time that perfectly encapsulated the near constant state of confusion and distress in which she lived.

Only recently, as she'd stepped out of "Ivy" and begun to grow into "Georgette," did she finally understand.

It was a joke. In her mother's mind, spanking her daughter for failing at an innocent game had been a hilarious joke.

The first thing Georgette saw when she regained consciousness was a dark, blurry shape. After a moment, she realized she was looking, without her glasses, at the left foot of the Bultungin. She remembered the moments before she expended the last of her power. He'd asked her—pleaded with her—to free him. The guilt she felt over not helping was compounded by the fact that she now realized she had never even asked him his name.

The moldy smell of the carpet pressed into her nose, making her wince, so she pushed herself up and glanced around. Though still tired, she no longer felt drained. She found her glasses on the edge of the bed and slipped them on—only to realize that their bags were gone, and that although the potted marijuana was on the nightstand, Mei-Xing was definitely not inside it.

Alarmed, she bolted to her feet.

"Where's my stuff?" she asked the Bultungin.

Standing perfectly still, he didn't even look at her.

Panic growing in her chest, she ran to the bathroom. "Mei-Xing! Mei-Xing!" It was empty. Ducking around the hyena-man, she leaped out the open door—and collided with the Nymph just steps from the room.

"Oh!" she exhaled in immense relief. "I couldn't find you!"

Mei-Xing gently pulled her close, and the witch pressed her forehead against a mossy patch on her shoulder. Georgette smelled something sharp but sweet arise from the moss. As it filled her lungs, she felt her muscles relax.

"You passed out," Mei-Xing said, "and I couldn't move you. The hyena refused to leave, and Kivuli Panon will come to find him. So while you slept"—she held up one hand and jiggled a set of keys—"I loaded up our luggage."

Georgette sniffled, wiping stress-induced tears from her eyes. "Whose keys are those?"

"I grew something to knock out the man in room 23 and stole his car keys." When Georgette gaped at her, Mei-Xing shrugged. "The last car we stole has a busted window now."

The witch nodded and straightened up. "Is everything in the car?"

"Everything but my plant," Mei-Xing replied. "We can leave any time."

"Then let's go now." Georgette looked over her shoulder at the hyena-man, tense and unmoving. "What about him? Should we . . ."

A sudden flash of headlights cut across her vision, stopping her mid-question. Startled, Georgette watched as a car roared into the parking lot, headed straight for them. Mei-Xing stepped back into the motel room, using the walls to shield her inhuman form—her glamour was still inactive. Georgette stood frozen in front of the open doorway as the car came to a stop. In the poorly lit parking lot, she couldn't clearly see the driver, but the dark silhouette behind the steering wheel made her stomach flutter and an electric sizzle in her skin danced across the tips of her arm hair. *Magic recognizes magic*, she thought.

The driver stepped out of the car, her jewelry jangling with every purposeful motion. The sizzle of mutual magic grew stronger with her approach; Georgette felt an urge to back away. Just out of arm's reach, she stopped short, her features just discernible in the dull light cast through the motel room door.

Kivuli Panon was a small woman, no bigger than Georgette, but certainly older. Deep crow's feet at the corners of her eyes and frown lines emphasized her expression. Her skin was sunscorched, a patchwork of burnt orange and charred brown. Wisps of reddish hair touched with gray hung loose from the green and gold wrap that covered her head. Beneath the graying tendrils, Georgette saw two eyes full of fermenting wickedness that skewered her before snapping to the open motel door.

"You," she hissed.

When the newcomer took another step, Georgette squeaked and jumped out of her path, heart thundering, but Kivuli Panon breezed past her. She stopped at the threshold of the room, her eyes darting over the interior.

She sees my spell coating the walls. Is that why she's not going inside?

"I'm at the Waldorf Astoria," Kivuli Panon said, her voice venomous, "and you force me to come to this shit-stain of a place?"

Peering over Kivuli Panon's shoulder, Georgette saw the trembling Bultungin shift his gaze to glare at the elder witch. Having grown up in a household of witches, Georgette had seen familiars defy the *Hathiya* brand before, though never for as long as this man. He had to be exhausted—yet she saw him snarl as he continued glaring at his captor. His anger heightened her guilt.

Mei-Xing was as still as a tree in the far corner of the room, clutching her plant to her chest. The intruder either didn't notice the Nymph or didn't care. Instead, she scanned the mystic residue, her face tight with revulsion. Then she turned to Georgette.

"Is this your spell?" she demanded. "Are you the reason my familiar is still here?"

Caught off guard, Georgette cocked her head. Was this woman blaming the situation on her? After a lifetime of accepting blame for others' faults, this accusation made her blood boil. She had left behind her family, her home, and her name to get away from this crap. Accepting her position as family scapegoat was what Ivy did. She wasn't going to be Ivy anymore.

"Pretty sure *you're* the reason," she said.

The festering poison in Kivuli Panon's eyes grew hot as her gaze bored into Georgette. The younger witch felt painfully uncomfortable, but she strove to ignore it. After several long seconds of a shared unblinking stare, Kivuli Panon turned away and swept her eyes over the motel room once again.

"You've got some nerve laying this trap for my familiar," she said. "Give him back."

Georgette held her breath. Only once before had she stood her ground like this, and it had ended with her sister Violet deep in a catatonic state. The angry expression on Kivuli Panon's face was a carbon copy of her mother's on that day. Kivuli Panon, like Hazel Nichols O'Reilly, was unaccustomed to defiance. She'd clearly come here expecting that if she threw her weight around enough, Georgette would give in. Georgette's refusal made her angry but it was also, as evidenced by her hesitation, making her doubt herself.

Emboldened, Georgette stood firm. "You sent him to steal from me," she said evenly.

Kivuli Panon lifted her chin and looked down her nose at Georgette. "I want my property."

Georgette noted that Kivuli Panon still had not stepped over the threshold. "Come get him," she said, slipping past her into the room. "I'm not holding him here."

It was a brash challenge. The room was painted in her spell, her power. For another witch to step into such a place would put her at a disadvantage. Unless she was much stronger than Georgette.

Georgette, of course, didn't know how strong Kivuli Panon was; her sole description of her came from a man who lived under her thumb. She was taking a risk by baiting the older witch.

Kivuli Panon held her breath as she stepped inside. Georgette held her breath too.

The light of the bedside lamp poured over the intruder's colorful clothes and wove a map of shadows across her face. After giving Georgette one more look with her slithering gaze, she turned her attention to the Bultungin.

"You are a pain in my ass," she said. "Most familiars accept their situation within the first two weeks. By the end of a month, they're as docile as kittens. Why is it that after four months, I'm expending twice the magic to control you than I do on any other familiar?"

His lips parted slowly, revealing gnashed teeth. A trickle of blood oozed from his nose as he kept his silence.

"You're more trouble than you're worth," Kivuli Panon scoffed. "I'm putting you back with the others until I find someone to take you off my hands."

"Is that what you did with his wife?" Mei-Xing suddenly asked.

Wrinkling her nose as if affronted by a horrible smell, Kivuli Panon shot a furious look at the Nymph, then shifted her gaze to Georgette. "Control your servant!" she shouted.

Georgette stiffened. It wasn't the first time another witch had called Mei-Xing her servant, but she hated it. She hated that every witch assumed Mei-Xing was a piece of property, hated that they hurt her friend. Most of all, she hated that she had to speak in her friend's defense instead of letting her speak for herself. As Ivy, she had kept her remarks to a minimum. But now, caught up in the evolving persona of Georgette, she spat out, "Screw you!"

Face twisted in fury, Kivuli Panon charged toward Georgette. Confronted with such rage, Georgette acted on instinct. Before Kivuli Panon could reach her, she threw out her hand and reactivated the cage spell. The magic lit up in all its iridescence.

Ignoring the cage, Kivuli Panon raised a hand to cast her own spell. Georgette gasped and backed away. Despite her attempts to maintain her new identity, she felt Ivy's insecurities overtaking her and she started to lower her hand, to let the magic dissipate.

A pair of arms suddenly seized Kivuli Panon from behind and yanked her back. Pinning her in his grip, the Bultungin crushed the witch against himself and held her inside Georgette's cage.

9 Ishak

"WHAT DID YOU DO WITH MY WIFE?" ISHAK ROARED.

Kivuli Panon yowled like a cat and kicked her heels at him, but Ishak, numb from hours of constant pain, barely felt it. He locked gazes with the young witch. The girl's eyes widened; then she nodded and kept her hand up, maintaining the spell. Ishak concentrated on squeezing his captor with what strength he had left. Kivuli Panon fought to turn her head, snapping her teeth at his face, but couldn't reach him.

He squeezed harder until she grew still.

"What did you do with my wife?" he repeated.

Though she was no longer struggling, Ishak felt her tensing up—and then, suddenly, he began to feel weaker, as if his remaining strength was being sucked from his body. Though the cage was stopping her from asserting full control, she was drawing away his power through the brand. Against his will, he felt his grip relax to the point that she was able to wriggle one arm loose.

Expecting her to claw at him with her nails or to cast another spell, Ishak braced himself, but the anticipated strike didn't come. Instead, he felt her fumbling and snatching at something with her free hand.

"Her coat pocket!" Georgette exclaimed. "That's where she keeps her familiars! She's trying to put you back!"

Alarmed, he flung Kivuli Panon to the floor, grabbed her coat with both hands, and tore it away from her, so forcefully that the sleeves remained on her arms. She shrieked and threw up her hands, fresh magic crackling on her fingertips. He fought to tear the pocket open, but the enchanted material remained intact.

Kivuli Panon flung her spell at him, and he dropped to his knees with a wail, a thousand invisible needles burrowing into his skin. He felt her seize the torn coat and try to pull it out of his hands, but he held fast to the pocket, teeth gritted, even as she tore away the surrounding material. Screaming obscenities, she threw the ripped cloth aside and waved her arms over him, weaving a new spell.

Ishak frantically clawed at the pocket but the spell that bound it would not give way. His eyes shot to the blonde witch, but he saw that her arm shook, and her breath was ragged. Soon, she would be too fatigued to maintain the cage and Kivuli Panon would have him.

"Put down that pocket," Kivuli Panon snarled, "or I swear I'll kill you."

Glaring defiantly, he hooked his fingers into the pocket. The cage might fall in a moment, allowing her to break his will, but he resolved that until that moment came, he would fight. He tensed his legs, ready to spring at her in one last attack.

Flapping like a sail in the wind, the torn, discarded coat suddenly flew into the cage, fluttered over the combatants, and flopped down onto Kivuli Panon's head. Her eyes abruptly covered, the witch jumped back, her impending spell thwarted.

Ishak twisted at the pocket with all his dwindling strength. It did not yield.

Another pair of hands reached for the pocket. Instinctively, Ishak threw out his arm to block them—but froze when he saw that Kivuli Panon, flailing under the coat, had stumbled over onto her back. He realized that the hands reaching out to him belonged to the Nymph.

As Kivuli Panon pulled free of her shredded coat, the Nymph's hands changed, their moss and bark enveloped in a human glamour. Snakish eyes blazing, Kivuli Panon threw what was left of the coat to the floor just as the Nymph grabbed the pocket in her magic-wrapped fingers.

Screaming in fury, the witch lunged. The Nymph, her *Hathiya* mark alight, easily tore the cloth in two.

When the fabric split, the magic that sealed it exploded in a glittery flash. From within the pocket, dozens of tiny lights erupted into the room like a swarm of fireflies, striking the sides of the magic cage and rebounding back and forth.

With an exhausted gasp, the blonde witch released her spell, dropped to her knees, and slumped against the side of the bed. Meanwhile, the magic broke and fluttered to the ground like sparkling confetti as the tiny lights spread throughout the room and quickly began to take their natural shapes.

The brand on Ishak's back burned white-hot, and he flinched—but an instant later, the burning stopped, all pain left his body, and his strength returned. With relief, he felt all trace of his captor's presence disappear from his thoughts. He watched the faces of the other familiars as the reality of their freedom dawned on them.

He turned to look at Kivuli Panon—standing just a few steps away, still as death, her arms still outstretched in a gesture of attack. He watched as her expression shifted from fury to shock and then to horror as, one by one, her former captives turned, facing her. A wave of fear filled Ishak's nostrils, and he realized with a grin that it came from her.

Cornered and outnumbered, Kivuli Panon's desperate gaze darted about until she spotted the blonde witch on the floor. Ishak saw the wicked stew in her eyes hide beneath a cover of sticky kindness as she reached out a hand and pleaded, "Help me, sister."

The ex-familiars hesitated and glanced at the girl, their eyes betraying that they had not realized there was another witch in the room. Ishak smirked at their concern and watched the young witch wrinkle her nose at the sound of the bitch calling her *sister*.

"Go to hell," the girl said.

Without a word, the familiars moved as one to encircle Kivuli Panon.

Later, after the screams and bloody satisfaction, Ishak stood in the motel parking lot. Though the sickly light in Kivuli Panon's eyes had vanished, her face sealed in eternal horror, a handful of the familiars still lingered. Many had fled, some so quickly that their mad dash had broken the motel windows and shredded the drywall. Ishak understood their frenzy: freedom was precious.

Of those who'd stayed, some were sucking up the blood from the carpet and picking the gobs of flesh and bone from the furniture. Those not feeding seemed lost in thought, staring into space.

The bird-woman was among this group. She kept absentmindedly reaching over her shoulder, feathered fingers stretching toward the center of her back where the witch's brand was newly gone.

The Nymph and the blonde witch transferred all their belongings to Kivuli Panon's car while the familiars skirted around them as if they were made of broken glass. After the Nymph buckled her potted plant into the backseat, the blonde witch drew her attention to the nearby road, where an ex-familiar dragged Kivuli Panon's shredded corpse into the distance.

Ishak looked at the retreating creature—a gaunt, ashen thing with every bone visible beneath its grayish skin—and heard the Nymph voice a string of choppy words. All were nonsensical to him, with one exception:

"Wendigo?" he repeated to the girls.

At the sound of his voice, they turned toward him. The Nymph nodded.

Wendigo, he thought. *It's taking the body to eat it.* He shot the creature one last look as it disappeared into the brush, dragging the mangled witch behind it. "She deserves no better than to be turned into Wendigo shit," he said with a grim nod.

In Fae language, the blonde witch asked, "Is there much blood left in the room?"

"Very little," he said. "Does it matter?"

"Yes," she said. "Familiars rebelling is something every witch is afraid of. If word gets out that that's what happened here, it'll put a target on your head."

Ishak looked back at the motel room. The red stains and lumps of meat were almost gone. He felt a swell of gratitude toward those who were consuming the evidence and wondered if they did so out of hunger or self-preservation. Regardless, by the time they finished, the room would look like any other, except for the structural damage—and from the looks of this filthy motel, this was likely not the first time that one of its rooms had been trashed.

"Thank you for your help," he said. "Both of you."

"It was all your doing," the witch said. She turned her eyes aside, her expression suggesting embarrassment. "I'm sorry. I should have—"

"What's done is done," he said curtly. "And you." He nodded to the Nymph. "Thank you for doing what I could not." He held out his hand. "I am Ishak Siad."

The Nymph took his hand in hers and he felt the rough bark of her skin. "Mei-Xing Ma."

"What you did with the pocket amazed me. I did not know a Nymph could have such power."

"It was Georgette's power," Mei-Xing said. "I just borrowed it."

"Then . . . you are Georgette?" He held out his hand to the witch. "Ishak."

The witch took his hand. Their handshake was lazy and slow; the night had exhausted them both. Ishak's eyes drifted to her wrist, where he saw the edge of the mark the women shared. It was this mutual mark that had allowed the Nymph to draw on enough magic to free him. *Remarkable.*

A large bat-winged creature emerged from the broken motel window and took flight over their heads. One of those shuffling about the parking lot followed its path across the dark sky with his gaze and then, as if suddenly remembering that he had wings, sprang into the air, and flew off as well.

Out of the corner of his eye, Ishak saw the bird-woman creeping closer. He waited, expecting her to approach, but her eyes darted to the two girls, her thin face blazing with distrust. Nodding his understanding, Ishak left the witch's side and took a few steps toward his fellow ex-familiar.

"I saw the other one," she twittered softly. "The other one like you."

"My wife?" he said, taking another step toward her. "When?"

She opened her mouth to respond but a veil of confusion dropped over her expression, and she shook her head. Ishak sighed. She didn't know. When held within the sealed pocket, time lost all meaning.

"What can you tell me?" he asked.

"Kivuli Panon sold your wife to a broker's agent she met on the road," the bird-woman said. "She wanted to sell you, but the man said he was only interested in a female. She took the deal. He took your wife."

"Where?" he asked, putting his hands on her shoulders and leaning in. "Where did he take her?"

"I don't know," she said. "Kivuli Panon didn't ask."

"Can you tell me anything about the agent?"

She drew a breath and let a soft, fluttery whistle leave her orange lips. "Young . . . ish. Pale skin but dark hair and beard. Glasses. Heavy, with a gut." Pausing to think, she sniffed and scratched a loose feather free from her neck. "I don't know his name but there was a word he said several times: Zamek."

"Zamek," Ishak repeated. "Do you know what it means?"

"I do," interrupted Georgette. "Sorry to listen, but . . . I know."

The bird-woman's feathers bristled and fluffed. Ishak squeezed her shoulders reassuringly, but she brushed his hands away and slid into his shadow.

"What does it mean?" he asked Georgette.

"It's a brokerage," she told him, "a big one. It's actually called *Zamek's*, with an apostrophe *s*. They have offices up and down the West Coast."

"Where is the nearest?"

"Las Vegas."

"How do I get there?"

Georgette furrowed her brow. "What do you mean?"

"Las Vegas," he said irritably. "Where is it?"

"It's here," Mei-Xing said. "This city, here, that we're in right now. This is Las Vegas."

Ishak's stood a little taller. He felt just as he did when he hunted and caught the scent of excellent prey.

"How do I find this brokerage?"

"I'm not sure," said Georgette. "But," she added in response to his snort of frustration, "I can find out." She gestured to the car. "Want a lift?"

Ishak stared at the vehicle for a moment. He remembered the last time he rode in that car, Kivuli Panon's sickening eyes staring at him through the mirror. Her scent still lingered there, drifting to his nose on the night wind. But stronger than that was a new smell: Georgette's guilt, which oozed from her every pore. *She's ashamed of herself for not helping me sooner*, he deduced. *She's offering to help to make herself feel better.*

Though he was disinclined to rely on a witch, he was stranded in a foreign country. He would need help. The mark on Georgette's wrist caught his eye again, rekindling his curiosity about this woman and the Nymph with whom she shared magic.

"I would," he said. "Thank you. And thank you," he said, turning to the bird-woman. "I will never forget your kindness."

The bird-woman shifted her eyes to Ishak and tried to smile, though the effort seemed to strain her face. Her hand drifted above her shoulder, reaching once again toward the erased brand. She stopped short, withdrew her trembling arm, and glanced around the parking lot. Ishak followed her gaze. The other familiars had all gone. He and this bird-woman were all that remained of Kivuli Panon's collection.

Tucking her feathered arms over her chest, the bird-woman shuffled toward the road, each step marked by the click of her talon-feet on the pavement. Once, she glanced back at him with hollow eyes; then she walked on, eyes trained on the horizon, until she was swallowed up by the darkness.

10 Georgette

IT WAS MID-AFTERNOON WHEN SHE WOKE, FACE DOWN ON a king-size bed. She was still in her clothes and shoes, and dried sweat covered her body, but she felt better than she had in weeks.

Georgette rolled onto her side and looked out the floor-to-ceiling window at the city. From this height, Las Vegas looked quiet, almost drab, in the sunlight.

When she and Mei-Xing had gotten to the Waldorf Astoria the previous night—using Kivuli Panon's key to gain access to her suite—the view from the room had been vibrant and colorful, a neon metropolis. But as intriguing as the mad bustle of activity was, all Georgette had been able to think of was sleep. After dropping her bags to the floor, she had flopped onto the bed and immediately conked out. Now, almost fifteen hours later, she finally felt rested.

When she sat up, she saw the Bultungin asleep in an armchair next to the window, his head leaning against the glass, gentle snores coating one pane in fog. When they'd arrived at the hotel, Ishak had changed to his hyena form and run off into the darkness. She wondered when he had returned.

The potted plant was on the floor near the bed, basking in the afternoon sun. Georgette sensed Mei-Xing inside the plant, relaxing and soaking up some nutrients.

Leaving both her companions to rest, Georgette slipped out of bed, gathered some clean clothes from her bag, and went to take a shower.

After washing away the sweat and dirt of the last few days, Georgette sat on the edge of the bathtub, her body wrapped in one fluffy white towel and her hair wrapped in another. For one wonderful moment, she felt like she was snuggled up in a cloud. Then she caught a glimpse of herself in the mirror.

Just look at those spots, she heard her mother say. *It must be from Michael's family. God knows no woman from my side ever had skin like that. And that hair!*—Georgette subconsciously patted her toweled head—*It's bad enough that she's as blonde as Michael, but those messy curls! No matter how many treatments I pay for, it's still a bird's nest.* Here her mother would roll her eyes. *It's like there's nothing of me in her at all.*

Georgette yanked her gaze away from the reflection. It wasn't fair that she was clear across the country and yet her mother was still lodged in her brain like a hungry parasite.

A soft tap on the door interrupted her lament; she rose to let Mei-Xing into the bathroom.

The glamour over her friend's flora body was fully restored, leaving her looking like the young human woman that she wasn't. She slipped inside and closed the door behind her. "The hyena-man came back at dawn," she reported. "I had just woken up."

"Where was he all night?" Georgette asked.

"Running around, trying to find his wife's scent." Mei-Xing cast a glance at the door, her head tilted. "He didn't find anything."

"She still might be here," Georgette said. "Brokers know how to keep their 'inventory' contained. Zach's family keeps a huge number of familiars on a very small property. It's just a matter of stocking the right magics to make the familiars noncorporeal. His wife could very well be in a shoebox on a shelf in the local Zamek's office."

Unsurprisingly, Mei-Xing's face twisted up at the mention of Georgette's ex-fiancé. She had hated Zachary from the moment she met him. Not unduly, Georgette knew, since the first thing Zach had done after seeing that Ivy had brought a Nymph back with her from China was to estimate Mei-Xing's dollar value. Ivy had long been numb to that sort of talk, but the horror she'd seen on her friend's face at Zach's casual assessment had stabbed her in the gut.

"How will you find the Zamek's?" Mei-Xing asked.

"I'll look," Georgette said. "The office can't be too hidden. You don't make money by being hard to find."

"True." Mei-Xing nodded. "Speaking of money—I went through Kivuli Panon's bags. I found about four thousand dollars in cash and some jewelry we can pawn. Will four thousand be enough to buy the Bultungin woman?"

"I don't know," Georgette said, "but it won't be a problem. Give me a day, and I can turn that four thousand into four hundred thousand in any of the big casinos."

Mei-Xing turned aside, muttering. Georgette nodded sympathetically. She'd known the casino plan would be a hard sell. Mei-Xing's husband, a Water Spirit, had run up a sizable debt gambling while they were married and forced her to overextend her powers to produce narcotic plants for sale. Suffering physically and emotionally, Mei-Xing had complained to her family, but they'd told her to obey her husband; they'd feared if she didn't, he would deprive their entire grove of its water supply.

"Winning in a casino is basic magic," Georgette said. "My four-year-old niece could do it." She put a hand on Mei-Xing's shoulder. "I can get us enough money to live on for years and free Ishak's wife."

Mei-Xing cast her eyes to the tiled floor. "Won't you need an ID to collect your winnings? Are you going to show them your license? It's got your old name on it."

"I'll use a glamour to change it," Georgette said. "If I run into any problems, I can shift the casino employees' memories." She chuckled humorlessly. "My mother was good at memory spells. She didn't teach me, but I picked it up."

"What name will you glamour onto the ID?"

"Georgette."

Mei-Xing shook her head, lifting her gaze. "What *last* name? You can't go by O'Reilly anymore."

"Oh." Embarrassed, Georgette realized she hadn't thought of that. "I don't know. Any last name is fine, I guess." Her eyes scanned the marble countertop, looking for inspiration, and her gaze fell upon the little bottle of lotion next to the sink. She reached for it and turned it over in her hand. "'Delaney Company,'" she read on the back. "That'll work. Georgette Delaney."

Nodding, Mei-Xing picked up the shirt Georgette had brought

71

into the bathroom and held it up. Her lips puckered and her eyes squinted, a look Georgette interpreted as thoughtful, though she couldn't be sure. Sometimes the glamour she put on Mei-Xing didn't translate Nymph facial expressions very well.

"Whose hand-me-down is this?" the Nymph asked. "It's clearly meant for a taller, bustier woman. Is it Holly's? Lily's?"

"Is it a designer brand?"

"No."

"Not Lily's, then," Georgette said. "Probably Clove's. Most of Holly's stuff went to Poppy and Daisy."

"If you're going to win so much money," Mei-Xing said, "then you should buy new clothes. Everything you have once belonged to your sisters." A shimmer flitted across her eyes. "You need to find your own look. Georgette's look."

Georgette's gaze swept over the shirt. Sleeveless, low-cut, and dark green with black polka dots, it exposed her freckled shoulders, drew attention to her flat chest, and gave her complexion a sickly pallor. But it was the most flattering shirt she had. She had never been allowed to develop her own sense of style, forced instead to rely on hand-me-downs and whatever other clothes her mother deemed "appropriate." The opportunity to choose something for herself, something that fit properly and complimented her, was enticing. Possible styles for the woman she wanted to be lit up her mind. Pastels, flowy skirts, peasant tops . . . and, she decided as she untwisted the towel from her head, she was done with hair straighteners.

"I'll do it," she said, "if you come shopping with me. You need clothes too. People don't usually wear the same thing every day. Pretending to be human means looking the part. Okay?"

"Okay," Mei-Xing said. "After the brokerage?"

"Sure." Georgette took the shirt from her friend's hands and pulled it over her head. "Let's wake up Ishak and go look for the Zamek's."

Stepping into a pair of shorts, she glanced at herself in the mirror. The clothes looked hideous, but she was okay with that. When she took off this outfit, it would be for the last time—and there wasn't a damn thing her mother could do about it.

11   Neil

THE LAPTOP'S GLOW COATED NEIL MACCANA'S THIN FACE, accentuating the dark circles under his brown eyes, and highlighting a day's worth of unshaven stubble. Clicking his tongue in an unconscious rhythm, he scanned the screen. The case study was ready to be submitted. It wasn't his best work, but he anticipated a good grade. He clicked to another tab and opened a sales report. He smiled. He was much happier with this document. His first sale to a deep-pocketed client gave him a better buzz than a stiff drink. Mr. Li would like it. Hell, he might even raise his chin, nod, and say, "*Hmm*." That would be high praise indeed.

Another two tabs showed his email accounts, personal and professional. He quickly sent off two emails—one to the office with the sales report attached, and the other to his professor with the case study—then grabbed his phone and deleted both items from his to-do list. Seeing them gone, he felt a burst of accomplishment.

His email auto-refreshed, and a message from his nephew appeared at the top of his inbox. Danny thanked him for the birthday gift he'd sent him, wrote a little about starting high school, and then complained about his parents. "Traveling Dad" and "Codeine Mom," Danny called them. Neil shook his head. He didn't want to badmouth his brother and sister-in-law, but the kid wasn't wrong. He added an item to his to-do list: find more local summer camps so Danny could spend a full three months with him next year instead of toughing through another summer at home.

The last tab displayed his bank account. Looking at his balances, Neil's sense of accomplishment dimmed. He was doing . . . okay. Okay kept the lights on and covered his rent and loan debt, but it didn't leave much margin for error. Okay paid for online classes but kept his progress toward an MBA at a crawl. Three more years at this pace? He clicked his tongue again, louder this time, and tried to focus beyond the numbers on his screen. The experience he got from working at Li International was worth a lot more than numbers on a page. Not just in making sales—Neil had never found a product he couldn't move—but gaining an understanding of the ins and outs of the company. Knowing how to run a real business was a skill he couldn't buy—and it was one he hoped to need one day.

He closed his laptop and stretched his back. With the glow of the screen gone, awareness of his surroundings returned. His bedroom was a mess worthy of a frat house—his entire wardrobe strewn about the floor and empty food wrappers everywhere but the trash can. The chaos was familiar, but it was starting to feel inappropriate. He had a full-time job, was getting an MBA, and was trying to set a good example for Danny. At some point, this sort of mess needed to be phased out of his life. *Tomorrow*, he told himself, not for the first time. *Tomorrow I'll get this squared.*

His stomach gurgled. Surprised, he checked his watch. It was late. He should have eaten dinner hours earlier but had opted to focus on work instead. Nothing motivated him like an empty stomach, particularly when he knew there were excellent left-overs in the fridge.

He pushed back from his desk and jogged from his bedroom to the kitchen. As he swung open the fridge, the front door opened, and he heard Nico come into their apartment.

"Hey," Neil said from deep inside the fridge.

"Hey."

He frowned, unable to find the box he was looking for. "Did you eat my pad Thai?"

"I ate something with noodles."

"Man," Neil said sharply, "that was my dinner." He slammed the fridge door and whirled around. "What the hell?"

Nico dropped his shoulder bag on the floor. Sighing, he peeled his coat off his stocky frame, tossed it over the arm of the sofa, and plopped down beside it. Then he kicked off his shoes and put his feet up on the coffee table. "I'm sorry," he said, rubbing a hand over his face and through his shaggy black hair as he leaned back into the cushions. "I was in a hurry. I figured if you were gonna eat it for dinner, you would have already. I mean"—he checked his watch—"it's way beyond dinnertime, you know?"

"I was working," Neil snapped.

"Sorry," Nico repeated. "Help yourself to anything of mine."

Neil cursed. He reached into the fridge, shoving things around to find some hidden feast in the corners, and discovered a Chinese takeout box. He snatched it up and popped open the top, hoping for fried rice or won tons. It was broccoli. *Well, that's life, isn't it?* he thought. *Your roommate eats your pad Thai, and you get broccoli.*

Broccoli in one hand, he fished out his phone and added an item to his to-do list: *Buy food.* Then, after a pause: *Learn to cook.*

He took a seat on a stool at the kitchen counter and tore into the broccoli. Nico groaned and slumped low in the sofa.

"Long day?" Neil asked.

"Yeah." Nico sighed. "Between classes, work, and my aunt, I don't get much sleep. Just as well, since I keep having the same dream every night." He squinted and cast a questioning look at Neil. "You expecting anyone?"

"Huh?" Neil looked at Nico as he chewed.

"Like someone stopping by from out of town?"

Neil shook his head. "My brother and his family are in New Jersey, my dad lives in Illinois, and my mom lives in Ireland. They wouldn't just 'stop by.'"

"Well," Nico said, "I think my dream's telling me that someone's coming, someone I'm gonna meet, and they're coming to me through you."

"A dream told you that?" Neil said. He suppressed a chuckle so as not to sound disrespectful. "Your dream say who?"

"Nothing I can make sense of. Feels important, though."

"Important?" Unable to hide a smile, Neil asked, "Is it a girl? Is she hot?"

Nico shot him an irritated glare. "Don't be an asshole."

His joking tone gone, Neil frowned. "I'm an asshole? You ate my dinner, left me week-old broccoli, and I'm the asshole?"

Scowling, Nico opened his mouth but then paused and shook his head. "Forget it," he said.

Exhausted silence settled into the apartment, disrupted only by the faint babble of their neighbor's television, a distant chitter of canned laughter. Neil stuffed the last chunk of broccoli between his teeth and tossed the takeout box into the trash.

"Wanna go get a drink?" he asked.

For a moment, Nico looked straight ahead, dark eyes glazed. Then he turned to Neil and smiled wearily. "Yeah."

12 Mei-Xing

ZAMEK'S WAS, AS GEORGETTE PREDICTED, EASY TO FIND. IT took only fifteen minutes of walking the Las Vegas Strip before Georgette stopped in her tracks, her eyes glued to an electronic billboard. Mei-Xing and Ishak stood on either side of her, looking up at the huge, glowing slab.

Mei-Xing squinted as the advertisement changed from a casino to a restaurant to a performance. "What do you see?" she asked in Mandarin.

"When the ad changes," Georgette said, "there's an extra ad in between the regular images."

"I don't see it."

"No, you wouldn't. It's visually tuned to witches' eyesight."

"And you see Zamek's?"

"That and other things." She continued staring at the billboard as the cycle of ads repeated. "I missed the address the first time around. Wait a minute, and I'll catch it."

"What the hell are you saying?" Ishak said irritably. "Speak Fae so I can understand."

Mei-Xing shushed him. "We make it a point not to speak Fae in public," she whispered. "We stick to English or Mandarin."

"I don't speak those," he said. "Do you speak Arabic, Kanuri, or French?"

"No."

"Then speak Fae."

Mei-Xing sighed. He was right, they should include him, but speaking Fae out in the open was an invitation for attention. Mei-Xing was passing for human, and Georgette was trying to avoid her old life. If the wrong person overheard them speaking an inhuman language, their covers could be blown. But she couldn't very well expect this man to speak a language he didn't know.

"We'll try," she said, "but Georgette will have to speak English at Zamek's."

"Why?" Ishak demanded, looking back and forth between her and Georgette. "Surely these brokers know Fae. It is the most common language spoken among their . . ." He wrinkled his nose. "Their . . . *merchandise*."

"That's true," Georgette said, still watching the billboard. "Many of them do speak at least a little Fae, but they'll refuse."

"Why?"

"They consider it beneath them. My ex-fiancé says any broker who speaks Fae has 'gone native.'"

A film of distaste crossed Ishak's features. "You intended to marry such a man?"

"My mother intended me to marry him."

"And how long did you go along with it?" he asked. When Georgette didn't respond, he took a step forward and peered down at her. "How long was your engagement?"

Eyes fluttering and lip trembling, Georgette brushed past the

Nymph and the Bultungin and walked up the strip. "I got the address. We can go."

Mei-Xing whirled on Ishak. "Don't be so unkind," she said sharply. "She is trying to help you."

A wave of suspicion quickly smothered the flash of remorse on Ishak's face. "She is still a witch," he said, "and I've never known witches to have an excess of generosity."

In his voice, Mei-Xing heard an old sentiment that she had long believed. But she remembered how a teenage Ivy O'Reilly had helped her escape from her abusive husband and willfully blind family—not to mention risked trouble with local Chinese authorities by carrying Mei-Xing's last living plant, a marijuana seedling, in her bag all the way from Shanghai to the US. She had even invented a new type of *Hathiya* bond solely for the purpose of saving a total stranger who was desperate enough to ask a witch for help.

She caught Ishak's gaze and held it. "You've never known Georgette."

13 Georgette

"I can," said Ishak. "They *will* speak to me!"

"You don't understand," she said. "In their eyes, you're not a person."

"A misconception I'll be happy to correct," he said.

"No!" Georgette balled her fists with frustration. "Absolutely everything and everyone in that office is there for the purpose of catching, holding, and selling Fae. When they see you aren't a witch's familiar, they'll snatch you." She uncurled her hands and flexed her fingers at her sides. "You won't do Kalilah any good if you're locked up."

The mention of his wife silenced him. His eyes drifted to Zamek's, just a few yards from where they stood, and hardened.

"I'll return at night," he said. "With my full power, I can tear this building apart."

"What if Kalilah's not here?" Georgette said. "If you wreck the place and don't find her, you'll put every other brokerage in the area on high alert, which will make it that much harder to find her."

"What would you have me do?" he snapped, making her flinch. "Smile in the faces of slavers? Ask politely that they grant Kalilah her God-given freedom?"

"No, just . . . just let me do the talking. Please. Let me put a glamour on you so it looks like you're my familiar."

"You would mark my skin like Kivuli Panon did?"

"No," she said quickly. "Just an illusion. They won't look twice if you act like a familiar."

His face twisted into a visage of pure disgust. Burned by guilt, Georgette lowered her eyes. In the corner of her vision, she saw Mei-Xing sitting on a bench, staring across the street.

"I'm sorry," she said sincerely, "but it's the only safe way."

Grinding his teeth, Ishak gave a curt nod.

Georgette glanced up and down the street. Seeing no onlookers, she swiftly laced a glamour from whispered words, conjured thoughts, and the latent energy all around. At her bidding, the woven image settled on the underside of Ishak's wrist.

The Bultungin held up his arm and examined the false, looping mark closely. "It looks quite real," he said, eyes wide, "but I feel nothing."

"Exactly." Georgette nodded. "And I can remove it just as easily. Now"—she pulled herself up straight—"let's go."

The foyer of Zamek's looked like any office entrance, complete with a sitting area, front desk, and uninteresting art on the walls. Georgette's trained eye saw more. Behind an oversized desk, magic coated a door leading to the rest of the office like a window protected by iron bars. More magic dwelled deeper inside the building—the feel of it was like the crackle of an electrical storm in the air—but the door obscured its exact nature. Most brokerages used the excuse that it kept their merchandise protected and compliant, but Georgette knew there was another reason. Zach had once told her that it stopped witches from knowing the particulars of their inventory. This gave the brokers an advantage when bargaining.

She assessed the man at the desk. He did not match the description the other familiar, the bird-woman, had given Ishak; this man was gray-haired, smooth-shaven, and had no glasses or gut. His eyes caught hers for a moment—just long enough for him to acknowledge her as a witch—before sweeping over every inch of Ishak. She saw him making a mental calculation of the Bultungin in exactly the same manner Zach always had.

Willing her heartbeat to slow, she approached the desk with a polite smile.

"I'm in the market to make a purchase," she said in an adopted voice that resembled her mother's, which made the words taste foul. "I have it on good authority you have something for sale that interests me."

"Excellent," said the clerk with a shopkeeper's grin. He nodded at Ishak. "Have you come to trade?"

Just over her shoulder, Georgette heard Ishak exhale slowly, a barely audible growl under the breath. Forcing herself to keep smiling, she shook her head. "No. I'll pay cash."

"All right then." He turned to the laptop on the desk. "What can Zamek's Brokerage do for you today, Miss . . . ?"

It was on the tip of her tongue to answer *O'Reilly*, but at the last second, she caught herself. "Delaney," she said. "Georgette

Delaney. I've heard that one of your agents purchased a female Bultungin. I'd like to buy her."

"Bultungin?" said the clerk, his forehead wrinkled. He typed, his eyes glued to the screen, but soon shook his head. "I'm not familiar with that term, and it's not coming up in our inventory. Would it be under another word?"

"Try *Werehyena*."

Moments ticked by in silence, the clerk's eyes scanning the screen of his computer. At last, he shook his head.

"Nope," he said conclusively. "I tried *Werehyena*, *hyena*, and *were-creature*, but I've got nothing like what you've said. Are you sure this thing came to Zamek's?"

The word *thing* triggered a sharp breath from Ishak, and Georgette heard him grinding his teeth.

"Yes," she said, "but maybe it wasn't this office. Could you check other branches?"

"Already did," he told her. "Nothing."

"I was told that the agent who bought her was a young, heavyset man with dark hair, a beard, and glasses," Georgette said. "Maybe he would know where to look?"

At her description, Georgette saw the clerk stiffen. Quickly, he closed his laptop and turned away.

"That man," he huffed, "doesn't work here anymore."

"Oh," she said. "Well, perhaps you could provide me with his contact infor—"

"Could I interest you in a different purchase?" the clerk interrupted, wheeling about in his chair to face her again. "We have some new arrivals from Eastern Europe. I can offer you a great deal."

"Did he join another brokerage?" Georgette said, shaking her head. "If you just tell me his name I—"

"Leave."

She blinked, her mouth hanging open in surprise. The man's expression had grown dark so quickly that Georgette was alarmed. "Excuse me?"

"If you're not going to buy," the man said, all pleasantness dropped from his voice, "then leave."

Ishak took a step forward, but Georgette held out an arm to block him. "Look," she said, "I just need to know where to find that agent. Tell me, and I'll go."

"Absolutely not." He stood up, placed his palms on the desk, and leaned forward. "I looked up your name. You've never made a purchase from Zamek's, Miss Delaney. Since you are not and have never been a customer, you can take your prying questions somewhere else. The man you're looking for no longer works here." He pointed at the front door. "Get out."

A flush of anger went through her. Though she'd always been mistreated within her own family, Georgette was accustomed to people affording her a measure of respect based solely on her name. With that name gone, so, apparently, was the respect that accompanied it. The reality of her new situation struck her hard. She was free but she was no one.

In that moment, a new thought came to her: Why was she trying to play by the rules of her old life? Who was that going to help? Not her, not Ishak, and certainly not Kalilah. Feeling unburdened, she turned to Ishak.

"I've given you bad advice," she said, "and I apologize." Throwing out one hand, she cast a quick but solid sealing magic on the door behind the desk. "You handle this situation however seems best to you. You've got about ten minutes before the other employees get through the door." She nodded to him. "I'll be outside."

Surprised, Ishak's eyebrows rose. A second later, he let out a puff of laughter. He nodded back at her, smirking, his dark eyes afire with respect.

Georgette headed for the exit. She paused at the door to glance back at the clerk and felt a swell of satisfaction upon seeing the man backing away from Ishak's advance, his every movement radiating fear.

14 Mei-Xing

THE DOOR OF ZAMEK'S DINGED, DRAWING MEI-XING'S EYE in time to see Georgette exiting the brokerage. Mei-Xing returned her gaze to the far side of the street as Georgette took a seat next to her on the bench.

"Where's Ishak?" she asked.

"The clerk wasn't helpful," Georgette said, "so Ishak's chatting with him."

After a moment's thought, Mei-Xing nodded. This was an abrupt departure from the plan, but since it was already done, she simply asked the most pertinent question. "Is it safe?"

"Until the spell I cast on the office door wears off, it should be fine."

After three years of close friendship, Mei-Xing had developed a sense for how long Georgette's spells would last. They would probably have to leave quickly in a few minutes, but until then, there was no danger.

Seconds ticked by in silence as Mei-Xing continued to stare across the street. Finally, Georgette nudged her with an elbow. "What are you looking at? The bird?" she asked. "Or those boys?"

Magic By Any Other Name

A large, sleek raven perched on an awning, its inky feathers ruffling in the arid wind. Its eyes never strayed far from the two teenage boys taunting each other in front of an alleyway just below. The young men were inching closer to each other while gesturing threateningly, their voices gaining in volume. Passersby eyed the argument nervously.

"Neither," Mei-Xing said. "I'm looking at the lady with the bird."

Georgette squinted. "Who?"

"There, under the awning. Look deeper."

Mei-Xing sensed the shift in her friend's perspective, a soft breeze of magic flitting over her like the cold breath of a just-opened refrigerator. Now she knew Georgette saw her—the armored woman. Tall, statuesque, and glittering in ethereal light, she leaned against the wall under the awning with her arms, covered in chain mail, crossed over her breastplate. Her wavy brown hair spilled out in tendrils from beneath her helmet, the rim of which obscured her eyes. One of her feet tapped rhythmically, jostling the joints of metal on her leg, and swishing the loose, gauzy fabric that draped over her form like a cloud-woven cloak. The sunlight seemed to parade over every inch of her in sparkles that looked too brilliant to be real. Mei-Xing was dazzled.

"She's a Valkyrie," Georgette said, her voice soft and awed.

"A Valkyrie?" Mei-Xing repeated, drinking in the sight. "I've never seen one."

"Me neither. Witches avoid them."

"Why?"

"Because they're powerful and well-organized. If a witch ever took a Valkyrie as a familiar, the rest of the Valkyries would know

89

she was gone, and they'd come for her. They'd *all* come for her."

The squabbling boys were toe to toe and eye to eye now. Their vulgar shouts had awakened a homeless man, who shakily rose from the floor of the alley and looked around in confusion.

One of the young men threw a punch, igniting a vicious fist-fight. As the boys yelled and grappled with one another, the Valkyrie continued leaning against the building and tapping her toes, not even raising her eyes. The raven overhead shuffled along the edge of the awning, peering over the side to watch the fight below.

The homeless man staggered toward the violent pair, his eyes on his feet, and the raven warbled.

There was a struggle, a flash of metal, a scream. Suddenly, two people lay bleeding on the ground: one of the boys and the homeless man. The other boy stood over them with a knife in his reddened hand—shaking, wide eyes locked on his gasping victims. When onlookers cried out, he jolted to attention, dropped the knife, and ran.

Bystanders rushed to the wounded or yelled the location into their cellphones. Side by side on the bench, Mei-Xing and Georgette watched as the Valkyrie pushed off the wall, drew a sword almost as tall as herself, and walked as gracefully as a dancer toward the fallen.

A shadow spilled out of the alley like black milk. It circled the two wounded men, sweeping around the unseeing crowd without touching their skin. The darkness amassed between the boy and the homeless man and swiftly inflated until it towered over the crowd. Mei-Xing and Georgette held their breath, their eyes glued to the scene. The shadow bent over the homeless man, extended a skinny limb from its core, and plunged it into his chest. The black arm passed through the hands of a woman applying pressure to the wound and she gave no sign of having felt it. The shadow withdrew its limb, and with it brought out a pillar of fog. The mist, a permeable collection of muted colors, quickly shaped itself into a human form. As the particles came to rest, Mei-Xing saw it had become a translucent copy of the homeless man that floated inches above its source, connected only by a thin silver thread, staring down at the scene below it with an expression of calm lucidity.

The dark column grew another limb, this one curved and edged like a sickle. It swung the blade in an arc, aiming for the silver thread. With a ghostly clang, the sickle struck the Valkyrie's sword. She looked up at the shadow, her dark eyes shining like gold coins.

"He is chosen," she said.

Her words echoed as if trickling down a long hallway, easily reaching Mei-Xing's ears.

The Valkyrie and the shadow remained locked together, weapon to weapon, for a long moment. Then the darkness withdrew its blade and drifted toward the wounded boy, a new dark limb already growing from its center.

The Valkyrie turned to face the homeless man's spirit.

"Corporal Timothy Emerson," the Valkyrie said. "Attention!"

It was as if a shockwave blasted through the spirit, and the ragged clothes vanished, replaced by a crisp, clean uniform. The scruffy beard and overgrown hair disappeared to reveal a clean-cut, strong-jawed man with bright, clear eyes. He stood up straight, his gaze set on the Valkyrie.

"Ma'am, yes ma'am!" he said.

"You have been chosen, Corporal," she told him. "There is another war to fight. Will you come?"

The corporal paused and glanced down at his body. Mei-Xing couldn't imagine what this lean, well-toned soul saw when he looked at the lifeless ruin that was left of him in the alley, but the corporal made no remark. Instead, he returned his focus to the Valkyrie and asked, "Do they need me, ma'am?"

"Yes, soldier," she said. "They need you."

The corporal drew back his shoulders and saluted her. "Then I'm ready."

She nodded smartly and returned his salute. In a fluid motion, she swung her sword under his spirit feet and severed the silver cord. Free of his mortal husk, Emerson floated into the air, rising above the heads of the crowd. The raven on the awning spread its wings and took to the air at the same moment that the Valkyrie sprang from the ground and hooked her arm through the soldier's. The bird grabbed her other hand with his talons and, much to Mei-Xing's astonishment, carried both her and the soldier up into the sky.

As if sensing the eyes on her, the Valkyrie glanced down and looked right at her and Georgette. Mei-Xing saw Georgette cautiously offer a little wave and duplicated the gesture. The Valkyrie stared blandly at them until, in a flash of light, she and her companions disappeared.

15 Ishak

THE BANGS AND SHOUTS FROM BEHIND THE OFFICE DOOR were becoming louder. Ishak guessed that Georgette's spell was wearing off. Leaving the clerk to whimper under his desk, Ishak strode out the front door, which jingled pleasantly in his wake.

When they spotted him, the two women immediately rose from a bench and fell into step next to him. To his left, Georgette muttered under her breath and gestured backhandedly at Zamek's. An instant later, someone inside the office slammed against the door. It didn't jingle.

"How long until that spell breaks?" he asked.

"Maybe another ten minutes," she said.

"What did you get from the clerk?" Mei-Xing asked.

"Threats, at first," he said with a smirk. "Then bribes. Then begging. And all that before I even laid a hand on him. When I finally grabbed him, he talked immediately."

"Do you trust what he told you?"

Ishak chuckled. "To convince me to leave, I believe that man would have told me where his grandmother keeps her jewelry."

———

Blocks from Zamek's, the three companions sat in a booth at a bar and grill. The sun was setting, and the city lighting up; they saw the gradual shift from natural to artificial glow from their window-side table. As night crept upon the city, Ishak felt his Bultungin senses grow increasingly sensitive.

The aroma of seasoned meat was painfully alluring. His scent memory, intricately woven in with the hyena part of his mind, began identifying the source of every scent he caught. Beef, chicken, fish . . . his mouth watered so fiercely he had to gulp down the saliva to keep from drooling. Looking at the menu, he had no idea what the English words meant, but the pictures, combined with the scents, told him what he wanted. When the waitress came to their table, he pointed to a particularly luscious-looking photo. The girl, unfazed by his nonverbal response, jotted down his order with a smile.

When the witch and the Nymph had made their own selections, and the server was out of earshot, they both leaned across the table toward Ishak.

"What did he tell you?" Mei-Xing whispered.

Ishak leaned forward and spoke quietly, although he wasn't sure it was a necessary precaution; the restaurant was quite busy and consequently it was also quite noisy—it seemed unlikely that anyone would notice or care that they spoke Fae.

"The clerk," he told them, "said that the man who bought my wife is a former agent of theirs named Christopher Barnes. Apparently, this man had been selling some of their 'merchandise' to a competitor at a discount, taking commission on the sales and also accepting a kickback. Zamek's found out and fired him. They suspect that he took several undocumented acquisitions with him when he left. Kalilah was likely one of these."

"Where is he now?" Mei-Xing asked.

"The clerk thinks Barnes took a job at the other brokerage. With your help"—Ishak nodded to Georgette—"perhaps I can track him down."

"What's the brokerage?" Georgette asked.

"Kett & Kadena."

"Kett & Kadena," she repeated slowly, sounding out the words. "Never heard of it."

Ishak took a deep breath and laced his fingers together on the tabletop. Disappointment gnawed at him, but he tried to suppress it. He had come this far with less information.

"Unless . . ." Georgette broke into his thoughts. "Maybe Kett & Kadena is KK Inc."

"KK Inc.?" Hope roared up within him. "You know it?"

"Yes. Well," she qualified, "by reputation."

Her hesitant tone made the hair on the back of his neck stand on end. "Reputation?"

"Um," she stumbled, "I only know what I've been told. My ex said no respectable broker does business with KK Inc. because they cheat other brokerages. And my aunt said witches only go to KK Inc. when they need something that . . . they don't want anyone to know about."

Visibly uncomfortable with the topic, Georgette's eyes darted back and forth between the table and the window. Every second she stalled, Ishak felt his alarm at the situation grow.

Mei-Xing put a hand on Georgette's shoulder and murmured

something in Mandarin. Georgette took a deep breath and continued.

"My cousin Daphne and two of my sisters, Clove and Lily, have used KK Inc. to get familiars," she said. "One of the three of them is most likely to inherit the family headship after my mother. They're super competitive to be Mom's favorite. Daphne buys from KK Inc. and pays under the table to avoid a bill of sale. That way she can claim that she caught them to make herself look more powerful than she is. Lily uses KK Inc. to steal familiars from other witches. For the right price, KK Inc. will abduct a familiar from the witch that caught it, rip out the brand—usually by removing the skin and muscle tissue that it's attached to—and give the familiar brain damage to erase its memory. A lot of Lily's familiars are missing chunks of their bodies and don't remember their own names." Georgette winced and shot an apologetic look across the table. "Clove goes to KK Inc. to buy creatures for blood sacrifices. Most brokerages don't give a damn what happens to a familiar once they've sold it, but they also don't like to be associated with dark rituals."

"And," Ishak said shakily, "this is the brokerage you believe now has possession of my wife?"

"If KK Inc. is Kett & Kadena, then yes."

Ishak's guts wrenched. His blood pounded in his ears. He thought of the last time he saw Kalilah—the twists of her hair wrapped in a scarf and her long fingers popping dates into her mouth. He thought of her in her hyena form, her thick fur an elegant quilt of gray and brown. Memories cascaded through his mind: her smile, her laugh, the warmth of her skin. He felt their absence like a hole in his chest. Misery, fear, and anger vied for his attention, and he fought with them all to keep a level head.

"If this is true, how do I find Kalilah?" he asked.

Georgette picked up her phone, glanced around the busy restaurant, and then waved two fingers over the screen. A distortion like a heat wave passed over the phone and Ishak smelled a whiff of magic. She was using witchcraft to tap into the kobold net, an online system created by, maintained, and used by witches. The library in his hometown of Kabultiloa possessed one computer that allowed access to the kobold net; the elders had paid a witch to install it. Kalilah had thought they wanted it just for bragging rights, a way to show just how important their city was. Until this moment, Ishak had never given it much thought. Until this moment, he had not considered that the kobold net would ever be relevant to his life.

"What are you searching for?" he asked Georgette. "Kett & Kadena?"

"Yeah," she said, eyes still on her phone. "They're smaller than Zamek's, which actually might be a good thing. That means fewer offices where they could be holding your wife."

"Is there an online catalog?" Mei-Xing asked.

"No such luck," Georgette said, "but the only KK Inc. office within a day's drive is in San Jose, California. In fact, they only have two offices west of the Rocky Mountains: San Jose and Spokane. I think San Jose would be the best place for us to start."

Ishak squinted at her, cocking his head a bit. "Why do you say that?"

"Because it's closer."

"No," he said. "Why do you say *us*?"

The sun was down, its last receding rays quickly eclipsed by the neon glow of the city. The hyena within Ishak smelled anxiety radiating from Georgette's pores. She looked at him, her pale eyes magnified by her glasses.

"I said I would help you find her," she said.

"We have already established that I can get the information I need without your help. Why—"

"I'm gonna use the bathroom," she said, dropping her phone and jumping up from her seat. "Be right back."

Without a backward glance, she weaved her way through the other patrons toward the back of the restaurant. The suddenness of her departure confused Ishak—but then, he reminded himself, many things about Georgette confused him. He looked to Mei-Xing, who was reading something on the witch's phone.

"When I first asked her for help," he said, "she refused because she was afraid of being discovered by her family. I forced her hand but, in the end, she helped. Then she insisted on playing nice with Zamek's people—and changed her mind after five minutes in there. She fluctuates wildly between acting like a witch and acting like . . . a person. Why?"

Mei-Xing sighed and set down the phone. "She's at war with herself," she said. "She was raised to be one type of woman, and now she's remaking herself into another. It's not an easy thing to be one's own creator."

"But why is she helping me?"

Mei-Xing spread her hands wide. "Purpose. Until we met you, we were running away from her old life. Now, we're building her new life. Which one do you think feels better?"

Ishak nodded slowly.

"You're also more likely to find Kalilah with our help," Mei-Xing added.

"That is true," he mumbled. With a sidelong glance in the direction of the washrooms, he leaned closer to the Nymph. "How far can I trust this witch?"

She looked at him strangely, the human glamour on her face scrunching up in an inhuman way. "In China," she said, "my husband worked me to the brink of death, forcing me to grow opiates and other drugs to pay his debts. My grove was dependent on his water supply; no one came to my defense. Then, three years ago, Georgette passed by. She was spending the summer traveling with her aunt and cousin. I told her my story and asked her for help. She helped me escape and snuck the last of my plants away—after I let all the rest die so it would look like I had died—and then designed an entirely new type of *Hathiya* to keep me alive and free when my last plant wilted, and I was in danger of actually dying. It was meant to be temporary, just until the seeds of my plants could grow, but we maintained the bond, and I have never regretted it." She returned her attention to the phone. "Make of that what you like."

Ishak inhaled deeply, slowly, and thought. He was in a strange country whose language he didn't speak. He also had only a limited knowledge of witch society. He needed Georgette.

Kalilah needed Georgette.

16 Delia & Senji

On the steps of Valhalla, the Valkyrie delivered the corporal to her waiting superior.

Perched on his partner's shoulder, the raven watched the officer lead the chosen soul up the steps to begin his afterlife on the battlefield.

With a sigh, she turned away from the towering front doors. "Back to work."

"It will be some time before our next chosen dies," he said.

"I know," she said, disinterested. "So much of what we do is waiting."

Through the connection they shared, Senji sensed her distraction. Since 1945, shortly after their deaths, when their memories and thoughts had merged, their minds had been inseparable. *What troubles you?* he thought.

That he knew her mind so well was not surprising. Delia barely remembered the short human life she had spent with no thoughts in her head but her own.

I'm not troubled, she thought, giving him a smile, *but there is something we should discuss.*

But not here, he finished her thought. *Let's return to the living plane.*

Together, they descended through stars and sky, through realms and worlds, to their assigned sector.

Together, they descended through stars and sky, through realms and worlds, to their assigned sector.

Via her connection to Senji, Delia felt the wind swirl around them, but on her own spectral skin she felt nothing at all. While his soul now inhabited a raven's form, she remained a ghost.

They landed atop the STRAT Observation Tower, him on her shoulder. Pausing to take in the fading afternoon, they watched the sun sink into the desert.

Before long, Las Vegas was an electric island in a sea of night.

"You saw them?" she finally asked.

"The two women on a bench? Yes."

"Did you feel the witchcraft?"

He tilted his head. "Yes. The simplest explanation is that they are witches."

"No, only one of them is a witch. Still, the other has witchery about her."

"A familiar, then?"

"No," she said firmly. "I can sense when they're branded. And yet . . ."

"I saw it too, when they waved," Senji said. "They are *both* branded." He flapped his wings. "What does it mean?"

"I don't know," Delia said. Her eyes swept over the city from beneath the rim of her helmet. "But those two could be exactly what we've been looking for."

Senji suppressed a chuckle. When Delia got excited, her Creole accent became more pronounced. Right now, it was unmistakable.

"How shall we proceed?"

"You should scout them— watch them for a stint and see what you can learn."

"Is that wise?" he asked skeptically.

"You can move less conspicuously than I can." She turned to face the wind, though it passed cleanly through her. "I'll stay near the next chosen, so Valhalla won't suspect. They're more likely to notice my absence than yours."

He croaked an acknowledgment. The Valkyries watched their own far more carefully than they did the beast partners who served them.

"If what I learn of the girls is favorable to our purpose," he told her, "I will come for you."

They looked at one another, each seeing both a partner and a reflection, their vision split between two sets of eyes.

"*Ganbatte kudasai*, Senji."

They looked at one another, each seeing both a partner and a reflection, their vision split between two sets of eyes.

"*Lâche pas la patate*, Delia."

The desert city glowed and shone like a star in the darkness.

The desert city glowed and shone like a star in the darkness.

17 Georgette

A COOL BREEZE RUFFLED GEORGETTE'S LONG, TIERED SKIRT. Yawning, she brushed her golden curls out of her face, the loose sleeves of her peasant blouse billowing. California weather was delightful! Back in Boston, she would have been bundled up in her winter coat by now. But here it was November, and she was still in sandals.

She dug her phone out of her purse as she walked. Though she had been in San Jose almost a month now, she still struggled to develop a sense of direction. Her phone's GPS showed she was close to Club Nocturne, but still, she was early. The interview wasn't until 5:00 p.m., almost half an hour from now. Well, she would make sure she knew exactly where Club Nocturne was and then find a place to wait. That would give her a chance to calm her nerves before meeting with her potential employer.

Initially, she had planned to follow Olive's advice and not put down roots until she had completely shed her old identity—but circumstances had changed. As she feared, Ishak interrogating the Zamek's clerk had resulted in her being blacklisted at every brokerage for hundreds of miles around. However, Ishak's actions had also produced an unexpected result: no one wanted to be caught in possession of the female Bultungin that had caused a crazy young witch to turn her familiar loose on a brokerage. As far as Georgette could tell, Kett & Kadena still had Kalilah—and, at least for now, wasn't trying to sell her.

Ishak had campaigned for a direct assault on the brokerage office, but Georgette had objected. While open warfare might get them through the door, it wouldn't help them find Kalilah once they were inside. Kett & Kadena might have a dozen storage facilities, any one of which could be holding Kalilah. In the time it took them to raid an office and steal the inventory records, KK Inc. employees could move Kalilah to a new facility or even kill her to avoid future problems. This second possibility had convinced Ishak to consider other options.

When Mei-Xing suggested using a third party to locate Kalilah, Georgette had remembered something: while looking at the Vegas billboard advertising Zamek's, she had seen other notices, including one from a nightclub in San Jose seeking a witch's services. A quick investigation on the kobold net had revealed that Club Nocturne had an odd reputation. Rumor had it that the owner, Ms. Kazimiera, was a weekend spellcaster who hired real witches to hide the evidence of her magical hobby. It was also a well-known secret that illegally-purchased familiars performed at Nocturne, which strongly suggested that Ms. Kazimiera was a regular customer of KK Inc. If Georgette could get a job at the club, she might be able to search Kett & Kadena's inventory under the guise of doing so for her employer.

Georgette sensed the nightclub half a block before arriving. The entire eight-story building was like a fountain of magic, ever-flowing and giving off a misty spray that she felt on her skin the closer she got. The spellcraft, though effective at masking what was inside, was sloppy as hell. It was a half-assed patchwork of spells, one magic laid on top of another without properly integrating them. No well-taught witch would work craft like this. *No well-taught witch would* work *here, either*, she thought.

At the corner, Georgette found a busy coffee shop and got in line. *No caffeine*, she sternly warned herself, *you're jittery enough already*. The aroma of cinnamon kissed her senses, and she felt her stomach growl. *Couldn't hurt to have a snack*. She didn't want to be thinking about food during the interview.

"Jeez," she heard a man's voice mumble behind her, "it's four thirty already? Where the hell did the afternoon go?"

Amused by his mystified tone, Georgette chuckled.

"You too, huh?" said the man.

Surprised, she turned around. "Sorry," she said, her heart at a gallop. "I didn't mean to listen."

"No big deal," he said with a smile.

His smile radiated such warmth that Georgette felt her cheeks flush. Self-conscious, she tossed her head a little to shake her curls over her face. He was not much older than her, trim and well-dressed. While not especially handsome, he was clean-cut, with rich brown hair that he had taken the time to style. Her immediate impression was that this was a man who made an effort to present the best of himself to the world. And that smile. It was a smile that rested not only on his lips but also in his eyes. Knowing that he had brought it out for her embarrassed her in the best way.

"Is—is it always so crowded here?" she said, stammering a bit.

"Don't know," he said. "I haven't been here in a while. I just wanted a quick caffeine boost before I head to my last meeting." He smiled again. "You too?"

"Oh no," she said with a nervous giggle. "No caffeine for me. I'm just killing some time until my interview."

"Job interview? Hey, good luck."

"Thanks. What's your meeting about?"

"Trying to make a sale," he told her. "I work for an import and export company, and I've got a meeting with a restaurant a couple of blocks from here about becoming a regular supplier for them."

"Sales," she said. "Oh God, I could never do that. I get anxious just *thinking* about trying to sell something to somebody."

"I get it," he said with a nod. "What kind of work are you looking for?"

His smile had her so flustered that she almost told him the truth. She caught herself in time and said, "IT," instead.

"Hey," he chuckled, "I could never do what you do. I know just enough about my computer to use it. When it breaks down, I break down."

"I get it," she said. His eyes were as rich and comforting as the coffee the baristas poured. Her ex, Zach, had gray eyes, a pale shade as dull and joyless as ice. Zach had also been a salesman of sorts, but his smile had held none of the warmth and charm this man's did.

The woman in front of her paid and moved to the end of the counter, allowing Georgette to step up to the cashier. "Good luck with your sale," she tossed out before placing her order.

"Thanks."

She felt his eyes on her as she ordered a pumpkin muffin and cinnamon tea, and it made her cheeks burn. Georgette wondered why she was comparing this guy to Zach. Maybe it was just that this man was the first to look at her with interest in a long time. Zach never had. Actually, very few men had ever looked at her like that. She'd grown up as the plain-Jane of her family. In a house of dark beauty, she'd been a pale stain—only noticed for how different she was.

When she received her drink and snack, she glanced around, but the young man was nowhere in sight. Though a little disappointed, she wasn't surprised. He was off to his meeting and didn't have time for a freckle-faced four-eyes. Well, with a smile like his, he was sure to do well.

Once outside the café, she immediately felt wisps of Club Nocturne's poorly-assembled magic assault her from down the block. She checked her watch: 4:50 p.m. Just enough time to wolf down the muffin and sip the tea while she walked.

While the magic outside the building was a patchy waterfall of concealment, the enchantment inside defied explanation. With every step, a different and more bizarre type of magic assailed Georgette. Ms. Kazimiera might collect illegal familiars to work in her club, but the mishmash of powers Georgette felt as she walked through Nocturne suggested far more Fae than she had imagined. *All those spells on the outside*, she thought, *are they a curtain to hide a witchcraft hobbyist, or a cage to keep her workforce trapped?*

The man who let her into the club—a normal human from

the look of him—led her down a long hallway and up two sets of stairs to an apartment area. He knocked on the first door they came to. A muffled voice answered. Opening the door, he silently waved at Georgette to enter. Once she did, he closed the door behind her, leaving her alone with the owner of the building.

At first glance, Ms. Kazimiera reminded Georgette of her sister Lily. Dark and sensual, the bounds of her skin scarcely contained the overwhelming femininity within. Art in every expression, poetry in every movement. At the far edge of youth, the creeping approach of middle age was just barely visible upon her. With one Lily-like smirk, the woman reduced Georgette to a shivering child.

At second glance, however, the resemblance melted and left Georgette with an entirely different impression. The sexy exterior, gussied up with tight, revealing clothes, hid a hardworking woman who, Georgette sensed, needed more help than she got. Her amber eyes were as sharp as cleavers—the acquired attribute of a businesswoman who needed to cut through bullshit in an instant—but they were bloodshot and carried heavy bags. Her corkscrew mane had the look of hair that had been well-kept in the past but had not been tended to recently. Kazimiera was stretched thin.

There was something else there too, something begging to be noticed, but Georgette couldn't figure it out. It was like a palmful of water that dribbled from the edges of her hand; the more she tried to tighten her grip, the more water slipped away.

Kazimiera flashed a sly but weary smile. "Never met a non-witch who looked at me like that."

"Sorry," Georgette said with a jolt. "I didn't mean to stare."

"You'd be no good to me otherwise." Kazimiera sidled around her desk and circled Georgette's chair, staring down at her with a gaze so sharp the witch felt she might draw blood. "So," she said, resting her rump on the edge of her desk, "now I know you're qualified for the job. Why don't you tell me why you want it."

"I need a job," Georgette lied. "I saw your ad in Vegas and—"

"Why do you want *this* job?" Kazimiera asked pointedly. "You must know that this isn't a typical business. Why would a capable witch take a job from"—she smirked—"a scandalous pretender like myself?"

Expecting a question like this, Georgette had prepared an answer but now that she was faced with Kazimiera's cutting eyes, she wasn't sure it would work. "I'm a college dropout with no family connections to tap," she said. "My craft is the only bankable skill I have."

The club owner stared, unblinking, at Georgette. When concocting her answer, Georgette had worried she would blush—but now, face-to-face with this woman, she felt all color drain out of her cheeks.

"You do understand that working for me will make you unemployable with most of your community?"

"Screw 'em," Georgette replied.

The honesty of her response must have shown in her expression. Kazimiera nodded appreciatively; her red lips curled into a grin.

"You remind me of the last witch to work for me," she said. "He had a 'screw 'em all' attitude too." Kazimiera sighed. "Martin worked here a long time. I was sorry to lose him."

"Well," Georgette jumped in, "he didn't do a great job on the exterior of your building. It works well enough but it's messy. I can clean it up."

"You think you're better than Martin?"

"No," Georgette said, horrified at her own forwardness. "It's just that it looks like he layered his magics. That's old-fashioned spellcraft. I know more modern methods. I'm guessing," she added, "that Martin is an older gentleman?"

"Was. He's dead."

"Oh," Georgette said. She couldn't help but be unsettled by Kazimiera's casual tone. "I'm sorry."

"I liked him," Kazimiera said, eyeing Georgette closely. "I especially liked that he worked for room and board."

"He lived here?"

"He did. Apartment 7B. It's been empty since he died."

"Is that a requirement of this job?" Georgette asked. "Because I don't—"

"It's a perk," Kazimiera said, "once I'm convinced that you're right for the job. Until then, you'll come here for regular hours—"

"Whoa, wait a minute," Georgette said. "I got the job? Just like that?"

"On a trial basis, yes." Kazimiera flashed another sly smile. "That is what you wanted, right?"

"Sure, but . . . I thought this was just an interview."

"It should have been," Kazimiera said, "but I've been running ads for eight months and you're the only one who's applied for the job. So do you want it or not?"

"Um, y-yes," Georgette stammered. "Yes, I do." Her mind reeled. She hadn't expected this to be so easy. "When should I start?"

"Tomorrow. Come in after 5:00 p.m. You'll start by fixing the spells that cloak the outside of the building. That should keep you busy awhile."

"Okay," Georgette said, "but why 5:00 p.m.? I mean, won't it be harder for me to examine everything if your employees are getting the club ready to open?"

"I work nights," said Kazimiera, her hatchet stare cutting off Georgette's questions. "My club, my building, my rules."

Nursing a suspicion, Georgette glanced around the room. The apartment that served as Kazimiera's office was lit exclusively by low-wattage lamps that kept the room in constant artificial twilight. The windows were covered by thick, heavy curtains that blocked out all hint of the setting sun. She looked again at her would-be employer's bloodshot eyes.

"Are you . . . ?"

Kazimiera smiled, her red lips parting to show her pointed teeth. The sight of them sent a shiver across Georgette's skin and put her hair on end.

"I," Kazimiera said, "am the boss."

18 Neil

THE TASTE OF COFFEE LINGERED ON NEIL'S TONGUE LONG AFTER the meeting. If he'd noticed it earlier, he would have taken a breath mint, but he had been distracted by thoughts of the girl from the coffee shop. Thankfully, if the client did notice his breath, it hadn't prevented him from signing on to the sale. In a good mood, Neil felt optimistic about seeing the girl again.

That halo of blonde curls had sparked his interest, but her unique face was what had caught him on fire. Her freckles were like a splatter of paint on a canvas, an abstract work of art. In the center of a small face, her blue eyes looked adorably big behind her glasses. And she'd blushed when she talked to him! *Too cute,* he thought.

After the meeting, he walked up and down the street several times, wondering where she was interviewing. Though tempted, he stopped short of ducking into any of the businesses to look for her; he didn't want to cross the line into stalker territory.

Moments away from designating the IT girl a "missed opportunity," he saw a cloud of gold exit Club Nocturne. The breeze caught her as she stepped through the door, whipping about her white blouse and blue hippie skirt. She turned her face into the wind and smiled as it played with her hair. *God, what a sweet smile!*

Seeing her again, his optimism faltered. A girl like that definitely had a boyfriend. Even if she didn't, she wasn't going to be interested in a skinny creeper she met at a coffee shop. He was setting himself up to get shot down.

Still, when she headed up the street, he drew a deep breath, exhaled, and steeled himself. "Come on," he said to himself. "Let's do this."

He jogged up the street, quickly closing the gap between them. "Hey!" he called out in what he hoped was a friendly tone. "IT interview, right?"

Whirling around, the expression on her face was one of instant distrust. Embarrassed, he wanted to cover his face and slide down a storm drain. But then he saw recognition in her eyes, and, to his relief, she smiled—and blushed again.

"Import sales guy," she said as he trotted up next to her.

"Neil."

"Also known as Neil," she chuckled. "I'm Georgette."

Georgette. God, that's so perfect. "Hey, uh . . . hey."

"Hey. How was your meeting?"

"Good! Just finished the sale, stepped out, and saw you," he lied. He looked up at the sign over the building's front door. "You were interviewing at Nocturne?"

"Yeah," she said. "Their system is really out of date. The owner wants me to update everything."

"So you got the job? That's great!"

"Yeah," she said, looking a little bewildered. "It happened kinda fast. I didn't expect to get hired today."

Alison Levy

"That's good though, right?" Dry-mouthed, he tried to swallow. "I guess you'll be going out to celebrate tonight?"

"I hadn't thought about it. I doubt my roommates would want to."

Roommates. Not boyfriend, roommates. With his heart pounding, he pushed through his fear and asked, "Can I take you out? Drinks or something?"

The naked amazement on her face caught him off guard. She stammered a bit, making his chest constrict; he was sure she was inventing an excuse to say no. But then she smiled and laughed.

"Yeah," she said, sounding a little surprised. "I'd like that."

He grinned, his fear dissipating. A swell of confidence filled him up like a rising tide.

Georgette.

19 ❦ Ishak

Ishak shook Mei-Xing as hard as he dared but her limp body did not respond. Muttering darkly, he wondered if her plant body had bones to break or if he could safely increase his force. Instead, he continued staring at her where she lay with corpse-like stillness on the hotel bed.

Every night, Ishak shifted form and swept the city, searching. Every day, the girls checked the kobold net and made discreet inquiries to the local magic community. And still there was no sign of Kalilah. Weeks had passed now, and his worry chewed at him like a tapeworm, devouring him slowly but steadily from the inside out.

"Wake up!" he bellowed directly into the Nymph's ear.

Ishak was itching to begin his nightly patrol of the city, but first he wanted to know how the witch's interview at the night-club had played out. And Georgette wasn't there, so Mei-Xing was the only one who could answer his questions.

With sudden inspiration, Ishak grabbed the lamp from the end table, yanked off the shade, and held the bulb close to Mei-Xing's face.

She is a plant, he reasoned, *so she might react to light more than to sound.*

After a minute of him holding blazing light just inches from her eyes, Mei-Xing stirred and groaned. Her lids cracked open, then slammed shut again. She turned her head aside, muttering in Mandarin.

Ishak took her chin in his hand and forced her to face the light.

"Wake up!" he shouted. "Where's Georgette?"

To his surprise, she spat out some vicious-sounding words before finally opening her eyes. When she did, she hissed like a cat and threw an arm over them.

"*Aiya,*" she said. "She's out."

"At the club?"

"No, she's done with the club."

"Done?" Alarm creeped into his voice. "Why? Did she not interview?"

"Interview's over," Mei-Xing said. "She got the job."

Relief cooled his body. "She did?"

"Yes," the Nymph said irritably. "She starts tomorrow."

"Where is she now?"

"On a date."

"A date?" He waited for the words to make sense. "Who does she know in this city but us?"

"She called the room while you were getting dinner. She met a guy, and they're going out."

"She's going out with a man she just met? Is that a good idea?"

"Dunno," Mei-Xing mumbled. She rolled away and curled into a ball on the far side of the bed. "Talk later."

"Where did they go, her and this man?" he asked. When Mei-Xing didn't answer, he stepped around the bed and brought the lamp close to her face again. "Mei-Xing!"

The Nymph rolled into a tight fetal position to escape the light. Tightly wrapped in her own arms, she had fallen back into her nightly hibernation.

Ishak set down the lamp and refocused his mind. Georgette was starting the job tomorrow. That was one step forward. And every step forward brought them closer to Kalilah.

20  Georgette

DEEP IN GEORGETTE'S DREAM, SEVENTEEN-YEAR-OLD IVY O'Reilly stared, slack-jawed, at her mother. "Wh-what did you say?" she stammered.

"You're not going to apply to any college west of the Mississippi River," Hazel repeated.

The O'Reilly family dining room reeked of formality with its pristine white tablecloth, crystal chandelier, and gold-trimmed plates. Seated at the heavy oak table, watching Ivy and Hazel's argument unfold, were two of Ivy's younger sisters, Daisy and Rue; her two cousins, Poppy and Daphne; and her father.

"But I'm applying to Irvine and Boulder!" Ivy cried.

"No, you're not," said Hazel, "because if there's an emergency, the time difference will make it too difficult for you to call home."

Every fiber of Ivy's being screamed that this wasn't true; it was ludicrous. No college west of the Mississippi? That was completely arbitrary! The river wasn't even where the time zones changed.

The look on Hazel's face—that amused glint in her eyes, the

tiny smirk on her lips—told Ivy that her mother enjoyed Ivy's frustration. Ivy turned to her father, but Michael O'Reilly avoided her gaze, looking only at the dinner he actively devoured. She understood at once: Michael's refusal to get involved meant that her parents had not discussed limiting her college search—it was a spontaneous decision of Hazel's that they were both hearing for the first time. In typical fashion, he was letting his wife wield absolute authority.

"But why?" Ivy asked.

"I told you why."

Poppy quietly got up from her seat and took Rue by the hand. Silent as ghosts, they kept their eyes on their feet all the way to the exit. One of Hazel's familiars—a small, green-skinned Kappa—cleared away their plates with its domed head bowed.

"The time difference isn't a real reason!" Ivy protested.

"Of course it is."

"It's totally not," mumbled Daisy, picking at her food.

Hazel didn't respond to the snark, but Daphne, sitting across the table from her cousins, shot Daisy a nasty glare, like someone in a theater silently warning a noisy neighbor to shut up.

"Bu-but . . ." Ivy threw up her hands. "It's completely arbitrary! It makes no sense!"

"It's just the logistics of it," Hazel said. "Actually," she added, a self-satisfied grin spreading over her features, "I would rather send you to school in Brazil because that's in a closer time zone."

"No, it isn't," Daisy said.

Ivy felt Daphne kick Daisy under the table. Daisy responded by making an obscene gesture. Hazel sipped from her wineglass. Ivy envied how Daisy lived in their mother's blind spot.

"Do you want to go to school in Brazil?" Hazel asked, her dark eyes shining with mocking delight. "I'll send you to Brazil."

"Stop it," Ivy said, fighting the lump in her throat. First, Hazel snuffed out her chance at independence, and now she was teasing her for it. "This doesn't make any sense."

"God Ivy, stop being dramatic." Daphne smiled prettily for Hazel, face alight with sycophantic joy. "You're still going to school."

"That's not the point!" Ivy cried. "You can't just make up a ridiculous reason like that!"

"It's the truth," said Hazel, smirking.

The absolute authority of her mother was beginning to assert itself over Ivy, giving her doubt. No matter what the truth might be, everyone would agree with Hazel's reasons, whether with verbal support or with silence. Knowing she was alone, Ivy's logic crumbled.

Daphne furtively stuck out her tongue at her cousins. Willfully deaf to everything around him, Michael calmly ate his dinner. Hazel sipped from her glass with smiling lips, watching tears of impotent misery roll down her child's face.

Georgette woke up with tears on her cheeks. As her mind fully emerged into reality, she suddenly realized that nothing in the dark room looked familiar. *Am I back in Boston!?* In a flash of panic, she scrambled out of the bedsheets.

A grunt to her left made her gasp. She looked and heaved a sigh of relief. Neil slept next to her.

We came back to his place after drinks, she remembered. *I must have fallen asleep after we had sex.*

Picking up her phone, she squinted through her tears and poor vision to check the time: 1:54 a.m. Since leaving Boston, it was a rare night that she slept more than three or four hours.

"*Hrm*," mumbled Neil, his face half-buried in his pillow. "Insurance flaps."

Flaps? She leaned over him, holding her breath.

"Imma catch up," he slurred. "Yeah. *Hrmpha* . . . Get a boat."

Georgette smiled. He was talking in his sleep.

"*Hrmph* . . ." he said. "That's cheese."

After grabbing her glasses off the end table, she slid out of bed to look for her clothes. There were piles of shirts and pants everywhere, making it difficult to distinguish her clothes from his in the dark. She gave up and grabbed one of Neil's T-shirts and some sweatpants. She didn't really need her own clothes right this second. All she wanted was to get some water and find a place where she could scroll through her phone until sunrise— and think about the events of the night.

Neil had taken her out to an Italian place for dinner. They'd eaten, drunk wine, and talked for well over three hours, only to follow up the long meal with a visit to a nearby bar. They'd stayed there until nearly midnight.

Georgette started the evening a little on edge, fearful of how many lies she would have to tell, but within minutes, a different issue sidelined her concern.

"I just can't get over it," Neil said with a grin.

"What?" she asked.

"That buying a coffee on impulse led to me having dinner with a pretty girl."

At this comment, the smile momentarily slipped from Georgette's face. She came from a family of pretty girls. They had taught her that she wasn't one of them. No one in her mother's house had ever called her "pretty" without a smirk or an ulterior motive. *Is he teasing me?*

The fleeting shift in her expression wasn't lost on her date.

"But you're more a tea drinker, right?" he asked brightly. "Is coffee ever on the menu?"

The tension drained from Georgette's body. Without pressing for an explanation, Neil, like the salesman he was, had shifted gears to create a positive environment for the company he kept. Her smile, her real smile, returned.

Thereafter, Neil stuck to casual topics: music, movies, books, and food. As she learned about him, Georgette also learned about herself. So much of her life had been lived through the filter of her mother's expectations, that her ability to develop an independent personality had been severely hampered. Now that she had put three thousand miles and three months between herself and her mother, she was becoming a real person, a better person, and she felt most like this new woman when she talked to Neil. It was an absolute delight.

Still asleep, Neil muttered incoherently and rolled onto his back, his brown hair spilling across his forehead. Georgette found him to be sweet—charming, kind, and genuine—and the two of them had chemistry. Making love had felt like the natural progression of the night; she didn't regret it at all. Now that her buzz had worn off, though, she was worried about what would come next.

It's fine, she repeated to herself as she slipped out the bedroom door, *it's totally fine.*

In Neil's living room, she snuggled into the sofa and started web-surfing. As often happened during her insomniac hours, however, her fear and guilt soon took hold, and her thoughts began to wander. What if her mother caught up to her? She would be so angry. Only one other time in her life had Georgette defied Hazel—and as a result of her defiance, her sister Violet was now catatonic.

It happened years ago. Ivy came home from high school one day, and her mother called to her. Eyeing her mother's smile with suspicion, she took a seat across from her at the dining room table.

Hazel placed a plate in front of her. On it sat a delicate, fragrant fillet of grayish meat. Without preamble, she cheerily ordered her daughter to eat it. The meat smelled a bit like salmon, but it looked unseasoned, maybe even raw. Ivy continued to sit, waiting for an explanation, but Hazel only repeated her command.

In the ornate mirror on the wall above her mother's head, Ivy saw a familiar lingering near the dining room entrance, Hazel's *Hathiya* brand emblazoned across his broad, scaly chest. The Naga locked his slit pupils on Ivy in the reflection, gave the meat a pointed look, and subtly shook his cobra-hooded head. The hair on the back of Ivy's neck stood on end; she shook her head.

Hazel's smile vanished. "Eat it!" she snapped.

Fourteen-year-old Ivy once again refused. Hazel tried grabbing and shoving her face toward the meat, but Ivy flung out her hand, knocking the plate aside. Hazel gasped and grabbed the plate, shielding it with her arms, as Ivy darted out of the room.

An hour later, thirteen-year-old Violet was a soulless shell.

Within minutes of eating the meat, her eyes became as dull and empty as old tin cans. Hazel tried dozens of spells, potions, and rituals, all of which failed. Eventually, she gave up and allowed her husband to take the girl to a hospital, where a fleet of doctors saw just as little success as she had.

The next day, through tear-drenched eyes, Ivy saw the lump of gray meat in the garbage. She wished she had eaten the damn thing so that Violet hadn't been pushed to do it.

A huge yellow snake tail coiled loosely around her feet. From over her shoulder, she felt a flickering tongue near her ear. "Stay away from it," hissed the Naga.

"What is that stuff, Saagar?" asked Ivy.

"*Ningyo.*" Saagar used his talon-like hands to steer Ivy away from the garbage can. "I warned Violet too. She didn't listen." Balancing his legless body on his long tail, he gathered up the trash bag, tied it shut, and held it at arm's length as he slithered out the back door. "Always so desperate to please her mother." He shook his head. "Much good it did her."

Ningyo. Mermaid flesh. It was said that consuming mermaid flesh could make the eater immortal—but only for one out of five million. For most, eating *Ningyo* meant death or, as in Vi's case, catatonia. But it made perfect sense that Hazel was interested in it.

Most people were afraid of dying, but Ivy's mother was terrified of aging. Once, after too much wine, Aunt Laurel said she believed that was the source of Hazel's resentment toward her daughters: she hated seeing them in the prime of life when she was deep into middle age. Having paid a hefty sum for the extremely rare *Ningyo*, Hazel had needed someone to test the meat to see if their bloodline might benefit from its positive effects.

Violet had paid the price for Hazel's vanity—and for Ivy's rebellion.

Who will pay the price for me running away? she thought. *The only ones still living at home are Daphne, Daisy, and Rue.* Anxiety roared through her body, constricting her lungs, and tearing at her stomach. *Daphne's one of the favorites. Mom's spent so long ignoring Daisy that she isn't scared anymore. No, she'll go after Rue.* Tears filled Georgette's eyes. *Oh God! Rue begged me to take her with me, and I left her there! Daisy won't protect her, and Daphne will pick on her just to make Mom happy.* She clamped a hand over her mouth to muffle her sobs. *How could I do this!? I'm so selfish, stupid, and ugly!*

In the throes of her weeping, she almost didn't see light flood out from a bedroom door across from the couch. When she did notice, she had only a moment to register surprise before she heard an unfamiliar voice say, "*Hola, Bruja.*"

21 Nicolás

NICO'S IMMEDIATE THOUGHT UPON WAKING WAS THAT THIS was the first night in weeks that he hadn't dreamed of the trip across the desert. *That means something.* Before he could think it over, he felt tingling under his skin. Magic stirred the air.

Curious, he poked his head out of his bedroom door.

For all his *tía*'s gripes about his *curandero* skills, he knew a *bruja* when he saw one. Magic coated the girl sitting across the room from him as thickly as frosting on a cake.

"*Hola, Bruja,*" he said, making her jump. "Who are you?"

The streetlight leaking through the blinds caught her pale face. "I'm sorry," she said. "I didn't mean to wake you."

"Answer me," he said, approaching her carefully. "Who are you?"

She turned toward him until the light from his room fell upon her face. "Georgette Delaney," she said softly.

Her glasses magnified her bloodshot eyes and the glow from his room highlighted her blotchy skin. She was crying.

Nico had met a number of *brujos* in his life. Most were *brujos pequeños*—those who used the art of *brujería* to gain wealth or power—but a handful were *brujos negros*, those who used their skills to inflict pain. But this *bruja*, sitting on his sofa at 2:00 a.m., was not using her powers at all; she was crying. Was it a trick?

His training told him it was safer to assume the worst at the outset rather than deal with curses after the fact, but when he crossed his arms and bowed his head, he heard his spirit allies assure him that she was not here to harm anyone. Trusting them, he softened his approach.

"You okay?" he asked.

"Yeah," she replied, her voice raspy. She pushed her curly hair out of her eyes and sniffled. "I couldn't sleep." Smiling nervously, she gestured toward Neil's bedroom door. "We went out last night."

He noticed for the first time that she wore Neil's old clothes. Even without his spirit allies whispering in his ear, he understood. Nico felt a twinge of guilt for his earlier tone. His friend had just gotten laid for the first time in who knew how long, and here he was snapping at the girl.

Nico made himself smile and approached the couch. "Sorry I snuck up on you. I'm Nico García." He pointed to the far end of the sofa. "Can I sit here?"

"Yeah, it's your home."

Sitting down, he noticed how Neil's clothes hung on her frame. Neil was a thin guy, so she had to be pretty damn small for his clothes to look that baggy on her. Small with freckles and glasses. Neil definitely had a type.

Nico saw something odd on her cheek—an astral mark of intricate swirls, invisible to the naked eye. It was something Mariana had told him about, but he had never seen. He reached out a hand toward it, fascinated.

She yanked her head aside. "What are you doing?"

"I can see *la marca* on you," he explained, pointing to her face.

She flinched and covered her cheek with her hand.

"Your family signet, right? You're a *bruja hereditaria*—a witch who inherits her powers from her bloodline."

"I keep forgetting it's there," she whispered, rubbing her cheek. "How can you see it?"

"My aunt's training me to be a *curandero*."

"Coo-ran . . . cur-unn . . . ?"

"*Curandero*," he repeated. "A traditional healer."

"Like a shaman?"

"Uh . . ." He scrunched up his face. "Close enough."

She nodded and dropped her hand, giving him a full view of the ghostly mark. "My aunt told me some shamans learn to see magic. But I wasn't sure if it was true."

There was bizarre lettering within the mark's design. According to Mariana, *brujas hereditarias* used the Fae language in their clan signets. If he could read Fae, he guessed the letters would indicate what family Georgette was from. Unfortunately, the letters meant nothing to him.

"Does Neil know about you?" he asked.

Her eyes widened in horror, and she shook her head. "This was our first date. I don't want to scare him off."

"First date, *hm*? So you're not planning on one-night-standing him?"

"No," she said, clearly surprised by the question. "I like him. I want to see him again. Just . . ." She trailed off, eyes pleading. "Just please don't tell him about me. Please."

While Nico didn't like withholding something this big from

his friend, he didn't want to ruin a good thing, either. Neil's last relationship had ended over a year ago after he'd found out she'd been cheating on him for months. He hadn't dated anyone since. This girl, despite the fact that she was a *bruja*, struck Nico as kindhearted, someone who might be good for his friend.

Besides, if he started talking about witches and magic, Neil probably wouldn't believe a word of it.

Nico nodded. "Okay."

Relief flooded the girl's face.

"But," he added, "you better not mess with him."

Nodding, she sniffled and lifted her glasses to swipe at her eyes.

He gave her a quizzical look. "You sure you're okay?"

"Why?" she asked.

"Because it's 2:00 a.m. and you're crying in my living room."

"Oh. Yeah. I just . . . I'm an insomniac, and when I wake up like this, I stress over crap."

Squinting, he peered into her face. What she was saying might be true, but it wasn't the whole story. Deep in his soul, he felt his spirit allies press their energy upon him and lift a thought from the mists of his mind.

"It's your family," he said.

She jolted. "What?"

"Your family," he said again. "You're stressing about your family."

For a moment, she just looked at him. Then, without warning, she burst into tears.

"Damn," Nico said, rubbing his hands over his face. "Your mom sounds like a piece of work. Some of your sisters, too."

Georgette had been filling him in on all the dynamics over the last hour. Now, clearly spent, she smiled unhappily through her drying tears. "And my cousin Daphne. She gets anything she wants. She wanted to live in the main house, so Mom gave her my bedroom and made me move into my aunt's place."

"What?" *Hell*, he thought, *I've read cases in psych textbooks about less dysfunctional people.* "And your mom almost killed your sister."

She nodded. "Because I wouldn't eat the mermaid."

Eat the mermaid, he thought. *To anyone else, it would sound like a sex thing.* To him, this whole experience, talking to Georgette, felt like a weird convergence of his dual ambitions: psychologist and *curandero*. Georgette had been born and raised in a culture that heavily overlapped with the one he studied with his aunt. It was unusual to find someone outside of the *Botanica* who could discuss these things with him. Though he wanted to talk more, that urge was in conflict with his professional training. Georgette was clearly in need of counseling, and he wanted to help, even if he wasn't qualified yet. Never before had he felt these two parts of his life meld together, and it felt bizarre.

"Your mother deliberately compromised her daughter's safety," he said.

"I should have done something," she said, eyes downcast. "I should have thrown out the meat or told my father or . . . something. It was my fault."

"Who has more responsibility: a teenager who didn't understand, or her mother who knew the dangers and ignored them?"

She stared at the floor, her eyes glazed and vacant. Nico wished he knew her well enough to offer a hug. The pain on her face was palpable. *Jesus Christ*, he thought, *I'm in way over my head. But I need to help her somehow.*

"I work part-time in a counseling services clinic," he said. "I could get you in with a counselor there, let you talk it out."

"How would that work?" she asked, suddenly animated. "Should I tell a therapist about how my mother would make me try a spell too difficult for me because she liked seeing me cry when I failed? Or about how she would send her familiars into my room to look for the things I kept hidden so she could make fun of me for having them? Think your counselors would understand what it's like to find imps in your underwear drawer?"

"Okay." He nodded slowly. "Solid point."

"If I'm going to get away from my family and stop them from tracking me," she said, "I need to fully immerse myself in my new identity. I can't do that if I'm constantly rehashing my old life."

Her breathing grew more rapid and shallow as she spoke, and he saw her clutching the sofa beneath her, digging her nails into the fabric. *Anxiety*, he thought. *She's triggered. How do I help?*

"I won't pretend to understand all the magic involved," he said, "but from a psychology point of view, there's no way to escape your past. No matter how you bury it, it will find a way to come back. The best way to avoid your past rising from the grave and going all zombie apocalypse on you is to face it. You know— go head-to-head with the zombie, chop it up, and bury it one piece at a time."

She looked at him askance. Unsure if she was questioning his logic or his zombie metaphor, he pressed on.

"The things you're describing to me—the guilt, the anxiety, the insomnia—those are all common symptoms of someone recovering from long-term abuse."

"Abuse?" she said with a start. "No, I—my mother spanked me once, but—"

"Emotional abuse," he said. "Messing with someone's head, especially while that person is a child, can cause trauma."

The shock on her face caught him off guard. It seemed blatantly obvious to him that Georgette came from an abusive home, but clearly that was news to her. For Nico, this was further evidence that she needed professional help.

"I think you'd be better able to break away from your family if you were to deal with your trauma constructively, through counseling," he offered.

"Trauma," she murmured. Sucking on her lower lip, she closed her eyes, drew a deep breath in through her nose, and exhaled. "I'm a witch. We don't bring non-witches into our culture."

"What I'm hearing is," Nico said, "'I'm a product of a family that keeps secrets and I was raised to believe that sharing my emotions is bad.'" He raised an eyebrow. "Am I close?"

She paused, her mouth slightly open. "I guess," she said. "I don't know."

"Tell you what: If you ever want to unload some baggage, come by my aunt's shop and talk with me. I'm not a licensed therapist yet, but you can visit me as a *curandero*. My aunt has some customers who come for tarot readings just so they can gripe about their problems. I can do that for you, without the cards. Okay?"

"Maybe," she said. "Thanks."

"Sure. And listen . . ." He leaned toward her. "With Violet . . . there was nothing you could have done."

She sighed, her glazed eyes once again staring down at the rug. He put a hand on her shoulder. "The only way you could have saved Violet was to eat the poison yourself. And that would have left Violet with a parent who poisoned her sister . . . just like you were."

Hand on her shoulder, squeezing gently, he watched as tears rolled down her cheeks.

22 Neil

NEIL WOKE UP AT 5:56 A.M. GRUMBLING QUIETLY TO HIMSELF, he reached for his phone to turn off the scheduled 6:00 a.m. alarm—and then remembered it was Saturday.

He rolled over and tried to sleep again.

Georgette!

A jolt went through him, and he scrambled up to a sitting position, all thoughts of sleep gone. Where was she? He'd last seen her next to him in bed, nodding drowsily against his arm, those golden curls spread over the pillow. Now her phone and her glasses were gone, as was she.

Did she leave? He thought unhappily. *Dammit, do I even have her number?*

As he walked around the bed, he stepped on one of her sandals. A quick glance at the floor boosted his spirits. Her skirt and top were there.

He threw on some clothes and hurried out of the room.

The smell of coffee welcomed him to the living room, as did the sight of Georgette curled up on the sofa. The mug in her hands breathed steam over her glasses, fogging them, as her halo of hair bounced with her tiniest movements. His T-shirt hung loose at her neck, giving him a glimpse of the splatter of freckles that covered her breasts. She saw him and smiled.

"Hey."

"Hey," he said, letting out a breath. "Been awake long?"

"Yeah," she said apologetically. "I should've mentioned, I'm an insomniac."

"Gotcha." He stepped up to her, brushed back her hair, and kissed her forehead. "Could've woken me up. I don't mind."

"No, I already feel bad that I accidentally woke up your roommate."

He followed her gaze to the kitchen, where Nico cracked eggs into a hot pan. A robust smell accompanied the resulting sizzle, making his stomach growl.

"I'm gonna have some coffee," he told her. "After that, how about we go out? Get a real breakfast somewhere?"

"Sure," she said, nodding. "I have to head home after that, though. I'm starting my new job later today, so I need to shower and change clothes." She sipped from her mug with one hand as she picked up her phone with the other. "I'll call my roommates, so they won't worry about me."

He headed to the kitchen to give her some privacy. Edging around Nico at the stove, he reached for the pot of coffee in the corner.

"Mornin'," Nico said.

"Hey. You been up long?"

"Yeah. Your date woke me up. We got to talking."

"Yeah?" A pinprick of jealousy stung him as he poured his coffee. "What about?"

"I asked her about her insomnia and, uh . . . I kinda struck a nerve." Nico glanced into the living room, seemingly checking on Georgette, and then leaned closer to Neil. "Your girl's working through some shit. I don't think even she knows how much."

"What do you mean?"

"Family trauma," Nico said. "She doesn't believe it's trauma, but now that she's gotten away from her family, she's starting to process it."

"Trauma?" Neil said. He glanced back at the girl quietly talking into her phone. She was so small, sweet, and gentle. He couldn't imagine anyone heartless enough to traumatize her. "What happened to her?"

"Emotional abuse from what she described, especially from her mother."

"Shit." He'd noticed that Georgette didn't seem eager to talk about her family and now he knew why. Despite having heard only a little about her mother, he now hated the woman. The depth of his ire surprised him. "She didn't tell me."

"I don't think she will any time soon."

"Why not?" He glared at Nico. "She told you."

"I know which questions to ask." Nico poked his frying eggs with a fork. "Psychology, remember? And listen, emotional abuse for twenty-odd years will mess a person up. She doesn't understand that she's been abused but she knows she's got issues. I think she doesn't want you to know."

"Why not?" Neil asked, his jaw set.

"Because she *likes* you, dumbass!" Nico chuckled. "She talked to me because in her mind, it doesn't matter what I think."

The jealousy nipping at Neil's insides eased off. Apparently,

Georgette liked him enough that she didn't want him to see any-thing unappealing in her. He couldn't fault her for that. Nobody sane highlighted their problems on the first date.

"Why are you telling me this?" he asked.

"Because I want you to have some idea what you're getting into." Nico forked an egg and dropped it onto his plate. "Every-body's got issues. Hers are gonna pop up in weird, uncomfortable ways. Not everyone would want to get involved with that." He forked the other egg and dropped it next to the first as he turned off the burner. "Just looking out for you, man."

Neil stared into his cup, his thoughts swimming, and listened to Georgette's muffled voice in the living room talking on her phone. It sounded like she was speaking another language, some-thing flowy and poetic. He thought about the previous night's hours of easy conversation between them, from the dinner to the bedroom. He thought about the sugar tone of her voice, the splatter of freckles across her breasts, and the taste of beer on her lips. She had this gentleness about her, a sort of airy softness like a dandelion seed, which made him want to cradle her in his hands. He couldn't fathom never seeing her again.

"What do you think?" he finally asked Nico.

"Honestly," Nico said, his mouth full of eggs, "she's nice. I mean, she's . . . unusual, but I think she's got a good heart. And lucky you, she's got terrible taste in men."

Neil chortled and sucked down his coffee. *A good heart.* That wasn't a description he'd heard from his roommate before. He would say that someone was "okay" or "a decent person," but "a good heart?" Never. Whatever they had talked about, Georgette had made a solid impression.

He dumped the rest of his drink down the drain. "This coffee sucks."

"You bought it," Nico said.

Neil stuck his head into the living room just as Georgette ended her call.

"Hey," she said, uncurling her limbs and climbing to her feet. "Are we going out?"

He crossed over to her, circled his arms around her waist, and kissed her. When she leaned into him, a thrill went through his whole body.

"Hell yeah," he said.

23 Delia & Senji

Outside the great hall, the smell of mead and roasted meat filled her nose. Only here, at Valhalla, did she become tangible enough to smell, taste, and touch.

He watched the wind rustle the red gold leaves of the ancient trees. A dappled pattern of their reflected light danced over the tall doorway framed by spear-shafts.

They had arrived at Valhalla for two purposes: to deliver a chosen and to appeal to the Counsel for the third and final time.

They had arrived at Valhalla for two purposes: to deliver a chosen and to appeal to the Counsel for the third and final time.

Delia entered, Senji on her shoulder. Cathedral ceilings echoed with the battle-cries of unseen warriors. The war was fought far away but the sounds of war were always near.

Golden eagles on the roof and wolves at the door watched them as they entered. Senji wondered if the beasts were here to guard against intruders or internal uprising.

"Sister Svanhild!" said a voice, calling Delia by her Valkyrie name. Some yards away stood a woman dressed in Valkyrie armor. This was Sigrun.

On a nearby ledge, there was a raven. This was Dag. Taking flight, Senji joined him.

"Sister Sigrun."

"Dag."

When Sigrun was a woman, Delia knew, she'd loved a man her family hated.

When Dag was a man,
Senji knew, his sister had
betrayed their family with
an enemy of their people.

They had eloped, only to be
followed by her brother,
who had tried to kill her
beloved.

To restore his family's
honor, Dag had followed
them, hoping in vain that if
he killed the man, his sister
would return with him
willingly.

When Sigrid tried to stop
the fight, her brother
stabbed her. She died
within minutes.

Plagued by guilt, Dag killed
himself and met her on the
other side.

Reunited in death, she
became a chooser of the
slain.

Reunited in death, he
became her partner as a
chooser of the slain.

Like every other Valkyrie, she was a murdered woman who would be served by her killers until she was dismissed and went to her rest.

"Sister," Sigrun said, "your chosen is delivered and accepted."

"Thank you, sister. What of my petition?"

"Denied. But you must have expected that."

"Dag, how is your partner treating you?"

"She never says a word to me," said Dag, "beyond what's necessary."

"After all this time?"

"I robbed her of life and love. Now she deprives me of human interaction."

"Can I appeal again?"

"No. Three is the limit. Frankly, it is unusual that you persisted this long."

Delia sighed.

Senji cawed.

"Is there nothing to be done?"

"To visit a dying one who is not a chosen is unheard of," said Sigrun.

"But—"

Let it go, Senji spoke in her head.

Are you sure?

If you persist, they might become suspicious. Don't tip our hand.

Delia swallowed her protest and nodded. "I understand. But Sigrun, may I ask a personal favor?"

Tread lightly, he warned.

"The constant lights and noise of Las Vegas are exhausting. Would you trade territories with me? I need a change of scenery."

Ah, yes, Senji thought approvingly. *San Jose is part of her territory.*

Since we cannot petition the Council, we will petition the witch.

"I understand," Sigrun said, smiling kindly. "Certainly we can trade."

The Valkyries gripped one another in a friendly embrace.

"Back to work, Dag."

"Thank you for speaking with me, Senji."

Stepping back, they both smiled.

"Thank you, Sister Sigrun. I'll see you again soon."

"Be well, Sister Svanhild."

The ravens took flight and perched on their partners' shoulders.

Delia and Senji left Valhalla. As they soared through the realms toward earth, they both felt their hope renewed.

Delia and Senji left Valhalla. As they soared through the realms toward earth, they both felt their hope renewed.

"Do you think they suspect us?" Senji asked as they sped along.

"Why would they?" she asked. "As far as they know, we've accepted their judgment without complaint."

The hot, dry air greeted them as they arrived in California.

Senji spread his wings and let the morning breeze comb through his sun-soaked feathers.

She closed her eyes and, through his physical senses, felt the sun and inhaled the fresh morning breeze.

"Find them again," she said with a smile.

"I will," he said. "Rely on it."

24   Ishak

A GLINT OF MIDDAY SUN CUT A LINE ACROSS THE HOTEL mirror, searing Ishak's eyes. He winced. Squinting against the glare, he stared at himself. In mere months, he had lost ten pounds and aged five years. More and more, the face in the mirror changed from his own to that of his father. If Kalilah was here, he would gripe about it, and she would tease him.

The thing he had to do disgusted him and went against all his instincts. The skin on his back prickled, as if he could raise his hyena hackles in human form. He didn't want another brand.

"I feel nauseous," he said.

"I'm sorry," Georgette said. She was sitting cross-legged on the floor, wearing a flowy blouse with the sleeves rolled up. "We don't have to do this."

"No," he said, "but it will help in the search." He looked into his own eyes. "If it gets me to Kalilah, I can do anything."

Until today, Georgette's contribution to the search for Kalilah had exclusively taken place during daylight hours, while Ishak slept. Once the sun set, he and the witch switched places, her taking the bed and him heading out into the city. It was a sensible division of labor, since his Bultungin abilities only worked after sundown. But Georgette's new job would require her to work nights, and that left no one to search during the day. Well, there was Mei-Xing, but there was only so much a Wood Nymph who avoided contact with other Nymphs could do. If Georgette was to be the night shift, Ishak must be the day. And that meant he needed Georgette's brand.

Ishak closed his eyes, leaned his forehead against the mirror, and took a deep breath. "Tell me again," he said. "Once more. Tell me."

"The typical *Hathiya* spell brands the familiar so that the witch can drain his or her power," Georgette said. She had explained this many times, but if the repetition was annoying her, she hid it well. "My *Hathiya* brands both the witch and the familiar. Instead of a one-way power flow, it creates a loop. I can use Mei-Xing's powers, and she can use mine. Also, either one of us can shut off access to the other's power at any time."

Ishak opened his eyes and met Georgette's gaze in the mirror. "I will be able to cut off your access to my power *and* use my Bultungin senses in the daytime?"

"Yes," Georgette assured him, "and you'll understand English."

"Will I be able to speak it?"

Mei-Xing said something in heavily accented English.

Uncomprehending, Ishak shook his head.

"I can speak it," she translated into Fae, "but not well." The Nymph crossed her arms over her chest. "English is stupid," she grumbled.

"You already speak four languages," Georgette said to Ishak, "and your daylight form has a human tongue. English will come more naturally to you than it does to Mei-Xing."

Maybe it would. That wasn't really the pertinent issue. If he was to find Kalilah, he needed his Bultungin abilities. To have those, he needed the brand. Given the circumstances, he could muster up some trust in Georgette. For Kalilah's sake.

Georgette had him sit on the floor while she marked the carpet with spectral runes. He couldn't see the runes, but he sensed the magic building around them as she whispered her spells. It was a sensation like sinking into water, the pressure on his skin and in his ears slowly increasing as he went deeper. Peering down at them from her spot on the bed, Mei-Xing watched the ritual silently.

After half an hour of whispers, gestures, and ethereal summons, Georgette pulled together the energies she had gathered and shaped them between her hands like potter's clay. A wraith-like form gradually emerged out of the air. From the formless, glowing mass, Georgette molded a pattern of elaborate, intertwining lines and twists.

Once the luminous design was complete, Georgette picked up a thorny stem—provided by Mei-Xing—and, flinching, pricked her thumb. With a little shake of her hand, she dropped the pearl of blood onto the glowing shape. It absorbed her blood like dry earth swallowing rain.

"Now you," she said.

Ishak stabbed his thumb on another thorn and squeezed a drop of his blood onto the glowing shape.

Georgette held out her left hand, exposing the brand on the underside of her wrist.

"Okay," she said, exhaling slowly. "Now we put our wrists together with this between them."

Ishak tensed. "And that will brand us?"

"Yep."

"Will it hurt?"

"Yep. Don't let go until the pain stops."

They clasped forearms, each grabbing the other just below the elbow and pressing the undersides of their wrists into the shining compilation of curves and loops. Ishak watched as the glowing curves lined up with Georgette's existing brand and sank into it like a key into a lock. The glow intensified—and a sharp, searing pain burned deep into his muscle and sent ripples of agony up his arm.

Ishak gritted his teeth and tightened his grip on Georgette. The pain amplified, filling him up from fingertips to shoulder. He grunted, groaned, and then cursed—through clenched teeth at first and then loudly, with brutal vulgarity.

The scorching sensation was so severe that he didn't notice Georgette digging her nails into him until he saw a trickle of blood running down his arm. He looked at her. Biting deeply into her lower lip, her screams were muffled but incessant, as though she hadn't once stopped to draw a breath. He remembered that she had endured this once before. That meant she'd entered into this pact with a full understanding of how badly it would hurt.

With a newfound level of respect, he put his free hand on her shoulder. She opened her eyes, releasing a torrent of tears, and looked at him. Understanding passed between them in that glance. She put her other hand on his shoulder, gave it a squeeze, and together, in their shared agony, they waited.

On the bed next to them, Mei-Xing whimpered, her face contorted in surprise and pain. She squashed her branded wrist between her thighs, her other hand clutching the faded comforter. Through his agony, Ishak took note of her reaction; she had not expected to feel the branding. Georgette's *Hathiya* was not just binding him to her, it was binding the three of them together.

There was one final flash of light and then the glowing shape vanished, along with the pain. Ishak let go of Georgette and yanked back his arm as the witch hugged her own arm to her chest.

He inspected the underside of his wrist. There was the brand, as crisp and clean as a new tattoo.

"Did it work?" he asked.

"Let's see," Georgette said.

Ishak suddenly felt a tug in his gut. The lurching feeling passed quickly, but before he could ask about it, he noticed a change in Georgette. In place of her blue eyes, he saw two dark orbs containing twin glowing pinpoints—reflections of the lamplight. Her glasses slid off her face as her ears moved up her head and her face lengthened. When her lips parted, he saw a row of pointed teeth in her mouth. She, a non-Bultungin, was shifting to hyena form in the daylight! With a snarl, he instinctively flexed the internal muscles he used to resume human form. In a heartbeat, Georgette was herself again.

"You were changing!" Ishak exclaimed.

"Yeah." She rubbed her face before sliding her glasses back into place. "That really stings."

He squinted at her. "Why did you stop?"

"Because you stopped me," she said. "You cut the power."

"Really? As easily as that?" Curious, he tried shifting forms—and couldn't. He tried again. Again, nothing. "It's not working. I'm branded, and I have nothing to show for it!"

Mei-Xing chortled, drawing a scathing glare from the Bultungin.

"Why do you laugh?" he demanded.

"Because," Georgette explained, "I've been speaking English all this time and you've understood every word."

Ishak drew back in surprise.

"If it worked," he said, frowning, "why can I not change form? *You* were able to do it."

"You haven't had as much practice using my *Hathiya* as I have," Georgette said. "Changing form takes a lot of energy. Start smaller."

"The noisy guy in the next room is on the phone," Mei-Xing said, making a face at the wall. "Can you tell us what he's talking about?"

The speaker's muffled voice, one they had heard many times at odd hours, drifted through their shared wall. Ishak tilted his head and focused his ears, just as he would at night. Slowly, he felt his hearing intensify until the man's voice became clear.

"His wife kicked him out," he reported. "He wants to go home." Ishak listened to both sides of the conversation, the man and the much fainter voice of his wife through the telephone. "She says she has pictures of him with his whore." He paused, listening. "He's begging for another chance." Pause. "She says she's tired of his lies." He pulled his hearing back, settled into his human senses, and shook his head. "He may be at this hotel in-definitely."

Mei-Xing muttered irritably, casting scornful glances at the wall. Rubbing her brand, Georgette climbed to her feet, went to her suitcase, and picked out a clean outfit.

"I'm gonna take a shower and get ready for my first night at Nocturne," she said. She took a few steps toward the bathroom, stopped, and went back to the suitcase. She dug out a handful of cash and thrust it at Ishak. "Since you're on day watch from now on, you'll need better clothes. You've been wearing the same thing for weeks."

Ishak nodded. That was sensible. Decent clothes were hardly a concern while in hyena form, but during the day he would need to blend in. Finding new clothes would also give him a chance to practice speaking English. He reached out toward her, but instead of taking the money, he took her hand and held it until she looked him in the eyes.

"Thank you," he said sincerely. "You have done well."

She blushed and quickly cast her eyes aside. "We'll find her," she said before dropping the money in his hand and rushing to the bathroom.

Puzzled, Ishak looked at Mei-Xing. "Is she embarrassed?" he asked.

"She's uncomfortable with praise," the Nymph said.

"Why?"

"In her old life," she said, "praise was currency. No one in her family ever praised her without expecting something in return. She's been conditioned not to trust compliments."

Ishak cursed and shook his head. "Is there something inherent in witches to make them as horrible as her family?" he said. "As horrible as Kivuli Panon?"

"I think," Mei-Xing sighed, "that's just the nature of power. It's easy to be blind to its horrors when all you see are its benefits." She offered Ishak one of her odd little smiles. "If Georgette had been one of her mother's favorites, I doubt she would be here with us now."

Ishak listened to the sound of the water running in the shower for a moment before looking at the fresh brand on his wrist. *I will put the power she inherited toward an honorable goal. A witch's power took Kalilah from me. It is appropriate that a witch's power should retrieve her.*

25

Delia
& Senji

❧

She waited in a hospital hallway, where Valhalla might see her at her post. Police lingered nearby, pacing, and pressing the hospital staff for updates. A fellow officer shot in the line of duty.

He perched on a hotel windowsill, looking inside through a rip in the curtain. After weeks of following the witch's group, he had learned their routine. The women left in the morning and returned at night. The hyena-man slept all day and left at night.

Delia would collect the policeman that night when his heart failed on the operating table.

This afternoon was the first time Senji had seen them together in one room.

All the chosen were pings on her internal radar, faint and slow. As their deaths grew close, the ping got louder and faster, guiding her to the target. The sound of this man was rapid and thunderous.

He watched the witch cast a *Hathiya* spell, listening to their conversation. In this way, he gleaned what the dual brand meant.

Delia? Do you see this?

Lost in her own thoughts, she was jolted to hear one of his.

She looked through his eyes, reviewed his memory, learned what he had learned.

Yes, I see.

You were right.

It was just as they had hoped.

They needed to act quickly.

I need you here, she told him, sensing the chosen's time drawing near.

I don't know. This situation has only ever been hypothetical. How much should we tell her?

Then it's best if the witch doesn't know the truth, she finished. *The less she knows, the less she can tell.*

It was just as they had hoped.

They needed to act quickly.

He spread his wings and let the air currents lift him into the sky. *What will we say to the witch?*

A gust of wind swept him upward, ruffling his feathers. Memories of his days as a pilot flitted through his mind. *Very little*, he insisted. *If we're discovered, and the Valkyries come for us—*

A nurse passed by, her eyes
glued to her phone.
Memories of her days as a
Navy nurse swam in the
periphery of Delia's mind.

Will she deal with us? she
wondered. *Our offer is
unique, but—*

*But we have nothing else if she
refuses,* he finished. *We have
no possessions and no identity
independent from Valhalla.
Aside from ourselves, we have
nothing to offer.*

She sighed. *Then we will
offer ourselves and hope it's
enough.*

26  Nicolás

"Boring," Georgette said with a sigh. "I'm redoing the spells outside the building. I haven't been inside since I interviewed."

Nico shook a large bag, emptying its herbal contents into a fat, air-tight container labeled ANGELICA ROOT. The peppery citrus smell, so strong it made his eyes water, assaulted his nostrils. As he quickly replaced the lid on the container, he let loose a series of brain-shaking sneezes.

Mariana's voice rose up from the far side of the Botanica, where she was conducting a tarot reading, in a brisk but sweet, "*Salud!*"

With a final sniff, Nico tossed the empty bag into the trash and carried the refilled vessel back to its spot on the shelf.

"So what's on your mind?" he asked over his shoulder as he picked up the neighboring container.

Leaning on the counter, Georgette pinched a sunflower seed out of a snack bag and popped it between her teeth. "Olive."

"Olives? Like, on a pizza?"

"No, my aunt," Georgette said. She plucked the empty sunflower seed shell from her tongue and flicked it into the trash can. "Olive broke from the family before I was born. Mei-Xing and I tracked her down to ask her how she stayed off my mom's radar all these years. She told me what I should do."

"Why's she on your mind?"

"Because I haven't been following her advice." As Georgette chewed another seed, she looked at her feet. "She told me, 'Go from place to place, change your appearance, and commit yourself to being a new person. Do not make friends. Do not fall in love. Do not use more magic than necessary.'"

"You feel like you haven't done that?" Neil asked.

"I definitely haven't," she said. "I mean, I started to. I bought new clothes, stopped straightening my hair, and changed my name. But I've also"—Georgette held up one hand and started counting on her fingers —"settled in San Jose, made friends, and started dating Neil, and I'm using magic almost every day. I'm scared Mom will find me." She crossed her arms over her chest and stared intently at the floor, her breath quickening. "I try so hard not to think about my mother while I'm awake, but as soon as I'm asleep, she's in my dreams."

Nico took down the jar of black cohosh and opened it. Turning his head away from the fetid stink of the herb, he asked, "Can you tell me about the dreams?"

"It's like I'm reliving memories." She uncrossed her arms, dropped the seed bag on the counter, and pushed one hand through her thick curls. "Last night, I dreamt about the time I wanted to study abroad."

"What about it?"

"It was a summer program in between my sophomore and

junior years. It was a chance to study data systems and computer graphics in Singapore." A sour look crossed her face. "My mother said she wouldn't pay for it because it wouldn't be fair to my sisters."

"Meaning?"

"My parents set aside money for each of our educations. If we went over that amount, it came out of our own pockets."

"Well," Nico said, "when you have a lot of kids, I guess that's one way of keeping things even."

"Except it's bullshit." Georgette took one sunflower seed between two fingers and dropped it into her palm. "They paid for Lily to spend a year in Paris, even after she dropped out of her fashion classes." She slowly spun her index finger over the seed in her hand, lacing magic around it. "They also paid for Clove to travel all over Europe for 'art appreciation.'" The seed split, releasing a tiny green sprout. "She wasn't even taking classes."

As he put away the black cohosh, Nico reflected that Georgette was describing typical traits of a narcissistic family. A parent like Georgette's usually had at least one golden child, a favorite who could do no wrong. From what Nico had learned, it sounded like there were multiples in this family: Georgette's sisters Clove and Lily, as well as her cousin Daphne. Every other kid—like Georgette—fell into the category of invisible child or scapegoat. Nico picked up the container of buckthorn bark and nodded at her to continue.

"Since my parents wouldn't pay for it," she said, "I looked into getting a loan." The seedling in her palm rose out of its shell and stretched upward, growing almost an inch. "When I mentioned this to Mom, she told me not to take out a loan because it would ruin my credit score. She said she would loan me the money at a low interest rate." The tiny sprout wilted and fell, its spidery roots drying up on her skin. "Why the hell did I listen?"

The self-reproach in her voice saddened him. It was a recurring theme of their sessions: Georgette blaming herself for things her mother had done. It was common behavior for a scapegoat child.

"It's normal to want to trust our parents," he said, quoting from a book he'd read recently, "even when past experience tells us not to."

Georgette smiled, her expression appreciative but doubtful. She flicked the dead seedling into the trash.

"I filled out all the program applications," she went on, picking another seed from the bag, "got accepted, and started making travel plans." Gently patting the seed in her palm, she began spinning another spell. "Then I called Mom about the money."

"She wouldn't give it to you."

Georgette shook her head. Before the sunflower seed cracked open, she dropped it back into the bag. "She said if she loaned me the money for the summer program, she wouldn't be able to help me with a down payment on a house someday." As she talked, anxiety crept back into her voice. "When I told her I was already signed up, she laughed like I'd said something cute and changed the subject."

"Had she ever mentioned helping you buy a house?" he asked.

"Never before," replied Georgette, "and never again."

As he poured the refill bag of buckthorn bark, enjoying the subtle, woody aroma, Nico tried and failed to imagine his own mother giving him such an excuse.

"What happened with the summer program?" he asked.

"By then it was too late to apply for a loan, and I was contractually on the hook for the cost of the program even if I backed out. I couldn't stop crying. I was still crying when Aunt Laurel called for our weekly chat. When I told her what happened, she got me the money." Georgette exhaled with remembered relief. "I usually spent my summers traveling with her and my cousin Poppy, so she gave me the money she would have spent on my plane tickets and expenses. That, combined with my personal savings, covered the cost." She chuckled quietly but her expression was humorless. "When I asked my mother why she didn't tell me sooner that she'd changed her mind, she said she didn't know what I was talking about." Georgette's blue eyes, magnified by her glasses, looked to Nico, full of pleading. "Was she lying?"

Her childlike desperation for answers tugged at his heart. Keeping his face impassive, he said, "You know the answer to that."

She looked down at the floor again, a fog of doubt surrounding her.

Nico put the buckthorn bark away and picked up a different container, giving her time to think, before saying, "You don't need my confirmation to know what's true. The reason you think you do is because your mother has been gaslighting you all your life."

"Gaslighting?" Georgette squinted at him.

"Gaslighting is a form of psychological abuse," he explained, "that involves making someone question their sanity, perception, or memory by using lies or misdirection to rewrite past events."

Georgette bore an expression halfway between horror and amazement. Before he could decide what to say, she exhaled in a whisper, "It actually has a name? Oh my God." One hand covered her mouth as she teared up. "I thought I was crazy."

"You're not," he said firmly. "You *can* trust yourself. These dreams you're having make sense. I think your subconscious is confronting you with memories because now that you're away from your mother, you can finally see how these things *really* happened—experience them without her coloring your perception. You know what you saw, you know what you heard, you don't need anyone to confirm it. The dreams may be traumatic, but they serve an important purpose: they're helping you heal."

"Doesn't feel like it," Georgette said softly.

"You say you're not changing yourself as much as your aunt told you to, but I disagree. You are undoing a life's worth of emotional turmoil. That's hard work. Don't sell yourself short."

"Maybe," she said, sounding unconvinced, "but Aunt Olive said I need to live as free of attachments as possible. I have Mei-Xing and Ishak, I've got a job at Nocturne, I've got these meetings with you, and I've got Neil."

Despite her obvious anxiety, Nico noticed how Georgette smiled when she mentioned Neil. Other names came and went in their conversations, but only Neil's made her so obviously happy.

"How are things with Neil?" he asked.

"Really good." She looked at him with sparkling eyes. "Spending time with him is refreshing."

"Refreshing?" he asked. "Why's that?"

"Neil's nothing like my ex-fiancé Zach," she said. "He's sweet, thoughtful, always asks for my opinion . . . Zach never wanted to hear my thoughts on anything. We were only together because my mother had made a deal with his family."

Arranged marriage? Nico wondered. His aunt had told him that *brujas hereditarias* often saw themselves as the royalty of the magic world. Maybe arranged marriages were a part of that culture. "Was it typical for her to do that?"

"Oh yeah. She's picked out boyfriends and husbands for my older sisters too."

"They didn't have a problem with that?"

"Clove did," said Georgette. "She brutally rejected the guy Mom pushed on her when she was sixteen. Said he was fat, ugly, and miles beneath her. Mom was pissed. The guy was from a wealthy, influential family and Clove ruined Mom's chances to connect our family with theirs. After that, she wouldn't let Clove date for years."

Damn, Nico thought in amazement. "And your other sisters?"

"Mom lets Lily pick her own men but only because Lily's already good at catching rich guys." Georgette rolled her eyes. "She's been the mistress of a married banker for over a year. And Holly never argued with Mom about David. Not a surprise, honestly." A joyless smile crossed her face. "Holly's kind of . . . docile. They got married five years ago when Holly got pregnant."

"Unplanned pregnancy?"

"Pretty sure the baby was planned."

"Really?" he said in surprise. "They didn't want to get married first?"

"Oh, I mean planned by Mom," Georgette told him. "Mom told Holly when to start having sex with David and when to stop using birth control. Holly's lucky, though," she added quickly. "David's a good guy. He cares about her, and he loves their daughter."

Holy shit.

Ordering her daughters to sleep with men they didn't choose for themselves . . . it turned Nico's stomach. *It must screw the hell out of their concept of consent.* The worrying thought came to him that Georgette had jumped into a sexual relationship with Neil very quickly. Had she slept with him because it was what she wanted or because it was what she thought he would want? With her upbringing, was she even capable of seeing the difference?

"How long did you and your fiancé know each other before your Mom told you to get involved?"

"We didn't. We met on our first date, which Mom set up. She told me to date him, so I did. For years. Then Mom announced our engagement to all her friends and Dad's associates at the family's Fourth of July party." She puffed a breath through tight lips, shaking her head. "I had no idea it was coming. I was alone in the middle of the applauding crowd with my mouth hanging open. In front of everyone, Zach gave my mom diamond earrings, gave my dad a box of Cuban cigars, and didn't even give me a look. I tried talking to Mom, but she was busy accepting congratulations. I grabbed my dad as he was leaving the party, but he just told me to mind my mother. Zach avoided me. He and I never really talked again."

"Wow," Nico mumbled. The vessel he'd taken off the shelf sat on the counter before him, its refill bag unopened beside it. "You've been through so much. You're strong."

Her freckled cheeks flushed and she looked away. "Olive said that to me," she told him. "She said that because I'm the only one of my sisters to run away, I'm the strongest."

"Believe her," he urged. "Believe in your strength. It's brought you this far and it will keep taking you forward." He smiled with all the encouragement he could muster. "You're doing well. You really are."

For a moment, he saw a glimmer of true confidence on her features. It filled him with professional pride.

27 Neil

AFTER COMPOSING AN EMAIL TO ONE OF LI INTERNATIONAL'S clients, Neil noticed that the office was almost empty. Mr. Li wasn't in; he was on a flight to Shanghai. Taylor, Mr. Li's secretary, was still at her desk but she was on her cell phone, chatting casually and looking at her computer screen. Neil guessed that she was using office hours to shop for her upcoming wedding again.

The rest of the employees had cleared out hours ago. That wasn't surprising. When Mr. Li left for the airport that morning, Neil had known his son, Jin Li, would be gone by lunch. The other employees, knowing Jin wouldn't be back, had left soon after. Neil would have taken off too if he didn't have work to finish. But once he wrapped up these last few emails, he could go. Then he would turn his full attention to the more interesting issue of how to schedule time with Georgette.

Neil worked full time five days a week at this job and dedicated most of his off-duty time to getting his MBA. Georgette worked six nights a week—including weekends, when Neil was off—at her new job. Each was often sleeping while the other was working, which made seeing each other difficult. They often managed to meet for early dinners in the short time between Neil getting off his job and Georgette starting hers—Mr. Li wasn't picky about Neil's work hours, so long as he put in a full day and kept making sales—but those dinners were too brief for Neil's liking. Today, though—today was Monday, the one day of the week Georgette was off, and he was counting down the minutes until he could leave work and spend time with her. He was determined to make the most of the night.

I deal with scheduling issues all the time, he reminded himself. *Plenty of couples overcome bigger hurdles than this.* He silently grinned, realizing that he already thought of them as a couple. *It'll definitely work.*

His last email sent, Neil shut down his computer and leaned back in his seat with a long exhale. He checked his watch: 3:30 p.m. Georgette would be getting up soon. He caught a glimpse of his reflection in the computer screen. He was smiling like an idiot. He didn't care. He hadn't felt this good in a long time. Not since before he caught Lyndsey messing around.

Lyndsey. Since their breakup, just hearing her name had been enough to send him spinning into self-pity. But not since he met Georgette. Suddenly, he didn't give a damn about Lyndsey.

"I'm heading out," he called to Taylor.

Taylor waved one hand without skipping a beat on the phone. As Neil exited the office, he heard her asking, in a voice that reminded him of his ex, "Should I hire a professional calligrapher for the place cards? It's expensive but so pretty!"

I can't imagine Georgette wanting something like that, he thought happily.

Headed up the street, he called her number. The phone rang twice and then cut to voicemail. He was about to leave a message when he got a text from her.

Five minutes, it read.

He reached the bus stop at the same time she called. "Hey," he said, leaning against the bus stop sign. "I wasn't sure you'd be up yet."

"I've been up for over an hour," she said. She sounded tired, as she often did, but even so hearing her voice was like listening to a favorite song. "I'm running errands."

"When will you be done?"

"Soon. I just have to stop by the Botanica."

"The Botanica?"

"It won't take long. I'll meet you later, okay?"

"Yeah, fine," he said, the smile gone from his face. "See you soon."

The Botanica? His heart sank into his gut. She sure seemed to go there a lot. He knew her boss was a regular customer, so maybe she was there on business. But this was her day off.

No, he thought, his inner voice full of resentment, *she's going to see Nico.*

The bus arrived and he boarded, lost in thought. Unwelcome images of Georgette and Nico together swarmed his brain. Flopping down in a window seat, he tried to shake it off. Even though he wasn't certified yet, Nico was a therapist through and through: he felt driven to help people who were suffering. *Georgette is seeing Nico because his counseling makes her feel better*, Neil told himself.

A feeling came over him—wormy, rotten, sticky. *Nico makes her feel better. Not me.* Flinching, he tried to bury the feeling deep.

She's not cheating, he scolded himself. *This isn't like how Lyndsey lied for months about that guy being her "tutor."* Both Georgette and Nico were completely open about the time they spent together. What they weren't open about was the subject of their therapy sessions.

I know we don't get to pick our families, he thought. *So why won't she talk to me about it?*

Staring vacantly out the bus window at the flowing river of city blocks, he reviewed all the things he knew about her family. Georgette was the fourth of seven sisters, only a couple of which she got along with. Their father was a bigshot in an aerospace and defense corporation and he traveled frequently. Georgette spoke fondly of the "sober summers" she spent traveling with her Aunt Laurel and the elder of her two cousins. Their relationship reminded Neil of his bond with his nephew, except he liked to think Danny would never describe him as a "seasonal alcoholic."

As Neil gradually put together the puzzle that was the woman in his life, one gap remained: her mother. Neil knew Georgette's mother was the reason she had cut ties with her family, but whenever he so much as mentioned it she got flustered and shut down. He sighed. If the abuse was half as bad as Nico had implied, he couldn't blame Georgette for having so much baggage around it. He just wanted her to talk to him about it.

Why am I already so attached? he asked himself. But the truth was, he couldn't seem to help himself. Just the thought of her thrilled him. He wanted all of her—the good, the bad, everything. And knowing that she was reserving some part of herself for someone else tore him up.

Neil's gut twisted and his chest tightened as a maelstrom of emotions roiled inside. Jealous, possessive, brooding—he didn't like himself like this. With great effort, he hauled his mind out of his emotional mire and swung it toward the subject of tonight. He would meet Georgette at the restaurant, they would eat and talk, and then see where the night took them.

At that thought a smile, albeit a small one, turned up the corners of his mouth.

28 Mei-Xing

MEI-XING GLANCED AT GEORGETTE AS THEY WALKED UP the street, watching how she spoke cheerfully into her phone, smiling brightly. It was a smile she saw on her friend often lately.

In the two weeks since they'd met, Georgette had spent a ridiculous amount of time talking to Neil MacCana on the phone. When she woke in the afternoon, she immediately checked her phone for texts. And they were always there, just waiting to make her smile.

Mei-Xing had never seen Georgette so happy. It worried her.

Georgette was not a trusting woman; within the Nichols O'Reilly family, trust was only ever rewarded with betrayal. For her to have taken to this Neil guy so quickly meant that he was either a very good man or a very convincing fraud. Not having met him, Mei-Xing couldn't say which—but she feared the worst.

Neil's roommate, the *curandero*, also concerned her. Right now, they were on their way to get spell ingredients from the Botanica. While there, Georgette would talk to Nico. Again. Twice this week she had visited the shop, and both times she had returned to their hotel room in good spirits. Mei-Xing wanted to believe that the *curandero* was being helpful out of the goodness of his heart—but in her experience, it was not a common motive. A combination of curiosity and a desire to protect her friend was what had driven her to tag along to the herb shop now.

Despite her worries, Mei-Xing was enjoying this outing. With Georgette working nights at Nocturne, sleeping during the day, and spending her free time with Neil, she often found herself alone these days—and she was unused to loneliness. She'd spent the majority of her life as part of a grove, and since leaving China she'd always had Georgette at her side. Distracted though her friend was at the moment, the Nymph was glad to have this time with her.

It was late afternoon as they approached the Botanica. Mei-Xing glanced at the sun sinking between the buildings and reflected that Ishak would probably be winding down his daily patrol about now. Ever since the branding, he'd spent all day every day walking the city streets and loitering near KK Inc., using his heightened senses to keep its employees under surveillance. With new clothes on his human form, he was free to explore areas he hadn't been able to access as a hyena. He had not yet been able to determine where the off-site storage facilities were, but he was confident that his wife had not been sold; he smelled the familiars coming in and out of the building, and he said he was sure Kalilah had not been among them thus far.

Georgette ended the call and dropped the phone into her bag just as they reached the Botanica's door. She pushed forward, and Mei-Xing followed her across the threshold.

A bell chimed, followed immediately by a woman's voice saying, "Welcome! How can I help you today?"

"Hello, Ms. García," Georgette said.

"Oh, Nico's *amiga bruja*!" said the middle-aged lady, her smile the very picture of congeniality. "So nice to see you again! Just a moment." She disappeared behind a beaded curtain, calling out, "Nico!"

The aroma of incense and herbs washed over Mei-Xing as she drifted deeper into the shop. She flinched at the intensity of the scents; it made her uncomfortable to smell so many plant-based scents at once. These plants did not all grow together in the wild. It was unnatural.

"Hey," said a man's voice, drawing her attention. "How're you doing?"

"Hey Nico," Georgette said.

Peering through a display of bottled oils, Mei-Xing inspected the young man behind the counter. Stocky, with messy dark hair and bright, sharp eyes, he gave her the impression of a man who cared more for his studies than he did for his looks.

She watched as he waved one hand at the stock behind him and said, "What can I get you?"

"I've made a list," Georgette told him as she fished a strip of paper out of her purse. "I'm beefing up my personal concealment spells."

"Okay," he said as he scanned the list. "I'll get these." He set the list on the counter and pulled out a paper bag. "Have you been doing those breathing exercises we talked about?"

"A few times," she said. "It's helpful when I work at Nocturne. I'm still on the roof, working on the outside of the building. Now that I've finished the preliminary work, I have to do spellcraft on a massive scale. It's stressful."

The pair continued talking as Nico gathered up Georgette's order. Mei-Xing's eyes swept all around the shop, taking in shelf after shelf of trinkets, a long glass display case topped with canisters, and a wall of boxes stacked floor-to-ceiling, each one labeled with the name of an herb. She ran her fingers over the display case, glancing inside at the beads, amulets, and figurines of holy men for sale. At the end of the case, she came to a small table covered by a colorful cloth, above which loomed a gold-framed painting of the Virgin Mary.

Hanging over every nook and cranny of the shop was an ethereal mist, invisible but tangible, made of a strange magic. Mei-Xing was from a world where magic permeated every aspect of life, as encompassing and natural as the air she breathed. Her people were *made* of magic, conceived and grown in it like seeds in soil. Witches like Georgette were grown from similar magic, but unlike the Fae, they were not constructed of it. They were humans who had brought magic into their lives and used it for so many generations that it eventually integrated into their blood, like a skin graft blending into flesh. The magic here in the Botanica—this was something else entirely. It was human-made, with no roots in the world of the Fae. The two types of magic were as like and unlike each other as a rose and a dandelion. This *curandero* magic would never be capable of the things Mei-Xing's or Georgette's magic could do, and yet it had a power all its own.

"Hey."

With a gasp, Mei-Xing whirled around to find herself face-to-face with Nico. He smiled kindly, but his eyes were intense.

"Hey," he repeated, holding out a hand. "I'm Nico García."

She took his hand and squeezed. His palms were sweaty. "Mei-Xing Ma."

"Georgette talks about you a lot."

"She a good person." Mei-Xing forced the choppy English from her lips. She hated the feel of it in her mouth. *Stupid English. I sound like an idiot.* "We good friends."

The level of concentration on his face made her fidget. She looked for Georgette, only to see that she was grinning at her phone screen. *Another text from Neil*, she thought as she squirmed.

"Sorry." Nico lowered his gaze, looking a bit abashed. "I shouldn't stare. Just, um . . ." He leaned a little closer to her. "What are you?" he whispered.

"What?"

"What are you?" he repeated. "Georgette never mentioned that you . . . aren't human."

A wave of panic rose up from her core and she backed away from him. "I-I don't . . ."

"Did she put this glamour on you?" His head tilted. "It's impressive. I mean, I can only see a little of what's underneath, and I'm really having to push myself to see it."

Frozen in Nico's inquisitive gaze, she couldn't move. Knowing he saw beneath her disguise made her feel exposed, a fish in a glass bowl. With every fiber of her mind, she instinctively reached for Georgette. She felt a pinch in the brand on her wrist—an elastic band snapping against her skin—and suddenly Georgette was at her side.

"Mei-Xing's a Wood Nymph," Georgette said to Nico as she gently inserted herself between the two. The two women looked at each other, silently exchanging a slew of emotions in an instant. "She understands English, but she doesn't speak it much."

"Oh, sorry," said Nico. He took a couple of steps back, embarrassment on his face. "That was pretty forward of me. I just, uh . . ." He smiled sheepishly. "I've seen non-humans before, but not up close."

With his eyes no longer pinned to her face, Mei-Xing relaxed a bit. She looked down at her body to assure herself that the glamour was intact. Georgette took her by the hand and gave it a squeeze.

"You're okay," Georgette said. "He can see you because he's *wu.*"

Wu. A shaman. Mei-Xing thought of the Chinese pharmacy she had stumbled into as a child. The old man who worked there had, like Nico, recognized her for what she was. Before any other human could lay eyes on her, the old healer had walked her to the edge of the forest and pointed her toward her grove. Young and ignorant then, it would be years before she would understand the compassion he'd shown that day. He could have made quite a lot of money from selling her.

"You're sure about him?" Mei-Xing asked in Fae. "If you're connected to the magic community, your mother could find out."

"His and my family's communities have very little overlap," Georgette said. "People like Nico and his aunt have well-developed insights but aren't hereditary witches. They've put one foot in magic and can adapt some of it to their lives, but it's not the same." A humorless smirk crossed her face. "My mother wouldn't condescend to look a shaman in the eye."

Mei-Xing nodded. Yes, that did sound like Hazel. A queen never mingled with peasants.

Georgette's phone buzzed. Turning away from her friend, she scooped it out of her bag with a silly grin. A mixture of impatience and irritation welled up in Mei-Xing as she wandered off.

"Is she as annoying as Neil?" Nico asked.

Mei-Xing glanced at him over her shoulder. She was irked enough by Georgette's distraction that it no longer occurred to her to fear him.

"She on that phone all damn time," she said.

"Yeah, Neil too."

Mei-Xing narrowed her eyes at Nico. "He bad?"

"What's that?"

"Neil. He bad?" She inclined her head toward the oblivious Georgette. "He bad to her?"

"Oh, no way," Nico said with a definitive hand motion. "Neil would never hurt any woman. And he's crazy about Georgette."

"Crazy," Mei-Xing said, staring at her friend. "She crazy, too."

"Guess they're good for each other, then."

Maybe, she thought. "And you?"

"Me?" asked Nico, pointing to himself. "What about me?"

"You good for her?" Mei-Xing asked him. "You help Georgette?"

"With the counseling, you mean?"

"Talking, yes. You help?"

Heaving a breath, he crossed his arms over his chest and squinted in Georgette's direction. "I hope so," he said. "It only takes a few minutes of hearing about her family before I feel like I'm in over my head."

Mei-Xing understood. She and Georgette had bonded while helping each other shoulder their traumas over the span of the last three years. She knew exactly how heavy her friend's burden was.

"I see her family," she said, "and she tell me everything."

"Yeah, Georgette has said how huge you've been in her life," Nico said. "She said she never would have gotten out if not for you." He smiled warmly, surprising her. "Thank God she has you."

Mei-Xing stared at him, silently weighing all she knew. Usually, when people who mistreated Georgette saw how she and Mei-Xing supported each other, they tried to drive a wedge between them. Zach had tried to convince Georgette to sell her. Hazel had blatantly looked down her nose at her, dismissing her as subhuman. But this man praised their friendship.

Pushing aside her lingering discomfort, Mei-Xing made a conscious decision to focus on the positive. "She doing better," she said.

"Glad to hear that. But, uh"—he leaned closer to Mei-Xing while simultaneously casting a nervous glance at the distracted witch—"why is she increasing her concealment spells?"

"I tell her to."

Nico's eyebrows jumped up his brow. "Why?"

"She supposed to hide after she run away," Mei-Xing told him. "She supposed to not live anywhere long until she safe. But she get job to help Ishak and she date Neil. Now she not hide so much. I tell her she need more spells."

Shaping her inhuman mouth to form alien words was less irritating to Mei-Xing than hearing how poorly they conveyed her thoughts. She was not the fool that English made of her. She might be foreign-born and non-human, but she was not an idiot, and she hated like hell that—to her ears, at least—she sounded like one.

To her relief and to his credit, Nico never gave her that look of annoyed superiority that she often saw when trying to communicate with English speakers.

"More spells," he repeated. "You didn't tell her to dump Neil?"

"No," Mei-Xing said, surprised. "Why?"

"Well, that would be easier, wouldn't it? Dump Neil and stay hidden?"

"Easy," she agreed, "but she happy like this." She looked at Georgette's goofy smile and blushing cheeks as she listened to Neil on her phone. "If she unhappy here like in Boston, we run for no reason." Mei-Xing suddenly thrust one finger at Nico's nose. "Neil make her cry, I make him cry!"

"Fair," he said, chuckling.

"Sorry!" Georgette's voice rang out, startling both of them. She tucked her phone away and grabbed the bag of spell ingredients from the countertop. "I'm just gonna double-check, make sure I've got everything." She started digging through the bag while casting apologetic glances at Mei-Xing. "I won't get on the phone again, I swear."

Though she knew Georgette meant what she said, Mei-Xing doubted it would turn out to be true. However, she wasn't as bothered by it now. Georgette *was* happier, and that was the whole point of this new life they were living. It was important for Mei-Xing to remember that.

As Georgette compared the contents of the bag to her shopping list, the Nymph gently tapped the *curandero*'s arm. "I go outside," she said, "take in light before sunset. You talk with her some."

Not waiting for a reply, she walked away. Behind her, she heard Nico approach Georgette and ask her how she was doing. Without waiting to hear the answer, she opened the door and slipped out into the fading sunlight.

29  Georgette

TWO WEEKS INTO HER EMPLOYMENT AT NOCTURNE,
Georgette concluded that she could do no more for the exterior
of the building. She called Kazimiera on the phone and asked her
to come outside to inspect her work.

When initially handed the task, she'd panicked. *That's much
too complex for her*, her mother's voice had asserted from deep in
her mind. *She can't do magic on that big a scale. She'll mess it up.*
Though she still heard that voice constantly even now—it was a
steadily whispered narration of her life—Nico had helped her
recognize it for what it was: a learned response. Georgette had
been taught that if she tried, she might make a mistake, which
meant her mother would mock her. The only way to avoid her
mother's scorn was to never push her limits. Nico had helped her
establish a new response to the voice: Focus in. Don't look at the
full scope of the job, just focus in on the first step. Smaller steps
were less likely to set off her anxiety, to summon the voice.

Breaking down the job at Nocturne in this way, Georgette
had gradually worked her way through without sliding into emotional overload.

She'd discovered that the foundational magic around the building was of sound structure, so she'd left that alone; she'd stripped everything else away and re-layered magic on top of it, building a comprehensive cross-hatching of concealment charms and containment spells designed to keep the building impenetrable to outside magic. What had before been an inefficient fountain of enchantment was now a tight system of electrical circuits that enclosed the entire building. The task had strained Georgette physically and mentally, but she smiled as she brought her employer to the sidewalk to see the results.

"*Hmm*," Kazimiera said. She shifted her parasol and raised the wide brim of her hat to squint up at her property. "It looks the same."

"It's using a fraction of the energy it used to," Georgette told her with pride. "And it's less conspicuous than before. The first time I came here, I could sense the magic from a block away. Now I have to almost touch it to know it's there."

Kazimiera scanned the building over the top of her sunglasses, her amber eyes sizzling with cool light. Georgette held her breath, awaiting judgment. Finally, Kazimiera nodded.

"Okay," she said. "I'm satisfied."

"Great!" Georgette said, exhaling. "What should I do next?"

Kazimiera turned to her and, through the tinted glasses, looked her up and down with an expression that made her spine tingle. As the last light of the evening died and the streetlights flared to life, Kazimiera folded her parasol, removed her sunglasses, and let the artificial streetlight paint her chestnut skin. She gestured to the front doors.

"I'll take you through the club," she said, "show you everything I need done. You can pitch some ideas, then I'll decide what takes priority."

"Okay." Georgette smiled. Finally, a chance to get a closer look inside.

"Don't wander off, and pay close attention," Kazimiera warned. "I don't like to repeat myself, and my club isn't a place you'd like to be lost in." Her glare sliced through Georgette's soul. "You go nowhere without me. Understand?"

"Yes ma'am," Georgette said quietly. "Perfectly."

The ground floor of Nocturne was a wide-open area with a stage, a dance floor, sitting areas, and a huge bar. The whole room was draped in royal purple and midnight blue, accented with gold and silver details.

As the pair walked across the room, a voice called out for a light check and the club suddenly plunged into darkness. Georgette's eyes widened with wonder as pinpoints of artificial starlight lit up the ceiling, walls, and floor. There were no spells involved, but the effect was magical, nevertheless. It was like walking through the night sky.

The lights came back on and Georgette scanned the employees, human in appearance only. One bartender was an Incubus, the other two were Succubae—all of them emanating magnetic sexual energy. The performer warming up on stage was a Siren, her animal features hidden by a glamour. Two waitresses—a Selkie without her sealskin and a Huldra without a tail—chatted near the bar. Georgette caught glimpses of *Hathiya* brands on several of these workers, but noticed that none of them matched.

Strange, she thought.

On the second floor was a dining room with a small stage for intimate performances and a corner bar with exclusive drink selections. Like the club below, this floor adhered to the blue-purple color scheme and starlight vibe. Unlike the club area, there was magic here. The windows, which should have looked out over the busy downtown streets, displayed images of moonlit lagoons, beaches, forests, and fields.

"Glamours," Kazimiera said. "They're . . . functional but haven't been changed in years."

"I'm good with glamours," Georgette said, taking notes on her phone. "I can make the image crisper and create a loop of action that's at least an hour long."

"For each one?"

"Yes ma'am."

Kazimiera nodded, a glimmer of approval in her eyes. Georgette felt a rush of confidence.

The kitchen, though cloaked in magic, was ordinary enough, except for the workers. It was here that Georgette saw the true diversity of Kazimiera's staff. A pair of Brownies—short, hairy little men—chopped up vegetables on either side of a large-footed, squat quasi-man Georgette knew to be a Pombero. At the stove, a Pooka—composed of various parts from a goat, a rabbit, a horse, and a man—sautéd something fragrant. Gathering up plates and silverware were a Banshee with long red hair and an Encantado, his aquatic form well hidden beneath the visage of a handsome young man. Both were dressed in black-and-white formalwear and both avoided eye contact with Georgette.

The magic was stronger on the third floor. Georgette had

initially assumed these would be the employee bedrooms, but the hallway was too fancy for living quarters: plush blue carpet, purple wallpaper with hair-thin gold swirls, and heavy, ornate doorknobs. They passed the first door—the office where she had interviewed—and continued toward the second. The door was open and Georgette, curious, glanced into the room, her witch's vision piercing the glamour draped across the door frame. Inside, she saw a wall covered with screens displaying images of the club and restaurant. Beside them, she saw what looked like a large, floating gyroscope with rotating wheels-within-wheels, each of which was covered with dozens of spots. As she gawked, the golden wheels suddenly stopped turning and every spot on them shifted in unison. Startled, she jumped back. The nested wheels were covered in big, lidless eyes, all of which were looking at her.

"Sorry," she mumbled. "Excuse me."

The creature's attention immediately returned to the wall of screens.

Impressive security, Georgette thought as she scurried to catch up with Kazimiera. *With that many eyes, I bet nothing gets past him.*

Kazimiera led her through the next door. As Georgette stepped inside, the spells within the apartment engulfed her like a fog of incense.

"What's this?" Georgette asked, glancing around through squinted eyes.

"VIP," Kazimiera said. "Private members only."

The dimly lit room was set up like an executive lounge: black leather couches, crystal ashtrays, and mahogany tables. Georgette's eye was drawn by the heavy curtains—thundercloud gray—blocking the outside light.

"There's a spell coating the windows," she said. "Why use curtains?"

"It makes the clients feel secure," Kazimiera said. "They can't see the magic, but they can see the curtains."

"The concealment spells are sturdy," Georgette said, looking around, "but there are also a lot of memory-obscuring spells. Why would—"

"Don't ask why," Kazimiera snapped. "Just take your notes."

Georgette lowered her eyes. "Yes ma'am."

Most of the other suites had a similar setup—a smoky lounge coated in a combination of magics. One exception was a room at the end of the hall, which turned out to be an impossibly large sauna. Peering through the steam, Georgette saw a greenish, claw-footed Akaname licking the floor clean with its snake-like tongue, and a bearded, shriveled old Bannik folding towels. Both paused briefly in their work to look her up and down.

The sauna's wood-paneled walls extended far beyond where the edges of the room should have been, easily as long and as wide as the entire building. The ceiling was also twice as high as the ceiling of the adjacent hallway. *Holy crap.*

"The expansion magic on this room is massive," she said, suddenly nervous. "I've . . . never cast a spell like this."

"Neither had Martin when he first started here," Kazimiera replied with a dismissive wave. "If the spell isn't maintained, the room will shrink to its actual size, which will make it unusable. I expect you to figure it out."

Georgette's gut twisted. For a moment, the room around her tilted, panic threatening to consume her. *Focus in*, she told herself, locking her gaze onto a distant spot until the room stopped sway-ing. *You can do this.*

The last suite on the third floor was a break room for em-ployees—the vast majority of whom were female. A Nagini with a delicate human face atop a long, striped body of green and black scales sat alone. Three Kitsune with fox ears and multiple tails conversed quietly with a deathly pale Yuki-onna, the snow demon's lips as blue as veins. Another Selkie, a male without shirt or shoes, weaved through the room, followed by a young woman whose wet hair and damp dress hem marked her as a Nixie. A cluster of sinewy Elves, gleaming like moonlight on water, combed and braided each other's silver hair. Nymphs of every element moved about the room.

Nursing an uncomfortable suspicion, Georgette asked, "What, um, do these employees do for your . . . VIPs?"

Ignoring her, Kazimiera turned to the group. "We're short-staffed downstairs. I need one of you to work in the club."

The Nagini slithered forward, her hand raised.

Kazimiera rolled her eyes. "Obviously not you," she said.

Georgette started in surprise as the rest of the room, including the Nagini, laughed.

"Someone who can pass." Kazimiera zeroed in on the Nixie. "You. Get gussied up, braid your hair so it won't look wet, and head downstairs. And you," she added irritably, pointing at the Selkie, "put some damn shoes on."

The Nixie brushed past Kazimiera and the Selkie wandered off while the rest of the group went about their business. The club owner shooed Georgette out of the room and closed the door behind her while Georgette's suspicion welled within her.

Nerving herself, she cleared her throat. "I know I'm not supposed to ask—"

"Then don't," Kazimiera interrupted. "Follow me."

Swallowing the question didn't agree with Georgette, but she obeyed and followed her boss back down the hall.

"You can sit here," Kazimiera said when they stepped inside her office, waving Georgette to a chair. "Figure out what needs to be done." She crossed to the window and peeked through the dark curtains. "Make a list of whatever you'll need to—"

Gulping down her fear, Georgette blurted out, "Is this a brothel?"

Kazimiera whipped around. "A brothel?"

"Yeah." Georgette swallowed hard, trying to stop her hands from shaking. "I-I-I don't know if I'm comfortable with—"

"Why," the owner asked, her eyes slicing through the objection, "would you ask that?"

"It's just, those rooms—"

"I provide entertainment and distraction, for a price." She walked up to Georgette, locking her in a red-shimmered gaze. "Does that bother you?"

Georgette smelled the telltale coppery aroma that clung to Vampires, making her unbearably conscious of the blood racing through her veins. But while she had never been face-to-face with a Vampire before meeting Kazimiera, she was well acquainted with feeling vulnerable. Memories of her mother's cold stare perforated her anxiety and, to her surprise, slowed her heartbeat. Being within striking distance of a dangerous predator was not a new experience. Hell, she'd take a dozen Kazimieras over one Hazel Nichols O'Reilly.

"Yes, it does," she said, though her voice trembled a bit. "I won't cast spells to help keep these people locked up just so you can rent them out."

Kazimiera's reddened eyes bore into Georgette, the shine of them made all the brighter by the frame of her dark face. The Vampire's lips parted. Slowly, she ran her tongue over her teeth, coming to a stop with her tongue pressing into one needle-sharp canine. Though keenly aware of her naked throat, Georgette crossed her arms over her chest.

"You don't scare me."

"Yes, I do," said Kazimiera. She tilted her head, smirking. "But that didn't stop you."

She's gonna kick me out, Georgette thought miserably. *I've thrown away this chance to find Kalilah. Oh God, what am I gonna tell Ishak?*

Kazimiera craned her neck forward until she was inches from Georgette's cheek and drew in a slow breath. When she exhaled, the air coated Georgette's exposed neck and made her shiver with fear.

Kazimiera chuckled, startling Georgette and breaking the tension of the moment.

"Go talk to my staff," she whispered in Georgette's ear. "See what they tell you."

"What?"

"Go talk to my staff," Kazimiera repeated. "Talk to whomever you like. They'll answer your questions." She kissed the air and sauntered to the door. "Take your time. Come back to my office when you're satisfied."

30   Ishak

WHEN A WITCH IN A THREE-PIECE SUIT STEPPED INTO KK Inc.'s downtown office around 11:00 a.m., Ishak decided on skipping lunch.

Even from across the street, Ishak smelled the stink of excess on the man. The witch spent twenty minutes within, and then emerged with an employee at his side who walked him to a car. Ishak found it difficult to stay inconspicuous as he followed the moving vehicle, but at least his new clothes—slacks, a button-down shirt, and leather shoes—made for good camouflage.

Eventually, the car rolled up to a gated community in Silver Creek. Here, Ishak broke off his pursuit. The security he saw around the walled perimeter was intimidating. Furthermore, a casual glance around the neighborhood made it clear that he had little hope of blending in: all the residents were gleamingly pale.

The car containing the witch and the broker rolled through the gate and disappeared behind the walls. Ishak whipped off his shoes and socks and transformed his feet into their hyena form. Using his claws, he quickly scaled a tree and watched over the wall until he saw the car pull into a driveway. The house was a three-story picture of modernity, complete with surveillance cameras attached to its eaves. The broker led the way to the door, used a key, punched a code into a glowing panel, and ushered the witch inside. The scents on the wind were mottled but unmistakable hints of magic hovered in the air. Significant spells protected this house.

An hour later, the pair exited the house. The witch had something in his hands—a box of some sort. As he climbed into the car's passenger seat, a distinctive whiff of Fae magic reached Ishak on the wind. *He's bought a familiar,* the Bultungin surmised as he watched the car drive away. The scent was vague but distinctive enough that he could reassure himself that it did not come from Kalilah. *This house is a storage facility.*

After marking the location of the house with immense care—writing down the address and even drawing a map—Ishak circled the community fence half a dozen times. The extensive security not only made getting into the neighborhood challenging, but it also guaranteed that any discovered intrusion would be investigated immediately. After breaching the wall, he would have to reach the house without anyone questioning him. Then he had to get into a house that required a key and a code to enter. Assuming he overcame those obstacles, there would then be all manner of security, both magical and mundane, to overcome within. And after all that, there was still the possibility that this was not the site where Kalilah was being held.

With the odds so heavily in the enemy's favor, he retreated. For now.

The smell of the meaty contents of the takeout container he carried kickstarted Ishak's growling stomach on the way home. It was a short walk back to the hotel but, hungry as he was, it felt like miles.

Today was a productive day, he told himself as he rode the hotel elevator, inhaling the mouthwatering aroma of stir-fried beef. *Finding the location of that house is a crucial step toward finding Kalilah.*

Feeling confident and optimistic, he whipped out his key card, unlocked the hotel door, and stepped inside. "Mei-Xing, are you here?"

"*Hmm?*"

"Success!"

"*Hmm.*"

Ishak set his takeout container on the desk and went into the bathroom to wash his hands.

"I've found a new KK Inc. storage location," he said, raising his voice over the sound of running water. "It has formidable security—"

"Ishak."

"—but we will find a way in."

"Ishak."

He dried his hands and moved into the room, his thoughts split between the house and his dinner. It wasn't until he saw the Nymph's expression that he registered the distress in her voice.

"What is it?" he asked.

Mei-Xing sat on the edge of the bed—her back straight, her fingers gripping the comforter. Her iridescent eyes darted between him and a far corner of the room. Ishak followed her gaze and blinked in surprise. A large, black bird perched on the lamp-shade. The animal looked at him and issued a croak.

"What is this bird?" he asked Mei-Xing.

"There's more," she said.

"More of what?"

"Look with your other eyes," she said.

He drew on his Bultungin senses and immediately saw what he had missed. Next to the bird stood a stately woman dressed in flowing robes and gleaming armor with an ornate helmet under her arm. A silver sword leaned against the wall, within her reach but sheathed.

Astounded, Ishak gazed at her slack-jawed until Mei-Xing nudged him with her foot.

"Madam," he blurted out. "Good evening."

She gave a regal nod. In the silence that followed, Ishak sized her up. She was strikingly tall for a woman—almost his height. What little of her skin was visible under her vestments was the color of desert sand. Her wavy hair was loose, hanging about her shoulders. Her features reminded him of his mother and aunts. Like them, she had full lips and a wide nose. Also like them, she presented herself with an air of calm authority. Very unlike them, however, she was not fully in this world, visible only to those who knew how to look.

"Who might you be?" he asked.

"My name is Delia Beauregard," she said. Her voice was firm but lyrical, the hint of an accent he couldn't quite identify laced through her aristocratic tone. "Or rather," she added, "my name *was* Delia Beauregard. I am now Svanhild of the Valhalla Sister-hood."

A Valkyrie. Yes, that accounted for the armor and ethereal form.

"This," she said, gesturing to the raven, "is Senji Nakamura, my partner." The bird cawed, rattling the lamp. "He greets you."

After exchanging a look with Mei-Xing, Ishak nodded to the bird and then to the Valkyrie. "I am Ishak Siad."

"*Konbanwa*," she replied with a slight dip of her head.

The smell of his takeout dinner beckoned to him, dampening his curiosity. Eager to get to his meal, he decided to cut to the heart of this encounter.

"Why are you here?"

"She and I were just discussing that." The Valkyrie nodded toward Mei-Xing. "I had hoped to come when all three of you were here, but you're rarely all together of late."

Suspicion prickled the nape of Ishak's neck. "How would you know that?"

"We've been watching you."

Ishak's jaw clenched. "Have you?"

"A necessary precaution," she said, her voice level and calm. "By coming here this evening, we're putting our heads on the chopping block. We had to be sure the three of you were worth the risk."

"And what is it you want from us?"

He didn't know what to expect when he asked the question, but he most assuredly did not expect the answer she gave. Without pause, without nicety, without ambiguity, she stated, "We want the brand."

"The brand?"

She pointed at his wrist. Ishak lifted his arm, showing the mark. The Valkyrie nodded.

"The brand," she repeated. "The witch brand. That's what we want."

"You want to be branded by a witch?" Mei-Xing asked, clearly just as confused as Ishak was.

"Not *a* witch," Delia said as the raven bobbed on its perch, "*your* witch. We want the *Hathiya* spell that lets you draw on your witch's power."

"Why?" asked Ishak.

Delia hooked a tendril of her hair with two fingers and flicked it out of her face. She glanced at the raven, which cocked its head at her and croaked.

"Personal reasons," she finally answered. "There's a matter that Senji and I wish to attend to, but Valhalla refused our request. If the Sisterhood learns of our intentions . . ." Delia's lips tightened and her eyes narrowed as Senji made a resonant sound deep in his throat. "They would not approve. After watching the three of you and seeing what the brand has made possible for you, Senji and I feel that it will give us the freedom of movement we need to complete our task without Valhalla's knowledge."

Personal reasons. Ishak didn't know a great deal about Valkyries, but his understanding was that they had no personal reasons because they didn't have their own person; their entire post-life existence revolved around Valhalla's war. And yet, Delia Beauregard and Senji Nakamura not only had personal reasons, they had some that were compelling enough to make them willing to defy their superiors.

Mulling this over, Ishak turned to Mei-Xing, only to see the Nymph's head bowed low. She had fallen asleep sitting up. He briefly considered waking her, difficult as that would be, but decided against it.

"Why should we do this for you?" he asked the visitors, casting a longing look at the bag holding his dinner.

"We're prepared to bargain," she replied.

"Bargain?" His eyebrows raised. "What are you offering?"

"What do you need?"

Ishak squinted at her. It struck him as an odd question. She was a Valkyrie, not a merchant. He couldn't imagine that she was in a position to offer very much. Delia seemed to recognize his confusion.

"Senji tells me that you appear to be on some sort of mission—that you spend your waking hours watching a brokerage. You clearly have a goal. What can we do to help?"

Immediately, Ishak thought of the KK Inc. house in the gated community. All the walls, locks, and cameras in the world couldn't stop an invisible woman like this one from entering.

"I cannot give the brand," he said. "Only Georgette can do that."

"We know," Delia said. "Please convey our offer to your witch: in exchange for the brand, we will offer our services in whatever capacity they are required." The Valkyrie swept her helmet onto her head in a quick, fluid motion. The raven hopped to her shoulder. "Senji will check in on you. You can reach me through him." She took a step toward the window, then paused. "In our particular . . . situation . . . time is of the essence. Please contact us soon."

And then she and the raven were gone. Ishak blinked, staring at the window. He wasn't even sure how the pair had exited the room, only that they had left.

With a shrug, he grabbed his lukewarm dinner, plopped down next to his sleeping Nymph friend, and began shoveling it into his mouth.

As he ate, he pondered the day's events. He imagined using Delia to get into the brokerage house. He imagined the Valkyrie, the brand on her wrist, leading Kalilah by the hand into his waiting arms. He imagined—and he hoped.

31   Georgette

THE SIREN SAT AT THE CLUB BAR, STIRRING HONEY INTO her tea. Her heart-shaped face contorted in discomfort; she kept scratching at her arms as if the sparkly material of her dress crawled with fleas.

"Can I help you with that?" Georgette asked, cautiously approaching her.

The Siren's pearly sea-green eyes darted toward her. "What do you mean?"

"Your glamour is deteriorating." Georgette pointed to the Siren's sleeve. "That's why it's irritating you. I can fix it."

The Siren looked the witch up and down, eyes narrowed. Finally, she nodded and said, "Go ahead."

Georgette gently dipped her fingers into the glamour. Envisioning a new look, she pulled a bit of the old glamour into herself and linked it to her inner power.

"What's your favorite color?" Georgette asked.

"Purple," the Siren said, and her face softened slightly.

Pouring her magic into the rips and holes, Georgette reconstructed the spell. The Siren's face and short dark hair remained the same, but her clothing quivered and changed. For a moment, the old glamour dissolved, flashing a glimpse of the Siren's feathers and scaly feet—then the new image solidified. The old dress, a tight, silver sequined number, transformed into a loose, gossamer purple material with reflective sparkles. Her scaled and taloned feet were newly coated in shapely human calves and spiked high heels.

Smiling, the Siren looked herself over, holding up her arms so that the dress twinkled in the light. "It's nice," she said. "Stopped itching, too. Thanks." She peered deep into Georgette's face as she took a sip of her tea. "I saw you earlier with Kazi," she said. "You're here to replace Martin?"

"I guess," Georgette said. "Um, can I ask you something?"

"*Hm?*" The Siren looked at her expectantly.

"How did you end up here?"

The Siren shrugged. "My song draws in the customers. Kazi thought it would be a waste to have me wait tables."

"No," Georgette said. "I mean, how did you end up in this building?"

"Oh, I see." The Siren flashed a smile at the Incubus bartender. "Hey handsome, bring the new Martin a drink, okay?"

The tall, dark man glided over to the women with a decanter of water in his hands. As he poured her a glass, Georgette's skin grew warm and her cheeks flushed. She became acutely aware of every slope of his face and the smooth motions of his hands. Though she knew this was a natural physiological reaction to have in the presence of an Incubus, she still felt flustered.

He placed the glass in front of her. "No alcohol for employees during working hours," he said, giving her a smile that made her heart flutter. "Kazi's orders."

"It-it's fine," she stammered. "Thanks."

He winked at the Siren and then returned to stocking the bar. As he moved away, Georgette felt her attraction wane. He was like a candle, lighting up only those close to him; once out of range, his allure lost its effect. Taking a sip of the water to wash down the last of her butterflies, Georgette reflected that he probably got great tips.

"I came to Nocturne," said the Siren, "like everyone else here: Kazi brought me in."

"Did she . . . buy you?"

"Not me, no. That one"—the Siren pointed at the Huldra sweeping the floors—"she bought. I came here after I escaped the witch who branded me." Her eyes grew unfocused as she stared into her tea. "I was too valuable to lose—she used the power of my voice to get men and money—so when I ran, she came after me. I thought I'd have to keep running forever, but then I met a Jotun who had once escaped from a witch as well. He was by then completely free of her, thanks to Kazi. He hooked me up with a series of others who passed me down the line from Brazil to California and right to Nocturne's door. Kazi had Martin link me to the concealment spells on the building and wrap me up in a glamour." Smiling, she took a sip of her tea. "That was five years ago, and I've been here ever since."

Dumbstruck, Georgette felt all the mystery of Nocturne vanish. The brands she had seen on the various employees were different because they had been inflicted by different witches. The powerful spells on the outside of the building, which Georgette thought were part of a system to keep the familiars prisoner, were actually designed to hide them from the witches who had enslaved them.

"What about her?" Georgette flicked her head in the Huldra's direction. "Why did Kazimiera buy her?"

The Siren curled her long nails around the mug, softly tinkling the ceramic. "She belonged to a particularly sadistic witch. The bastard cut her up, used her blood in spells, sold pieces of her flesh . . ." She shuddered. "The glamour hides it, but she's covered in scars. When the witch decided there were no more profitable body parts to remove, he tried selling her. None of the reputable brokerages would buy her all cut up, so he sold her to Kett & Kadena. Someone at Nocturne got wind of her situation and talked Kazi into buying her. Poor thing is so traumatized, she's afraid to leave the building."

Georgette's stomach lurched at the sudden memory of one of Clove's acquisitions. She had seen the creature—an old, gray-haired Faun—only once from her bedroom window. As she watched, Clove led her limping, goat-footed purchase from her car to the shed at the edge of the yard. The whole house knew what was in that shed; Hazel Nichols O'Reilly wouldn't allow messy rituals in the house. Just before entering, the Faun glanced up and met her eyes. Startled, she'd ducked and stayed that way until she heard the shed door bang shut.

"Is that how everyone got here?" she asked.

"More or less." The Siren drank the last of her tea and slid off the barstool. "I have to get ready for opening," she said. "Thanks for the glamour, New Martin."

The Blemmye towered over Georgette, but since his large eyes were embedded in his chest, they spoke face-to-face. Broad and headless, the creature smacked his wide lips—situated over his paunchy stomach—and continued cleaning smudges off wine glasses as he spoke.

"I have been at Nocturne," he said in his deep, oddly accented voice, "for eight years. Before that, I was chained to a witch for, oh . . ." His chest rumpled as he sniffed thoughtfully. "I think thirteen years."

A loud crash exploded through the kitchen, followed by inarticulate shouts. A Brownie, giggling wildly, scurried across the floor with a carton of milk in one hand and a glob of choco-late cake in the other. He darted into the dining room just in time to avoid a wooden spoon that struck the door and clattered to the floor. Georgette turned to see where the spoon had come from and spotted the Pooka chef shaking his rabbit paw fist at the door. When the chef saw the rest of the staff looking at him, he bellowed like a foghorn through his horse mouth. The noise star-tled everyone and sent them scurrying back to work.

"How did you escape?" Georgette asked the Blemmye.

"I didn't." He held a wineglass to his chest, just at eye level. "It is difficult to navigate this human world, big as I am. I broke a lot of glassware when I first started in the kitchen here, but Kazi encouraged me. She was short on kitchen staff, and at the time I was the only Fae available who had thumbs. Since I was the only option, she told me to go slow until I got a feel for the work. The witch who branded me did not have the same patience." With slow, careful movements, he set down the glass and picked up another. It looked like a doll's cup in his huge hand. "One day I broke an expensive bobble, and the witch flew into a rage. She beat me with a bat—broke my nose and two of my ribs. Then, using the binding power of her brand, she commanded me to march into the desert and wait there until I died."

Georgette wished she felt shocked by this cruelty but it sounded like something her mother or Lily might do. Too often she had noticed a colorful bruise or bandaged gash on one of their familiars. She'd learned at a young age to never ask about the injuries. In the Nichols O'Reilly house, unexplained wounds were expected to remain unexplained.

"How long were you in the desert?" she asked.

"I'm not sure," he said. "I kept passing out. At some point, a Rain Bird flying overhead saw me and took pity on me by letting loose a downpour. The rain revived me, but I was still trapped there by the witch's command. The Rain Bird visited Nocturne and told Kazi what it had seen. She paid someone to fetch me. By the time they found me, I was too near death to move—which was fortunate. Had I been able to, I would have been compelled to obey the witch's command, and they wouldn't have been able to budge me. Once Martin connected me to the spells of Nocturne, the witch's brand lost its power over me."

"Have you worked in the kitchen since then?" Georgette asked.

"Mostly," he said. "I also work security and help unload the supply trucks. But I've gotten comfortable with kitchen work."

"Are you paid?"

The Blemmye laughed, the crinkles of his eyes extending into his armpits. "What would I do with money?" he asked. "I work for my bed, my food, and my safety."

"If you didn't work, would you be allowed to stay?"

"There have been some who didn't want to work," he said.

"Kazi let them stay but only gave them the minimum of supplies they needed. 'This is a business, not a resort'—she says that all the time. But anyway, most of them eventually asked for work, just to pass the time and to be part of our little community."

"How long are familiars allowed to stay?" she asked.

"Until the brands wear off and we can leave the building without fear of being tracked. That usually takes about . . ." He pursed his big lips. "Oh, ten years, give or take." He set down his latest glass and lifted his left arm into the air. "See? My brand is fading." The mark on his side was indeed very faded, like a photocopy of a photocopy. "In another year, I might be able to go home." He smiled sadly. "I haven't seen my mother in over twenty years."

A Kitsune adjusted her green kimono while muttering under her breath. Her five fox tails did not fit well under the restrictive skirt.

"Why a kimono?" asked Georgette.

"Customers expect it," she said. "The VIPs don't pay good money to see a Kitsune in a pantsuit."

Her five tails were so smooshed together under her clothes that the tips were crowded around her ankles like red and white fur socks.

"Can I help?" Georgette asked.

"If you can, yes," the Kitsune said, still tugging at the skirt.

Georgette remembered helping her big sister Holly get dressed on her wedding day and discovering that Holly's newly showing pregnancy made the gown too small. Holly burst into tears, wailing that their mother would be furious that the expensive wedding was ruined by her "fat" daughter. Desperate to help her sister avoid their mother's ire, Georgette had woven a spell that duplicated the fabric of the dress, expanding it in necessary places without changing the seams. It hadn't hidden Holly's belly, but it had allowed her to fit in the gown.

Now, on the third floor of Nocturne, Georgette used the spell again, expanding the lower part of the kimono to give the Kitsune's tails room to swish. The Kitsune sighed with relief and offered Georgette an appreciative nod.

"What, exactly, are the VIPs paying for?" she asked.

"To see us and what we can do," the Kitsune told her. "To see the magics our various species are capable of. To have us wait on them for an evening—serve them drinks, listen to them talk, and flatter them."

"That's all?"

"Most humans aren't you," the Kitsune said. "They aren't used to Fae."

"Isn't the whole point of the spells on this building to keep hidden?" Georgette asked. "How can you let them see you and expect to stay safe?"

"You saw the rooms, didn't you? The memory spells? They filter out the details of what happens in the room but leave them with the feelings of awe and excitement that they experience. They leave happy and wanting to come back."

"Are they allowed to touch you?"

"If we let them. Mostly they ask to touch my ears or the Nagini's scales. They just want to be sure we're real."

"But . . . nothing sexual?"

"Any customer who tries gets kicked out. Or"—she smirked—"they get taken to Kazi's office. Those guys wake up on the curb at 4:00 a.m."

Probably suffering from blood loss, thought Georgette. *Draining customers' blood must be a regular part of the VIP experience—a part that gets filtered out. That would explain how Kazimiera keeps herself fed.*

"So no one here is ever pushed to do anything sexual with the customers?"

"No," the Kitsune said firmly, looking a bit offended. "Kazi wouldn't do that."

"I just meant—"

"Kazi wouldn't do that," she repeated, emphasizing her words. "She knows what we've survived."

The Yuki-onna took hold of the Kitsune's long, wide sleeve and said something to her in Japanese. The Kitsune nodded, replied in kind, and pointed toward the back of the room. The snow demon headed in that direction, her long, white robe leaving a chill in her wake.

"She and I were branded by the same witch," the Kitsune told Georgette. "He collected women for a harem. Yuki and I spent months planning our escape. One night, while he was drinking wine, we added a little more to his glass from the bottle every time he looked away. He kept drinking, getting drunker all the time, never realizing that his first glass was actually an entire bottle. Once he was asleep, all of us—her, me, and all the other familiars—ran. Well," she corrected herself, "first, we tried to kill him. But we could only get the knife within six inches of his skin before the brand incapacitated us." She shot Georgette a harsh glare. "You witches and your *Hathiya*."

Heartsick, Georgette nodded in agreement and waited for the Kitsune to continue.

"Yuki and I made our way to California," the fox woman said. "We heard rumors about Nocturne and decided to approach Kazi for help. She took us in, Martin hooked us to the building's magic, and we've been here ever since." The Kitsune locked eyes with Georgette. "Look, Kazi is a hard woman; she's here to run a business, not to be our friend. However, she understands what we've all lived through, and she would never ask us to go back to being what we were. She fosters rumors about her being a wannabe witch on purpose, but those are just a cover story." She looked Georgette up and down, nostrils flared. "She's not any kind of a witch."

The Kitsune padded her way toward the door, all of her tails twitching under her skirt. Even after she had left the room, Georgette still felt that judging gaze, stripping her down to her fragile, naked core.

With the heavy curtains of Kazimiera's office swept aside, Georgette saw a flowing river of headlights on the street casting fleeting shadows on the crowd of people waiting to get into the club. The Siren's enticing voice alternatively grew louder and softer as the front doors opened and closed to admit new patrons. The alluring vibrations of the music pleasantly tickled Georgette's ears.

She looked at her notes. There was a lot to do. Some of it fell outside her experience, but she felt deeply motivated to learn.

The office door opened, and Kazimiera slipped inside. The metallic shine of her tight dress refracted the light of the hallway into the dim office like a disco ball.

"Satisfied?" she asked, closing the door behind her.

"Yes," Georgette said. "I'll start with the glamours in the dining room and the individual glamours on those that need them. After that, I'll need some time to figure out how to keep the sauna the way it is, but the memory filter spells shouldn't be too—"

"So you still want the job?"

Georgette looked up from her notes. "Yeah, I do. But I have questions."

The club owner slid into her chair, crossed her legs, and folded her hands in her lap. "Such as?"

"Why did you trust me to talk to your staff? I mean"—Georgette shook her head—"there are a lot of witches who would blow the whistle on you."

"Not you."

"What made you so sure?"

"Because," Kazimiera said, "you called them 'people.' In all my days, I've only ever met a handful of witches who called familiars 'people,' and damned if they weren't all like Martin."

"Like Martin," Georgette murmured thoughtfully. "How many witches have worked for you?"

"Sixteen. Seventeen if I include you." The Vampire brushed back her hair from her forehead, letting the corkscrew coils run through her fingers. "Some of them were with me for only a few months while others, like Martin, stayed on for decades."

"Decades? Has Nocturne been around that long?"

"In various incarnations." Kazimiera ran her tongue over her pointed teeth, never taking her eyes off her. "I have questions for you, too."

"What can I tell you?"

"First, let me explain something. Martin worked for me because when he was young, he fell in love with an Iara."

"Iara? What's—"

"A subspecies of mermaid," Kazimiera said. "Martin could talk about her for hours. To hear him tell it, she was the most beautiful, most amazing, most *everything* in the whole world. They'd been happy together for almost a year when she disappeared. After months of searching, he learned she'd been caught by a brokerage and sold. She had changed hands multiple times before Martin found her, and by then it was too late. She was dead."

"That's horrible." Georgette's voice fell to a frail whisper. "But why are you telling me?"

"Because I know why Martin came to work for me," Kazimiera said. She leaned closer, her amber eyes locking Georgette in their forceful light. "Why are *you* here?"

32  Mei-Xing

THROUGH THE RESTAURANT WINDOW, EARLY-MORNING sunlight spread over Mei-Xing's skin, feeding her as the diner fed her friends. Georgette had woken her up before sunrise—not an easy feat—so she could fill both her and Ishak in on the previous night's events. She had spent the dark hours of the morning struggling to be alert—a draining effort. Only now, drinking in the first sun rays of the day, did she feel relief.

"What did you tell her?" Ishak asked.

"That my reason wasn't my secret to share," Georgette replied.

"And what did she say?"

Mei-Xing watched Ishak drain his coffee cup, his eyes on Georgette—who, in turn, was staring at her half-eaten breakfast of yogurt with berries and granola. She kept picking up a spoonful of the glop and dropping it back into the bowl. Mei-Xing found the repetitive motion strangely hypnotic.

"She said that wasn't good enough and she needed to know the reason. I said I would get back to her."

Their waitress appeared with a hot pot of coffee. Ishak held out his cup for a refill and, smiling, thanked her. Mei-Xing saw the young woman blush slightly, probably a response to the Bultungin's good looks and exotic accent. The waitress then gathered up the empty plates in front of Ishak and Mei-Xing. The Nymph had not eaten, but she had ordered steak and eggs to avoid looking out of place. Ishak, who had ordered the same thing, had eaten his own meal and then switched his plate with hers. He seemed to have a bottomless appetite.

The waitress walked away with the dishes, leaving the trio alone in the otherwise vacant restaurant.

"What now?" Ishak asked.

"I won't tell her your secret," Georgette said. "Not without your permission."

The Bultungin exhaled over the rim of his cup, dispelling the steam. Mei-Xing knew he didn't understand the significance of what Georgette was saying. Nichols O'Reilly children kept their own secrets, but not each other's. Given the opportunity, they eagerly traded those secrets for favors, praise, or escape from punishment. For Georgette to come to Ishak for permission to share his secret went against everything she was raised to do.

"What do you think of this woman?" he asked.

"She intimidates the hell out of me," Georgette said.

"And her club? What the staff said? Is it true?"

"I think so." Georgette stirred her yogurt, creating a spiral of granola within it. "Kazimiera took a big risk in letting me talk to them. So many witches would either expose her out of tribal loyalty or blackmail her. She had everything to lose by opening up to me."

Mei-Xing took a long drink from her water glass, reflecting on what Georgette had told them: Nocturne was a club, a restaurant, a private entertainment site, but it was also a refugee camp. Ishak seemed skeptical but Mei-Xing was elated. All her life she had been warned that being taken as a witch's familiar was a life sentence, but that wasn't true. Familiars were escaping and finding freedom. She wondered if there were other places like this one.

"I will think about it," Ishak said.

"Meanwhile, we have some news too," Mei-Xing said. "And it might be the key to finding Kalilah."

Georgette leaned forward in her seat. "Tell me everything."

By the time Ishak and Mei-Xing were done telling Georgette about the Valkyrie, the witch was wide-eyed and open-mouthed. She made them repeat Delia's request to be branded several times. She was not, however, surprised to hear about the broker's house in the gated community; in fact, she was annoyed with herself for not thinking to look there sooner.

"What do you think we should do?" Ishak asked.

"Well," Georgette said, "if we confide in Kazimiera, she could go to KK Inc. directly and maybe find Kalilah overnight."

"But then she could conscript Kalilah into her service." Ishak glowered.

"I don't think so. None of her employees are forced to be there."

"What about the Huldra who never leaves the building?" he argued. "You took the Siren's word that the Huldra stays because she's traumatized, but that might not be true."

Georgette shook her head. "I deconstructed and rebuilt the spells on the outside of the building. There's nothing holding her in."

"A locked door is not the only way to hold someone prisoner. Up here"—he tapped the side of his head—"is the real prison. Kazimiera may have convinced the Huldra that she can't leave. She is," he added, "a Vampire."

Vampires are supposedly deceptive by nature, thought Mei-Xing. *Fair point.*

"Why mess with the minds of a few familiars when she could just stick to taking in runaways who have to stay in the building for ten years?" Georgette countered.

Also a fair point, Mei-Xing thought. *The Vampire is a business-woman. She's probably inclined to do what's most practical.* She drank some more water and laid her arm on the table, trying to maximize surface area touched by the sunlight coming through the window, as she listened.

"All right." Ishak nodded thoughtfully. "But would she be willing to do such a thing on my behalf?"

"We won't know unless we ask." Georgette stirred the bowl of yogurt again and Mei-Xing watched the chunks of fruit and granola sink into the white swirl. "At least we know what Kazimiera gets out of this arrangement. We don't know what the Valkyrie wants."

"She was vague," Ishak agreed, "but I feel the possibility of her assistance outweighs the concern of not knowing her intentions. Should it really matter what their 'personal reasons' are?"

"Here's the thing," Georgette said. "Witches don't interfere with Valkyries, they don't interact with Valkyries, and they never, ever brand Valkyries. Making a familiar of one Valkyrie makes enemies of the rest, and an enemy of Valhalla is a dangerous thing to be." She finally put down the spoon and leaned back in the booth, resting her hands in her lap. "Capturing a Valkyrie would be a huge status symbol. My mother lives for status symbols, but she still avoids Valkyries like white after Labor Day."

"This wouldn't be capturing a Valkyrie, it would be partnering with one."

"I promise you, Valhalla won't see it that way."

"Surely they would be angry at her, not us."

"Are you willing to bet your life on that?"

Ishak sat back in the booth, eyes closed. "Delia and Senji may be my best chance to free Kalilah. Am I willing to bet my life on that? Yes. Without reservation."

"Okay," Georgette said to Ishak, "but let me ask you this: is it worth asking for Kazimiera's help so you might *not* have to risk your life?"

Intrigued, Mei-Xing eagerly looked to Ishak for a response. If bringing the Vampire on board kept Georgette safe from Valhalla's wrath, then she was all for it. She saw a wrestling match of emotions take place on Ishak's face as he considered his answer.

"Only," he finally replied, "if I am not increasing the risk to Kalilah's life by doing so."

Georgette sighed. "So what it boils down to is this: I'm inclined to trust Kazimiera, you're not. You're inclined to trust the Valkyrie, I'm not."

"That is the sum of it." Ishak lifted his cup to his lips, drank, and then exhaled over his coffee. "How do we move on from here?"

Mei-Xing waited with bated breath to see what they would do. However, her expectation turned to befuddlement when both of them turned and looked at her.

"What?" she asked, pulling back in surprise.

"I think you're the tie-breaker, Mei," Georgette said.

"Yes," Ishak said with a nod. "We need your thoughts."

"My thoughts?" Her mind froze. With her mouth hanging open, she looked back and forth between the two of them for several seconds before casting her eyes down at the table. "No thoughts," she said in her heavily accented English. "None."

"That's never true," Georgette scolded her.

"Please," Ishak said, leaning closer to her. "What do you think?"

Mei-Xing didn't want this responsibility. She understood both arguments and didn't feel suitable to judge which was worthier. She had met the Valkyrie and had also, like Ishak, seen the possibilities her help would open for them. She had not met the Vampire, but she trusted Georgette's assessment. *My friends have both been through a lot and aren't willing to trust someone sight-unseen. No matter which way I vote, one of them will resent it.*

"You meet both," she blurted out, catching herself by surprise. "Bring them one place, meet both. You talk. Then choose."

They stared back at her for so long that she worried her English was incomprehensible. Trying to suppress her embarrassment, her mind raced to construct a better sentence. But before she could pull together the words, Ishak turned to Georgette and nodded.

"She has a point," he said. "If we're to make this decision properly, we should each talk to them first."

"It's not a bad idea," Georgette said, "but I'm not sure Kazimiera will let me bring you into the club. It took two weeks before she let me into her secrets. Pretty sure she spent that time watching me to decide if I was worth the risk."

"Will she agree to meet with us outside of the club?"

"Maybe. But it would have to be somewhere she knows."

"Botanica," Mei-Xing chimed in. "She regular there."

"That might work," said Georgette. "What about the Valkyrie? Would she meet us there?"

"Why wouldn't she?" Ishak replied, sounding mildly surprised. "According to you, even witches fear her kind. Is there any place she could meet us where she wouldn't be safe?"

Mei-Xing watched this truth sink into Georgette. Drawing a deep breath, the witch locked eyes with the Bultungin and nodded. He returned the gesture, his conclusive expression mirroring hers.

"Then we're decided?" he said.

Georgette glanced at Mei-Xing for confirmation. Mei-Xing gave her a tiny nod.

"We're decided," Georgette said.

Mei-Xing looked from one friend to the other. Both awaited her final word on the matter. Her fears smothered by their trust, she nodded smartly. "Decided."

33 🜏 Neil

"HEY, BABE!" NEIL SAID WITH A GRIN. HE CAUGHT GEORGETTE AROUND the waist and kissed her smiling lips. "Real glad to get your text!"

"Hey," she said, returning his embrace. "Sorry for the short notice. I just needed a break before I have to jump into my next assignment."

The mid-afternoon sun warmed Neil's skin through his light coat, but the feel of Georgette in his arms warmed his soul. The unexpected joy of meeting up for a meal—late lunch, early dinner, whatever this was—washed away the doldrums of his mundane morning.

"Don't be sorry. Glad I had a break between meetings." He smiled sympathetically. "Work got you down, huh?"

Sighing, she shrugged. "Today's just been a lot of back and forth, a lot of juggling different things. Exhausting."

"I know how that goes." He turned, one arm still around her, and gestured at the food trucks up the street. "What sounds good to you?"

It made him happy to see her eyes sparkle with childlike wonder at the dozen or so colorful rigs lining the block.

"So many!" She lowered her gaze to the sidewalk. "Mom wouldn't let us eat from trucks," she confided. "She said they were for laborers who had to eat on the job. Once, in college, I told her that couldn't be true because the trucks were also at street festivals."

Neil felt her flinch under the arm wrapped around her.

"She got upset," Georgette said in a subdued tone. "Said she wasn't paying tuition for me to waste my time at festivals. She started tracking me after that. She'd call me up at all hours, asking why I was where I was. It got to the point that I jumped every time my phone rang."

While she talked, Neil just looked at her, hardly blinking. She had never opened up to him about her mother before. It was an upsetting yet tantalizing glimpse behind the curtain.

Unexpectedly, her gaze darted to him, and they locked eyes. Georgette quickly turned aside, cheeks flushed. Neil's heart skipped, flooded with panicked adrenaline. *I screwed it up!*

"Sorry, I didn't—I mean, your mom," he said, fumbling with words that all felt wrong, "she sounds intense."

"Yeah," she said after a pause. Turning away, she said, "Let's eat, okay?"

"I—"

"How about Ramen Roadtrip?" she asked, pointing to the truck in question. "That looks good."

"I, uh, didn't mean to—"

"Do you like ramen?" she interjected, her eyes landing on him only for a moment before darting away. "I don't think I've had it before."

Without waiting for his reply, she trotted off toward the red and brown truck, clutching her purse to her chest. Misery and exasperation roiled in Neil's chest as he watched her go. *She talks to Nico about her mother*, he thought, clenching his jaw. *Why not me?*

Forcefully swallowing back his churning emotions, he followed her to the ramen truck. Afraid that a wrong move from him might send her running, he kept his gaze locked on the cartoonish logo next to the truck's serving window. That smiling bowl of noodles irritated the hell out of him.

"I do like ramen," he said, still avoiding her eyes. "Never had it here, though. Want to try it out together?"

For a second, she looked nervous, as if uncertain that he meant what he said—but a heartbeat later, her expression softened, she smiled, and took his hand. The warmth of her touch once again filled him with delight, allowing him to willfully ignore the persistent doubt that gnawed at the back of his mind.

34   Delia & Senji

Delia sat on the gym steps, watching the chosen's last day unfold.

Senji perched on a shrub near the hotel while the Bultungin spoke to him.

The boxer, a compact powerhouse of a woman, was on her phone, arguing with her estranged husband about child custody.

He funneled the conversation to Delia, giving her access with one ear while she kept the other on the chosen.

Within hours, the man would arrive at the gym to shoot her dead. When his rage subsided, he would turn the gun on himself.

The Bultungin was agreeable to their deal. According to him, the Nymph was also willing, but the witch was unsure. She wanted to meet with him and Delia, Ishak said, before she could agree.

Delia?

Yes? she thought with a start.

The witch wants to meet us. Shall I agree?

Yes. We'll meet her when and where they like, so long as it's soon.

Soon. Time was slipping away.

The boxer thrust the phone into her bag. Delia heard her grumble as she headed into the gym for her last workout.

Senji bobbed to convey assent. Ishak nodded. The raven then cocked his head and squawked a wordless question.

"There is a shop Georgette frequents, the Botanica," the Bultungin said. "You have been following us, you certainly have seen it. Can Delia join us there this evening?"

I'll be there.

Senji bobbed again.

"Good," said Ishak. "We will meet then. I hope for the best."

As do I, Senji thought.

As do we both, Delia agreed.

The chosen's killer is on his way. Death is imminent.

The image of a wild-eyed man driving a jeep with a loaded gun in his lap flashed through her mind.

We'll deliver her and then meet with the witch.

On my way.

Senji let the wind lift him into the sunlit sky.

Delia closed her eyes,
following the flight
through her partner's
vision.

He thought about their
impending meeting.

She thought about what
they would say to the witch.

It had to go well.

It had to be convincing.

They needed this deal.

They needed this deal.

Ganbatte kudasai, *Senji*.

Lâche pas la patate, *Delia*.

35   Ishak

THE BOTANICA'S OVERHEAD LIGHTS WERE DIM THAT EVENING, creating a dusty haze of shadows in the shop. Ishak stood beside the tarot card table, beside the seated witch and Valkyrie. Mei-Xing sat opposite him, her backside planted on the edge of a display case. Her feet dangled limply in the air as she rested her chin in her hands, elbows on her knees. From where Ishak stood, she seemed to be stealing sleep a few minutes at a time while the others talked. A sliver of streetlight pierced the gap between the door window and the roll-down shade covering the glass. The light cut a clean line up the floor and onto the back wall, slicing through the cheek of the Virgin Mary and tapering to an end an inch above her eye.

Minutes ago, Delia had entered the shop clad in silver robes and armor. The raven was not with her; the Bultungin presumed Senji was keeping watch outside. When Ishak greeted her, Delia nodded politely before removing her sword and helmet and leaving them on the display case next to Mei-Xing.

Georgette and Delia introduced themselves. Then they sat. Then they talked.

Georgette listened silently and politely to the Valkyrie's pitch, her hands resting on the purple and gold tablecloth, until Delia reiterated her request for the brand.

"Why?" the witch asked. Her blue eyes narrowed slightly behind her glasses. "Why would you want me to brand you?"

"For personal—"

"Personal reasons, right," Georgette muttered. "But what you're asking for is . . . it could be risky. I need more than that. Tell me why you want it."

Though there was no change in her expression, Ishak saw Delia's fists clench under the table. Instinctively, he sniffed the air, searching for a tangible indicator of emotion. When all he detected was a whiff of Georgette's anxiety and Mei-Xing's drowsiness, he remembered that the Valkyrie was a spirit, not flesh and blood.

"Our motives are our own," Delia said. "There's no reason to—"

"I'm not a powerful witch!" Georgette said, her voice surprisingly sharp. "I'm already testing my limits by sharing magic with both Mei-Xing and Ishak. Extending my *Hathiya* to cover you and your partner might be too much for me. I need to know what you're planning in order to know if I have enough magic to go around, let alone whether I want to be a part of it."

Delia's nostrils flared. Ishak saw her fingers flex under the table. For all her poise, Delia struck him as uncomfortable with her current position.

"If I thought you weren't strong enough for our purposes," the Valkyrie said, speaking slowly, "I wouldn't be here."

"Only I can decide that," Georgette replied, "and only after you've told me what your 'personal reasons' are."

The witch folded her arms over her chest, staring at Delia, her jaw clenched. On another woman, the expression would look like a show of anger; on her, Ishak recognized it as an attempt to subdue an anxiety attack. Wishing to offer her his support without disrupting the conversation, he flexed his wrist. A feeling like an elastic band snapping made his brand sting, and her eyes darted to his. In the split second they locked gazes, he somehow poured a dose of his confidence into her—not enough to drown her anxiety but enough to calm it.

Unclenching her jaw, she looked away and refocused her attention on the Valkyrie.

Delia stared down at the floor, her eyes glazed. A moment of thick silence took hold of the room; Ishak guessed that she was conferring with her unseen partner. *They have their own sort of* Hathiya *link,* he thought, *and theirs allows them to communicate more effectively than ours.*

"Our business is private," she finally said, "but I can tell you what we need the brand to do. Will that suffice?"

"Maybe. Tell me."

"We need to be able to leave our designated district without alerting my sister Valkyries."

Georgette shot Ishak a look of mild surprise. *Is that all?* the look seemed to say. *Simple concealment? That's hardly worth so much fuss.*

"And," Delia added, "we need Senji to appear in his human form."

Ishak heard Georgette draw a sharp breath, saw her eyes widen. His hopes for enlisting the Valkyrie's help began to dwindle.

"His human . . ." Mouth agape, Georgette shoved one hand into her thick curls and pushed them back from her face. "Do you have the slightest idea . . ." She drew a series of short, choppy breaths. "To do that," she said, "I'd have to break the bond between you. A bond that was forged in the hearth of Valhalla—transcending time and space, life and death. I can't override that! I doubt there's a witch alive who could."

Ishak felt a maelstrom of panic, grief, and anger. Faced with the loss of this powerful ally, his mind churned with thoughts of Kalilah in chains, Kalilah cut to pieces, Kalilah in a grave. *If Georgette was stronger*, he thought with a stab of resentment, *then maybe, just maybe.* With great effort, he shoved those feelings aside. *She's doing everything she can to help, I must remember that.* But gratitude was elusive.

"We don't want to break the bond," Delia said. "We only want to loosen it just enough to show Senji as he was. We want to . . . put a damper on it, not to shut it down completely."

Ishak looked nervously at Georgette, hoping but doubting that this semantic shuffle would change the situation.

The witch tapped her fingers on the table, drumming the colorful cloth softly.

"For how long would he need to look human?" she finally asked.

"Perhaps an hour."

"That's not too long," Georgette mused. "Dampened . . . ." She adopted the sly expression of a co-conspirator as she asked, "And would I have to make you solid?"

"No," the Valkyrie answered, "not at all. That would, in fact, run counter to our needs."

Seeing the witch's eyes alight with calculation, Ishak allowed himself to hope. This deal was happening. It had to.

"What would you be willing to do for us?" Georgette finally asked.

"What do you need?"

Georgette immediately turned to Ishak, nodding expectantly.

Heart racing, Ishak told Delia about Kivuli Panon, about meeting Georgette and Mei-Xing, about confronting the Zamek's clerk, and about KK Inc.'s house in Silver Creek. Through it all, he told her about Kalilah, the love of his life. Delia listened with the slight glaze in her eyes that he had seen earlier, presumably relaying all of his information to her partner.

When he finished, she sat in silence, still and unblinking, for what felt like eons.

"You need us to get you into the house," she finally said, "and help you get your wife out."

"Yes," he said, "that's it."

"Easily done."

He blinked; his lips parted in surprise. He pictured the gated community—guarded by walls, security systems, and suspicious residents—and felt awe for the Valkyrie.

But also doubt.

"Easily?" he asked. "Are you sure?"

"The walls, cameras, and locks you describe are meaningless to me," she said.

"But the brokerage," Ishak said. "If they catch you—"

She cut off his protest with a chirp of laughter. He was as surprised by the ladylike tone of her laugh as he was by the suddenness of her response.

231

"I'll be impressed if they have a way to contain a Valkyrie," she said, still laughing.

Delia's eyes shone with delight; her lips spread in a fearless grin. Somewhere outside the shop, a raven's amused squawk rang out—likely audible only to Ishak's inhuman ears.

"I'll be even more impressed if they have the balls to use it," Delia said.

The coarse language surprised Ishak even more than the laughter had. *Not as regal as she first seemed*, he thought, amused.

The smile on her face gone, Georgette asked, "And what if your sisterhood finds out?"

The smile melted from Delia's face as well.

While a part of him understood the need for the question, Ishak silently cursed Georgette for turning the tide of the conversation when it had been going so well.

"If Valhalla learns of this," Delia said softly, "I will be in far more danger than you."

"But we will be in danger?"

". . . Yes."

The scent of fear came off Georgette in waves, sparking a sympathetic response in Ishak. Though nothing frightened him more than losing Kalilah, he understood Georgette's horror of unknown consequences.

Looking for support, he glanced at Mei-Xing—but the night had finally done its work on her. Though still sitting upright on the Botanica display case, the Nymph was unconscious. *The hell,* he thought irritably. *Why did we bring her if she was just going to sleep?*

"What, *exactly*, could happen to us?" he asked the Valkyrie.

She shrugged slowly. "This is uncharted territory. If any Valkyrie has ever made an alliance with a witch before, I've never heard of it. I don't know how Valhalla might react. I only know that they will certainly view it as an affront."

"An affront?" Georgette repeated. "Are you waging war against Valhalla?"

The Valkyrie closed her eyes and let out a slow breath.

"Senji and I were chosen by Valhalla," she said. "We accept our position without reservation. But this matter concerns our pre-death lives, which is forbidden to Valkyries. We are not interested in waging war against Valhalla, but . . . to do as we plan . . ." She trailed off with a sigh. "The sisterhood will see it as an act of war, yes." She locked eyes first with Georgette and then with Ishak. "We will continue to perform our duties. You have our word that we will give Valhalla no reason to suspect us. And if the sisters do learn the truth, we will try to protect your identities. They would far rather punish a traitor than a solitary witch, a wandering hyena, and an uprooted Wood Nymph."

Rising from her seat, the Valkyrie collected her sword and helmet from the display case counter. In the doorway, she stopped and glanced back. "Time stops for no one, living or dead," she urged. "We need an answer soon."

Two steps past the threshold, she vanished into silver light.

Kazimiera arrived for their meeting sporting a form-fitting mini-dress the color of wild roses and matching spiked heels that clicked with every step. While Georgette sat at the tarot table, Ishak standing beside her, the Vampire sauntered around the

Botanica. Puckering her painted lips, she brushed her long, French-tip nails over the display cases, feather-touching the glass. A gossamer wrap draped loosely around her shoulders glistened like morning dew.

In the Vampire's presence, Ishak experienced an unsettling contradiction. The woman he saw was a bundle of life: full hips, ample breasts, and a youthful-yet-wise energy. Every liquid motion she made was pure, sensual power. He could easily imagine men and women being caught in the wake of this force of nature, swept along in her footsteps, helpless to escape.

That was what he saw. What he smelled told a different story.

A living body gave off a variety of scents—some of them robust, others subtle. But a Vampire's body, while not exactly dead, was not alive. When inhaling the air around Kazimiera, Ishak smelled decay. It wasn't rot, such as he would smell from spoiled meat, but it seemed to belong to something newly dead.

His eyes told him he should pick up lusty, fertile scents. His nose told him he should see a fresh corpse. The disagreement of his senses made him uncomfortable.

"So Kett & Kedena bought your wife from the witch who caught you," Kazimiera said. She walked along the side of the display case, pausing when she reached the sleeping Nymph. "Now you're using this one's"—she pointed to Georgette—"*Hathiya* to access your abilities during the day." She wound a section of Mei-Xing's hair around her long finger and sniffed it as if smelling a flower. The Nymph's glamour wobbled, revealing that the hair was actually a small, leafy vine. When Kazimiera dropped it, it merged back into the imaginary curtain of straight black hair. Mei-Xing never stirred. "And Georgette came to work for me because she hoped to covertly use my connections to find your wife."

"Correct," Ishak said.

As she turned to sashay toward them, she crossed a beam of light spilling in from the street. For a moment, it lit up her eyes. The light reflected from them in a green, catlike glow.

Kazimiera put her palms on the table and leaned over. The sheer wrap slowly slid down her bare arms, exposing her cleavage. Her visual appeal tugged at Ishak, stirring arousal—until he inhaled. Her honeysuckle perfume couldn't fool his hypersensitive nose. She was temptation incarnate, but her body promised no warmth.

"What are you offering?" she asked.

"Offering?" Georgette asked. She and Ishak exchanged looks—hers puzzled, his irritated. "What do you mean?"

"Well," the Vampire purred, "obviously your cover is blown. You won't be sneaking around to use my connections now."

"Sorry," Georgette murmured, her cheeks flushed.

Kazimiera stood up and tossed her hair with a *tsk!* sound. Then she pinned Ishak with a pointed gaze. "If I get in touch with KK Inc. about your wife, what will you give me?"

"Give you?" Ishak's cheeks began to burn. "Georgette told us that you rescue enslaved creatures and protect them. Why would you ask us to give you something for Kalilah?"

"Because I'm not running a charity," she said, placing her hands on her hips. "When I bring in new rescues, I don't just save them, I also gain new employees."

Ishak narrowed his eyes and gritted his teeth. His hyena half growled, rising into his throat. If Kazimiera weren't a woman, he would have struck her. "Slave labor."

"Oh honey," she chuckled, gliding to his side, "no one is forced to work. If they opt to hide in their rooms to wait until their brands fade, I let them. But if all of them did that, I couldn't keep the doors open. I can't take care of all of them and also pay salaries. The labor my employees provide allows me to save others." She cocked an eyebrow at him. "If you see that as slavery, that's on you."

Her charm invaded his personal space, sizzling into his skin. The tingle it sent through his body made him remember Kalilah. At moments of peace and rest, Kalilah often smiled just like the Vampire smiled now. It was a proposition—a spark to light a fire. Maybe it would lead to a night of hunting, or maybe to sex, but it always led someplace he was happy to go.

He didn't want to go anywhere with this woman.

"If you blind yourself to the truth," he said, "that is on *you*."

Her smile faltered for the briefest moment. She recovered so quickly that, if not for his extraordinary sight, he might have believed it was just a trick of the light.

"Well," she said with an exaggerated shrug, "if you aren't interested in my help . . ."

She smirked at him before turning her back. Slowly, deliberately, she walked toward the door, hips moving with the steady twitch of a cat's tail.

Georgette's head jerked up toward Ishak, eyes wide with alarm, but the Bultungin couldn't help but grin. He had conducted enough trade with the Toubou and Fulani tribesmen to see this for the bluff it was. *Negotiations*. Though an ocean apart from his home and family, this was familiar ground.

"What do you want?" he asked.

"I want," Kazimiera said, swiveling and taking a step toward him, "a replacement for your wife."

"Someone to work in place of Kalilah?"

"Exactly." Strolling about the room, she scrunched up her face as if deep in thought. The clicks of her heels echoed faintly as her long fingers drummed on her arms. She glanced at the sleeping Mei-Xing. "What about that one? She doesn't look like she's being a productive member of your little team, and many of my VIPs are Chinese businessmen. I'm sure they'd enjoy her."

Georgette made a squeak of protest, but Ishak put a hand on the witch's shoulder to keep her quiet. Under his hand, the panic riding her scent faded. With a swell of gratitude, he realized that she was trusting him to deal with this. He looked first at Mei-Xing—deep asleep and still as a tree—and then at Kazimiera. The Vampire stared back at him, waiting expectantly.

"I won't give you a slave," he told her.

"Employee," she corrected. "A temporary employee. The longest any of them has worked for me is twelve years."

"Indentured servitude is slavery."

"Not when the one in question is free to leave at any time."

Anger bubbling up from his gut, Ishak opened his mouth to snap at her—and then he saw her smile and stopped himself. He was doing exactly what he'd sworn to himself he wouldn't: following where she led. She was making him angry to keep him off balance. Drawing in a deep breath, he exhaled slowly and steadied himself.

"I cannot give you what you ask for," he said calmly. "Perhaps something else."

Her amber eyes swept over him with an assessing gleam. Then all air of playfulness slid off her like an unzipped dress. When next she spoke, she assumed a no-nonsense, businesslike tone of voice.

"I can use my contacts to find your wife," said Kazimiera, "but that's just a first step. KK Inc. doesn't give out freebies."

"Free bees?" Ishak repeated, brow furrowed. *No one mentioned bees.*

"She means," said Georgette, "that they won't just let her go. We'll have to pay for her."

Ishak nodded, filing the strange word away in his growing English dictionary.

"I think it's safe to say that she won't be cheap," the Vampire said. "Nymphs like her," she gestured at Mei-Xing, "are a dime a dozen. Werehyenas aren't something you see every day."

"We can pay the broker's price," Ishak said, "if money is the only way."

"This is America, handsome," the Vampire said. "Money is always the way. Now," she continued, "let's discuss *my* payment."

Ah, we have come to the meat of it. Now we will learn what she really wants.

"Do you want money?" Ishak asked, knowing this was unlikely.

"Oh," the Vampire said with a swish of her hands, "I guess we could do it that way. But it's not my preference."

Everything about Kazimiera, from her stance to her voice to her ever-present smile, was annoyingly casual. Finding his eyes unhelpful, Ishak drew a breath and examined her scent. The smell of her was still unsettlingly stagnant, but now there was an element of hunger underlying it—not the red hunger her kind were known for, but something far more human. She did want something, wanted it badly.

"Perhaps payment on a sliding scale?" he suggested. He expected her to refuse but wanted time to feel her out. "The better the deal you make with the broker, the more we pay you?"

In what he took for a show of disdain, she slowly turned her back to him and ran her fingers through her corkscrew curls. Her sheer, sparkling wrap slipped over her arms and shoulders, frictionless as water, as she moved.

With her attention momentarily diverted, Ishak raced to figure out what she was thinking, grasping for an advantage.

She would not come to us for something so simple as money, he thought. *Could she want blood? But a fresh supply comes through her club every evening. Perhaps she really does want an "employee," like she joked.* His eyes shot to Mei-Xing, Kazimiera's opening request in the negotiations. *No,* he immediately thought, *Nymphs are a dime a dozen—she said it herself. She will want something rarer.*

Kazimiera completed a full rotation, still teasing her hair. As she came around to face him again, her catlike eyes coasted over everything in their path, as lightly and thoughtlessly as mist across a garden—except when they arrived at Georgette, at which point she shifted her eyes to skip over the witch.

Suddenly, Ishak understood.

Georgette.

A cooperative witch was much harder to come by than a Nymph. Readily accessible magic was worth more than any fee they could offer. It was the thing Kazimiera needed the most to keep her business running. *She thought she had found a suitable replacement for her last witch, only to learn that Georgette never intended to stay. Now she hopes to secure her service via Kalilah.*

His stomach turned. It was unacceptable. He would not give up Georgette to servitude. The very thought was abhorrent.

The Vampire opened her mouth to speak but stopped without uttering a sound. For a moment, she looked at Ishak through squinted eyes, her painted lips tight and unsmiling. The Bultungin felt a crawling sensation under his skin, a nervousness he usually associated with the prey he hunted. The feeling stopped at the same instant that her expression softened.

"Clever man," purred Kazimiera, the sexy smile back on her face. "I think you know what I want."

Anger rumbled through Ishak. Somehow, she had seen right through him.

"I can be flexible on the terms—but, honestly," she said, looking him up and down, "you have nothing else of value to me."

Damn you, he thought, struggling to keep his face impassive. *The thing you want isn't mine to give.*

Kazimiera looked back and forth between Ishak and Georgette, her smug smile widening into a predatory grin that exposed her pointed teeth. "Do we have a deal?"

After seeing Kazimiera out, Ishak stood by the door and waited until his Bultungin senses lost track of her. Sighing, he glanced back at Georgette and Mei-Xing. The Nymph's arms had fallen to her sides; her hands dangled limply over the edges of the display case.

Georgette shook her by the shoulders but got no response.

"Perhaps she should have waited at the hotel," he said.

Georgette shook her head. "She wanted to come. Besides, this is partly her decision to make. We're all sharing the brand. I just need to drop her glamour. Once she's not using my power for that, she'll have enough energy to stay awake." She reached out, fingers inches from Mei-Xing's face, then paused. "Um, could you double-check that all the blinds are closed? It'll freak her out if she thinks somebody might see her without the glamour."

He obliged and walked the perimeter of the shop. When he returned, Mei-Xing's human visage was gone, replaced by her true, mossy, grass-sprouting form. Georgette shook the Nymph again and this time, she awoke with ease. Though Mei-Xing accepted their assurances that she was safe, when she took a seat at the tarot table, she pulled her legs up to her chest and wrapped her arms around them, making herself as small as possible. Her iridescent eyes repeatedly scanned the room over the tops of her knees as if she was expecting to spot some hidden threat in the shadows.

"Your Vampire employer," Ishak began, standing near the table, "has questionable morals."

"More so than I realized," Georgette agreed. "But whatever her motivation, she's definitely doing good."

Ishak thought of the months he'd spent under Kivuli Panon's control. Enslavement had made him desperate to the brink of hopelessness. If he had come upon Kazimiera's club while in that situation, he did not doubt that he would have viewed the Vampire as a savior. However, as things stood now, his view of her was less generous.

"I don't like her," he said.

"I still think she's our best shot at finding Kalilah. She could end our search with one phone call."

A very expensive phone call, he thought. "What about the Valkyrie?" he asked. "She could get us into the building I found."

"I'm not going into a brokerage house," Mei-Xing said, speaking Fae into her knees. A shiver racked her body, sending a ripple through the greenery that covered her back, as she tightened her arms around her legs. "I don't care if Delia is with us. I won't do it."

Though he didn't have much experience in deciphering floral-based emotions, Ishak would have understood Mei-Xing's scent as fear even without seeing her posture. The idea of being caught by KK Inc. frightened him, too. But Kalilah's life was at stake. He hadn't come this far to be scared off now.

"I will go," Ishak said. "I won't ask either of you to join me."

"I'll go with you," Georgette said. She spoke quickly, and with a flashy confidence that rang false to him.

"You have expressed concerned about getting caught several times," he said. "Wouldn't you rather—"

"If you go, I go," she insisted.

What a change from the witch who refused to help me when first we met, he thought. She had stunk of fear that night, but he did not smell fear on her now. Instead, waves of guilt emanated from her every pore. *Is she offering to do this because she refused to help me then?*

They had never discussed the night they met. It seemed to be a point of silent agreement between them that as long as she continued to help him, he would not mention her earlier failure to do so. But every time they were in a room together her guilt was there, sneaking up on him like a clumsy pickpocket.

He was comfortable with that. She had earned that guilt, along with the chance to remedy it. Guilt was not a negative emotion, or so his father had once told him. Guilt was an agent of change, a chance for growth. Ishak had not understood his father at the time but since encountering Georgette, it made perfect sense. Moved by her guilt, Georgette had grown out of the restrictive bonds imposed on her by her upbringing. She had taken up his quest, shared her money and magic, and done everything she could to help find Kalilah. It was certainly a sign of growth. Her efforts had gone so far above and beyond, in fact, that he now considered her a friend.

"Still," said Georgette, breaking into his thoughts, "it would be easier to have Kazimiera arrange to buy her." Her face crinkled. "Except that we didn't agree on a price."

Ishak's stomach sank. If he told her what Kazimiera wanted, he suspected Georgette would agree. That could mean that he would get Kalilah back in his arms—but at the cost of his friend's freedom. If they shared the brand with the Valkyrie, Ishak would accept Georgette's help in raiding the house without reservation and would stand at her side through it all. But he couldn't ask her to submit to the very thing he had rebelled against, the thing he was trying to save Kalilah from.

Do I tell her? he asked himself. *If I do and she agrees to the Vampire's terms, can I live with that? Since we threw our lots in together, she has shouldered her guilt and grown as a person. Can I outgrow the weight of my own guilt if I trade her for Kalilah?*

"The Vampire wants you," he blurted out, almost against his will.

Georgette's brow furrowed as she tilted her face to look up at him. "What?"

He explained, quickly but thoroughly. With every word, he felt guilt burrow into his gut like a rodent preparing its den. Though he hated the feel of it, Ishak accepted its presence and steeled himself to carry its weight forward.

"Makes sense," Georgette said once Ishak had told her everything. She sounded calm, thoughtful. "She'd been looking for a witch to replace Martin for months, and I was the only one who applied."

Mei-Xing spouted off a string of Chinese words from behind her knees. Though he didn't know the language, their shared *Hathiya* provided him with some notion of their meaning. Her shimmery rainbow eyes shot daggers at him. Georgette, however, continued to look at the tablecloth, her eyes bright but unfocused.

"I will not ask you to agree to her price," Ishak said. "I want us to join with the Valkyrie instead."

"*Hmm*," the witch murmured, still lost in thought.

"Can you meet Delia's conditions?" he urged. "Can you give them what they want?"

"Oh, sure," said Georgette, lifting her face to meet his gaze. "Actually, I think it would be pretty easy."

Both he and Mei-Xing looked at her in surprise. Shaking his head in confusion, Ishak asked, "How so?"

"Well, she wants two things," Georgette said, "the ability to hide from the other Valkyries and to allow Senji to temporarily resume his human form. The first one is simple. That can be accomplished simply by sharing the brand with them. Our *Hathiya* mark causes all our powers to bleed together. As long as at least one of us stays in Delia's designated area, Valhalla should detect her presence here and see nothing amiss."

"And the second requirement?" he asked. "Can you make the raven look human?"

"I think so," she said with a nod. "I can use the brand to drain off some of their power and dampen their link with Valhalla. If I take away some of the magic that makes them what they are, they should revert to what they were. It may take some effort to figure out the right balance, but I should be able to drain just the right amount of magic to make Senji look human while allowing Delia to stay as she is."

"And it won't reduce your magic at all?" Ishak said.

"Just the opposite," she said. "If it works the way I think it will, it should make me—make us—stronger."

The guilt eased its hold on him. They could share the brand with the Valkyrie pair without putting a strain on Georgette's magic? Better than that, bringing Delia and Senji into their *Hathiya* loop would actually strengthen the witch? It all sounded almost too good to be true.

"Excellent news," he said, eyes bright. "So you are willing to make the deal with them, then?"

"It's still risky," Georgette told him, shaking her head. "Clashing with Valhalla is a stupid thing to do. If we're found out, I promise you, it won't end well for us."

"Won't end well for *her*," Mei-Xing clarified, pointing one woody finger at Georgette but speaking only to Ishak. "She's the one who gives the brand, not us. If Valhalla decides to punish someone, it will be Georgette."

Ishak reluctantly admitted to himself that she was probably right. So, he thought unhappily, *making a deal with the Valkyrie might put her life in danger, while making a deal with the Vampire en-*

Alison Levy

dangers her freedom. The only way she stays safe is if she walks away and leaves me to find Kalilah on my own.

"What do you want to do?" he asked, his voice barely more than a whisper.

Georgette's eyes slipped downward, drifting lightly over the tabletop as if swimming in the tablecloth's pattern. A fresh aroma of guilt met Ishak's nose, causing him to internally cringe.

"I think," she said, "we should make the deal with the Valkyrie. But I still think we should ask Kazimiera to contact KK Inc."

Mei-Xing exploded into a tirade of Chinese. Dropping her feet to the floor, she grabbed Georgette's hand and tugged at her arm as she ranted. Georgette repeatedly broke into to her friend's outburst with short responses, also in Chinese, but the Nymph would not be calmed.

After nearly a minute of constant chatter, Mei-Xing threw up her hands and brought her fists down on the table with a loud thump. Ishak jumped, startled by the sound, but his heart leaped again when the Nymph fixed him in a vicious stare. *This is your fault,* she seemed to say, *so fix it!*

"But you know what she will want in return," Ishak said. "If we just use the Valkyrie—"

"Kazimiera said she could be flexible on terms," Georgette said. "I won't sign my life away to her, but maybe if I offer to work without pay for five or six months—"

"No," Ishak interrupted. "No, I can't—"

"You're not," Georgette said. "I am." Ignoring Mei-Xing's unhappy mutters, she looked up at him and offered him a smile. "I went to work for her to take advantage of her contacts. I never cared about the money. This is no different."

"It's very different," he said. "The first situation was your choice."

"This is my choice too."

So she said. But the air was once again laden with guilt, as was Ishak.

I am using her remorse for my gain. I have earned this guilt.

"You need not make this choice at all," he persisted. "If we ally ourselves with Delia, we will not need the Vampire."

"We don't know that," Georgette said. "Delia could get us into the brokerage house you found, but what if Kalilah isn't there? Kazimiera is our best chance to find her. That said, I still think it's worth having some Valkyrie firepower in our back pocket. I think we should share the brand with Delia and Senji for however long they need for their 'personal reasons.' After that, I can remove the brand so Valhalla will have nothing to connect us to them. Even if we end up not needing their help to get Kalilah, I wouldn't mind having a Valkyrie out there who owes me one."

Mei-Xing made a starkly inhuman sound, something akin to the fizz of a freshly opened soda can.

Georgette clucked her tongue and reached out a hand to her friend. "Don't be like that," she said. "It's no big deal. We don't need the money, and I was expecting to work at Nocturne anyway."

Slumped low in her seat, Mei-Xing refused to look Georgette in the eye. Instead, the Nymph turned her frigid gaze on Ishak.

"Are you sure?" he asked.

"Yes," Georgette said, "as long as you two agree."

Mei-Xing shot Ishak a look that pierced Ishak's soul.

"I agree," he said, "and I will do my best to negotiate a short time of service with the Vampire on your behalf."

Georgette nodded, smiling.

Mei-Xing made another fizz noise but seemed resigned. "Do what you want," she said. "I'll cooperate any way I can, so long as I don't have to go into the brokerage house." She narrowed her eyes at Ishak. "I hope this bargain is worth the price."

So do I, thought Ishak, but he said nothing.

36  Delia & Senji

Only when they arrived at the hotel did the witch realize that she could not burn the mark into a bodiless spirit.

I will take the brand. Hopping to the witch, he put forth his left leg. *Will this do?*

"Will this do?" Delia asked.

"Yes."

He watched Georgette twist the solidified magic into a funnel-like shape, wide on her end and tiny on his, though both sides had identical curves.

She leaned on her sword as the witch wove her spell of words, signs, and power.

The witch brought his leg to the small end as she positioned the wide end on her wrist.

The mark seared into his skin. He stifled his pain into a single, throttled croak.

Delia felt it just above her left ankle, the scorching of ghostly flesh.

The pain grew stronger as the mark sank deeper. It burned white-hot.

The pain subsided. Relief washing over him, Senji looked down at his leg. His mark was pea-sized, far smaller than the witch's, but otherwise identical—a looped, intricate pattern.

Delia looked down at her leg. Her mark was a ghostly gray, paler than the witch's, but otherwise identical.

I feel no different.

Nor I.

"What went wrong?" she asked the witch.

Georgette blinked, blank-faced. "Nothing," she said. "The brand's done. I feel the bond."

"We feel nothing," Delia said, her voice taking on a sharpness that both she and Senji felt.

"Okay," the witch said through a slow exhale, "let's see what I can do."

Senji felt a sensation like a magnetic pull that seemed to draw away some part of him.

Delia felt energy begin to trickle out of her, siphoned through the mark. She froze.

What's happening?

What's happening?

Delia and Senji looked at each other and realized that for the first time since joining Valhalla, each saw with only with one set of eyes. The dual existence they had experienced for so many decades had vanished in an instant.

Icy fingers gripped their heart, horrific isolation trapping them within their skin.

"The brand's working," Georgette said. She flexed her fingers, her eyes locked onto her left wrist. "I can feel your power," she said in amazement. "Wow, so much power!"

"What happened!?" Delia lunged forward, hands reaching for her partner. "Senji!"

Cawing in alarm, the raven leaped into the air and alighted on her arm.

Senji?	*Delia?*
	He felt a rush of relief, as well as Delia's relief.
"You've cut the power," Georgette said, getting to her feet. "If you want me to really test the brand, I think you need to put a little space between you."	
	What does she mean?
"Space between us? What do you mean?"	
"I was taught," the witch said, "that the first post-death touch is what binds a Valkyrie to her partner. Is that right?"	
Memories.	Memories.

She, a Navy nurse, standing
on the deck of her ship,
feeling the salty air,
smelling the odor of oil and
men.

He, a pilot, on his final,
fatal flight.

Shouting, gunfire, the roar
of a foreign engine.

Plunging down through an
onslaught of bullets, aiming
for the deck.

Locking eyes with Senji.

Locking eyes with Delia.

She did not remember the
explosion.

He did not remember the
explosion.

Then nothing.

Death.

And then . . .
New memories pouring in.

In mere moments, living
one another's life.

Then Delia, feeling a primal
urge to hear her mother's
voice, flung herself away.

His ghost-self was caught in
her wake, yanked along as if
by a tether.

She found her family. She saw her parents and sisters mourning for her—and then saw *him* at her side. Awash in her family's heartbreak, a grief he had caused, anger overtook her. Boiling with fury, she lunged.

As she grabbed him, he transformed from a fleshless man to a sleek, black raven—and they were both transported to Nagasaki, his home.

Rubble, bodies, survivors crawling with skin hanging from them in long strips. The air rang with wails of pain and misery. The shock of what her people had done—deliberately—blew away her anger.

His home destroyed. His parents and two brothers dead, their skin burned to char. One brother, the last of them, missing altogether. It was *Jigoku*. Hell.

In the face of loss, they stood together—found strength in one another.

And it began with a touch.

"That is correct," Delia said.

"Touch establishes and maintains the link between you," the witch said. "If you're touching, I can't siphon any energy."

I suppose that makes sense, she thought, fighting hesitation.

And I suppose it's necessary, he agreed, equally reluctant.

Since death, they had existed as two halves of a unit, so entwined that they didn't differentiate their thoughts and experiences.

All that one was, the other had become; there was no future for one alone.

They were of one mind.

Even about this.

Delia crossed the room and stood by the locked door.

Senji took flight and perched on top of the television.

As the witch siphoned
away their power, their
consciousness divided.

Like raw bread dough
pulled apart, their two
minds clung to each other
by thinning, fraying strips.

Delia's memories of Senji's
life dropped away.

Her knowledge and skills
faded away until . . .

Eyes squeezed shut, Delia grabbed her head with both hands as if to hold on to what remained within.

"My mind is half gone," she groaned. "I feel as though wind could blow through the holes in my head."

"Is this what we once were? Did I live twenty years with such gaps in myself?"

That voice! Delia's eyes popped open.

"Senji?"

He stood on the far side of the room, staring at his hands. *Hands.* The sight of them shocked him almost as much as the sound of his own voice. A sense of loss, nostalgia, and excitement overwhelmed him. He had forgotten so much of himself, of the man beneath the raven.

"Look, Delia," he said, turning toward her. "Can you . . ."

The question died on his lips when he saw her. The shock in his eyes made her look at herself. Her Valkyrie armor was gone, replaced by the white nurse's uniform she had worn the day she died. The sleeves were still rolled up from when she had scrubbed blood from her hands shortly before the crash. Both shoes were badly scuffed but perfectly molded to her feet from long shifts. There was a small rip in the hem of her uniform she had not had time to mend and sweat stains in the armpits.

She looked again at Senji. He wore a flight suit, army green with a flag insignia on the sleeve, and an aviator's cap, its goggles pushed up on his forehead. Below the cap, his human face was young and pale.

"You looked like this," he said, his words heavy, "on that day."

"Yes," she agreed, "we did."

Senji looked again at the uniform he had died in. The left boot was too small. He had been issued a mismatched pair but had not spoken up since he'd known he would not wear them long. These were Masao's goggles. Senji's had cracked right before his final flight, so Masao had given him his.

He yanked open the top button of his flight suit, and his hand dove for the inner pocket, trembling with anticipation. There! He pulled out the photograph. For the first time in over seventy years, he looked on the faces of his family.

Delia could not see through Senji's eyes, but she sensed his turmoil. It gave her a peculiar comfort to know that though the bond between them was weakened, it was not broken. She moved toward him, hand outstretched. "Are you—"

"No," he said, stepping back. "Don't touch me . . . not yet."

She stopped and lowered her hand. After being linked for so long, she did not feel a need to question him.

"Look at them," Senji whispered. He turned the photograph

so she could see. "This was taken just weeks before I died. It's the last picture of the six of us together." He thrust the picture toward her. "Look at my mother, Delia," he said, louder. "See her? I was afraid I had forgotten her face."

"She is just as you see her in your mind, Senji," she said, smiling gently. "You haven't forgotten anything."

"Whoa."

The sudden sound of a third voice in the room made them both jump. They whirled and saw Georgette standing alone near the bathroom door. In her hand, a Valkyrie sword glittered silver in the artificial light.

"Wicked," she murmured, eyes wide. She slowly swung the weapon from side to side. "It's light as a cloud."

"Give it to me!" Delia shouted, already diving toward her. She tried to grab the weapon; her hand passed through the witch's flesh like air, but she still succeeded in knocking the sword to the floor.

"Sorry," Georgette said. She carefully picked up the sword and set it tip-down in the carpet, leaning it against the wall. "You okay?"

"I'm not solid," Delia said, examining herself from hand to foot. "For a moment, I thought I might be." She glanced at her partner. "You?"

Senji carefully pocketed the photograph. He reached his hand to the wall and stepped forward; his arm disappeared up to the elbow. "Not solid," he said.

"That's what you wanted, right?" Georgette asked nervously. "I mean, we'll have to practice a bit to make sure I'm draining exactly the right amount of your power—what a rush, by the way," she added with a grin. "I feel JUICED."

Under their silent regard, her smile shrank.

"Will that work for you?" she asked in a more subdued tone.

Senji and Delia locked eyes. Though their minds were now connected by only the thinnest fibers, they both instantly flashed to the moment of their death. The explosion of gunfire, the chaotic screams, the smell of the ocean and engine fumes . . . it all seemed to be happening again. This time, however, they each felt each other's horror and resignation, like faint vibrations through a tightly stretched string.

Through the bombardment of emotions, Delia raised an eyebrow and pushed a tiny smile to the surface.

Drawing a long breath to steady himself, Senji nodded and returned her smile.

"We can make it work," he told Georgette. "You have upheld your end of the bargain. We will uphold ours."

Relieved, the witch stood a little taller. "When will you need to look human?" she asked. "For your 'personal reasons'?"

"We'll let you know," Delia said. "We don't know exactly when yet—but when it does, we will need you to be ready."

She hesitated a moment, then nodded. "Okay. I'll do my best."

"What do you need from us?" Senji asked.

"I don't know yet," Georgette said, "but I should soon."

"We'll wait," Delia said. Then she stepped forward, hand outstretched toward her partner. Meeting her gaze, he did the same.

Their minds reknit.	Their minds reknit.
In a shimmer of silver light, Delia became a Valkyrie once again.	In a shimmer of silver light, Senji became a raven once again.
Ganbatte kudasai, Senji.	
	Lâche pas la patate, Delia.
They were whole.	They were whole.

37  Mei-Xing

MEI-XING STARED DOWN AT THE EMPLOYMENT CONTRACT
on Kazimiera's desk. The words—half English, half Fae—were
inscribed on ordinary paper with Club Nocturne letterhead, but
the writing was composed of phantasmal red smoke. The letters
floated and swirled, clinging to the paper with wispy, vein-like
tendrils. Their strange appearance did not unsettle her half so
much as their meaning did.

Upon reaching an agreement with Ishak, who had negotiated
on Georgette's behalf, the Vampire had insisted on something
firmer than an ordinary contract: a geas. Mei-Xing had never
heard of such of thing. According to Georgette, a geas was a magical contract that would inhibit the signer from acting against its
conditions. This particular geas forbade Georgette from leaving
her job at Nocturne for one year. If she tried, it would make her
suffer by gradually shutting down her motor functions.

Mei-Xing scowled. She was brimming with fury but didn't
know who was most worthy of it: Kazimiera for demanding the geas,
Georgette for accepting it, or Ishak for putting it all in motion.

Under the terms of the contract, the geas would be sealed

only when Kazimiera delivered Kalilah alive and safe. Ishak was very firm on that point.

He's selling out Georgette to get what he wants, Mei-Xing thought bitterly. She glared at the Bultungin's unseeing back. *I ought to make a seed sprout in his ear canal. Partial deafness would give him a lasting reminder of what he's done.*

Kazimiera made a purring sound through puckered lips as she sauntered around her office. For all her efforts to look flirtatious, Mei-Xing saw a sharpness to her movements that suggested frustration.

"I don't know if your woman is even alive," the Vampire said. "You're asking me to put time and effort into this arrangement without any guarantee of a payout." As she walked up to Ishak, her painted lips curled up to expose her long fangs. "That's a bad bargain."

Bad bargain? Mei-Xing's rage flared up. *Georgette is just a business deal for her.* She narrowed her eyes at the Vampire. *With a handful of dirt, I could sprout garlic in her vents. That would give her a vicious rash and months of respiratory problems.*

"It is the only bargain we will make." Ishak crossed his arms over his chest. "Do not waste any more of our time with these pointless arguments."

With a tsking noise, Kazimiera signed the geas.

Mei-Xing shot Georgette one last, pleading look but the witch just smiled.

You went from letting your mother control you to letting Ishak do it, she thought, her eyes fixed on her friend. *You'd only been out from under Hazel's thumb for a few weeks when you threw your lot in with* him. *You never learned how to live independently.* Rage boiled up through the cracks of her core. *This man's troubles were none of your business. Why didn't you leave him at that motel?* In a rush that startled her, the anger she was directing at Georgette suddenly did an about-face and struck her head-on. *Why didn't I protect you? I knew you were fragile. Why was I so useless?*

The misty words writhed on the contract, red and ghostly except for the solid ink signatures at the bottom. Georgette Delaney. Kazimiera Bowen. However much the deal enraged Mei-Xing, it was finished. And there was more than enough blame to go around.

"Well," Kazimiera said, setting her pen down next to the paper, "that's done." She flashed a saucy smile that disgusted Mei-Xing. "Have a seat, everyone. I'll make a call."

"Gary," Kazimiera cooed into the phone, her voice honey-soft, "why are you being coy with me? Baby, I know you've got a hyena-woman. I heard through the grapevine that Christopher brought her in for you."

She paused, listening, as Ishak, Mei-Xing, and Georgette, seated side by side on her couch, held their collective breath.

"Never mind how I found out." The Vampire laughed. "I want to buy her."

Unable to hear what the broker said, Mei-Xing turned to Ishak on her right. The Bultungin had partially shifted form, lengthening his ears, and elongating his nose to better listen to the conversation. It gave him a bat-like appearance.

"Gary, sweetie, I don't care about some witch nobody's heard of scaring a Zamek's receptionist. I'm not calling Zamek's, I'm calling you."

An unhappy whine squeaked through Georgette's lips. Her guilt seemed misplaced to Mei-Xing; it was Ishak who had terrorized Zamek's, not her.

She slipped her left hand into Georgette's right and squeezed. The witch's palm was clammy and damp, and the salt from her pores caused Mei-Xing's floral skin to shrivel slightly, but that discomfort was offset by the rush of gratitude she felt flood her body via her brand.

"No, no, honey," said Kazimiera, playing with her corkscrew locks, "a Deer Lady won't do. My customers want the 'werewolf experience,' you know? They've seen TV shows with werewolves, it excites them, and they come in here with their freaky-deaky kinks. But you and I both know how unpredictable werewolves are. A little bit of moonlight and they're all teeth and claws! I don't need a liability like that. I hear hyena-people do the shapeshifting thing but keep their brains when they change. Sounds like a perfect fit, doesn't it?"

The broker's faint mumbling continued as Kazimiera paced behind her desk. Mei-Xing watched Ishak's expression for clues as to the tone of the conversation. For several seconds, his face stayed tense but emotionless. Then, suddenly, he caught his breath.

At the same moment, Kazimiera stopped in her tracks, her lips drawn tight.

"What's the problem?" she asked the broker. "Is it the mess at Zamek's? If you sell the beasty to me, you won't have to worry about the witch anymore. What's your asking price?"

Georgette squeezed Mei-Xing's hand again, her fingers

trembling. The Nymph wondered if Georgette had drawn on Ishak's power to sharpen her hearing, or if she was just sensing the tension in the room.

"Gary, I don't understand what the issue is," the Vampire pressed. "You do still have the hyena-woman, don't you?"

The Nymph waited, her eyes moving between Kazimiera and Ishak, watching for a sign. If KK Inc. didn't have Kalilah, then everything they had done was a waste.

"Great!" Kazimiera exclaimed. She winked at the three of them, making an OK sign with her free hand.

Mei-Xing felt Georgette's hand unclench and heard Ishak exhale.

"So how much?"

Georgette let go of Mei-Xing, reached around her back, and laid a hand on Ishak's shoulder. The Bultungin turned toward her, his distorted features slowly shrinking into human form. His breath was choppy, as if he had run miles in the last few minutes. He gave the witch's hand a quick pat and nodded to her and then to Mei-Xing.

"*What?*"

As one, all three snapped their attention to the Vampire. Hand on her hip, Kazimiera stood stick-straight at the end of her desk. For the first time since Mei-Xing had met her, the curvy woman looked like she was made of angles.

"Is this a negotiating trick, Gary?" the Vampire snapped, her tone utterly lacking its usual playfulness. "I don't get what you're fishing for."

An echoey growl emanating from his throat, Ishak leaped up from the couch.

Kazimiera whipped out one hand in an unambiguous *Stop!* gesture.

Ishak began pacing the office frantically, like an animal that had suddenly found itself caged. Mei-Xing saw panic, horror, and fury rampaging through his eyes.

"Okay . . . fine." Tapping the toe of her high heel shoe, Kazimiera sank one fang into her lip, puncturing the skin but not drawing blood. "In that case, can I at least do a pre-sale inspection? I've got big plans for her; I want to make sure she's a sound investment."

Whatever the broker said in response, Mei-Xing saw that Ishak did not approve. With his fists clenched, he circled the desk, eyes blazing. Georgette whimpered. Mei-Xing put a hand on her friend's knee as the witch stared at the floor, clutching fistfuls of her skirt.

"Well, when *will* you be taking offers?" the Vampire said. "Gary, you're not being helpful."

"I'll kill him," Ishak snarled, his face distorting into rippling flesh and skin. "I'll kill him."

Kazimiera shot him a glare and held one finger over her pursed lips.

Ishak grew in bulk and sprouted fur; he was transforming from human to hyena. Concern escalating, Mei-Xing frantically smacked Georgette's leg. It took several hits before Georgette raised her eyes—but when she registered Ishak's changing form, she bolted up and jumped in front of Ishak, placing herself between him and Kazimiera.

"Wait," she urged the now fully transformed Bultungin in a low, urgent voice. "Just wait." She glanced over her shoulder at the Vampire. "They're still talking."

266

Beast-Ishak said something—not words but huffs and growls. Though Mei-Xing couldn't understand the noise, she knew intuitively that it was speech. She had a hunch that if she drew more power from the *Hathiya* link, she would understand—and Georgette, the source of the link, seemed to understand perfectly. The witch nodded along to Ishak's sounds, her expression solemn but kind.

"Killing that guy won't help anything," she whispered to the growling hyena. "There's always another one like him. Please just keep your voice down and be patient."

Ishak snorted, blowing a glob of snot onto Kazimiera's lush carpet. The Vampire wrinkled her nose at the mess but kept her voice professional.

"Put my name on the hyena-woman's file," she said. "When you do sell her, come to me first, you hear? I'll make it worth your while." She paused, nodding. "Of course, honey. Sure. Talk to you soon, Gary."

She made a loud kissy noise into the phone before hanging up. As she set the phone down, she eyed the steaming mucus on the floor with a hiss of disgust.

"Well," she said, looking Ishak up and down, "today has been disappointing." She turned her eyes to the contract on her desk. "For all of us."

"What did he say?" Mei-Xing asked. "Why won't he sell her?"

"*Ugh*," Kazimiera scoffed. "He hemmed and hawed, kept trying to dodge my questions and distract me. What it boils down to is, they won't sell her."

"WHY?" bellowed Ishak, inhuman voice reverberating off the walls. Mei-Xing cringed at the sight of his gaping, tooth-filled mouth. The Bultungin's eyes gleamed red as he pushed Georgette aside and thrust his face within an inch of the Vampire's. "WHY?"

Kazimiera looked down her nose at the hyena, an expression of disdain souring her face. "Gary only said KK Inc. was not prepared to sell her at this time. 'At this time,'" she repeated, slowly, as if talking to a child. "They will sell her, I'm sure of it. I just can't say when."

Ishak roared, his claws digging holes into the floor. Mei-Xing jumped up from the couch, grabbed Georgette, and backed away from him. She had a sick feeling in her core, like the feeling she got traveling up from her roots when the weather made a violent change. Seeing Ishak be this animalistic stirred a primal fear in her. And Georgette felt it too. The brand they shared told her as much.

"You," Ishak growled murderously at Kazimiera. He squared his body, muscles bulging under his fur. "You."

He launched himself at the Vampire, mouth open. Before Mei-Xing could gasp, Kazimiera flung out one arm and seized him by the throat. Ishak grunted in surprise but recovered quickly and swiped at his target with his front paws. His long claws tore apart the club owner's sparkly dress and ripped her abdomen open. Mei-Xing pulled back at the sight of Kazimiera's bloodless, ragged flesh, and then recoiled a second time when the rotten smell of the Vampire's internal organs hit her.

Kazimiera, however, looked unfazed. As Ishak spat and fought, her annoyed expression never changed.

"Do I look like prey to you, little man?" she demanded.

Mei-Xing saw her tighten her grip around his throat. Within

seconds, the hyena-man stopped struggling and started gagging.

"I'm keeping my end of the bargain and what do you do? You trash my carpet, you ruin my dress, and you tear a hole in my stomach." She looked down at her wound. "I'm going to need gallons of blood to heal this mess. And where do you think I should get that meal?"

When the Vampire lifted her face, Mei-Xing was horrified by the change in her. The warm amber irises and the whites of her eyes were gone, replaced by stony onyx. Kazimiera's jaw had unhinged, becoming the razor-filled maw of a shark. As the Nymph watched, the Vampire's cocoa skin paled, turning the sickly, greenish-gray hue of a corpse. The curvy weight on her hips and chest melted to expose a sinewy, long-limbed body of bare muscle on bone.

Terrified, Mei-Xing turned to Georgette—only to see her friend rushing into the fight.

"Stop!" Georgette shouted. Not giving the Vampire's unsettling new form a second look, she grabbed Kazimiera's arm and tried to pull it away from the Bultungin. "Let him go!"

"I'm hungry," Kazimiera intoned, black eyes locked on Ishak, "and that's his fault."

"He's afraid," the witch said. She ducked under the arm and wedged herself between the two, putting herself much too close to the Vampire's distended jaw for Mei-Xing's liking. "Haven't you ever been separated from someone you love? Didn't not knowing if they were okay drive you to the edge?" Slowly, she placed her hands on the Vampire's shoulders and gently walked toward her, pushing her back.

After a moment's hesitation, Kazimiera released her grip on

Ishak's throat. The Bultungin fell to the floor and quickly shifted to human form. As he recovered, drawing in ragged breaths, Mei-Xing dropped to the floor beside him, and Georgette kept talking.

"I wonder about my baby sister every day," she said. "I hate like hell that I had to leave her behind. You're a Vampire, you've been on this earth longer than any of us here. There must have been someone, at some point, who you had to leave behind too."

Kazimiera's black eyes regarded Georgette's with doll-like disinterest. Then she plucked the witch's hands from her shoulders and let them drop.

"I'll make some more inquiries," she said in a hollow voice. "The geas stands until I say otherwise." She looked down at Ishak, who lay panting on the floor. "You're lucky."

As he coughed, rubbing the emerging bruises on his neck, Georgette joined Mei-Xing at his side.

"We'll contact Delia and Senji," she whispered. "They can check out that house you found without anyone knowing. Maybe they'll find her." She held her hand to her lips and whispered into her wiggling fingers. A wispy green light filled her palm. She blew the light toward the Bultungin like a child blowing bubbles. The glowing wisps settled on Ishak's skin and spread, covering the injury—and he heaved a sigh of relief, his body relaxing from head to toe.

He looked up at her. She smiled.

"We'll find her," she assured him.

Mei-Xing stared at Georgette in wonder. *So much emotional damage, and yet she stepped between a Vampire and her prey,* she marveled, shaking her head. *There's some steel inside that squishy shell.*

38 Neil

NEIL CHEWED A MOUTHFUL OF CHICKEN PARMESAN, THE tomato and cheese lifeless on his tongue as he stared across the restaurant table. Georgette gazed down at her plate, poking at her shrimp linguine with her fork. Dark circles nestled under her eyes, and her freckles stood out starkly against her pale, sunken cheeks. Despite her weary appearance, however, her jaw was tight and her jabs with the fork were sharp. She looked simultaneously exhausted and on edge.

She's not here, he thought. Irritation and concern waged a war behind his thoughts. *She's a million miles away.*

"What's up?" he asked.

The sound of his voice startled her into dropping her fork. It clattered on the edge of the plate, splattering butter sauce on the tablecloth. Her eyes flitted to his, wide with alarm. "What?"

"You seem distracted," he said.

"O-oh," she stammered, plucking up the fork in two fingers. "I'm sorry."

"It's okay," he quickly assured her. His previous irritation vanished in a blink, replaced by a piercing stab of remorse for upsetting her. "Just seems like something's on your mind."

"Yeah." She sighed. "There was this . . . argument at work."

He set down his fork and leaned forward. "What happened?"

"My boss got into it with somebody in her office yesterday," she said. "I ended up having to jump between them."

"Damn," he said, shaking his head. "That's awful. What was the fight about?"

"It was . . . *um* . . ." She squinted down at her plate as if she was trying to read very tiny words in her pasta. "It's kinda hard to explain. I guess it just boils down to a personality clash."

Neil nodded. No matter how intelligent two people were, sometimes they were just too different to get along. He'd seen Li Sr. get into multiple arguments with his son for just that reason.

"I get it," he told her. "I've seen a few clashes like that at work. Never had to get between anyone, though. Sounds bad."

"Could've been worse," she said. "At least I got them to stop."

"Being able to defuse that kind of situation is a skill." He smiled warmly at her. "You should be proud."

Georgette flushed pink, and a sweet little smile transformed her face. Her eyes, sparkling, looked at him full of appreciation. The girlishness of the expression tickled him. *God, she's cute.*

A low buzzing sound cut off his thought.

"Oh!" Georgette exclaimed, lunging for her bag. "Sorry, that's my phone! I'll turn it off, okay?"

"It's fine," he said with a chuckle, returning to his meal.

She yanked out the rumbling phone; it slipped through her fingers, but she caught it with her other hand just before it hit the table. When she looked at the screen, though, she froze.

Neil cocked an eyebrow. "Something wrong?"

"It's Nocturne," she said, brow furrowed. "I think I should answer this. Sorry."

He nodded. *Work calls*, he thought with half a smile. *Ah, well. What can you do?* But then a sudden memory of his ex texting while they were at restaurants intruded on his thoughts. *She always claimed it was work-related*, he thought, clenching his jaw. With a conscious effort, he suppressed the tension skittering through his muscles. *Georgette isn't Lyndsey*, he repeated to himself as he forked another piece of chicken. *Georgette isn't Lyndsey.*

"I can't understand you," she said quietly into her phone. "What's all that noise?"

An electronic clatter burst from her phone, causing Neil to freeze mid-chew and Georgette to yank the device away from her head. They locked gazes, mutually startled and confused.

"What's that about?" he said through a mouthful of cheesy chicken.

"No idea," she said. "There's a lot of shouting." She put the phone to her ear again. "Hello? Are you there?"

Even from where he sat, Neil heard a steady chatter of sound from the far end of the call. It was such an absurd amount of noise that he wondered if the club was on fire.

Georgette put a finger in her other ear and pressed the phone harder against her skull. "I don't know what you mean," she said, a little louder than before. "Delivery? That's not my department." She paused, shaking her head. "Forget it. Can I talk to Kazimiera please? What? No, Kazi. Kazi!" she repeated, her voice increasing in volume with every word. "Put Kazi on the phone!"

Geez, Neil thought, *every business is its own brand of crazy.*

Hearing a muffled whisper over his shoulder, Neil's gaze

darted to a neighboring table, where a pair of senior patrons were shooting Georgette irritable glances. Neil leaned into their eye-line, cleared his throat, and raised his eyebrows. The husband huffed, nostrils flared, but returned to his meal. The wife pursed her lips and glared at him.

"So rude!" she hissed as she turned away.

"Back atcha, lady," he whispered.

"I don't understand," Georgette said into the phone, speaking quietly again. "Who's with Kazi in the office?"

Suddenly, her expression underwent a dramatic shift. She sat up straight, and the color drained out of her cheeks until she was the palest Neil had ever seen her. Her lips drew to a thin line as her eyes went wide, quivering like eggs on a skillet.

"Oh my God," she murmured.

Alarmed, Neil reached out to her. The moment his hand touched her arm, she jumped, and the phone slipped from her grasp and thunked down onto the table.

"You okay?" he asked, ignoring the phone, and taking her hand. "What the hell's happening at Nocturne?"

Georgette looked at him, lips parted as if about to speak. Then she closed her mouth and looked away. "There's an emergency," she said woodenly, snatching up her phone. "I have to go."

"Go?"

"To the club." She stood and slung her purse over her shoulder. "I'm so sorry."

The phone to her ear again, she took two hurried steps, almost rushing past him, but he jumped up.

"Whoa!" he said. "What kind of IT emergency could they be having that's got you so freaked?"

"I have to go," she said again. Before he could reply, she kissed him. "I'll call you later, okay?"

Without another word, she fled for the door—but he heard her say, "Ishak!" into the phone before she exited. His throat constricted. Ishak. That was one of her roommates. Was there really an emergency at Nocturne? Was Ishak even a roommate? An onslaught of memories—a lengthy string of Lyndsey's lies—threaded their way into his mind.

That guy wasn't a tutor, he thought as he shoved away his plate. *Maybe Ishak isn't a roommate.* And what did that mean about her "sessions" with Nico? Was that all bullshit too? Past and present ping-ponged around in his brain until his head hurt. Nothing made sense. None of this was okay. Eyes resting on Georgette's well-stabbed shrimp, nausea ripped through his gut.

"God dammit," he said under his breath.

39

Ishak

ISHAK SCOOPED UP A LARGE DOLLOP OF MEI-XING'S PUNGENT salve and applied it to his bruised throat. Georgette's spell had repaired most of the damage, shrinking the inflammation and opening his crushed windpipe, but the pain still lingered. The Nymph's homemade balm numbed the ache for an hour or so, but it always returned.

His mind returned to the moment when the Vampire seized him in her cold, bony fingers: black, soulless eyes; the stink of rotten entrails; endless rows of razor teeth. It was the only time in months that he had feared for himself more than Kalilah. A shiver spread through his body. *She would have drained me in minutes.*

With the contract that would deprive her of freedom freshly signed on the Vampire's desk, Georgette had still saved him. The guilt in his gut rivaled the ache in his throat. He had accepted his guilt over the contract, but he was disgusted that his temper had forced the witch to defend him.

He pulled aside the hotel curtains and looked out the window. The late-afternoon sun cast long shadows over the cars in the parking lot. He saw Mei-Xing below, reclining poolside, soaking up the fading sunlight. Still no sign of the raven. Valhalla had apparently sent the Valkyrie and her partner a hefty "chosen" list for the week. Senji had assured Georgette they would investigate KK Inc.'s house as soon as possible but could not say when. They could not afford to draw Valhalla's suspicion by straying from their assignments.

That was yesterday. Not a word since.

Sighing, Ishak sat on the edge of the bed, elbows on his knees, his face in his hands. KK Inc. still had Kalilah but refused to sell her. Kazimiera kept making calls but thus far had made no progress. After living off anger and hope for so long, Ishak's reserve of emotional fuel was running dry. His love for Kalilah would soon be the only light left in the encroaching darkness.

The phone on the end table rang. Muscles aching with the effort, he forced himself to reach for it, pluck the receiver from the cradle, and lift it to his ear.

"Hel—"

"Ishak!"

It was Georgette. The firestorm in her voice stirred him from his depression.

"Yes?"

"Get to Nocturne," she commanded. "Now!"

Her words were choppy, forced from her lips in between gaspy breaths, like she was running.

"Why?" he groaned. "Is that woman going to throttle me again?"

"She's got her."

"Who?"

"Kalilah!" Georgette exclaimed, panting. "Kazi has Kalilah!"

An electric bolt shot through him, lighting up every inch of his body. He found himself standing, legs shaking and hands trembling. "What?!"

"Kalilah's at the club!" Georgette yelled. "KK Inc. sold her to Kazi! She's there now! I'm on my way! GO!"

He heard the last word as he dropped the phone and charged toward the door. He was into the hallway before the receiver hit the floor.

The world passed in a blur as Ishak sprinted to the club. Vague images crossed his vision—Mei-Xing jumping up from her lawn chair, a car swerving to avoid him, startled strangers leaping out of his path. It happened so fast and yet so painfully slow.

The guard at Nocturne's front door tried to stop him, but Ishak shoved him aside and yanked open the door, breaking the lock in his haste. After a crazed race up the stairs, he entered the hall of Kazimiera's office and immediately smelled his wife. The beloved scent warmed and thrilled him, sending a heat wave through his already sizzling body.

A crowd of Fae creatures loitered by Kazimiera's door, talking in hushed tones. When they saw him, the crowd parted, giving him a clear path inside.

The first thing Ishak saw was Kazimiera standing by her desk, one hand on her hip and the other holding a phone to her ear. Her fangs were clearly visible through a vicious snarl. Then Ishak's eyes locked onto three figures on the floor. One, facing away from him, was a woman in flowy clothes that hid most of her stout form but not the peacock-feathered wings sprouting from her back. Another woman, clad in a short dress that exposed much of her nearly-transparent skin, gazed up at him with wide doe eyes. Wine-red streaks that he recognized as bone marrow ran through her body under the pearly sheen of her skin.

"You are Ishak?" she asked in a thick accent.

Ignoring her, his eyes fell upon the third woman on the floor. There, behind the Peri and the Houri, in her human form, was Kalilah. Instantly blind to all else, Ishak plunged between the two creatures and gathered his wife into his arms. He drew a deep breath, overwhelming his nose with her scent as he pressed his face into her matted hair.

Only then did he smell the blood.

Ishak loosened his grip on his wife's limp body until he saw her face. Her cheeks were sunken, her closed eyes framed in dark circles, and her breath as faint as a whisper in a hurricane. Alarmed, he brought a hand to her face, only to see that his palm was wet and red.

"Kalilah," he said frantically, giving her a gentle shake. "Kalilah."

A feeble groan leaked from her cracked lips. Ishak felt the immensity of the situation overtaking him, tilting him off solid ground. He pulled her to his chest, pressing her to his racing heart. "*Habibti*," he whispered into her crown, rocking back and forth. "*Hayati*."

"She was cold," said the Peri in Arabic, drawing her colorful wings around her shoulders. She picked up a crumpled blanket from the floor and wrapped it around Kalilah. The fresh blood-stains on the fabric burned Ishak's eyes. "She asked for you."

"What happened to her?" he demanded.

"No one knows," the Houri said. "The broker dropped her off like this. She was delirious, babbling in Arabic, so Kazi called us to talk to her. But she keeps passing out."

"Where's the blood coming from?" he asked with increasing horror. "Was she cut?"

"No," the Peri said. "The injury is internal." Her dark eyelashes lowered over her eyes as she turned her head aside. "The blood . . . it's from between her legs."

"What?" He fought against the implication of the Peri's words but soon, with a fiery burn in his eyes, he accepted it. "Was she raped?"

"We don't know," said the Peri.

"She wouldn't be the first," the Houri said matter-of-factly. She used one white hand to brush Kalilah's hair out of her ashen face. "Most of us came here bruised and bloody."

"GARY!" Kazimiera shrieked, her shrill voice slicing the hallway chatter to ribbons. "WHAT THE HELL HAPPENED TO THIS HYENA-WOMAN?" She paused just long enough to draw a breath. "YOU'VE GOT SOME BALLS TO SELL ME DAMAGED GOODS!" Panting, she bared her teeth as she listened. "I KNOW WHAT AN 'AS-IS' CONTRACT IS, GARY! DO YOU HAVE ANY IDEA HOW MUCH MONEY I'VE SPENT WITH KETT & KADENA? HOW DARE Y—"

Her tirade came to a screeching halt as she held her phone before her eyes, glaring at it in fury and indignation. When the screen went dark her jaw dropped, opening far wider than a human jaw could, and she let loose a primal scream that shook the walls like an earthquake.

A terrified silence stretched through the room and adjoining hallway until Kazimiera huffed a sharp breath and tossed her phone onto her desk with a loud clatter. The sound broke the unnatural stillness, and the crowd heaved a collective sigh.

Pulling the blanket around Kalilah, Ishak pressed his face to her forehead. Her scent filled him with a lifetime of memories and dreams. "It's all right," he whispered to her in Kanuri, fearful tears in his eyes. "It's over now. I'm here. We'll go home and put all this behind us. Everything will be the way it was. Just open your eyes, Kalilah. Open your eyes and speak to me. Please."

"Let me through!" Georgette's voice shouted from the hallway. Ishak heard her pushing through the crowd. "Where's Kalilah?"

"Here," Ishak called over his shoulder. "She's bleeding."

Panting heavily, Georgette crouched down beside him. He watched her cast the same spell she had used to heal his throat—blowing wisps of magic over Kalilah, covering her body in green light.

A flush of color came into Kalilah's cheeks and her body inflated with a deep breath. Eyelids fluttering, she mumbled something.

"Kalilah?" Ishak said, cradling her face in his hand. "Can you hear me?"

"*Hmm,*" she murmured. She stirred but didn't wake.

"I'll make a stronger dose," Georgette said, preparing a fresh spell. "Just give me a second."

"Magic isn't enough," Kazimiera hissed, and stomped her foot so hard that her high heel snapped off. She teetered slightly before catching her balance. "She has a severe infection."

"How do you know?" Ishak asked.

"I tasted her blood."

He glared at the Vampire, his hyena teeth emerging from his mouth. If not for the fact that his wife was in his arms, he would have launched himself at her—no matter the ache in his throat reminding him of the consequences of doing such a thing.

She shot him an irritated look. "I taste the blood of every ex-familiar that comes into my building," she said, kicking off her shoes. "You never know what diseases they might pick up while in storage. I don't need an epidemic in here. But she's not contagious. She has sepsis."

Ishak didn't recognize the word but saw Georgette's eyes flicker with alarm. The spell brewing in her hands grew, swelling to twice the size of the previous one. *It's serious*, he concluded. *My God, it's serious.*

"We need to take her to the ER," the witch said. "Right now."

"It won't help," Kazimiera said, plopping down in her chair. "Those idiot brokers must have seen she was sick. They put a seal on her—probably to stabilize her condition long enough to get her treatment, but they bungled it. They sealed the bacteria into her blood." She snarled, tightening her grip on the armrests until the wood cracked. "They only sold her when they realized how badly they'd messed up." With a red-eyed bellow, she ripped both armrests from the chair and hurled them across the room. "They've got my money, she's got a death-sentence, and the geas is void!"

Death-sentence. Ishak's limbs felt like lead weights. *No.*

"That can't be." Ishak stared at Georgette as she spread her new spell over Kalilah's body. "Georgette? That can't be."

After several failed attempts to speak, she finally said, "It can."

"Fix it. Remove the seal."

Georgette raised her eyes to meet his. In them, he saw a smothering misery.

"No," she whispered. "The seal . . . it's like—like a tourniquet. You know, like you lose a leg and tie off the stump to stop the bleeding? The tourniquet may or may not save your life, but if you take it off, you'll definitely bleed to death. The seal can't save her, but if I take it off . . ." She trailed off, dropping her gaze to the stained, ripped carpet.

Ishak looked down at Kalilah in his arms and realized he was trembling. Georgette's spell sank into Kalilah's skin, and once again the greenish hue faded. His wife moaned and opened her eyes.

Ishak's heart leaped. "Kalilah!" he exclaimed, pulling her closer. "*Habibti!* Can you hear me?"

"Ishak," she whispered, her voice raspy and weak. "Where . . .?"

"You're safe now," he told her, stroking her hair. "I have you. No one will hurt you again."

Her bloodshot eyes drifted over his face, unfocused and weary. "Cold . . ." she murmured. "Cold."

"I'll keep you warm," he said. He kissed her forehead as he pulled the blanket tighter around her. The smell of fresh blood brought more tears to his eyes. "We'll go home and soak in the sun."

He meant every word and yet he knew it was all lies. This was the closest she had been to him in months, yet she slipped farther away by the second. The knowledge wrought a desperation and grief so great that he felt his body too small to contain it.

This is the last time I will speak to my wife.

"Ishak," she whispered.

"Yes, *hayati*? What is it?"

"Where is Ziya?"

"Ziya? Your cousin?" Confused, he hugged her tighter. "She died, Kalilah, many years ago."

"I was with Ziya," she murmured. Eyes sliding shut, she nestled her face into his throat. The gesture was preciously familiar, a sweet thing she had done a thousand times before—and yet never would again. "Find Ziya."

"Of course," he agreed sadly. "Anything you say."

Her eyes opened a fraction, two sliver crescent moons casting dim light on him. "My love? It's cold. Isn't it harvest time still?"

"No," he croaked. "The rains have come by now."

"I'm cold." She sighed and her eyes closed. Her head fell against him, and her arms went limp. "I'm cold."

"It's all right, Kalilah," he said, kissing her hair. Tears flowed down his face as hot as lava, dripping off his nose and chin. "It's all right."

The light inside her slowly fluttered out, sliding through his embrace into darkness. He remained, drained and adrift, a lone, strangled howl leaking from his open mouth.

40  Georgette

THE RUMBLE OF ENGINES AND CHATTER OF PEDESTRIANS filled the streets and sidewalks, the sound rising up to where Georgette stood on the roof. The sun had fled, leaving a fading pink and purple stain at the horizon. Lampposts glowed to life, lines of headlights and taillights crisscrossed through the streets, and office windows grew dark one by one.

Georgette's ragged breath misted the air. Her eyes were so full of tears that she could hardly see, and her ears heard nothing but Ishak's soul-devouring wails. She knew she shouldn't be able to hear him—he was inside the building and several floors down —but she did, and every mournful howl drowned her in ever more pain and misery.

A peel of laughter split the night air. Startled, Georgette stepped to the edge and looked down at the street. A line had formed in front of Nocturne—young men and women dressed for a night out. It was past opening time, but because Kazimiera's staff had been delayed from their usual duties by Kalilah's arrival, the club doors were still locked.

"Everyone out," Kazimiera commanded when it was clear that Kalilah was gone. "Get to work."

Ishak gave no sign that he heard; his attention and his arms were full of his late wife.

Angry on his behalf, Georgette prepared to lash out at the Vampire, but Kazi cut her off.

"There are dozens of Fae here who depend on my business," Kazimiera said. "Should I shut it all down for one man?"

"He just lost his wife," Georgette said. "How can you be so—"

"Heartless?" Stepping over the sobbing Bultungin, Kazi picked up her shoes before walking, barefoot, into the hall. "A bleeding heart won't pay my bills."

Laughter emanated below from a gaggle of girls in weather-inappropriate clothes. Enraged, Georgette fought the urge to curse them all with severe acne. It was so unjust that the world went on turning like it was any other night. Her anger gradually dissolved into miserable frustration, until finally she sank to her knees and cried.

The roof access door creaked open behind her.

"I'm here," Mei-Xing said as she stepped up and crouched down beside her. "Are you okay?"

Georgette shook her head, swiping at her eyes underneath her glasses. "Kalilah died," she whispered.

"I know." Mei-Xing laid a hand on her shoulder. "Everyone in the club is talking about it. But even before I got here—I felt it,

I think, through the brand. I felt Ishak losing her. It was like . . . a shiver in my soul."

Georgette wiped her nose on her sleeve. "I was there."

The Nymph put an arm around her shoulders and stroked her hair while whispering soothingly in Mandarin.

A new wave of grief broke over Georgette and she collapsed, sobbing, against her friend.

"I'm sorry," Mei-Xing said, "and I wish I didn't have to burden you further, but . . . this can't wait."

A throaty croak drew Georgette's attention to the raven perched nearby, the buttery glow of streetlights reflecting off his sleek black feathers.

"Senji showed up right after Ishak left the hotel," Mei-Xing said. "It took a while, but eventually I was able to use the brand to hear words instead of bird noises when he spoke." She brushed curls of hair out of Georgette's face. "Delia went to that house in Silver Creek."

"It doesn't matter anymore." Georgette took off her glasses to dry her eyes. "Kalilah's not there now."

"I know, but . . ." Mei-Xing released a weighty sigh. "They found something."

"Yes," came Senji's voice through his avian squawks, "and someone needs to address it. Immediately."

The rhythm of the club's music vibrated up through the floor as Georgette stepped into Kazimiera's office. Ishak knelt on the carpet with his back to her, eerily still. Kalilah's body was on the floor, covered head-to-toe by a bloodstained blanket. Ishak held one uncovered hand, brushing the knuckles with his thumb.

Georgette sank to her knees beside him and placed a hand on his shoulder. Slowly, as if every movement hurt, he twisted his head to face her.

"I failed her," he said, his tone low and hoarse.

"I'm sorry." Tears filled her eyes yet again.

"Those brokers . . . those *murderers* . . ." His bloodshot eyes flashed red with predatory rage. "I'm going to kill them. And God help you if you try to talk me out of it."

Georgette shook her head. "I won't. We'll go to the house in Silver Creek and bust it wide open."

"No," he said. "I'm going to the downtown office. I want the men responsible for this."

"Help me with Silver Creek," she said, "and I promise you'll get them."

"Why Silver Creek? Kalilah's not there."

"Senji and Delia investigated the house." She tightened her grip on his shoulder, her jaw clenching. "They found something."

After what Georgette had learned from Senji, all the confusion she'd suffered over the last few months had been knocked away, leaving her uniquely clearheaded. Every struggle she'd experienced since leaving Boston—every fear, every panic, every guilt—had all boiled away into righteous anger. Now, kneeling by Ishak, she felt that rage radiate through the *Hathiya* brand, transmitting her anger to him.

Through his own fury, she saw a flicker of surprise.

"What?" he asked, brow furrowed. "What did they find?"

She drew in a sharp breath and exhaled through her bared teeth. "Children."

Ishak blinked. "What?"

"Children," she repeated. "The KK Inc. house in Silver Creek is full of Fae children."

41   Delia & Senji

How much do you know about the witch-familiar brokerage business?

I know what you know. Senji attacked a security camera, pecking at an exposed wire until it sparked. The camera's red eye went dark.

She swung her silver sword upward in a smooth arc. It passed through the thin space between front door and jamb, kicking up a spray of ethereal orange mist. The spell protecting the entrance ruptured and leaked energy like a deflating balloon until the magic was spent.

No. But it's not surprising.

With a one-armed swipe, she cut through the back door. The sealing spell broke with a flash of light. She sheathed her sword.

On an adjacent roof, Senji dug his talons into another camera. *It's a sound investment from their point of view.* He snapped his beak through a wire. *One born into bondage or brought into it so early in life that they've never known anything else is easier to control than one who remembers freedom.* The camera emitted a high-pitched whine that quickly petered out, leaving it blind and deaf. *One cannot miss what one has never had.*

The Valkyrie passed through the back door and walked into the kitchen. *I'm sure that's part of it. But it's also supply and demand.* A heavyset man with glasses walked past her, oblivious to her presence. Ignoring him, she walked on. *There wouldn't be so many children for sale here unless they were in hot demand.*

291

But if underage Fae are in demand, wouldn't all brokerages have them?

Perhaps, but it's risky. Stealing children is more likely to provoke a response. And witches must know that they're vastly outnumbered by Fae.

The fear of rebellion must haunt them, he agreed. That would account for the secrecy. And it would explain why this is the only brokerage the witch knows of that does it.

Possibly. Delia strode past a television blasting unrealistic gunfire. Down a hallway, she approached a padlocked door and thrust her sword into the knob. The Valhallan blade did not touch the knob itself but pierced the spell woven into it, cutting it to ribbons. The spell fluttered into the air like confetti.

Taking flight, Senji swooped low and glided over the gated neighbor- hood, searching for any other cameras that might have a view of the house.

Delia walked into a room
identical to one she had
seen just hours earlier. As
before, the sight filled her
with rage, compassion, and
restless agitation. Floor-to-
ceiling, wall-to-wall shelves:

Elf, female, age 2.

Tengu, male, age 18 months.

Cyclops, male, age 4.

There were hundreds in
this room, and five other
identical rooms in the
house.

Satisfied that all relevant
cameras were disabled,
Senji flew to the front door.
He perched on the railing
that lined the front steps
and cocked his head to get a
good look at the security
system keypad.

Are the cameras down?

*Yes, but this keypad is a
different story.* He pecked
lightly at the casing. *If I
damage it, the company might
receive an alert. The witch
must deal with it when she
arrives.*

Understood.

She stared at the boxes, at row after row of labels. KK Inc. had a rainbow of species aged fourteen to newborn, all dematerialized, sealed in limbo inside shoeboxes.

"Poor babies," she murmured.

Valhalla often sent them after people of questionable morality. Some of the chosen warriors turned her stomach. But however questionable their actions, when facing an enemy,

the chosen were convinced of their moral superiority.

KK Inc.'s morality was below questionable; it was for sale. Senji hopped about on the railing, anticipation sizzling through his body.

We have witnessed action over the years but have had little of it for ourselves. Delia, when was our last battle?

1972, she replied excitedly.
*An enemy combatant broke
through our ranks of chosen
and entered the atmosphere.
Valhalla summoned every
Valkyrie to drive it back to
Muspelheim.*

The memory of the fire
giant filled her mind,
bringing with it the taste of
joyous battle-lust.

Today is different. Senji
spread his wings and took
flight. *I have doubted the
righteousness of Valhalla's
cause. I doubted our success
against that fire giant. In my
final moments of life, I
doubted my purpose.* He
circled the house twice
before perching on the
roof. *But here and now?* He
cawed triumphantly. *I do not
doubt. The battle is at hand.*

Delia laughed joyously. She
brandished her sword,
smirking at her eager-eyed
reflection in the silver
blade.

Lâche pas la patate, Delia!

Ganbatte kudasai, Senji.
Let's give 'em hell.

42  Georgette

THE SCREEN ON GEORGETTE'S PHONE FLASHED WITH THE intensity of a strobe light. Page after page of coded information blipped across the phone at an unreadable pace, streaming via magic directly into her brain.

"How much longer?" Ishak panted.

"Not long," she monotoned, never breaking eye contact with the phone.

The screen jostled, almost breaking her concentration. Out of the corner of her eye, she saw the city whooshing by as Ishak, with her on his back, leaped from rooftop to rooftop. Georgette tightened her grip around the giant hyena's torso. Sensing a pending panic attack, she pushed her surroundings away and plunged back into the data stream. *Don't look down, don't look down, don't look down . . .*

"I could have ripped the main office into bite-size chunks by now," the Bultungin said, heaving.

"That office is closed for the night," she said, her cheek pressed into his rough fur. "If you want the broker who sold her, this is how we'll get him."

Ishak skidded to a stop, his claws scraping through stone,

making her suspect that he had run out of tall buildings. *Now approaching suburbia*, she thought. *Next stop, Silver Creek.*

After a moment of listening to Ishak gulp air, Georgette lowered the phone and rubbed her eyes to clear away the strobe effect. Lifting her gaze, she saw that they had landed on a roof in the middle of a shopping center. At a glance, she saw Little Caesars, Wendy's, and the ever-present Starbucks. An evening crowd milled about the parking lot, but the fact that no one was staring up at the huge hyena with a girl on his back told her that her hastily assembled glamour was holding. Anyone who looked would just see a flock of birds.

The glamour is draining, she thought. *I'm exhausted. When tonight's over, I'm gonna feel like shit for a week.*

"What have you found?" Ishak demanded.

"That we're in luck," she said. "Looks like KK Inc. doesn't let ordinary security guards work the Silver Creek house." She smiled humorlessly. "I guess the merchandise is too sensitive. That man Barnes, the one who bought Kalilah from Kivuli Panon, is on duty at the house tonight."

Ishak turned his head toward her, a murderous glint lighting up his eyes. "What about the other one? The man who sold Kalilah to the Vampire?"

"Gary Cooke. I've found his private number."

"And you can get him to the house?" he asked.

The hunger in Ishak's eyes made her skin crawl; a fight-or-flight urge pinged through her body.

"Immediately?" he insisted.

Georgette punched the number into her phone. "Let's find out."

As the phone rang, she whispered a spell into the signal, sending electronic magic through the radio waves that would scramble the caller ID. Her magic was already spread too thin for her liking, but the last thing she needed was for anyone to know who had really placed this call.

"Yes?" answered a male voice on the other end.

Georgette closed her eyes, as horrified and panicked as if an eighteen-wheeler was barreling straight toward her. Thinking back on her sessions with Nico, she breathed deeply and tried to slow her heart. *Anxiety is a chemical response. Don't let it hijack your brain.*

"Mr. Cooke," she said, trying to keep her voice from trembling.

"Yeah. Who's this?"

"My name's Sara Elliott. I work for Long, Pijara & Ruszt."

Georgette heard Cooke inhale sharply—exactly the effect she'd hoped for. Long, Pijara & Ruszt was one of the largest and most prestigious international familiar brokerages in the world. A brokerage like Kett & Kadena—smaller and with a poor reputation—would never expect to receive a call from them. Cooke was caught off guard. *Hopefully,* she thought, *too off guard to wonder how I got his private number.*

"How can I help you, Miss Elliott?" he asked in a formal tone.

"I was recently contacted by someone named Christopher Barnes," she said. "Is he an employee of yours?"

"Yes."

"This Mr. Barnes offered to sell me some of your inventory. I told him that our firm does not do business with Kett & Kadena, and he informed me that he was not acting on your brokerage's behalf. He implied that he wanted to sell me the merchandise under the table." Channeling her mother, Georgette tossed her hair and turned up her nose. "Do you sanction this sort of behavior from your people, Mr. Cooke?"

On the other end of the line, she heard another quick inhale. She smiled. *Cooke believes me.* Of course he did. Selling his employer's product under the table was exactly how Barnes had come to work for KK Inc. in the first place.

"What," Cooke asked tensely, "did he offer to sell you?"

"Several items that were"—she let disgust leak into her voice—"how shall I put this . . . unripe."

She let the word hang in the silence. *That's right*, she thought. *How's it feel to be reminded that even other slavers look down on you?*

"And when was this sale supposed to take place?" Cooke asked.

"At the start of business tomorrow morning," she told him. "He said he was acquiring the merchandise tonight."

C'mon, she mentally urged, *do the math.*

"Thank you for the call, Miss Elliott," Cooke said, speaking faster than before. "I apologize for my employee's behavior. I assure you, he will be dealt with."

"That's good to hear," she replied. "Have a pleasant evening, Mister Co—"

The line clicked, cutting her off. She gave Ishak a grim smile. "I think he did the math. He should be on his way to Silver Creek right now."

The Bultungin's muscles clenched underneath her as he crouched, ready to jump.

"Hang on," he commanded.

She dug her fingers deep into his fur and gripped his sides with her knees. Ishak launched himself forward, soaring through the air toward the Starbucks roof. From the back of Georgette's mind, a little voice said she was helping Ishak commit murder. The little voice scolded her, warned her, and made a feeble but earnest attempt to derail her course of action. She quashed it.

I'm not Ivy anymore. I'm Georgette.

43 Ishak

GEORGETTE HAD SENT SENJI AHEAD TO SILVER CREEK WITH instructions for him and Delia to remove all the security, physical and magical. Then she had begged Mei-Xing to go somewhere the Nymph did not want to go—Ishak wasn't sure where, he had stopped listening. Their argument, whatever it entailed, was irrelevant to him.

For months, he had spent every waking minute trying to return his life to what it once was. All his thoughts had revolved around going home to Kabultiloa arm in arm with his wife. Now Kalilah was gone—and with her, his purpose.

Except revenge against the two men he held responsible for Kalilah's death.

And then? Nothing. He tried pushing his thoughts beyond revenge but found he could summon nothing. So he stopped thinking about it. He had a temporary purpose. That was all he needed. For now.

44  Mei-Xing

MEI-XING SHIMMIED DOWN THE CONCRETE EMBANKMENT, her unglamoured feet pressing lightly into the soggy dirt at the water's edge. The sound of traffic on the nearby roads drowned out the ambling flow of the river, which spanned barely the toss of a stone in front of her. This urban stretch of the Guadalupe River looked so unimpressive, yet it filled the Nymph with dread.

Stripped of her human mask, she felt ludicrously naked, though she knew the glamour would not have been much help in this scenario. Every touch of her feet to the soil sent tiny signals to the network of roots that ran through the earth. The roots recognized what she was—as would their owners, were they awake. For the first time in years, she was one Nymph among many.

Even if they are awake, she reminded herself, *they don't know me or the family that thinks I'm dead. I'm not in danger.*

Mei-Xing knelt at the river's edge and dipped her fingers into the water.

"Guadalupe River!" she called out. "I request an audience!"

She heard the soft trot of the water over loose rocks and the faint whisper of a breeze through the shrubs, all of it underneath a heavy rumble of vehicles.

"Guadalupe River!" she shouted again. "Please speak with me!"

A ribbed golden fin, many meters long, emerged from the river. As it lifted from the water's surface, the gold color shifted to a brilliant green with leopard prints of blue. A pair of gray-feathered heron wings stretched and shimmied away water droplets; the wingspan was wider than Mei-Xing was tall. The tail, capped with a fin of sunny orange, flipped up, sending a spray of droplets into the air that splattered over Mei-Xing's mossy bark. All along the body, Mei-Xing saw tiny speckles of white that she found repulsive and distressing. She had met enough of her Water Spirit husband's people to recognize the telltale signs of pollution.

The front end of the body, still underwater, snaked its way toward the concrete shore. Mei-Xing shivered, shrinking into herself but not budging from the spot.

Will it look like my husband? she thought, distressed. *Will it have his big black eyes? His huge, webbed ears? The same irritated expression when I speak?*

Slowly, the head of the River Spirit emerged. Long, wide grasses sprouted from its crown and draped over its head like a wet mop. From between the green and brown blades, the Nymph saw bits of the River Spirit's face—little flashes of sky and ocean blue. Two big golden eyes, rimmed by rings of pure midnight, locked onto her. As the head cleared the surface, Mei-Xing caught her breath. The River Spirit's face was that of a great blue puma.

"I am *Thámien Rúmmey,*" he said to her, his inhuman mouth forming words over his finger-length fangs. "Also called Guadalupe River."

His voice was both cavernous and distant, like a thunderclap echoing through a canyon. Tremendous though it was, the sound eased Mei-Xing's nerves. This River Spirit was nothing like her husband.

"I am Mei-Xing Ma," she said, bowing her head. "I've come to ask for your help."

The mountain lion's face turned upward, eyes scanning the dark sky. "The hour is late," he said. Slowly, his head and body began to sink back into the water. "Come back at dawn and speak to your own kind."

"This can't wait," she said quickly, putting up a hand toward the River Spirit. "The matter is urgent."

With a sigh, the River Spirit coiled up his long body like a snake, lifting his head higher into the air. The Nymph noted with sadness and nausea that its underbelly, too, was pockmarked with the white pollution stains.

The golden eyes looked down on Mei-Xing. "You are branded," he said. "Were you sent by your master?"

"I have no master!" Mei-Xing spat back. She leaped to her feet and glared at him, eye to eye. "I share this mark with friends and allies only."

The river blinked and pulled back in surprise. *Wood Nymphs don't talk back to their water source*, Mei-Xing thought, full of bitter memories. *Heaven knows my family never did.*

"Peace, little sister!" he said, sounding bewildered. "I meant no offense." He sent a shiver down his long body, throwing off a shower that rained down on the water surface in a soft patter. "What troubles you and your allies this evening?"

His soothing voice cooled her temper. She took half a step back, remorseful that she had lashed out. "You have a wide watershed in this area," she said, resuming the respectful tone with which she had begun their encounter. "Your influence must spread to multiple Fae communities."

"True," he replied, a hint of pride in his voice.

"We—my allies and I—want to ask you to deliver a message as far and wide as you can before morning. To every grove, to every creek, to every nook and cranny where Fae might be found."

"That's a lot of work for one night," he said after a moment's consideration. "Is your message so important?"

He's showing me great kindness, considering I'm a stranger who's intruded on his home and raised my voice. Mindful of this, as well as the importance of the favor she asked, Mei-Xing held her arms before her, folded her right hand over her left, and bowed before the Spirit. "It concerns a great many Fae children who have been abducted from their homes and families," she said, her eyes upon the muddy water's edge. "Would you spare a night's work to help us set things right?"

Mei-Xing kept her head bowed, waiting for a response. For long seconds, she heard nothing but the traffic of the city that surrounded them. Though little time had passed, it felt long enough that she wondered if the Spirit had slipped away without a word. But then she heard a throaty rumble and the click of river stones under the Spirit's shifting weight.

His blue face and golden eyes crossed her vision as he ducked his head into her lowered gaze.

"Speak, little sister," he said, "and explain."

45 Ishak

INSIDE LIGHTS SHONE OUT THROUGH THE WINDOWS AS Ishak dropped over the wall behind the Silver Creek house. His four large feet landed solidly on lush green grass, then carried him forward until his claws clicked on the stones of a small patio. He would have galloped ahead to crash through the window if he hadn't felt Georgette grab fistfuls of his fur and yank backward as if reining in a horse.

"Wait!" she said. "We need to make sure the security's down."

"I hear a man inside," he said irritably, "but just one. You promised me both."

"Cooke's coming. We got here by jumping from roof to roof. He has to make his way through traffic." She slid off his back, glancing around. "I'm gonna find Senji and Delia. Wait here."

He snorted and swiped at the ground, breaking away chips of the patio with his claws. "I warned you not to try to stop me," he snarled. "I'm here for blood."

"I'm not trying to stop you," she said calmly. "I'm asking you to wait two minutes while I make sure Delia and Senji have taken down all the security." Without any of the nervousness which he had come to associate with her, she placed a hand on his shoulder and met his eyes with a steady gaze. "You will have blood. I promise."

Her tone was at once reassuring and peculiar. Georgette's hand was still, her voice smooth, her scent utterly devoid of anxiety. She seemed more solid than before, as if he had just now found the real woman after only seeing her shadow for months.

"I will wait," he said, settling back on his haunches. "For now."

"Thank you." She jammed her hands in her jeans pockets and pulled out a stick of chalk. "I'll signal when it's safe."

Without another word, she walked through a row of shrubs, crossing from patio light into darkness.

Ishak stared after her. The transformation in Georgette was astounding.

I wish Kalilah could have known her.

He shook his head, forcing himself to be numb, and all thoughts of Georgette's growth and wishes for what could not be left him. He waited, dead to all but his thirst for revenge.

A high-pitched whine broke the air. Perking up his ears, he turned his gaze toward the sound just in time to see an ethereal blue spark burst from the back door's security system keypad. The numbered buttons flickered, their green glow blinking erratically. Then the buttons went dark, and the whine ceased.

Georgette's disabled the system.

It was obvious at a glance that his enormous hyena body would not fit through the doorframe, so he held the form just long enough to crush the knob. As the door flew open with a bang, he walked through, fully human but for his blazing red eyes.

Immediately, he was bombarded by living scents. With only a

307

sniff, he knew this house held hundreds of individuals from dozens of different species. He pressed on, deeper into the house, searching by sight and sound for his prey.

The living room looked empty, but someone had been there recently. A half-eaten pizza was on the coffee table next to an open can of soda. A smartphone sat on the arm of the sofa, the screen still glowing.

Growling under his breath, Ishak swept his gaze around the room, eyes narrowed for any sign of movement.

"There."

The Bultungin turned his head to see Delia, barely more than a transparent shimmer, at the far end of the room, pointing at a closed door.

"He's in this closet," she told him. "He heard you smash through the back door, panicked, and shut himself in there." She leaned over, plunging her ghostly head through the wooden slab. "He's trying to load a gun," she said from inside the closet. "The bullets are the wrong caliber, though." She chuckled. "He's peeking at you from under the door."

As Ishak advanced on the closet, the door suddenly flew open into his face. Huffing like an asthmatic hippo, Barnes exploded into the room and bolted toward the front door. Ishak pushed aside the door but didn't hurry after the unkempt, overweight man. One bound would close the distance between them and put his hand on the broker's throat.

On his way to the door, Barnes tripped over the hallway carpet runner and fell on his face with a grunt. Ishak approached him, drinking in fresh waves of fear, as the frantic man scrambled to get to his feet. Halfway up, he stumbled and fell again.

This time, instead of trying to stand, he rolled over and pointed his handgun at Ishak.

The report of the weapon reverberated off the walls. Ishak dove to the floor, but the bullet flew wide, lodging itself in the ceiling.

Panting, Barnes frantically crab-walked backward, and with quivering hands took aim again. Ishak tensed, ready to spring, but when Barnes pulled the trigger, the gun didn't fire.

Gasping, he pulled the trigger again. Nothing happened.

"It didn't eject the case," Delia, standing over Ishak, reported gleefully. "With the case from the first round stuck in the barrel, the second round couldn't chamber." She grinned down at him, transparent eyes glimmering. "That gun's nothing but a paperweight."

Teeth bared, Ishak lifted himself off the floor and changed his form. As the hyena emerged from the man, he watched a familiar shift occur in Barnes's eyes. It was a thing he had seen in the eyes of prey in the past—the realization of being outmatched—and was usually followed by one of two actions: giving up in despair or trying to run.

Barnes chose the latter. With a surge of energy Ishak would not have thought him capable of, he hurled the gun at his pursuer, leaped to his feet, and bolted for the door.

Ishak roared and gave chase.

The front door suddenly opened, and Georgette stepped inside, seemingly deep in thought. Barnes raced ahead, charging toward the door as if he would go right through the witch. Georgette's eyes alighted upon the broker as he barreled toward her, but Ishak saw no concern on her face. Instead, she waved her hand at Barnes as if shooing away a fly.

With that casual movement, a shockwave rippled through the air and struck Barnes in the chest. The undulating distortion lifted the broker off his feet and hurled him, bellowing, to the far end of the hall. He landed with a thud and skidded across the hardwood, the rug bunching beneath him. He came to a stop at Ishak's feet, eyes wild with fear.

"I'm gonna need this space." Georgette pointed to the living room. "I've drawn runes all around the outside of the house in chalk, but I need a large indoor area to finish setting up the spell."

"It's all yours." Ishak smacked one paw on the mewling broker's chest, pressing him firmly to the floor. "I have what I came for."

"Hey," Barnes babbled, hands tugging at the hyena's foot, "I just work for them. If you're here for the merchandise, help yourself, man."

"No." Ishak lowered his massive head to bring his eyes close to Barnes's face. "I'm here for you."

"Whoa," Barnes said, eyes darting around the room, "you're making a mistake. I don't know you."

"You"—his chest burned with fury—"bought my wife from a witch named Kivuli Panon. If you had not bought her, I would have freed her when I killed the bitch. If you had not then taken her to Kett & Kadena, I would have stolen her from Zamek's without incident. If not for you, she would not have died." He leaned on Barnes's chest, forcing him to gasp for air. "Do you remember now?"

The quivering fear in Barnes's eyes leaked from the corners and trickled down his unshaven cheeks. He stammered a few broken pleas for mercy which quickly degenerated into single-syllable whimpers. The fight-or-flight reflex drained from the broker's eyes. His quivering muscles went limp, and he sagged back on the floor, eyes closed and mouth agape. He looked as if someone had unplugged his power supply.

Ishak huffed, snout wrinkled in disgust. "I thought so."

46 Delia & Senji

Delia watched impassively as Ishak took apart his victim piece by shrieking piece. Blood and gore covered the rug, splattered on the walls, dripped from Ishak's lips and claws.

Georgette sat cross-legged, eyes closed, hands on her knees, quietly chanting. Four runes marked the cardinal points of a chalk circle around her, each topped with an elemental item: a handful of Earth, a bowl of Water, a feather for Air, and, oddly, a table lamp for Fire.

Seeing the scene through Delia's eyes, Senji asked, *Is there no candle?*

*She says electricity is the
aspect of fire she knows best.*

Delia sensed the magic, a
sphere of power gathering
bulk like a ball of yarn
winding its loose end. As
the power grew, so did the
circles under Georgette's
eyes.

Senji flew around the
house. The chalk markings
the witch had drawn on the
outer walls glowed faintly.
They seemed to seal off the
house, preventing anyone
from seeing or hearing
anything within.

"Are you all right?" Delia
stepped toward the witch.

"*Shhh!*" Georgette hissed,
her cheeks pale. "I need to
concentrate. This is a
complex spell, damn it."

"You look ill. Maybe I
could—"

"Maybe you could shut up,"
the witch snapped. "Back
off and let me work!"

Delia was surprised and
impressed by the witch's
spunk.

Senji chuckled—but his laughter was cut short when he saw a gray sedan turn the corner. It came down the street, turned into the driveway, and parked.

There's a car out front. There are three men inside.

Three? The Bultungin only wants the one.

Two spares for us, then. Excellent. He flexed his talons. *I'm bored.*

"Your target has arrived," she told Ishak. "He's brought two others with him."

The Bultungin snarled. "I'm not finished with this one."

Though still drawing shallow breath, Barnes was now little more than a bloody torso covered in gashes and wounds. His severed limbs, all four in multiple pieces, were scattered and resting in pools of blood.

The three men exited the car, the driver muttering darkly under his breath.

"He looks finished to me," she said. "Is it worth keeping him alive another few minutes if it means losing Cooke?"

The driver approached the front door, pausing only to bark at the other two men to hurry up. One of the pair, the younger, trotted up to his boss while the second ambled behind, yawning.

Ishak grumbled as he looked at the broker, unconscious and still. "Very well."

With a halfhearted swipe, he tore through Barnes's throat. The ragged hole spurted a feeble stream of blood that drained quickly.

The limbless torso emitted
one last croak—a faint,
soulless sound that faded
unceremoniously into
silence. The hyena snorted
at the corpse and skulked
away, leaving enormous,
bloody pawprints in the
hallway.

They're at the door, Senji
said, leaning over the edge
of the roof to get a good
look.

Why haven't they come in yet?

*They're arguing about who
has the keys to the house. They
think Barnes left the security
system offline.*

*Then he doesn't suspect it's
fried. Good.* Delia drew her
sword and squeezed the
hilt,
fingers tingling with
delight. *By the time he figures
it out, it'll be too late.*

47 Gary Cooke

COOKE ENTERED THE SECURITY CODE ON THE PUNCH PAD twice before he realized that the damn thing wasn't even turned on. The fury simmering in his gut boiled up into his head, sending a deep red flush into his cheeks and up the back of his neck. *Barnes didn't even activate the goddamn security system?* It was either extreme negligence or confirmation that Miss Elliott was telling the truth. Cooke was betting on the latter.

"Backstabbing piece of shit," he muttered.

"Sir," said one of the security guards he'd brought along, "there's some vandalism on the side of the house."

Cooke looked where the man was pointing and saw white chalk markings on the bricks. Some of the drawings looked like backward letters or upside-down numbers, while others looked like random assortments of lines and angles. *Are those . . . concealment runes?* he wondered. He wasn't sure. But if they were, it was just further confirmation of Barnes's guilt; why put concealment runes on the house unless he had something to hide?

"Later," he said with a dismissive wave.

Think you can steal from me, Barnes, you prick? he thought, stabbing the key at the lock. *When I'm done with you, no brokerage in the world will touch your ass with a ten-foot pole.*

When he felt the lock click open, Cooke glanced over his shoulder and gestured for the two men to follow him.

The one who had called his attention to the chalk glared at the markings, stubbly jaw clenched. Cooke suspected he knew he would be the one to have to wash them off tomorrow. The other, a baby-faced youngster, gazed around the neighborhood, drinking in the large houses and manicured lawns. Cooke cleared his throat, and the two men snapped their attention to him. He pushed open the door.

The smell hit him first. It was rotten and metallic, like bad meat left on a rusted grill, but there was also a stink of shit and piss. The odors turned his stomach, but they also set his hair on end. This wasn't the smell of Silver Creek. It was the smell of a slaughterhouse.

"God damn," he said, covering his nose with his hand. "What the hell is that—"

As the door swung wide, he choked on his question. The entire hallway was red. He blinked, confused. *Paint?* Then his eyes fell upon the body. *My God, it's blood.* Though shock and horror did arise within him, his first thought was, *This is going to be a PR nightmare.*

A legless, armless torso, its throat in tatters, was in the center of the chaos. Chunks of flesh were strewn about, none of the body parts recognizable except for the hands, each of which sat in a pool of blood with their fingers curled up like the legs of a dead insect. On the floor, mere feet from the entrance, Barnes's lifeless eyes stared up at Cooke from the remnants of a torn, splattered face.

The corpse's mouth hung wide open, frozen in an eternal scream.

"Jesus," Stubble-Jaw said, low and breathless. "The hell kind of animal made those?"

"What?" said Cooke. He ripped his gaze from the carnage and glanced back at his men. "Animal?"

"The prints," Stubble-Jaw said, pointing. "In the blood."
Cooke saw them. Huge, beastly pawprints, red and sticky, all over the hardwood. A shiver passed through his skin, sending an electric current up the length of each body hair. *Did something from my inventory get loose?* It wasn't unheard of for a broker or guard to pull something out of stock to "entertain" him for an hour or two while he was on duty, but he'd never known any man to have tastes this dangerous. *What do I even have in this house that's so big? Whatever did this must be full-grown, and there's nothing stored here that's out of puberty.*

"I don't understand," Baby-Face said, shaking his head. "I looked through the window when we were outside. I didn't see any of this." Wild-eyed, he ducked back through the front door and peered through the window. "It's not there!" he shouted. He stepped over the threshold again and Cooke saw on his face a mess of terror and denial. "I can't see it from outside at all!"

"Mr. Cooke"—Stubble-Jaw drew his weapon—"the animal might still be in the house. We should go."

"Screw that," Cooke snapped. "If it's still here, it might be damaging the merchandise. Find it and kill it."

The guy looked at Cooke like he had asked him to assassinate the president. "Not unless you've got a bazooka with you."

Baby-Face backed away from the mess, shaking his head. "I'm outta here."

Cooke jabbed a finger at the young man. "Leave now and I'm not paying you a dime."

"No paycheck is worth this," Baby-Face said, already halfway through the open door. Hands twitching, he pulled out a cell-phone. "I'm out."

Cooke started to shout—paycheck or not, the kid was still bound by the confidentiality clause of his contract—but was stopped by a loud shriek as, in a mad rush of feathers and squawks, a large black bird attacked the kid. He screamed and flailed his arms at the bird to no avail. Frozen in shock, Cooke saw the kid's face disappear underneath a swamp of blood.

Stubble-Jaw charged forward and swiped at the bird, knocking it back. With a croak, it tumbled to the ground just outside the door—but leaped right back up, spread its wings wide, and trilled loudly a second later. Baby-Face kicked his feet, bellowing as if trying to scare the bird, but it lowered its head and made a hissing sound like a cobra. Looking at the animal, Cooke thought with amazement that it actually had murder in its eyes.

What. The. Hell.

Stubble-Jaw yanked the kid back inside and slammed the door. Immediately, the bird's jet-black face appeared in the nearest the window and it rapped on the glass with its bloody beak.

Eyes wide, the kid shimmied out of Stubble-Jaw's grasp and bolted toward the hallway. Cooke watched as he slipped in Barnes's blood, windmilling his arms for balance, and then hy-droplaned into the living room. There, he collapsed to the floor, panting and swiping blood out of his eyes.

Just beyond Baby-Face, Cooke noticed the girl.

Cross-legged on the floor, surrounded by markings like the

ones outside, a small, blonde, freckle-cheeked girl sat perfectly still with her eyes closed. Though he heard nothing, her lips were in constant motion. *She's casting a spell*, he realized—and suddenly, the weirdness of the last few minutes made perfect sense. *This witch used familiars to kill Barnes and trash my storehouse!*

"Hey!" he shouted. "Hey, you! What the hell are you doing!?"

The witch continued chanting, eyes closed, palms up, as if she hadn't heard him.

Cooke scrunched up his face in fury. "Shoot her," he ordered Stubble-Jaw.

The guy gave him a worried glance. "You sure?"

"Did I stutter?" he yelled. "Shoot that bitch!"

With a resolute sigh, Stubble-Jaw took aim. Cooke returned his gaze to the girl, eagerly waiting for the shot that would drop this would-be thief.

Instead, from behind him, he heard a growl.

He and Stubble-Jaw whirled around simultaneously, only to be confronted with glowing red eyes and a muzzle stained with dripping blood. Shadowy and huge, the animal stalked its way toward them like a living nightmare.

With a nauseated gulp, Cooke realized it was standing between them and the door.

48   Ishak

FUMING WITH VENGEFUL RAGE, ISHAK ADVANCED ON HIS prey with his teeth bared. Cooke, rank with fear, backed away down the hall until his shoes were soaked in Barnes's blood.

The other man, however, stood his ground and aimed his gun right between Ishak's eyes.

Ishak ignored him. The gunman didn't know it yet, but he was already dead.

"Sh-shoot it," Cooke stammered as he backed away. "Shoot the damn thing already!"

The guard set his jaw and stared down the length of his handgun—then lurched and dropped the weapon. As the gun slipped from his fingers and clattered into the gore at his feet, his arms dropped limp to his sides, his eyes glazed over.

Dumbstruck, Cooke stared at his employee, now slumped forward with his head bowed low, like a marionette dangling from its strings.

Ishak's inhuman vision allowed him to see what Cooke could not: the Valkyrie. Delia stood with her hand gripping the back of the gunman's neck and her sword deep in his chest. A wry smile played on her lips as she tightened her grip on the hilt, her eyes dancing.

"I've often wondered what effect this would have on the living," she said.

In one liquid motion, she removed the sword from his chest and gave his body a brisk shake. The gunman's body trembled its way downward, inch by inch, until it was facedown on the bloody floor, but the soul—identical to the body but for its transparency—remained in Delia's grasp, its expression befuddled. With a flick of her wrist, she used her sword to sever the ghostly silver thread that tied spirit and flesh together. The body went limp—eyes still open, heart still beating, chest still rising and falling with shallow breaths, but entirely void of self.

Looking at Cooke—staring, mouth agape, at the comatose man—Ishak felt pain and fury flood his veins. This man was standing here, alive and useless, while Kalilah was dead.

Snarling, he lunged forward, smacked Cooke onto his back, and planted one paw squarely on his chest. The broker screamed, punching and kicking at his captor, but Ishak barely felt the blows. Finally, he leaned into the foot on Cooke's chest, applying more and more pressure until he squeezed every last speck of air from his lungs.

"You," Ishak said, nose to nose with his prey, "took everything from me. I'm here to repay you."

Silent and trembling, Cooke stared up at him with the mortal dread of a man with his head on the block.

49 Delia & Senji

The disembodied soul dangling from Delia's hand stared down at its still-breathing husk. By stabbing a living man, she had divided body and soul without damaging him physically. It fascinated her.

Focus, Delia! Where's the other one?

Other one? She turned to look behind her.

The other guard. Through her eyes, Senji saw the young man scrambling toward the back door. *There.*

Ah. Shall I?

I have him. Senji flew around the house, dove through the back door, and shot himself at the man's head, shrieking a battle cry. The moment Senji got his talons into his skin, the guard threw himself facedown on the floor, covering his head and flailing blindly.

Delia dropped the older guard's spirit, letting the soul drift down to the floor like an autumn leaf falling from a tree. He whispered something, half a question, half a prayer,

but he didn't look at her as he settled to the floor next to his body.

Facedown on the floor, crying, the younger guard began crawling toward the exit.

I can't stop him, Senji said, annoyed. *He'll reach the door at this rate. He's yours.*

325

He managed to climb to his knees before Delia plunged her sword through his back.

As its silver point emerged from his chest, the young man's eyes slid shut and his head bobbed. She grabbed the boy by the neck as she retracted her blade. Then, with a quick yank of her arm, she pulled his soul from his body. The spirit stared in astonishment as she let his body drop

and cut the thread that bound him to it.

Senji peered into the hall. Ishak was still there, leaning so close to Cooke's face that Barnes's blood dripped from his jaws onto his chin. He seemed to be talking to his quivering prey through snarls.

What should we do now? Delia asked, drumming her fingers on her sword hilt.

Wait, I suppose, Senji said. He took flight and alighted on her shoulder. *I was hoping for more action.*

326

Yeah. Delia looked at Georgette. Her spell had gathered so much power that the room crackled with energy. *It won't be long now. I'll make a sweep of the perimeter.*

I'll stay here and keep an eye on things.

Delia turned to go but was stopped by the young guard's spirit.

"What happened?" he wept, his transparent cheeks streaked by ghostly tears. "Am I dead?"

"Your body is still alive," she replied, "but you can't return to it."

The spirit's lip trembled, his eyes darting wildly between Delia and his husk.

Delia exchanged an annoyed look with Senji.

They usually catch on quicker than this.

The spirit rocked back and forth on his heels. "Why did you do this to me?"

She cocked her head. This
boy was so naive, so unsure,
so fragile. In him, she saw
every serviceman she had
treated as a nurse, all those
she had patched up, all
those she had seen expire.

In him, he saw every airman
he had served with, all
those he had welcomed
home, all those he had
never seen again.

She felt a flash of pity. But
only a flash.

"I didn't do this to you, son.
Your employer sells
children. I'm here to exact
justice. You're collateral
damage." She walked on,
stepping through his spirit-
form as if he were not there.
"Watch your employer's
end and decide for yourself
if you got such a raw deal."

Senji watched the young man's spirit sink to its knees, racked with sobs. He watched the other guard's soul lie still next to his body, eyes eerily blank. He watched Delia calmly leave the house. And he watched as Ishak enacted his final revenge.

50 Ishak

ISHAK PINNED COOKE TO THE FLOOR WITH HIS FOREFOOT, glaring down at him. The blood already on the floor seeped into the man's clothes, turning his blue shirt a sticky purple. The stench—death mingled with Cooke's fear—was not as satisfying as he had hoped. Still, he was determined to do right by his wife in the only way he now could.

Their eyes met for an instant, but Cooke immediately looked away, glancing first at his fallen security guard and then toward the living room, where Georgette quietly chanted her spell.

"Miss!" Cooke shouted. "Miss! Let's talk! Call off your familiar!"

"I am no one's familiar," Ishak growled.

The broker frantically looked him over, his twitchy eyes searching for something. Suddenly, his expression shifted from alarm to recognition.

"You're a Werehyena!" he said. "Like the other one!"

Ishak summoned a rumble from deep in his throat, a primal vibration that made Cooke flinch. Even then, however, he didn't blubber or beg as Barnes had. Though Ishak smelled fear, the man seemed to be in full command of his reactions.

"She's not here," Cooke said. "I-I sold her. She's at Nocturne, downtown. If you go there—"

"She's dead," Ishak said.

"Oh," Cooke mumbled. "That's . . . unfortunate. I-I warned that woman, the club owner, that she was in a fragile condition—"

"Lies," Ishak said. He shifted his weight, applying more pressure to Cooke's chest. "You sold her," he spat, "with an infection and severe blood loss." He flexed his toes until his claws dug into Cooke's skin. "Instead of getting her proper care, you gave up and sold her, knowing she would die." He curled his lips, enjoying the sight of his fully exposed teeth reflecting in Cooke's wide eyes. "Her life meant less to you than a few dollars."

He felt Cooke's heart racing through the pads of his foot. The broker's lips were moving, fighting to form words despite having no breath with which to do so. His eyes began to roll back into his head.

Too soon. Ishak shifted his weight to his other side, allowing his prey to breathe again. *Kalilah suffered longer than this. So should he.*

"Business," Cooke rasped, his voice as raw as meat on the bone. "Just business."

The words sparked a mad fury in Ishak, overwhelming every inch of his body until he felt like one huge, electrified nerve. He snapped his teeth inches from Cooke's face.

"Her death was 'just business' to you?"

"Yes," Cooke said. His body had been so starved of oxygen that the scent of his fear was muted, though still present. "Cost analysis is part of the job. If I don't make a profit, I can't feed my family." As his breathing steadied, the broker managed to look Ishak in the eye. Much to his disgust, Ishak couldn't help but be impressed with the man's self-control. "I didn't build the system," he said, sounding weary and defeated, "and I don't make the rules."

It occurred to Ishak that Cooke might very well believe what he was saying. Selling familiars was a lucrative international business. Thousands of employees worldwide relied on it for their livelihood, just as witches everywhere had spent generations pouring their money into it. While it was likely that he was putting on a show to save his life, it was equally likely that Cooke really did see himself as just one piece of a larger whole. Either way, it didn't matter.

"You sell intelligent beings," Ishak replied. "You sell children." Seething, he reapplied his weight to Cooke's chest, forcefully deflating his lungs again. "You raped Kalilah and sold her, bleeding and infected, to a night club, knowing full well that she would die."

Despite his lack of air, Cooke looked confused. Shaking his head, he tapped the foot holding him down—not as a man fighting for his life but as one person trying to get another's attention.

The bizarre change in his prey stirred Ishak's curiosity. Watching Cooke closely, he lifted his foot again. Cooke inhaled deeply as he held up one finger, requesting a moment to catch his breath.

"No one raped her," he panted. "Stock in her condition is strictly off-limits until post-delivery."

Ishak shook his head. "Condition?"

"Yes. She was nearly halfway along when Barnes brought her to us. I separated her from the other merchandise to keep her safe."

"Safe!" Ishak roared. "She was gushing blood from between her legs!"

"From the birth," Cooke gulped out. "Not rape."

"Birth?" In context of the moment, the word sounded eerily foreign. "What are you talking about?"

"I always give the ones that come to us pregnant extra care," Cooke explained. "A healthy baby is worth a lot more than a sickly one, and a mother that dies in childbirth is worth nothing."

"Baby." The word flew wild about his mind for several long swoops until it finally perched. *Is it true?* he asked himself. *Was Kalilah pregnant?* "Baby?"

"The birth seemed to go well," Cooke babbled on, his voice growing fuzzy in Ishak's ears. "It wasn't until we saw how heavily she was bleeding that we realized there had been complications. By then, sepsis had already gotten ahold of her."

"Baby," Ishak repeated mindlessly. He wobbled and fell back onto his haunches. Staring off into space, he racked his brain. *If she was halfway along when she came to them, she must have been pregnant before we were abducted by Kivuli Panon. Then . . . it's my child.*

"We wanted to help her," Cooke said. "We did the best we could, but we don't have a witch on staff. We couldn't save her. But we did protect the health of the baby."

Ishak vaguely felt himself swaying from side to side, as listless as a drunk. *Kalilah had a baby. Kalilah had our baby.* The darkness that had shrouded his future when he watched Kalilah die lifted, chased out by a rising light. *I have a—*

"Baby," he said—firmer, louder, this time.

Taking advantage of his distraction, the broker had shimmied his way out from under him and was sliding his way toward the front door. When Ishak locked eyes with him, however, he froze.

"Where is the baby?" Ishak demanded.

"Upstairs," Cooke said nervously. "Healthy, full term."

Ishak's eyes darted to the ceiling, his entire body tense and alert. *Kalilah's made me a father and our child is here.* Lively fire filled his soul. A part of Kalilah still lived. Still lived and needed him. Having a purpose made him feel weightless. He wanted to fly from this house, away from the blood, with his child safe in his arms.

"Boy or girl?" Ishak asked.

"What?"

"The baby," he bellowed, startling Cooke. "Boy or girl?"

Blinking rapidly, Cooke opened his mouth but only sputtered nonsense. Suddenly, Ishak realized he didn't want him to answer. Kalilah was gone. This was the only child they would ever have. He didn't want this slaver to be the one to tell him if he had a son or daughter. He didn't want that man's voice in his head for the rest of his life.

Ishak slammed a huge paw into the side of Cooke's head, hurling his body ass over elbows. The broker skidded in Barnes's blood until he thudded against the far wall and his body crumpled to the floor. Though his eyes continued to follow Ishak's every move, he didn't budge an inch. He opened his mouth, looking like he wanted to scream, but no sound escaped.

Broken neck, Ishak guessed. *I wonder if he still feels pain. Ah well,* he thought with a smile, *no matter. Better to honor Kalilah's memory by raising our child than through torture.*

Ishak put his bloody foot on Cooke's head and applied all his weight until he heard and felt the skull crunch.

51  Georgette

THE SPELL GEORGETTE CHANTED FILLED THE HOUSE LIKE water, muffling sound and distorting sight as if she sat on the bottom of a swimming pool. The magic she'd gathered was nearly ready, but it was also oppressive. The weight of it pressed against her skin, relentlessly hugging every inch of her body until it was hard to breathe. If she had to chant much longer, the spell might crush her lungs—but if she missed even a single beat, the magic would dissipate, and all her work would be for nothing.

So, lightheaded and nauseated, she carried on.

Every muscle in her body ached, but she was so close. Another few minutes, maybe even less than that, and the house would be full from foundation to rooftop. Then all she had to do was recite the final incantation. *I've got this, I've got this, I've got this.*

Oh, indeed! chuckled a voice in her head. *Can't you feel how drained you are? That's what happens when you work above your skill level. Honestly,* the voice scoffed, *what made you think you could handle a spell this size? You're embarrassing yourself. God, how did such a weakling come from me?*

Her mother's judgmental comments, even when they were

only in her head, always sent a painful sizzle through Georgette's nerve endings. At every other time in her life before now, it would have been enough to break her concentration entirely. But she wasn't that girl anymore.

She plunged ahead with her spell, determined to finish what she'd started.

A wave of dizziness swept over her. Her head bobbed and her eyes rolled. A teaspoon of vomit leaped into her mouth. The acidic taste made her gag, snapping her to attention.

Cringing, she swallowed it and forged on.

Almost. Almost. Just . . . one . . . more . . . minute.

Faintly, she heard a crash, followed by a wet crunch. *That's the broker, Cooke,* she thought. *Ishak's killed him.* She was relieved. That was one less living body she had to transport. With Cooke dead, she could flip the switch on this spell a tad earlier.

"S'time," she said. Her tongue felt heavy and unresponsive, like a slab of meat on a butcher's block. Though she could hardly hear her own words, she felt how badly she was slurring them. "Le's go."

Immediately, her cloudy vision filled with black feathers and silver armor. Delia and Senji knelt nearby, well inside the circle she'd drawn on the floor. A moment later, she heard two loud thumps, one to either side of her, followed by an influx of body heat that warmed her back; Ishak was close behind her.

"Hurry," the Bultungin said in her ear. His voice was lively, excited. "I have so much more to do."

Georgette drew a deep breath into her strained lungs. The magic was all around, compressed and thick and charged with her purpose. Tired and shaky, she spread her fingers and pressed their tips together, summoning all the energy she could from her core and forming it into one concentrated, apple-size ball. That ball spun like a top between her palms, crackling with electric sparks.

This is it.

She yanked her hands apart, and the ball fired into the room like a bullet.

The magic orb broke through the fabric of reality, boring a tunnel through space and time. As it ripped its way along the path Georgette had set, it pulled her gathered magic in its wake. The energy in the house began to pour outward, draining from the rooftop down and flowing through the tunnel at a breakneck pace. Obeying the instructions laid down by Georgette's spell-craft, it seized hold of every living thing it touched—Ishak, Georgette, and every Fae child held in suspended animation—and yanked them toward the tunnel.

As the spell lifted them off the floor, Georgette felt her *Hathiya* mark also snatch up Delia and Senji and pull them along.

They sailed through the air and into the tunnel as if swept up by a raging river. Georgette felt tingling ripples go through her as the spell distorted her size and mass to make her fit through the small opening.

The journey through the portal was a maelstrom of color and wind-whistles that whipped about and pressed in on her so intensely that she didn't dare breathe. Several times, she felt Ishak's fur brush over her skin, saw flashes of Valkyrie silver, and heard muffled raven squawks; hundreds of boxes, sealed by magic, rode the spell along with them.

Desperate to close her eyes, Georgette fought to stay alert. It was almost done.

Slick with magic, she slipped cleanly from the tunnel, returned to her proper size, and landed in the Botanica with a thud. The boxes from the Silver Creek house rained down around her, their edges and corners punching and scraping her skin. She was so numb with exhaustion that she made no move to protect herself; all she could do was lie on the cold floor, inhaling the dizzying scent of herbs that filled the shop.

She only barely registered it when Ishak stepped over her, his hyena body shielding her from the onslaught. Over his shoulder, she dimly saw the tunnel's opening on the ceiling, an apple-sized, pulsating hole with boxes still pouring from its inner depths, returning to their true size as they exited the tunnel and dropped down to the floor.

The kids are okay, she told herself. *The containers keep them safe. They'll sleep until we can release them.*

The cascade of boxes finally ceased. Ishak stepped away and Delia moved into view, Senji on her shoulder, their heads craned upward toward the ceiling.

"Is that all?" Delia asked. "Is everyone through?"

Straining, Georgette stretched out her senses. Most of her magic had flowed through the tunnel with them and dissipated after carrying all the passengers to their destination, but residual spellcraft still coated the Silver Creek house like the silt left behind after a flood. Even so far away, she felt it and everything it touched.

"Ev'one's through," she whispered.

"Let's finish it then," the Valkyrie said.

Georgette initiated the last part of the spell. The flow of the tunnel reversed. In the house, she felt the magic residue shift in essence, awakening from its dormant state, and growing volatile. She looked at Delia and nodded.

Helmet in one hand and sword in the other, the Valkyrie placed the flat of her blade on her gleaming headpiece and, with a horrific sound, scraped them against each other. Golden sparks sprang from the metal, whipped through the air, and soared into the tunnel.

Fatigue sucked the last remaining energy from Georgette's bones and she went limp on the floor. Her eyelids fluttered shut and her head lolled to the side as her consciousness began to fade. In her final moment before losing touch with the world, she heard a crackle and smelled a whiff of smoke.

52  Mei-Xing

UPON ARRIVING AT THE BOTANICA, MEI-XING HAD TO CLIMB and push through a pile of brown shoeboxes to get past the threshold. The boxes were everywhere, cluttering the floor, shelves, and countertops. She also saw what appeared to be two human bodies underneath the boxes. It took her aback, but since neither Ishak nor Delia seemed to care, she ignored them.

Sprawled out on the floor of the Botanica, Georgette was cut and bruised, her breathing shallow. Mei-Xing rushed to her side, and found her pulse distressingly slow.

"Georgette!" she shouted, shaking her.

Georgette didn't respond.

"Is she okay?" Mei-Xing asked frantically, wiping blood from her friend's cheeks.

"She's fine," Delia said, standing by the door. "Just sleeping. The spell drained her strength."

At the far end of the shop, Ishak, in his human form, examined the boxes one by one. Like Georgette, he was bloodied and battered, but when Mei-Xing offered to clean him up, he curtly refused and continued digging through the boxes. She wondered what he was up to but, busy with Georgette, she opted not to ask.

Delia peered out the window at the dark street. "How long until they arrive?"

"I don't know," Mei-Xing said.

"But the river agreed to deliver the message?"

"Yes."

Delia glanced back at her, one eyebrow cocked. "Will they come?"

Mei-Xing met her gaze. "How could they not?"

Ishak's constant shuffling came to an abrupt stop. Mei-Xing looked his way—and saw that he was frozen in place, a box in his hands. He seemed to be reading the label.

"It's a girl," he whispered. "A girl."

"Ishak?"

He whirled around, and there was a strange light dancing in his eyes—an eager, joyful light. Mei-Xing found it startling. In the short time she had known him, she'd never seen Ishak happy.

The Bultungin held up the box. "It's a girl!" He let out a loud whoop, then held the box up in front of his face. "How do I open this?"

Mei-Xing shook her head. "I don't know."

Ishak fumbled with the box, trying without success to re-move the lid. "It's as solid as a brick." He scanned it carefully. "No hinges, no lock." He turned his excited gaze to Delia. "Can you open it?"

"I don't know what effect my sword would have on the box," the Valkyrie replied. "To be safe, it would be best to wait for the witch to wake up. She'll be able to open it."

"But I have to meet her."

"You will," Delia said. "She's in your hands, where she belongs." The Valkyrie's face softened, and she offered him a kindly smile. "Your daughter is safe. Let her sleep for now."

Daughter? Before Mei-Xing could ask anything, her eye was drawn by Delia suddenly straightening up.

"Senji says they're coming."

"How many?"

Delia grinned. "He's already lost count."

53   Georgette

GEORGETTE AWOKE FEELING GROGGY, UNRESTED, AND SORE. Groaning, she pushed herself up, straightened her glasses, and looked around the room.

The Botanica was packed.

There were so many individuals of so many species of Fae surrounding her that her tired brain reeled at the sight. Fairies, Elemental Spirits, Nymphs of every kind . . . and so many more. They moved through the shop, elbow to elbow, chattering noisily, as they edged past each other and between the shelves. A petite Faun woman stepped over Georgette, still sprawled on the floor, on thin, hoofed legs. In her hands, Georgette saw a stack of boxes. She clopped her way to the open door, where she handed the boxes to a squat, pointy-eared Goblin.

Feeling something on her leg, Georgette glanced down. One of the boxes was in her lap. The witch squinted, trying to read the label through cracked and smudged glasses. Werehyena, female, newborn. *A newborn Bultungin?* she thought, brow furrowed. *Does that mean—*

"You're awake!"

Georgette turned her head to see unglamoured Mei-Xing pushing her way through the crowd. The Nymph threw her arms around her friend.

"How long was I asleep?" Georgette asked. Her own voice sounded thunderous in her head; the sound emphasized the pounding in her skull.

"Not long," Mei-Xing said. She cupped Georgette's face in her hands and brushed her cheeks with mossy fingers. "How do you feel?"

"Everything hurts." Georgette looked up at the ceiling to where she had last seen the tunnel. It was gone. In its place, a Jorogumo, six of her spindly eight legs holding on to the ceiling, was accepting boxes from Fae on the floor and passing them out the door. "Did I mess it up?" she asked. "Did I pass out too soon?"

"No," said Delia's voice.

Georgette turned her head to the right and found the Valkyrie standing above her.

"The children are here, and the house is in ashes," Delia assured her. "You saw it through to the end."

For a blissful moment, a sunny warmth filled Georgette and all her pain washed away. *I did it! I got it right!* She looked around again at the dozens of Fae sorting through boxes, reading labels, calling out the species of children within, and handing them off to those waiting outside. *These children won't be sold,* she thought, tears creeping into her eyes. *They're going home.*

Mei-Xing helped Georgette to her feet. Her legs wobbled like overcooked noodles and the Nymph had to hold her up, but she didn't loosen her grip on the baby Bultungin box for a second.

"Can you use your magic?" Mei-Xing asked.

"Do I have to?" Georgette sighed.

"Everyone here"—Delia gestured to the lively crowd—"came for the children, to take them home. But no one can get the boxes open. Can you do it?"

Georgette's muscles screamed at her to refuse. The bruises and fresh scabs on her arms throbbed, reminding her of how much she had already done that night. *Do I even have the strength to do this?*

Then she looked through the front door and saw, to her amazement, that the street in front of the shop was mobbed with Fae. Many were just milling around, their arms full of their imprisoned children. *They can't go home yet*, she realized. *Having the children means nothing if they aren't free.*

"I'll do it," she said.

"Are you sure?" Mei-Xing's iridescent eyes shimmering with concern.

"It's okay," Georgette said. "The spell on brokerage containers is pretty simple. I can break it easily." *At first, anyway*, she thought. *But after I do it a thousand times, I'm gonna be a mess.* She held up the box in her hands. "She's Ishak and Kalilah's?"

Mei-Xing nodded.

Georgette smiled. "Where is he now?"

"He took the two comatose guards to Club Nocturne," Delia said. "He said he had a debt to pay."

"He left his daughter with you," Mei-Xing added, "for when you woke up."

"Sure," Georgette said. "That's fine." She took a deep breath, exhaled it slowly. Then she nodded at the crowd. "Let's get started."

54  Nicolás

WHEN GEORGETTE HAD CALLED NICO EARLIER IN THE evening, she'd been vague about why she needed to use the shop. Though he'd eventually agreed, hours later, their interaction wasn't sitting well with him—especially now that she wasn't responding to his texts.

So he went to the shop.

She had promised that the Botanica wouldn't be damaged. After walking in from the back entrance and looking around at the state of the shop, it was clear to Nico that she hadn't kept that promise.

Boxes. Brown shoeboxes with handwritten labels piled all over the floor and countertops. Boxes blocking the herbs, boxes where the candles should be, boxes on top of the saint figurines, and, presumably via magic, boxes floating through the air. Hundreds of boxes.

Through the front windows, he saw Georgette seated on the curb outside, a heap of open boxes surrounding her. A steady stream of closed boxes kept floating through the air and landing in her lap. Nico couldn't see what she was doing—her back was to him—but within seconds of getting a box, she tossed it aside, empty.

Nico stepped into the center of the Botanica and scanned the shop. The air was laden with magic—it was as thick and gummy as pudding. Faint undulations in the air glided around the store and the sidewalk out front like concentrated mirages. He squinted at them and tilted his head back and forth, trying to pull a solid image from the distorted air. Unable to do so, he grunted in frustration and headed toward the front entrance, carefully avoiding the moving boxes, intent on confronting Georgette.

Before he got to the threshold, something came in through the door from outside. At first glance, he saw an upright, walking log covered in patches of moss and long grass. Blinking rapidly, he forced his eyes to focus closer on the log so his brain could assemble the details. It was a person . . . sort of. A better description was that it was a human-shaped being with two mossy arms, two bark-covered legs, and a head covered in grass and sprouts. Within the brown and green face, he saw two eyes shimmering like rainbows on an oil slick.

"Nico García," the being said in an accented voice. "Hello again."

The soft, choppy voice was familiar, but he couldn't immediately place it while looking into the alien face. A moment later, it clicked. "Mei-Xing?"

She nodded, sending the long grasses on her scalp waving and rustling. "Why you here?"

"I work here!" he exclaimed, agitated by her nonchalance. "What the hell is going on?"

The bark on her face constricted, making her face thinner. "What you mean?"

"The boxes? The . . . air things . . . I don't know what they are!" Seeing a Nymph unglamoured for the first time ever only added to his confusion and alarm. "I need to talk to Georgette."

Mei-Xing glanced in her friend's direction and then looked back at Nico. "She busy," she said. "She open boxes."

"What the hell's in these?" he shouted.

He snatched up a box from the floor and grabbed at the lid. He was stunned to find that it wouldn't budge. It looked ordinary enough but, try as he might, he couldn't make a dent in it. He shoved it toward Mei-Xing.

"What's in these?" he demanded.

"Fae children," she told him.

Startled, he looked at the box again. Now cooler-headed, he felt the magic vibrating through it. He read the label aloud: "Centaur, male, age eight." Staring at the description, he was caught off guard by the sudden touch of his spirit allies. In their wordless voices, Nico heard them urging him to let it be, to let the *bruja* work.

He drew a deep breath but couldn't settle his nerves. It was the first time the spirits had ever spoken to him without being summoned.

"Children," he said. "Why?"

"For sale at broker house," Mei-Xing explained, taking the Centaur box from him. "We steal, give back to Fae."

At her words, Nico's senses twitched, forcibly expanding in a manner he had only experienced before under the influence of a deliriant. Bizarre colors and shapes popped into his vision, quickly taking form.

From one of those weird air ripples, a tall woman emerged. Surprised as he was to see her and her naked breasts appear out of nowhere, Nico was more surprised to see that her human torso was connected to a pair of hairy goat legs. On her head, half-hidden by her wild brown hair, he also saw two curved horns, each one a foot long. She approached the door with several boxes in her arms, her goatish eyes—blue with horizontal, rectangular pupils—sweeping over Nico. From her human lips came a sharp bleat that made him jump.

A moment passed in silence, then she snorted and repeated the sound.

Mei-Xing took Nico's arm and gently pulled him aside. Stunned, he didn't resist. Once he was out of her path, the Faun woman stepped through the door, her cloven hooves clicking on the floor.

Dazed and awestruck, Nico followed her.

During his *curandero* training, Nico had experienced many things. He'd learned how to recognize when a person had been bewitched and how best to help. He had projected his astral-self through unseen realms, he had conversed with spirits, and he had formed bonds with otherworldly creatures. So much of his life was outside of the ordinary that he had become comfortable with the bizarre. But nothing in his life had prepared him for what he saw outside the Botanica's front door.

In the street, stretching for an entire city block, was a crowd that would rival any masquerade carnival on earth.

The first thing he saw was a beastly looking man-creature with enormous teeth protruding from its mouth and many horns on its head. There was also a large eagle, its gray and blue wings crackling with sparks, perched on the streetlamp across from the shop, a box held in its beak. An ugly old woman with pendulous breasts stood near Georgette, her sagging arms covered in a fog of gray hair. A dog-like thing with ape hands stood behind the crone, swishing tiny glowing Fairies away from its rump with the hand growing out of its tail. A huge, bulbous shadow loomed over everything, its glowing satellite-dish eyes looking down on the crowd.

"Holy hell," Nico whispered. His last lingering concern about the Botanica vanished. Far from worrying about what his aunt would say when she saw the mess, he wished she was here to guide him. She was the only one he knew who might help him process this experience.

Mei-Xing called out a string of foreign words and held a box up in the air. Nico caught his breath at the sight of a bare-chested man approaching the Nymph, his waist disappearing into the body of a dappled gray horse. Mei-Xing handed the Centaur the box and exchanged a few words with him, after which the Centaur bowed his head. Then he trotted up to Georgette, pushed aside a tortoiseshell creature with a large dent in its skull, and plopped the box onto the witch's lap. Georgette, without a glance at the Centaur, mechanically raised two fingers to her lips, blew a pale green light onto the tips, and then tapped the box. The green glow flashed bright and the lid popped open like a jack-in-the-box.

Nico heard a soft *whoosh* and saw a flurry of color fly out of the open box. He blinked, and just like that, there was a young Centaur standing by the adult, the boy's head barely reaching the other's elbow. Crying, the child held his arms up to cover his face and rocked his human half back and forth until the grown Centaur put a hand on his shoulder. The boy flinched but then looked up and gasped with relief. With a kindly smile, the Centaur leaned down and spoke to the child.

"What's he saying?" Nico asked Mei-Xing.

"He ask what herd boy from," she said. She turned and headed back into the Botanica. "He say he take boy home."

Nico looked out over the crowd, at all the creatures and all the boxes they held. He looked back through the shop window at all the boxes still inside. *Each one is a child,* he thought. *My God, there are so many.*

His eyes drifted back to Georgette, who was working with the steady rhythm of a factory machine. For the first time, he noticed how sickly she appeared. Like a candle left sitting in the sun, she seemed melted, droopy, and spent. Behind her glasses, her eyes were glazed. Swimming in a sea of psychedelic weirdness, he zeroed in on her as the one familiar aspect of the night he could latch on to. He took a seat beside her on the curb.

"You okay?" he asked.

"Busy," she mumbled.

He put a hand on her shoulder. Very little body heat came from her skin. She tossed the two halves of her most recently opened box aside as another creature dropped a closed one in her lap.

"You should rest," he told her.

"Busy," she repeated, her tone weary and mechanical.

"You don't look great."

"Hafta finish," she said. "Important."

Nico sighed. Yes, it clearly was important. If she wanted to work herself sick, there wasn't much he could do to stop her. He certainly wasn't going to physically remove her from the spot— not when all these beings, many of them terrifying to look at, were waiting for her help. He squeezed her shoulder again. "Okay."

"What the hell, man?"

Jolted, Nico leaped to his feet and whirled around. Through a mingling group of Fae, Nico saw someone—someone human—standing in front of the store. He couldn't see the guy's face through the crowd, but he knew the voice.

"Neil?"

The group of Fae walked ahead until Nico clearly saw Neil's face—which was twisted up with an unmistakable mixture of hurt and fury. He glanced down at Georgette; stock still, she was looking at Neil through wide, horrified eyes.

"What the hell?" Neil asked again. He pointed at Georgette and then at Nico as he stepped forward. "You gonna try to tell me this is a therapy session?"

"Neil, come on, man," Nico sputtered. He waved his hands around, gesturing at the Fae. "You can see—"

No, he can't see, he realized, his stomach sinking low. *He can't see any of it. All he sees is me sitting on the curb with his girlfriend.*

Tears leaked from Georgette's eyes as she tried to rise, a still-closed box sliding from her lap. "Neil!" she cried. "I didn't . . . I wouldn't . . ."

"I knew something was wrong," Neil said to her. Shaking his head, he put a hand over his face. Behind the hand, Nico saw his jaw tighten and tremble. "Why did you do this?"

"It's not like that," Nico said calmly. "I came to check on the store. She's here to help . . . her community."

"My ass." Neil glared at him with such vitriol that it made Nico physically uncomfortable. "Dammit, you're the last person—how could you do this?"

Georgette's sob cut him off. Tearing up, Neil turned away. Nico looked down at the witch. She was curled up in a ball, her face in her knees, sobbing.

Ignoring her distress, a male Fae, ape-like and naked but for his dirty fur, kept grunting and trying to push a box at her.

"You've got it wrong, Neil," Nico insisted, though he felt his argument losing steam. Neil couldn't see what they saw, and there was no way to describe it without sounding insane. "You're projecting your anger at Lyndsey onto Georgette."

Neil snapped his head around, his expression pure rage, and rushed at Nico. Bracing for a punch, Nico held up his hands to protect himself, eyes squeezed shut. But the punch never came.

Nico eased his eyes back open. Neil had stopped short and was staring at something over Nico's shoulder, mesmerized.

Mei-Xing—the only Fae on the street visible to the average eye—was walking toward them, one hand out, a trumpet-shaped white flower growing from her palm. Though her inhuman features made her expression a mystery, Nico sensed anger.

"Make her cry," she hissed. "Bad man."

Though he doubted Neil had even noticed the plant sprouting from the Nymph's hand, Nico recognized it at once. It was on the tip of his tongue to stop her—but without knowing exactly why, he clamped his mouth shut.

Mei-Xing ground the plant between her wooden palms. "You hurt her," she spat at a flabbergasted Neil. "I show you."

She opened her hand and blew the *datura* powder into Neil's face.

The dust flew into his wide eyes and gaping mouth. Caught by surprise, Neil did exactly what Nico expected: he drew in a sharp breath, pulling the loose powder into his lungs. Nico scampered out of the way of the dispersing cloud and caught only a tiny whiff of its sickly-sweet odor as he escaped.

Coughing, Neil stumbled back and bumped into the Botanica's front window. Nico jumped forward and caught him before he fell.

"The hell?" he sputtered. "What was . . ."

Neil's voice drifted away as his pupils dilated. His arms flopped to his sides and his legs went out from under him, leaving him limp in Nico's arms.

"You might feel your heart racing," Nico said, lowering Neil to the sidewalk, "or your muscles spasming. You also might feel like time is moving in weird ways. More importantly"—he held Neil's head up, directing his face to the Fae crowd—"you're going to see things you couldn't see before." He leaned in and spoke directly into Neil's ear. "You're not hallucinating. What you're seeing right here is *real*."

Still holding Neil's head, Nico felt electricity from the spreading *datura* flow through Neil's sweaty skin. Though he couldn't see through Neil's eyes, he sensed his friend's perspective shifting.

A trio of squat, green-skinned Goblins in baggy black robes stepped over Neil's twitching legs. Neil yanked his feet out of their way and slurred, "*Ssshhhiiittt*. Who're . . . I . . . are they *people?*"

Nico glanced at Georgette, who was now sobbing into Mei-Xing's shoulder. The Nymph, meanwhile, was clutching her protectively and glaring at Neil.

"They're Fae," Nico told him. "They're here for Georgette's help. See those boxes?" he asked, directing Neil's face to the pile of empties. "They need her to break the magic seal on those to free the Fae children inside. She's a witch, Neil—born with powers it'll take me my whole life to acquire. That's what she was keeping from you." He gave Neil a quick shake. "She's not cheating on you; she's draining herself dry to help others. And you *know* I wouldn't do that to you, MacCana." He smacked the back of Neil's head. "You idiot."

With that, Nico let go of him. Neil fell back against the Botanica's wall—eyes wide, mouth slack, body shivering like he was waist-deep in snow.

Nico looked back over at Georgette and saw the ape-man still shaking his box at her, irritably mumbling and gesturing. Several others in the crowd, waiting just behind him, started to do the same.

The witch, oblivious, continued to press her face into Mei-Xing's mossy shoulder.

A flash of silver burst into the street, and a tall woman in shining, ethereal armor appeared at Georgette's side. The witch didn't react, but Mei-Xing nodded to the warrior woman as Nico looked on in astonishment.

"I already told you," the woman boomed, a bit of a southern accent emerging from her voice, "form a line and *wait your damn turn!*"

All eyes on her, the crowd grumbled, some of them gesturing, others pushing forward. The silver woman pulled a sword and swung it in a wide arc. The glimmering metal sang like a delicate but powerful chime, the vibrations hammering Nico's eardrums.

The crowd fell silent. Slowly, the Fae shuffled back into line.

"She upset, Delia," Mei-Xing said, stroking Georgette's hair. "Bad man hurt her."

The warrior looked down at the pair. "If she needs a break, let her say so," she said. "Otherwise, there are dozens more boxes."

"She's had a nasty shock," Nico jumped in. "She should rest awhile."

Delia looked at him, her eyebrows arched. Nico thought she either hadn't noticed him or was surprised that he would speak to her. "You are?"

"Nico García. My aunt owns this store."

Above Nico's head, a sharp caw broke the air. Startled, he looked up at the awning. A raven peered down at him, the nearby streetlight illuminating its inky feathers and reflecting from its beady eyes. It cocked its head as if examining him, then turned its attention to the silver woman.

"Yes," she said to the bird, "I agree." She leaned down toward Georgette and Mei-Xing. "Siphon off some of my power, mine and Senji's," she said to the witch. "You've done so much tonight, and you never asked to borrow any energy from us. We are strong. Use us."

"Strength not problem," Mei-Xing snapped, cradling Georgette's head. "Bad man problem! He make her cry!" The Nymph pointed in Neil's direction—and her expression transformed into confusion. "Where he go?"

Nico whirled around. Neil was gone. Alarmed, he looked up and down the street. He saw the grousing crowd but no sign of his friend.

Swearing under his breath, he ducked back inside the Botanica. A handful of Fae remained hard at work sorting the boxes of captive children. Neil was not among them.

Nico sighed and rubbed his face. Wandering the streets

under the influence of *datura* was dangerous. *I have to find him.*

When he emerged from the shop, he saw Georgette back at work—still crying quietly, Mei-Xing's arm around her shoulder.

Her face streaked with tears, she discarded an empty box and reached out to receive another.

55 Neil

UNABLE TO SLEEP AFTER GEORGETTE RAN OUT ON THEIR DATE,
Neil stared blankly at the Netflix show playing on his computer,
his brain bombarding him with unhappy memories and unhappier
possibilities. The only break he got from his misery was when
Nico got up around 11 p.m. and surprised him in the living room.

"The hell?" Nico said. "Didn't know you were awake."

"Likewise," Neil muttered, eyes barely budging from the
glow of his laptop screen. "Where you going?"

"The Botanica," he said, pulling on his coat.

"Now?"

"I've got a weird feeling. I'm gonna check it out." Nico gave
Neil a quick nod. "See ya."

It wasn't the first time Nico had left the apartment at a crazy
hour due to a "weird feeling"—but this time, thanks to his sleep-
deprived paranoia, Neil's brain immediately belted him with the
notion that Nico was going out to meet Georgette.

He spent twenty minutes arguing with himself—until, against
his better judgment, he finally closed his laptop, got up off the
sofa, and headed out the door.

Paranoid though he was, Neil wasn't really expecting to find anything but his friend alone in his aunt's shop, checking for a nonexistent burglar. He figured he'd either slink away unseen after verifying that this was the case, or perhaps even talk him into getting a late-night drink.

Finding him with Georgette caught him completely off guard. The moment he saw the two sitting next to one another—Nico's hand on Georgette's shoulder, their heads close together—a tidal wave of emotion overtook him. Feeling betrayed, foolish, and crushed, his emotions exploded and flew uncensored from his mouth.

Only something as strange as the human-shaped thing made of bark and moss could have silenced his brokenhearted rage. Thoughts of Georgette and Nico vanished, replaced by the notion that this creature looked like an animated version of the weird trunk faces he sometimes saw on trees. It was so alien that he just kept staring at it, blinking rapidly, his brain refusing to accept what his eyes saw. Then it advanced on him, calling him a bad man. All he could think was how un-treelike it was behaving as it leaned forward and blew some kind of powder in his face.

As he choked on the powder, the light of the streetlamps became too bright, forcing him to close his eyes, and his entire torso heaved violently with coughs that created air-wobbling vibrations. Confused, he shook his head like a dog, stumbling.

His throat was bone dry. He opened his eyes, looking for something to drink, and realized that he was on the ground. Nico stood over him, saying something about time and muscle spasms, but he couldn't absorb the words. He felt disconnected, like his mind was floating in a bubble.

Neil glanced around, but his eyes refused to stay focused. Georgette was nearby, the tree-creature with her, but they looked like they were made of television static. Perplexed, he tried to speak, but his dehydrated throat wouldn't cooperate.

His eyes suddenly focused and locked onto some small, grotesque green men with long ears and droopy noses passing in front of him. As one stepped over his leg, a jolt of panic went through him, and he yanked his leg back, trying to scramble away.

It was then that he realized there were hundreds of shadowy fairy-tale things on the street. While staring at one, something else—was that a *Centaur?*—popped into the periphery of his vision. His eyes darted to the newly appeared creature, only for it to vanish into shadow again. Heart punching his chest, he felt trapped and surrounded.

He tried speaking again, but all he heard of his own voice was a series of record scratches.

Suddenly, Nico's face filled his vision. Neil saw that he was speaking again, but like before, he had trouble gathering the words together.

"Fae," Neil heard. "Help. Boxes. Magic. Children." Nico directed Neil's gaze to Georgette, still wrapped in a shroud of static. "Witch. Witch. Georgette." He smacked Neil in the back of the head, jostling his vision.

The world of shadow men bounced and bobbed as Neil slumped against the wall.

Witch.

The weird creatures seemed to be staring at him. Some were crying, others laughing, smiling, their mouths full of strange teeth. He shivered. Looking up and down the street, he didn't see any place where he could hide. He glanced up at the sky. A black bird looked down at him, its eyes dripping blood. It squawked—an ear-biting, technicolor sound. Neil cringed and put his hands over his face. His fingers felt metallic and smelled like sulfur.

Goawaygoawaygoawaygoaway—

He opened his eyes and saw that he was walking. The shadow-creatures were gone. Now orange-skinned people walked past him. Many of them had blood leaking from their eyes, streaking down their elongated faces.

Heart racing, he looked down and saw that he was wading through an ankle-deep mass of black-furred animals. He couldn't tell what kind of animals they were, but they looked wet and angry.

Why are they wet? Is it raining?

Desperate for water, Neil turned his head upward. The sides of the buildings breathed in and out, their windows blinking like eyes. Sparkling blue fish swam through the walls high above him. Captivated by their beauty, he watched for a while. Every time he moved his head, the fish image, like an animated GIF, reset and started again.

Magic.

The world skipped, yanking him out of sync with time and space.

As he came back to himself, he was in a new place, his cupped hands full of water. It was pitch black outside—darker than before, and colder. He quickly gulped down the water. Gritty and lukewarm, it barely soothed his parched throat. Still, it was better than nothing. He leaned over the waist-high concrete edge before him, plunged his head underwater, and gulped down as much as he could.

Resurfacing, he found he was surrounded by trees, each one pulsating with ghostly essence. The water he'd taken was from a dead fountain, just a stone basin full of still, dirty water. Too thirsty to be bothered by the filth, he lowered his head to the water and drank deeply a second time.

Echoing, unsettling voices filled the air. Lifting his head, Neil saw creatures with twisty faces, enormous eyes, abnormally long arms, and large feet with newt-like toes flitting about in the trees. The things sprang from branch to branch, as busy as cars on a superhighway. Amazed, Neil felt he was glimpsing through a veil of secrecy—but every time he tried to look at them directly, the faces disappeared, absorbed into the leaves and bark.

Magic.

Dizzy, he closed his eyes, but behind his lids, where there should have been blackness, he saw an entirely new, entirely real scene.

Though he could still feel the concrete fountain with his hands, with his closed eyes he saw himself standing on the side of a desert highway. A rusted parked car on the shoulder honked, startling him. Neil saw something in the car's passenger seat, took a step toward it, and froze, his blood hardening in his veins. It was a pale creature, hairless, with a triangular head that sported large, lidless eyes. Its piercing, malevolent stare tore deep into his soul. The thing had no lips on its red gash of a mouth. It said nothing, only sat in the car and glared at him.

Screaming, Neil opened his eyes.

The creature was gone—but so was the fountain. Trembling,

he put his hands on the step where he now sat, gripping the cold stone edge. Gazing around, he saw plant life growing up through sidewalk cracks, creeping out of streetlamps, and bursting through concrete walls. At some distance, beyond the sprouting forest, he saw steam rising from a pool of dark, nonreflective water. Though he was still parched, Neil felt repulsed by it. Beyond the pool, he saw a large black wolf with search-beam eyes walking along the edge. It was looking at him.

Follow me, its motions conveyed. *I'll show you things.*

From the unseen land beyond the pool, Neil heard wordless voices—crazed, pornographic, murderous. His unwilling eyes saw pulsating silhouettes of human forms in the distance, all of them copulating wildly. Frantic though their movements were, they seemed angry, as though none of them enjoyed what they were doing.

"No," he murmured, on the verge of tears, "I don't wanna see anymore."

It gestured again. *Come with me.*

"Go away," he cried.

A pair of hands took him by the shoulders and shook him firmly. Tearing his eyes from the circling wolf, Neil turned to see Nico standing over him.

"Did you see it?" he asked, breathless.

"Time to go."

Neil stared out at the steamy pond, at the wolf pacing back and forth in the darkness. He was somehow able to see every individual hair on its sinewy body.

"I'm scared!" he sobbed, quaking with horror. "Where did these things come from?"

"They've always been here," Nico said. "It's you who doesn't belong."

When Neil looked again, it wasn't Nico with him but a tall woman, white and luminous as the moon. A crown of green vines writhed around her head, trumpet-like flowers blooming and fading from the dark leaves. Shining gray eyes watched him as her silver lips parted.

"You're trespassing," she said.

Her voice was authoritative but sounded well-intentioned. It calmed him.

"What should I do?" he asked, wiping away his tears.

"Leave," she commanded.

Drawn to her, Neil reached out to touch that shimmery skin. An inch from her, he stopped. She had become a still image painted on tall grass.

"Don't come here again," she commanded.

"Never," he agreed. "I just wanna go home."

"We *are* home, dipshit."

Neil blinked rapidly. He was on the sofa in his apartment. Jumping to his feet, Neil scanned the living room. The wolf and the lady were gone.

Nico came out of the kitchen with a glass of water. Neil seized it and downed the liquid in two huge gulps. It was clean, cold, and absolutely amazing.

"Oh, thank God," he gasped.

"Jesus Christ," Nico mumbled, rolling his eyes. "Sit down. I'll get more."

With a huge sigh, Neil plopped down on the sofa. He felt much better. "I don't remember coming home."

"Not surprising," he heard Nico say over the sound of running water. "*Datura* screws with your perception."

"*Datura.*" The word felt smoky and exotic in his mouth. He repeated it several times, rolling it around on his tongue. "How did it happen?"

"Mei-Xing blew it in your face." Nico returned to the living room and handed him another glass. "You inhaled it."

"Oh yeah." He drank the water. His thirst finally eased. "Mei-Xing was the tree?"

"Wood Nymph."

"Oh." Not long ago, he would have scoffed at that. "Why did she do it?"

"She was angry that you hurt Georgette."

Georgette? Neil scrunched up his face. The harder he tried to remember, the more jumbled his memories became. He couldn't picture Georgette very clearly, not as clearly as the wolf and the lady. *What's real?*

Muttering some non-English words, Nico threw his arms out wide and brought them crashing together in one thunderous clap barely a foot from Neil's nose. The violent collision blew a wind through his head, cleaning away the clutter. Thoughts began falling in line.

"You showed up at the Botanica yesterday," Nico said, impatient and angry, "and screamed at her like a psycho. Remember?"

Unfortunately, he did remember now. Seeing Georgette next to Nico had triggered something horrible in him. All those weeks of powerful attachment and self-doubt had overwhelmed him. Instead of taking a moment to think about things rationally, he'd lashed out. He'd had no idea he was even capable of feeling so much pain. Or shame. But he felt it all now, crashing over him in waves.

"Shit," he muttered, pinching the bridge of his nose. "What the hell's wrong with me?"

Nico snorted as he sat down beside him. "You want the full eval?"

"I gotta—wait." His disoriented brain brought him back to what Nico had said and underscored a word he'd missed. "Yesterday?"

"Yesterday. About five hours ago."

"Five?" Neil stared at Nico in disbelief. "No way. One or two hours, maybe, tops."

"Five," Nico repeated, rubbing his eyes. "It's almost 4:00 a.m."

"But I was just talking to that moon lady a few minutes ago."

"Queen Toloache," Nico said, "spirit of the *datura* plant. You've been babbling about her since I found you. Damn lucky she pulled you away from that wolf."

"You saw them?"

"Not last night, no, but I've seen them on my own journeys."

"So all that shit I saw was real?" Neil whispered, a shiver running down his spine.

Nico shrugged. "'Real' is a matter of perspective."

"But . . . are those things I saw actually there, or were they just in my head?"

After a pause, Nico answered, "Yes."

"I don't understand."

"I know. Don't worry about it. All you need to know right now is you had a bad trip and you need to sleep it off."

"Sleep?" An alarm went off in his head, causing him to sit bolt upright. "I'm supposed to be at work in a few hours!"

"I'll call the office for you." Nico collected the two empty water glasses and carried them to the kitchen. "I'll tell 'em you have the flu. That should buy you the time you need to recover. The effects of *datura* can last three days."

"*Dammit.*" Neil groaned. "I have to call Georgette. I need to . . ." More of the previous night suddenly came into focus. Confused, he stared at Nico as he returned to the living room. "She's a witch? Like, a real witch?"

"Yeah."

Just a day ago, it would have sounded like horseshit. A day ago, Neil would have rolled his eyes and wondered how Nico could believe such crap. Today, well, things were different. His eyes had been forcibly opened to a truth he didn't understand and couldn't ignore.

Despite Nico's help, weirdness was creeping back into his brain; he thought he heard the sound of cows mooing and he saw blood oozing from a book on the coffee table. Neil closed his eyes and took a deep breath. At least now he knew why he was messed up.

"Did she put a spell on me?"

Nico tilted his head. "Huh?"

"A spell," Neil repeated. "Did she put a spell on me? Is that why I've been so obsessed with her ever since we met?"

Nico burst out laughing.

Shocked and annoyed, Neil scowled.

"I'm not laughing at you, man," Nico said, taking a seat on the sofa. "Just . . . think about it. If she could make someone obsessed with her, who's the best choice? Famous actor, rich CEO . . . or an imports salesman who's just scraping by?" In reaction to his friend's glare, he chuckled. "No offense. I'm just making a point. No, she's not controlling you. Your emotions are your own." He leaned closer. "Anything you feel for her, and she for you, has nothing to do with her magic. Understand?"

Though still peeved, Neil admitted that Nico was making a fair point. Even if Georgette was that type of person, he wouldn't be an ideal choice. No, Georgette was the best thing in his life, and he had ruined that. *God, I hate myself.* He wanted to make it right. Even if it meant living in this bizarre and horrifying world opened up by the *datura*, he still wanted to be with her. Nevertheless, he knew he would have a lot of questions once he was sober. If only those damn cows would shut up.

"I get it," said Neil. His throat was drying out again, and his mind was detaching from his body. "I wanna talk to Georgette."

"Not a good idea. You probably can't tell, but you sound drunk and your pupils are huge. You shouldn't be talking to anyone but me right now."

"Why d'we have cows?" Neil slurred. "Th' apartment's too small for cows."

"Jesus." Nico took him by the arm and pulled him to his feet. "Get back in your room and go to sleep."

56   Ishak

THE TINY FUSSING SOUND ON HIS DAUGHTER'S LIPS WAS the sweetest thing Ishak had ever heard. She squirmed in his arms, flexing her little legs inside the hotel towel he'd used to swaddle her. The baby's miniature hand wrapped around his finger, squeezing with such strength that it made his heart swell. She was absolutely perfect.

"Ziya," he whispered, smiling. "I thought your mother was asking for her beloved dead cousin, but now I know she was asking for you. It's the name she gave you with her last breath." The baby cracked open her smoky topaz eyes. He chuckled. "Ziya means *light*. You are the light that brought me out of darkness."

Minutes after holding his daughter for the first time, Ishak had the realization that he was completely unprepared for her; he had nothing to feed her, no clothes, and no cradle. He wasn't even sure what sort of supplies he needed. He and Kalilah had talked about having children, but not so soon. He had assumed there would be time to plan, to learn. But now time was up, and his mind boggled at all he did not know.

Where in his small Kabultiloa house would he put the nursery? While Ziya was young, she could sleep at his bedside, but she would eventually outgrow that arrangement. Yet he didn't want to leave the home he had shared with Kalilah. Perhaps his family could help him build an addition to the back of the house once Ziya was old enough to need privacy.

He had to start preparing for her education. This girl would need intellectual challenges, he was sure of that. No child had eyes so bright as Ziya's unless she had a spark in her mind. He should also plan for her wedding. He knew his parents would come up with half a dozen prospects for an arranged marriage. He would refuse them all. He and Kalilah had chosen each other, and he wanted their girl to have the same experience.

Exhaling slowly, he leaned back with the baby against his chest. Thoughts roiled about in his head, but when he stared at his daughter, all he could do was smile. He held her, grinning and cooing, until the sun rose. Then, reluctantly, he acknowledged that he needed to go out for supplies.

His first instinct was to bring Ziya with him, but he didn't like the idea of taking her into town when she was so small and helpless. Walking into a store with a baby wrapped in a towel was also likely to provoke questions he wasn't prepared to answer. It would be better to leave her at the hotel with Georgette.

Unfortunately, Georgette was sleeping hard, flopped face down across the hotel bed, still in her clothes from the previous day. Mei-Xing, meanwhile, was nowhere to be found. Though he couldn't be sure, he suspected she had dissolved back into her marijuana plant for some rest.

"Well," he said to the sleeping Ziya, "the girls won't be any help this morning. We cannot fault them for it. But"—he caressed the baby's cheek—"I still must find someone to watch you. And I do have someone in mind. It's not an ideal solution, but . . . ah," he sighed, "you may as well know now, *sokar*, that very little in life is ideal. We can only do the best we can with what we have, and"—he nuzzled her—"hold fast to the things that matter most."

There was much to do. First, he owed Kalilah an honorable burial. It would break his heart to bury her this far from Kabultiloa, but tradition demanded that she be buried quickly. He tried not to let it trouble him. Kalilah was a great hunter. Her spirit would find its way home.

Ishak brought Ziya's face to his and hummed a tune he had heard his father sing when he was young. He had hardly thought of his father since arriving in America. His parents must be worried sick over their missing son and daughter-in-law. He must get in touch with them as soon as possible. That computer in the Kabultiloa library with access to the kobold net, the one he had scoffed at as a useless vanity, might be just what he needed. Hopefully he would be home soon, sitting at his parents' table, sharing all the hardship, struggle, and tragedy of these last months with them. Until then, he would have to share the news of Kalilah's passing via cyberspace.

Kalilah would not be forgotten. Through him, Ziya would know her mother—the brave, beautiful woman who'd survived a march through hell to bring their child, free and limitless, into this world. Through Ziya, Kalilah would live on.

57 🦂 Nicolás

WHEN HE FINALLY FOUND NEIL—CRYING AND BABBLING ON the steps of a public library—Nico dragged him home to bed. Then, despite wanting nothing more than to go to bed himself, he staggered back to the Botanica to deal with the mess.

Just half an hour until the Botanica was due to open, Georgette, Mei-Xing, and all the Fae were gone. The empty boxes tossed aside by Georgette littered the sidewalk in front of the shop, forming a knee-high cardboard maze that passersby had to either wade through or cross the street to avoid. Inside the shop, canisters of herbs lay overturned, their contents scattered. Figurines of saints lay in shattered pieces on the tile, some of them crushed into white dust. There was an arm's-length crack in one of the display cases and chips in several others. Entire shelves of candles had been knocked down, one of which had rolled onto the heating vent and melted into a puddle of sage-scented wax. The painting of the Blessed Virgin had been knocked off the wall and stepped on by something that had left a three-clawed footprint on her face. Worst of all, Mariana's beloved tarot cards were spread all across the shop—torn, trampled, and splattered with mud.

Faced with so much damage, Nico gave up the idea of making repairs before opening. Instead, he sat down at the tarot table, put his chin in his hands, and waited for Mariana to arrive and chew him out.

She didn't disappoint.

The barrage of Spanish exploding from her mouth was too fast for Nico to follow. Nevertheless, he understood her perfectly.

"I'm sorry, *Tía*," he said again and again, looking down at his shoes. He wanted to tell her everything, but he knew her: Mariana needed to vent her fury before she would be ready to listen. "I'm sorry, *Tía*."

Minutes ticked by, full of Mariana's angry rebukes. Nico watched for signs that she was running out of steam, knowing that moment would come if he just let her yell long enough.

"*Irresponsable!*" she bellowed. "*Descuidado!* A complete disregard of everything I have taught you!"

"There were Fae here, *Tía*," he said, finally meeting her gaze. "I saw them."

"You saw them, you saw them," she snarled, gesturing wildly at the mess. "You saw Fae do this to my shop? Were they having a midnight mass? Throwing a birthday party?"

"Mariana!" he snapped. "I. Saw. Them."

He watched the tension in her jaw and shoulders uncoil and her eyes grow wide with comprehension. She rushed forward and took his face in her hands. "Tell me."

He told her. About Georgette, about the children, about everything. "My sight opened," he said. "I saw all of them at once, as plainly as I'm seeing you."

"How many?" she asked.

"Dozens!" he said. "Hundreds! All types, all sizes—old and young, male and female . . ." He ran out of breath and had to pause to gulp in air. "The world of shadows opened to me, *Tía*. I have never made so much progress so quickly before."

"*Increíble!*" Her dark eyes dancing with inner light, Mariana knitted her hands together before her chin, her pointer fingers pressed over her lips. "How long did it last?"

"Most of the night. It only faded about an hour ago."

"Oh, *mijo!*" she exclaimed, smiling. "*Que buen presagio!* I'm so proud of you!"

Nodding, he smiled back at her. "It was amazing, *Tía*. I've never experienced anything quite like it." His smile faded slightly as his eyebrows pinched together. "Have you?"

"Well," she said, her voice drifting into nostalgic tones, "I have seen Fae. Several times. But not recently. And I have never been witness to a gathering like the one you describe. Oh! What a sight that must have been!"

Seeing his aunt get starry-eyed over his *curandero* training spread warmth through his body and lightened his mind.

"I'm sorry about the shop, *Tía*. When I let Georgette use it, she promised not to cause any damage. If I'd known—"

"*No importa, no importa,*" she interrupted, waving her hands around like a cop directing traffic. "Your intentions were good. But your *bruja* friend"—a stern frown creased her face—"was not honest with you. She should make amends."

"She may not have known that her spell would cause this much damage."

"Of course she did!" Mariana rolled her eyes. "The *bruja* is no fool. She planned this theft from a guarded house. She knew her spell would cause at least some damage. I expect her to make restitution, and I will tell her so."

"Please don't be angry with her," Nico said. "This girl's like an egg; you have to handle her gently or she cracks."

Mariana clucked her tongue. "I won't yell. She had good intentions. No one could deny that."

Nico nodded and sighed. *Shit happens. With magic, shit happens more often than not.*

"I wanna help clean up, *Tia*, but Neil's back at our apartment sleeping off a dose of *datura*. I need to keep an eye on him."

Annoyance bubbled over her face, but she didn't forbid him from going. She knew as well as Nico what *datura* did to an unprepared mind. Mumbling, she waved him off.

He turned to head out the back, planning to grab a few medicinal herbs on the way for Neil, when something caught his eye. At the foot of a display case, camouflaged by the mess, sat a collection of grass-woven baskets. Nico scooped up a small one and stood up with it in his hand.

"*Tia*," he called over his shoulder, "are these yours?"

Mariana approached and inspected the basket. "No. Just more mess to clean up." With a *hmph*, she reached out and flicked away the grassy lid, sending it spiraling across the room like a flipped coin—but when the light hit the basket's contents, she gasped, snatched the basket from him, held it to her face, and inhaled deeply.

"Ambergris!" she exclaimed.

"What's that?"

"A product of whale intestines," she said.

Hearing this, her excitement baffled him. "Um, gross?"

"It's a rare, very expensive ingredient for perfume." Her eyes drank in the shapeless gray lump. "This is worth thousands!"

Without warning, she shoved it into his hands and lunged at the other baskets. Tearing the lid off the largest, a keg-size container, Mariana exposed an enormous brown-and-white pile of parsnip-like tendrils.

Nico recognized them at once. "Ginseng root."

"*Wild* ginseng root." Mariana shook her head in wonder. "This is wild American ginseng." She inhaled deeply. "It smells like money!"

Nico pushed back another lid, revealing a hefty amount of needle-thin red fibers.

"Saffron threads!" Mariana exclaimed. "Pound for pound, saffron is worth more than gold!"

Diving into the remaining baskets, they uncovered obscene riches. One basket had white truffles the size of potatoes. Another contained albino caviar, a delicacy that—Nico pulled out his phone and did a quick Google search—was priced in the tens of thousands. He found an identical pair of Yubari Kings, a type of melon that sometimes sold for thousands. Mariana next discovered dried cordyceps, the most expensive mushroom in the world. They found pearls, white and black, all beautifully shaped and lustrous. There were also several skeins of cloud-soft vicuña wool, a bag of Kopi Luwak coffee beans, and a bottle of red wine so dark it was almost black.

The last container—a wooden jewelry box—held dried, shriveled leaves. Nico took a guess. "Tea?"

Mariana took the box from him and sniffed. "I think that's Da-Hong Pao," she said, breathless, "the most valuable tea on the market. One kilo can retail for over a million dollars. *Mijo*"—she was grinning like a madwoman now—"there is a fortune here!"

"Hold up," he said, "we can't keep these things."

"Why not?" she demanded, pulling the wood box close to her chest. "They're in my shop."

"These were clearly left by the Fae as thanks for helping the children," he said. "They belong to Georgette, Mei-Xing, and anyone else who was a part of it."

Nose wrinkled and eyes shooting daggers, Mariana opened her mouth to reply, but Nico spoke first.

"It would be bad karma to keep them. You know I'm right."

Cursing under her breath, Mariana's eyes eventually softened, and she nodded. "But I won't give her all of it!" she insisted. "She owes me for the damage. Besides, if I sell them, I deserve a cut . . ."

Trailing off, Mariana locked on to something beyond him. Turning to look, he spotted a bundle of newspaper tied with a strip of white lace. Mariana snatched it up and tore away the paper. He looked over her shoulder; it was a stack of tarot cards. The top image, The Fool, depicted a Satyr with a jug of wine in one hand and long flute in the other, a two-headed dog nearby. Nico was awestruck by the hand-painted detail and vibrant colors.

"I'm definitely keeping these," Mariana whispered, her voice full of delight and wonder. Her long fingers gently brushed the image. "My deck is ruined; I need a new one."

"I doubt Georgette will object to that," he said.

"Good." Mariana scanned all the gifts with the air of a priestess inspecting temple offerings. "Tell your *bruja* friend I forgive her."

"What about me?"

She flashed an impressive side-eye at him and then, after a pause, smirked. "I forgive you, too, *mijo*. Just don't do it again."

What the hell are the odds of this shit happening twice? he thought but, sensibly, did not say.

58  Kazimiera

"NO CHILDREN!"

The gaggle of Fae in the break room jumped at the sound of her voice.

"But Kazi—"

"No children!" the Vampire shouted, pointing to the baby in the five-tailed Kitsune's arms. "Children are unpredictable! Unpredictability puts all of us at risk!" She strode forward, pushing aside a Selkie and an Elf, to examine the baby. The fox spirit gently jiggled the child, holding a half-filled bottle to its lips. Tiny and wrinkled, it looked like a newborn.

"Which one of you had this baby?" Kazimiera demanded, her accusatory glare darting from one creature to the next. "Who the hell had the audacity to hide a pregnancy from me?"

"It's not ours, Kazi," said the Yuki-onna. "The Bultungin man brought her here."

"The hyena? When?"

"This morning," answered the Encantado, his uncombed hair exposing the blowhole on his head. "He asked us to watch her while he went out."

"And you agreed?" she asked, fuming.

"We all did," said the Siren. She smiled wide and babbled happy nonsense at the feeding infant. "It's been so long since any of us have seen a baby!"

"He's been back many times to check on her," said the Huldra. "Look."

Kazimiera looked where she pointed and saw a portable bassinet, bottles, formula, clothes, diapers, and sundry other baby things. "Are we holding his packages for him, too?"

"He said you wouldn't mind." The Kitsune repositioned the baby in her arms. "He said he'd repaid his debt to you."

Oh, she thought irritably, thinking about her exchange with him the previous night. *I see.*

It was a few hours past opening when Kazimiera walked into her office to find the hyena-man inside with two limp, breathing bodies slung over his shoulders.

"Here," he said, dropping the bodies to the floor. "The blood in these men should be enough to heal the injuries I gave you."

She knelt, putting her hands on the bodies, and sniffed the two men. They were warm and smelled of good health; their hearts pumped with the regularity of sleepers. "Who are they?"

"Employees of KK Inc." He crouched next to his dead wife's body, which was still covered with a blanket. When she had died hours before, his howling grief had driven everyone from the room, Kazimiera included. She'd left the body untouched even after he'd gone, busying herself with running her club rather than deal with the consequences of her bad investment. There was always work to do; business didn't stop for one death.

The Bultungin held his wife's cold hand. "Their souls have been removed from their bodies. You can consume them at your leisure."

Brushing her fingers over her abdomen, Kazimiera felt the lingering discomfort of her ripped flesh. Since her scuffle with Ishak, she had consumed just enough blood to regrow skin over the wound. Her body looked whole, but the internal injuries remained. The chance to properly repair that damage was extremely appetizing.

Ishak laid a hand on his wife's covered forehead. "I'll be back to bury Kalilah."

The peaceful look in his eyes bothered her far more than the fresh scent of death that surrounded him. She had known many killers, and none of them had ever looked this serene with blood still on their hands. Ishak had the look of a man who had had a lifetime to come to terms with the lives he'd snuffed out—like a man who no longer carried the weight of them on his conscience. His calm was mysterious, and Kazimiera, a businesswoman through and through, hated mysteries.

"Fetch her soon," she said. "I need my office back."

The Bultungin took off, leaving the bodies at her feet. After putting one into her bathtub—where it would spend the day—she consumed the other immediately, piercing the throat and letting the heart blindly pump its juice into her mouth. The flow was strong for a while but eventually waned, forcing her to tear into the torso to get the rest. She sucked up the fluid in each organ and muscle before cracking open the bones to get at the marrow. By the time she finished, all that was left was a shriveled pile of skin, dehydrated meat, and bones.

Grinning, Kazimiera sat back in her office chair, delighting in the sensation of a full stomach and a fully healed body. It had been a long time since she'd feasted on an entire human being in one sitting. *Glorious!*

She'd gone to bed early that morning, slept well, and had awoken just twenty minutes ago to find Kalilah's body gone. Pleased to see her orders had been obeyed, and anticipating a second full-body meal, she'd forgiven the Bultungin.

Then she'd heard a baby crying and found her employees not working.

"Where's the hyena now?" she demanded.

The loitering Fae exchanged looks, shrugging.

"Last time he came back to see the baby," said the Peri, "he took his wife's body for burial."

"When was that?"

"A couple of hours ago."

Kazimiera sighed, but the sound came out like a growl. The club would be opening soon, and there were far too many employees cluttering up the break room and cooing over this baby instead of doing their jobs. Half her waitstaff was here—not prepping for service, not even dressed. The entertainers weren't prettied up like they should be, and guests would be arriving soon.

Agitation tickled her body like tiny rodent feet running over her skin. "This won't stand," she said as calmly as she could. "There's work to be done."

An absurd look of panic swept through the room. "B-but,"

stammered the Nagini, wringing the end of her serpent tail like a handkerchief, "the little one can't be left alone!"

"One baby," Kazimiera snapped, "does not require my entire staff!" She pointed at the Kitsune, who was still holding the infant. "You watch her. The rest of you get to work."

Grumbling with disappointment, they shuffled off, leaving a grinning Kitsune alone in the break room with Kazimiera and the child.

"*Arigatou gozaimasu*, Kazi," she said.

"This is temporary," Kazimiera replied, taking her time to emphasize each syllable. "When the hyena comes back, you return to work."

Setting down the now-empty bottle, the fox-woman lifted the baby to her shoulder, and patted her back until she burped. The ease with which she handled the infant made Kazimiera wonder if she'd ever had a child of her own. Almost every Fae who passed through Nocturne told Kazimiera his or her story at some point, but after so many stories over so many years she couldn't be bothered to remember details. She did remember a few stories clearly, but most were a hodge-podge of common themes. Stories, faces, names, and years all bobbed about like flotsam and jetsam on an eternal sea.

The Bultungin, however, she was sure she would remember.

59 Georgette

GEORGETTE AWOKE AT 4:28 A.M. FIGHTING HER ACHES, SHE put her feet on the floor and stood up slowly. Though weary, her wobbly legs held her weight. The film of dried sweat that covered her skin felt like an icy paste as she tottered to the bathroom. Her clothes stuck to her body in one long, constant, unwanted touch.

A warm shower invigorated her. As her body became more alert, she realized that she was ravenous. *I burned a shit-ton of energy,* she thought, *and I haven't eaten since . . . geez, maybe two days. Yeah, my last meal was at that Italian restaurant where Neil and I—*

Neil's accusing shouts resounded through her head, bringing tears to her eyes. Seeing him lash out like that had made her realize she didn't know him very well. They had hooked up on their first date and formed an emotional bond, one that made Georgette happy, but they hadn't taken the time to truly get to know each other. Georgette had so little experience with healthy relationships that she didn't know what one should look like.

I did everything Aunt Olive told me not to do: I stayed in one place, I made friends, I used a lot of magic, and I fell in love.

Slowly, she slid down to the tiled floor of the shower stall and hugged her legs tight, burying her face in her knees. Water rained down around her. Now that Ishak's revenge had been exacted, it would be better if she did what she should have done in the first place: keep moving.

Back in the bedroom, she put on a flowy skirt and a peasant blouse. With her hair wrapped in a towel, she pulled a chair up to the window, gently put an arm around Mei-Xing's plant, and stared out at the night, her cheek resting against the cool clay pot. As she gazed out at the streetlamps and headlights piercing the darkness, she sensed Mei-Xing shifting slightly, like a sleeper twitching in a dream.

"Where should we go?" she asked the sleeping Nymph. "I mean, I guess we'll have to stay in the area until Delia and Senji do whatever it is they need us for. And we should ask Ishak, too, since he's still linked to us by the *Hathiya*. And," she realized, "we can't leave until I pay for whatever damage I caused at the Botanica." She sighed. "We might be here longer than I thought."

Sitting up straight, she unwrapped her hair and let her damp curls fall to her shoulders. She turned her head back and forth, looking at her reflection in the dark window glass. She looked so different from the girl who fled her family home in August. Here it was, November—*Wait.* She checked her phone. *December.* Time had flown, yet her old existence felt like a lifetime ago. She had left the Nichols O'Reilly home in ill-fitting hand-me-down clothes, and hair gone frizzy from unwanted straightening treatments. She smiled at her reflection. She didn't feel like that girl anymore.

A soft knock on the door startled her. *Ishak,* she thought. After giving Mei-Xing's plant a little squeeze, she stood up, steadied her weak legs, and walked to the door.

"Hey," she said as she turned the lock. "Did you forget your k—"

The door swung open to reveal a face so pallid and haggard that it took a moment for her to recognize it. When she did, her heart galloped.

"Neil."

At the sound of his name, Neil jolted and jumped back. When his eyes locked on to her, he blinked as if in surprise.

"Oh," he said in a voice as rough as burlap. "Hey."

Georgette had forgotten about Mei-Xing drugging him until she saw his huge pupils. He looked dazed.

"I never told you where I was staying," she said. "How did you know to come to this hotel? To this room?"

He squinted, his eyebrows knitted together, and shook his head. "I don't know. I don't remember how I got here." Looking perplexed, he ran a hand through his sweaty hair. "I was at home. Nico kept waking me up to give me water with some nasty-smelling herbs in it. He said it would help . . ."

It wasn't the first time Georgette had seen someone tripping on *datura*. Georgette's older sisters had occasionally raided their mother's supply—kept for spellcrafting purposes—during parties. More than once, she had seen her sisters' friends high as a kite and wandering the house with eyes dilated just like Neil's. Like him, they had also known things they shouldn't have. One boy had talked at length about their grandmother Rose, who had died before they were born. *Datura* was a hell of a thing.

Slowly, Neil patted his jeans pockets and then retrieved his phone from their depths. "I wanted to call you," he said, holding it up. "But I can't read. I called the name I thought was yours, but it was my brother." He pocketed the phone, shaking his head. "He was pissed. Yelled at me for calling so late." He sighed. "Can't read my watch, either."

This man didn't fit Georgette's image of Neil. This person was a shrunken shadow of the man she knew, a pale imitation both physically and emotionally. She couldn't help but feel sorry for him.

"Do you want to come in?" she asked.

His gaze was trained on the floor, his brow scrunched up as if he was trying to remember something. When Georgette touched his arm, he looked up and started, as if seeing her for the first time.

"Georgette!" he said. "I wanted to talk to you!"

To her surprise, he flopped down in a heap, his knees and hands on the floor.

"I am so sorry. I had no business talking to you like that. My ex cheated on me, and when I saw you with Nico it felt like it was happening all over again. It's my issue, it has nothing to do with you. I was way out of line." Pulling himself up into a sitting position, he glanced up and down the hotel hallway with a bewildered expression. "W-where are we?"

"My hotel room." She leaned down and took his hand. "Get up, okay? Let's go inside."

He let her lead him inside without protest. As the door closed behind them, he scanned the small room. "This is where you live?"

"Yeah, with my two friends." She gently steered him to the edge of the bed so he could sit down. "Mei-Xing gave you a hell of a dose, didn't she?"

Neil didn't answer. He just kept staring at the wall, muttering, "Sorry."

This conversation isn't going to get very far while he's still drugged, she thought. As badly as he wanted to apologize for his behavior, she was just as eager to explain the secretive way she'd conducted herself. She collected a tiny spark of magic into her fingers. *Maybe I can clear his head for a few minutes.*

"Hey," she said, "look at me."

When he raised his chin, she flicked the blue spark into his pupils. He was so glazed that he didn't blink as the magic entered his eyes, snaked back behind his lids, and disappeared. Casting even such a tiny spell, drained as she was, sent a wave of dizziness through Georgette's head; woozy, she plopped down beside Neil on the edge of the bed.

Heartbeats passed in silence, and then Neil shook his head, eyes pinched shut, and said, "Feels weird." He pressed his palms to his eyes. "What is that?"

"It's kinda like a shot of pure caffeine, but for your brain."

"Damn." He sighed with relief, his eyes slightly less dilated. "I feel a lot better. Thanks."

"It won't last very long. I just wanted us to be able to talk."

"Magic, right? 'Cause you're a witch?"

She looked at him strangely. "You remember Nico telling you that?"

"Kinda," he said. "Damn *datura*. I've seen some shit." Despite his evident exhaustion, he smiled. "You're a witch? Okay, that's unexpected—shakes up my assumptions about the universe—but, y'know, shit happens."

Georgette let his words sink in for a long beat—and then let out a sputtering giggle.

Neil looked at her, calm and unsurprised.

She put a hand over her smile. "Sorry," she said from behind her fingers. "That's just—it's not how I thought you'd react."

"Yeah, same here," he replied. "Honestly, as crazy as witchcraft is, it doesn't seem half as bad as cheating. Is that weird?"

"Yes. But that's okay."

Sighing, he ran both hands over his face and back through his hair. "We, uh, went too fast, didn't we? I mean, everything seemed so good from the start that we didn't get to know each other as well as we should have, right?"

Georgette nodded. "It didn't help that I was hiding a big part of myself from you."

"And I was dealing with my own shit." Hesitant, he started to reach for her hand but then pulled it back.

She reached over and intertwined her fingers with his.

"Could we try this again?" he asked. "Go a little slower, do this thing right?"

It was on the tip of her tongue to agree immediately—but then she remembered. "I . . . may be leaving town soon," she admitted.

A flash of pain crossed his eyes, but he nodded. "Could we do the long-distance thing?"

She felt a flood of warmth course through her body. All the good feelings she had come to associate with Neil came back to her, washing away the hurt of their last encounter. "Yeah, we could try it."

Neil was blinking rapidly, his pupils swelling. The quick-fix spell was already wearing off. "I'm gonna have a lot of questions," he said, his speech a bit slurred.

"I'll try to answer them," she said. "I won't hide anything this time."

"Cool." Smacking his dry lips, he slid back on the bed and rolled onto his side. "I'm just gonna stay here for a minute, okay?" He put a hand over his face, shielding his eyes. "Why do walls ooze blood? I don't like the blood."

Smiling, she reached over and stroked his hair. "It won't last much longer. Don't worry. We can talk more later."

Still hiding behind his hand, he mumbled something incoherent and rolled over.

He got himself here in this state, she thought, impressed. *Apologizing to me meant that much to him.* Fluttery hope spread through her chest. *He's a good guy, he really is.*

A knock on the door broke into her thoughts.

Ishak.

She leaned over to kiss Neil's head, then went to the door.

"Hey," she said, turning the knob. "I just woke up a little—"

As the door fell open, so did Georgette's jaw. A bolt of numbness went through her body; it was as though her spirit had jumped out of her flesh, leaving her hollow. Then, just as quickly, adrenaline thundered through her veins, making her lightheaded and nauseous. Her knees quaked so wildly that she staggered into the wall to her right.

Through it all, her wide, horrified eyes stayed glued to the face that had just reduced her to jelly.

"Mom."

60  Georgette/ Ivy

HAZEL NICHOLS O'REILLY BREEZED OVER THE THRESHOLD on spike-heeled pumps. The dim lighting twinkled off her gold earrings, gold rings, and gold necklace. She wore a wine-red pantsuit, the blazer of which buttoned over a white silk blouse with a plunging neckline, somehow both covering and emphasizing her curves at the same time. The light shimmered through the maple highlights of her brunette hair as she walked—not a gray root to be seen.

Georgette leaned against a wall, shaking, as her mother's designer perfume engulfed her. The smell brought back twenty-two years' worth of memories—thousands of smirks, raised eyebrows, and offhand remarks. The progress she'd made after hours of therapy with Nico vanished in an instant. In her mother's presence, the young woman Georgette Delaney faded into mist, replaced by the child Ivy O'Reilly: small, fearful, and trapped.

Her French tips smoothing back her hair, Hazel walked toward her daughter as the stunned girl stared at her in wide-eyed shock.

"Well," she said, "here we are."

She crossed her arms over her chest and stood before Ivy, frowning.

What are you doing here? How did you find me? All the questions came to her in Georgette's voice, but when she opened her trembling lips, Ivy couldn't form a single word. It was as if the identity she had lived since striking out on her own no longer fit her—like she was a toddler trying to walk in adult shoes.

"Nothing to say for yourself?" Hazel raised an eyebrow. There was a bite to her voice—an edge of anger and resentment—that horrified her daughter.

When Ivy didn't respond, Hazel *hmphed* and strode deeper into the room. "I've spent a lot of time looking for you. You gave us all a scare." She looked her daughter up and down. "Oh," she groaned, wincing, "what are you wearing? This hippie-dippy look is beneath you. And God, your hair!" She sighed. "You looked nice when I was looking after you."

Tell her to leave. Tell her to go to hell. Tell her anything—just speak!

Hazel's eyes fell upon Neil, still curled up on the bed, mumbling. "Lovely," she muttered.

"Mom," Ivy finally forced from her tongue. "I—"

"Is *this* why you left?" Hazel said, pointing at Neil. As she leaned closer to him, a flitting gleam went through her brown eyes that told Ivy she was inspecting Neil through a veil of magic. "No craft on him," she said. "What even *is* he? A waiter? A valet?" She turned back to Ivy, her expression dripping disdain. "You turned your back on Zachary Thayer for this man?"

"I didn't want Zach!" she managed, half-choked with tears. "You picked Zach and never asked what I wanted."

Staring at Neil, Hazel said, "You know, he's not going to marry you."

The nonsensical remark momentarily stunned Ivy into silence. "W-what?" she finally stammered.

"He's not going to marry you," Hazel repeated. "He's not our kind. You're wasting your time with him."

"Why are you here?" Ivy finally asked, pulling herself away from the wall. Her legs shook but she managed to stand. "What do you want?"

"What a question!" Hazel exclaimed, the picture of indignance. "I came to find my daughter." Hazel opened her arms and glided forward to embrace her.

Ivy felt a rush of panic as her mother stepped into her personal space. Feeling like she could do nothing else, she loosely hugged her mother back. The soft, smooth material of Hazel's suit made Ivy uncomfortable. For every memory she had of her mother hugging her, she had twice as many of her mother pushing her away to avoid getting her clothes wrinkled. Still, the closeness of the only mother she had filled her with an old longing—a painful desperation to be loved and accepted—that was as familiar to her as her own heartbeat.

Hazel pulled away from the hug and held Ivy by the shoulders, smiling.

"Moving away was very selfish of you," she said in a motherly tone. "You disappeared without a word, young lady. Why would you want to scare us like that?"

"I-I-I'm sorry." Ivy felt just as pitifully small under Hazel's eyes as she always had. "I just—I just wanted . . . I wanted to—"

"And you stole quite a bit of money that was meant to go

toward your education, too." Hazel leaned closer. "What was I to think?"

"I can pay you back," Ivy said quickly. "I have money of my own now, and I can repay everything I took—with interest."

A shadow passed over Hazel's face and her fingers tightened on Ivy's shoulders, alerting her that she had said the wrong thing. For a moment, she thought her mother was insulted at the suggestion that she wanted to be repaid—but then the truth sank in. *She assumed I've been living off that money all this time. She doesn't like being wrong.*

"I know what's best," Hazel declared. "You belong at home with the family. This little vacation is over. You're coming with me." She relinquished her grasp on her daughter, strode to the dresser on the far wall, and began opening drawers, pulling out clothes, and tossing them onto the bed. The fluttery *whoosh* of clothes soaring through the air and flopping onto the comforter filled the room, faintly underscored by Neil's mindless mumbling.

For a while, Ivy watched all this happen without any sense of agency. She kept trying to speak, only to have her voice catch in her throat each time. After several attempts, she mustered all her strength and finally pushed the sound past her lips.

"No."

"Where's your suitcase?" Hazel asked as she pulled out a tie-dye T-shirt with a peace symbol on the front. Nose wrinkled, she tossed it into the corner of the room, just missing the wastebasket. "You had a suitcase. Where is it?"

Louder now, she said, "I'm not going back to Boston." Ivy, her heart pounding, stood up tall, struggling to grow into Georgette again. "I'm not going with you."

Hazel gave her a condescending look. "Of course you are. Get packed."

"No."

She shot her daughter a stop-wasting-my-time glare. "Ivy," she said firmly, pointing at the pile of clothes. "Get packed."

"No." Though her limbs felt wobbly, Ivy walked to the bed, scooped up her clothes, and carried them back to the dresser. "I won't."

Hazel closed her eyes, clenched her jaw, and exhaled through her nose. "Young lady," she said, "I came a very long way to collect you. And not a moment too soon." Her smirk made Ivy's heart jump. She'd seen that smirk a million times; she knew it heralded an emotional blow. "Really, you have gotten in over your head out here. Why else would my daughter's magic light up the West Coast like a brushfire?"

Hazel's smirk deepened, bringing out the smile lines she fought so hard to keep at bay. She was enjoying the surge of superiority that her "playful" jab at her daughter had stirred.

I didn't use any masking spells to hide my magic at Silver Creek. God, I'm so stupid! Ivy felt an urge to curl up in a corner of the room and cry until she melted into a puddle—but to her amazement, the urge passed in seconds. *It's too late now*, she thought. *Like Nico said, I can't change what's past, I can't control the future; I can only deal with the here and now.*

"Why didn't you find me sooner?" Georgette asked. "Couldn't you track me with this?"

Lifting one hand to her face, she illuminated the Nichols clan mark on her cheek. As she'd hoped, Hazel's expression betrayed surprise. Georgette enjoyed a fleeting flush of satisfaction—then fell into worry. *I promised Olive I would keep her secret,* she remembered. *If Mom asks who told me about the mark, I'll have to lie. Dammit! She'll see right through me!*

But Hazel only asked, "Did my sister tell you about that?"

"Yes," she replied honestly, relieved. *Oh, thank God. She thinks it was Aunt Laurel.* If confronted, Laurel wouldn't bat an eye; she'd just assume she'd disclosed the information while drunk. "You put this thing on me when I was a baby so you could *control* me."

"Oh, for God's sake, Ivy!" Hazel tossed up her hands. "Every witch carries a signet. It's perfectly normal. Having one is no big deal."

"If it's no big deal, then why didn't you tell me?"

At this, Hazel's mask of calm authority slipped; her face twisted with ugly fury and she snapped, "You always take things the wrong way! Stop being so damned dramatic!"

I always overreact, Ivy's voice miserably agreed. *It's always my fault. I'm sorry.*

No, Georgette's thought cut in. *She's angry because I called her out on her bullshit.*

The child Ivy once was slipped back into the past, giving way to the adult Georgette had become.

"I'm over eighteen," she said. "An adult. I make my own decisions now. You don't get to force me to do anything anymore."

Hazel smirked again.

Oh crap, she can totally force me. Hazel hadn't brought any luggage with her to the hotel—not even a purse. *She used magic to transport here.* Panic consumed Georgette, making her dizzy. *Even if I wasn't drained, she's way stronger than me. If she tries to transport me by magic, I won't be able to stop her.*

Hazel's painted lips pulled up at the corners in a Cheshire cat smile as she opened her mouth to speak—but before either she or her daughter could make another sound, a loud rustling filled the room, followed by a sharp, "*Aiya!*"

Georgette glanced behind her to see Mei-Xing, newly emerged from her plant and glaring at the bed. Neil lay there, still hiding his eyes behind his hands. The Nymph moved toward him, her inhuman face glowering.

"You again," she said. "*Fàntǒng!* I . . ."

Her iridescent eyes spotted Hazel. For a moment, the sight rendered her mute. Then Mei-Xing uttered a squeak and vanished, dematerialized into her plant.

Hazel clucked her tongue as if annoyed at the interruption, then jabbed a finger at Georgette. "You have obligations. You agreed to marry Zachary—"

"No," said Georgette, "I didn't."

"And our two families have plans."

"Not my problem."

"Oh really?" Hazel said, her voice dripping sarcasm. "The Thayers have expectations of us. I have to honor the agreement you made."

"*You* made!" Georgette exploded, surprised by her own anger. "Not me!"

"An agreement was made!" Hazel bellowed, making Georgette jump. "If you don't marry that boy, what am I supposed to do?" The smirk returned. "Should I have him marry Violet?"

Georgette flinched. An image of her catatonic sister burst

into her mind. It was supposed to be Ivy in that hospital bed, drooling and staring vacantly out the window. If she hadn't refused to eat the *Ningyo*, Violet would be in her junior year of college instead of getting turned several times a day to prevent bedsores. If she had eaten that meat . . .

The meat she gave me! Boiling anger filled her. *I was a child! Mom knew the risks, and she didn't tell Violet or me!* She shoved the memories aside and met her mother's cool stare.

"Have him marry Lily," she shot back. "It's a good match. They're both snobs. Or how about Daphne? They're both immature brats."

That one landed; her mother's smirk disappeared. Lily and Daphne were favorites, two of the top contenders to inherit the role of matriarch one day. The very idea that they take Ivy's place was sacrilege. "When you disappeared," she said, "I suggested Zachary marry Poppy."

I guess I know who the next least-favorite is, Georgette thought bitterly. "Poppy's a lesbian, Mom. I know she's told you."

"Is she still in that phase?" Hazel rolled her eyes. "She should have outgrown that nonsense by now. Well, it's irrelevant; the Thayers aren't keen on her." She preened. "She's Laurel's daughter, after all."

Meaning they'll want to renegotiate the agreement if they get your niece instead of your daughter. It was on the tip of Georgette's tongue to keep arguing, but she stopped. *I ran away to escape this drama.*

"Good luck with that," she said.

"Good luck, indeed," Hazel hissed. "I worked hard to make this deal for you, and you ruined everything! After all the time and money I've spent raising you, protecting you from the hardships of my childhood, you put me in a position where I have to break my word? You spoiled, ungrateful child! I expect you to make this right!"

I embarrassed her, Georgette realized in amazement. *When I ran off, I tarnished her image.* The last slip of hope that her mother would ever accept her shriveled. *I'm never going to be more important to her than what other people think.*

"If you force me to marry Zach," Georgette said, her voice calm, "you'll have to physically drag me down the aisle." Managing to control her racing heart, she stepped forward, into her mother's personal space. "That'll be a great show for all your friends, won't it, Mom? Can't you just imagine them whispering and pointing?"

To her amusement, her mother clearly didn't know how to respond to this. Hazel's usual scolds and glares weren't working, and she didn't have a backup plan. All she could do was stand there and fume, her lips a hard line of bitter rage.

As time ticked by, Georgette marveled at her own resolve. She was doing this! She felt like she might puke, but she was doing it!

Still, the uncertainty of the situation pressed in. Not knowing what her mother's next step would be was nerve-racking. And there was always a next step.

With a sudden huff, Hazel pointed a long finger at her daughter's face. "I didn't come here to argue with you. You're not ready to be on your own. You're coming home. Now."

The air around Georgette grew prickly, as if she were being assaulted by tiny needles. *She's going to transport us both back East right now!* she realized, her stomach dropping.

Too drained of magic to counteract the spell, she lunged toward the window, threw her arms around Mei-Xing's pot, and drew on energy from their shared *Hathiya*. Gratitude flooded her as she felt the Nymph respond. Mei-Xing slipped halfway from the pot, her upper body materialized out of the dirt and leaves, and hugged Georgette tightly. Together, they began enmeshing their personal energies. It was unlikely to stop the transport spell, but Georgette hoped that their entanglement would make it take longer for Hazel's magic to get its hooks into her alone. Meanwhile, she tugged urgently at the *Hathiya*, pleading internally, *Help, help, help!*

"Oh, for God's sake," Hazel said. "Throwing a tantrum? At your age? I thought you were better than this."

On the bed, Neil stirred and raised his head. He rolled onto his stomach and started to push himself up. "Georgette?" he mumbled. "I can't . . . I don't know what . . ."

Cursing under her breath, Hazel threw out a hand toward Neil in a nails-on-a-chalkboard stance. Ethereal threads like long gold ribbons shot out of her fingers and wrapped themselves around his head with a wet slap, sealing over his mouth. Through muffled yelps, Neil clawed at his face, but his fingers passed through the ribbons without effect.

Hazel returned her attention to Georgette, who was still clinging to Mei-Xing's shivering form. Shaking her head, she said, "I am so disappointed in you."

A flash of silver suddenly cut between the witches. Georgette looked up to see Delia standing face-to-face with Hazel. The Valkyrie had responded to her tug on the *Hathiya*.

Hope filled Georgette to the brim. Delia was her best and possibly only chance to escape this situation.

"Step away from her," the Valkyrie commanded.

Delia's tone of unquestionable authority seemed weirdly out of place with her mother in the room. In all Georgette's life, no one had ever taken that tone in Hazel's presence, not even her father.

Hazel's eyes swept over the armored woman. "Why is Valhalla coming between me and my daughter?" she demanded.

"Valhalla is beyond your mortal concern," Delia replied.

Hazel put her hands on her hips and turned her back. Though Georgette couldn't see her mother's face, she sensed that Hazel's spell had begun dissipating. As she'd hoped, the presence of a Valkyrie had dented her mother's confidence.

"What do you want?" Hazel demanded, whirling around. "Tell me!"

Delia chuckled. At the sound, Hazel's eyes blazed with fury.

"That's none of your business, little witch," the Valkyrie said.

Georgette stood up, letting Mei-Xing slip fully out of her pot. Slowly, the two of them moved to the bed, where Georgette put a gentle hand on Neil's shoulder. His huge pupils darted to her, but his hands continued swiping at the ribbons around his mouth. There were bloody marks on his face where his fingers had passed through the magic and scratched his skin.

She drew a deep breath, and on the slow exhale tried to break the enchantment. Almost at once, she felt dizzy. This was going to take longer than she'd hoped.

"I need you to stay calm," she whispered to him. "Just breathe, babe, okay? Breathe."

With his eyes on her, Neil lowered his bloody fingers and stayed still as she continued to work. Glancing up, Georgette saw her mother scanning Delia using a veil of magic—probably looking for a weakness. Her gaze fell on the Valkyrie's ankle, where the *Hathiya* mark was, and she blanched. Then she looked at Georgette with an expression peppered with disbelief, concern, and, to her daughter's surprise, resentment.

"You didn't mark a Valkyrie," she said. "I don't believe it."

"It's true," Georgette said quietly. She showed her the matching *Hathiya* on the underside of her wrist.

Hazel stared at the mark, her eyes darting twice back to Delia's ankle, before she tightened her jaw and looked away. Georgette held her breath. Was the matching brand enough to convince Hazel that she had the behemoth power of a Valkyrie at her command?

"Even overlooking how crass it is to brand yourself like a common familiar," Hazel said, glaring, "marking a Valkyrie is stupid and dangerous. You cannot—"

"Stop," Georgette interrupted. "I'm not a child."

"Yes, you are," Hazel said, "and everything I've seen here today proves it." Tossing her head, she turned and walked toward the door, weaving a spell as she went. "I raised you better than this."

The transporting spell her mother was in the process of crafting was small, only enough for one. Georgette blew out a quiet breath of relief. Her bluff had worked. Whatever her calculations, Hazel didn't think it was worth it to press her luck today. For now, she was leaving by herself.

"This conversation is not over, young lady," she said over her shoulder as she strode to the door. "We *will* discuss this further."

"I have nothing more to say to you," Georgette said.

After stepping into the hallway, Hazel turned around to face her daughter. "Ivy—"

"That's not my name anymore."

Hazel pursed her lips, eyes shooting daggers. Half-hidden behind Delia, Georgette steeled herself against the coming verbal barrage. Suddenly, a blur of movement cut across her vision, charged the entrance, and slammed the door in Hazel's stunned face.

It took Georgette a moment to recognize the blur as Neil. Turning the deadbolt with one hand, he leaned against the wall and looked at Georgette with eyes still wide from *datura*. The last remnants of the spell over his mouth finally dropped away.

Neil drew a breath through his cracked lips as he pointed at the door. "What a bitch!"

Mei-Xing murmured assent while Delia laughed aloud.

For a moment Georgette could only blink, her mouth hanging open.

Then, slowly, her lips crept into a smile.

61   Mei-Xing

THE UBER DRIVER KEPT HIS SILENCE FOR THE ENTIRE DRIVE.
Mei-Xing was glad. Not many people needed an Uber to take
them and all their luggage to a nightclub at 5:30 a.m. The driver
could have asked a dozen legitimate questions, but he chose not
to. He didn't even ask what was wrong with Neil, who was visibly
under the influence. Thanks to his discretion, Mei-Xing, Georgette, and Neil rode in relative peace to Nocturne.

The club was closed, but the staff let them in when they saw
Georgette. The two girls held Neil between them as they followed
a helpful Pixie upstairs. It was slow going since Neil kept stumbling. When they got to the right floor, Georgette found a spot
in the hallway and gently lowered him into a sitting position on
the carpet. Mei-Xing wasn't sure he even knew where he was.

In a nearby room, they found Ishak asleep on the floor next
to a portable crib. When they entered, he immediately awoke,
put a finger to his lips, and gestured to his sleeping child. They
beckoned him toward the door; he got to his feet, quietly ushered
them back into the hallway, and pulled the door shut behind
him.

"How did you find me?" he asked them. "I forgot to leave a note."

"Delia told us," Georgette explained.

"That's your little girl?" Mei-Xing asked.

"Ziya," he said with a grin. Then he hesitated, seeming to struggle with something internally. "Can you . . . open a portal like you did at Silver Creek to send us home?"

"Home?" Georgette repeated.

"To Kabultiloa."

"Oh," she said, deflating. "No, I—I don't think I can. It took everything I had to move all those boxes just a few miles. Even fully rested, I don't think there's any way."

Though Georgette looked upset, Ishak didn't seem surprised. "I will find another way." He glanced at the baggage and Mei-Xing's potted plant. A puzzled look on his face, he asked, "Did you move out of the hotel?"

"We had to," Mei-Xing said.

He tensed. "Why?"

"A bitch," slurred Neil, drawing all their eyes. "A bitch witch." He moved his lips back and forth, opening and closing his mouth. Mei-Xing thought he looked like he was swirling something around in his mouth, trying to decide whether he liked the taste. "Witch bitch," he said, sounding out the words. "Itch switch hitch bitch witch."

"Hush," Georgette said, trying not to laugh. She knelt next to him and he flopped against her, his limbs rubbery. "Nico's on his way here. He'll take you home."

"Home," Neil droned, his head in her hair. "Dome foam roam comb."

405

Ishak looked at Mei-Xing, eyebrows raised. "Who is this man?"

"That's Neil. And we left the hotel because Georgette's mother showed up. Delia scared her off, but she'll come back."

"Is she as bad as that?"

"Like Kivuli Panon," Mei-Xing said simply.

Ishak inhaled sharply. The look in his eyes told Mei-Xing that no further explanation was necessary.

"We will have to find a new place." Sighing, he rubbed his temples. "Give me a few hours. I need to sleep while Ziya sleeps. She cries when she's not being held."

"We?" Mei-Xing asked. "Are you staying with us?"

"Yes."

"Are you sure?" She held his gaze with solemn intensity. "Hazel would love to add a Bultungin or two to her clutch of familiars."

"I understand," he said, nodding, "and it does worry me. But, quite honestly, I have no one else in this country." He glanced at Georgette, seated next to Neil and talking to him softly. "I trust her." He looked at Mei-Xing. "I trust you."

Mei-Xing did not reply. She was still uneasy with the knowledge that Ishak had been willing to sell Georgette to Kazimiera, but after everything she had seen in last few days, she wasn't prepared to carry a grudge. They had been through too much together.

Ishak opened the bedroom door, stepped just inside the room, and gave his daughter a tender look. It amazed Mei-Xing that this was the same man who'd been hellbent on revenge just a day earlier. All the anger and drive seemed to have melted away, leaving behind a weary but solid man ready to do right by his child.

"Let's talk tomorrow," he said.

Mei-Xing nodded, and he pushed the door shut.

A chime drew her attention to Georgette, who was reading the newly arrived text on her phone. "It's Nico," she said. "He's out front."

With each of them hefting one of Neil's arms around her neck, Georgette and Mei-Xing guided him back to the club entrance, where Nico was waiting. Mei-Xing helped Neil get into Mariana's car while Georgette apologized profusely for the damage to the Botanica.

"Where'm I going?" Neil slurred as Mei-Xing buckled his seat belt.

"Home," she said in English, "to sleep."

"*Hmm.* 'Kay." He looked up at her, squinting. "Cool face you're wearing," he said. "S'at magic?"

"Yes. Glamour."

"Huh." He pointed a shaky finger at her. "You did this, right? *Datura?*"

"Yes," she said flatly. "You hurt her. Not sorry."

"S'okay." He patted her hand. "Won't hurt her again. If I do, hit me harder."

Despite a lingering annoyance, Mei-Xing smiled. Neil recognized his bad behavior and intended to be better. No man in her life or Georgette's had ever done anything close. Not only that, he had slammed the door on Hazel. That was unprecedented. She couldn't help but be impressed.

"Behave," she told him. "She see you soon."

She closed the car door and made it back to where Georgette and Nico were talking in time to hear him say something about gifts and money. Mei-Xing was intrigued, but her friend seemed more interested in apologizing than asking questions. She made a mental note to ask about it later.

Empty of guests and staff alike, the only light on Nocturne's ground floor came from the propped-open door to the stairs. Listening to their echoing footsteps, Mei-Xing and Georgette ambled across the nightclub floor, eyes sweeping over the tables and stacked chairs.

"Mei." Though Georgette was whispering, her voice bounced off every wall. "I wanna stay here."

"In San Jose?"

"Yeah." She put her hands in her hair and shook her curls. "After Silver Creek, I thought we'd have to leave, but . . . I like it here."

That didn't surprise Mei-Xing. They had created a life in San Jose. It wasn't the life either of them had thought they wanted, but they had grown into it and from it.

"What about your mother?" she asked. "Are you worried?"

"Terrified. But . . ." Georgette put out her hands, palms up. "She found me. She came to get me. And I'm still here." She smiled, eyes alight with pride. "Screw her." A moment after she spoke those words, her lips drooped, and tears leaked down her cheeks. "Screw her," she rasped.

Mei-Xing pulled her friend into a hug. Georgette clung to her, her body shaking with quiet sobs.

"I know," Mei-Xing whispered. "You mourn the loss of a relationship you wanted and now know for sure you'll never have. I cried when I got to Boston, remember? That was when I was finally sure I would never see my grove again. You're allowed to cry."

With a throaty wail, Georgette unleashed her tears. She wept furiously, hanging on to her friend. Mei-Xing gently lowered her to the floor, never letting go. They huddled together as Georgette's exhausted grief filled the room.

62
Kazimiera

ISHAK'S SECOND DEBT PAYMENT WAS AS DELICIOUS AS THE first. Finishing the meal, Kazimiera felt younger than she had in decades. In all the years she'd spent running this business and others like it, she had seldom had the opportunity to eat her fill in one sitting. Draining a man of every last drop was a luxury that she, a respectable businesswoman, couldn't often afford. A nip of the neck here and nibble of the wrist there kept her healthy, but it didn't satisfy her.

When she emerged from her private bathroom, looking forward to a long day's sleep, she was annoyed to see Georgette in her office, a stream of red magic flowing from her hand, through the pen, and onto a piece of paper. *Sitting at* my *desk, writing on* my *letterhead with* my *pen! The nerve!*

"What are you doing here?" she demanded, hands on her hips.

"I won't stay," Georgette replied without taking her eyes off the paper. There was a harshness to her voice, like she had a sore throat. "I just want to make a deal before I go."

Though petulant and logy, the word "deal" perked up Kazimiera's ears. "What deal?"

Georgette handed her the paper. On it, Kazimiera saw a geas.

"Here's the gist," the witch said, twirling the pen in her fingers. "I will work for you for free on a month-to-month basis, renewed on the first of each month by mutual agreement. In exchange, you will allow Ishak and his daughter to stay in your building and extend to them the same protections and courtesies you give all those under your roof, with no expectation that either one will work." She leaned back in Kazimiera's chair, still twirling the pen. "How does that sound?"

The Vampire swept an appraising eye over her. This was striking behavior. Kazimiera had never known the witch to be so self-assured. She noted that Georgette's eyes were puffy and red—signs of crying. The girl had been through something, but she had come through with fresh determination. Kazimiera respected that.

"The hyena-man and his girl?" she asked. "Not you?"

"I can't stay here," Georgette said, placing the pen on the desk. "My mother will come looking for me. If I'm living here when she does, it puts everyone in this building in danger. She won't look too closely at this place if it's just where I work—but if I'm living here too?" She sniffed and pushed her hair back from her face. "I can't risk that."

The strain on the young woman's face spoke of a complicated history. The particulars didn't interest Kazimiera; simply knowing it existed removed the mystery about Georgette's motivations. That was enough for her.

She let the geas drop; it fluttered to her desk. "Children behave unpredictably," she said. "It's not safe to have an unpredictable element in here."

"She's not even a week old. Hardly a hazard; she can't even lift her head yet."

"Month-to-month creates a lot of uncertainty," Kazimiera pressed. "Commit to six months to start out. We can go month-to-month after that."

"Three months."

Kazimiera sauntered across the room, arms crossed over her chest. "Three months isn't long enough. Six—"

"Three," the witch said, low and clear, "with the caveat that if Ishak complains about unsatisfactory living conditions or poor treatment, the deal's off."

The Vampire turned away to hide her scowl. She was not in a good bargaining position: she needed a witch and Georgette was her only option. *Well*, she thought, drawing her lips into a professional smile, *I've made worse deals.*

She turned around. "Done."

63  Mei-Xing

ON HER PREVIOUS VISIT, MEI-XING HAD SEEN ONLY THE first three floors of Club Nocturne, which were strictly for the business. Things got more interesting on the fourth floor and above, where the living quarters were housed—every inch devoted to the Fae and their particular needs.

The temperature, humidity, and lighting varied wildly from room to room. One room had no furniture, only large, flat rocks under heat lamps. Another was kept so cold that the windows were heavily frosted, icicles dangling from the water taps. The room Mei-Xing found most appealing was one shared by a herd of tiny fairies where moss grew on the walls, ferns sprouted from a wall-to-wall floor mat, and vines dangled from the ceiling. While allowing the fairies to groom her by peeling her chipped bark and moisturizing her brown moss, the Nymph finally understood why all who lived there spoke so highly of Kazimiera: she might be using the Fae as free labor, but she was also spending oodles to keep them comfortable. She was certainly a complicated woman.

Some hours after dawn, when the staff was settling in to

sleep for the day, Georgette returned carrying a bag full of Ishak's clothes.

"She agreed?" Mei-Xing asked.

Georgette nodded.

"What terms?"

"Three months, and then we go month-to-month."

Mei-Xing sighed. It was not ideal, but that was expected. "Which apartment?"

"7B." Georgette pointed down the hall. "It's the apartment that the former witch-in-residence, Martin, used to live in. Did you clear it with Ishak?"

"He doesn't love the plan, but he admits there's probably no safer place in the city for his little girl."

Georgette opened the door to 7B, revealing a perfectly ordinary one-bedroom apartment. It was sparsely furnished and had plain white walls, but it was warm and inviting nevertheless—perfectly suitable for a widower father and his child. Mei-Xing opened the blinds, letting in the light. The sun warmed her skin and brightened up the bare room.

"Once he wakes up"—Georgette dropped Ishak's things to the floor—"we'll help him get Ziya and her crib set up in here."

Mei-Xing nodded. "Then we'll go find a place of our own."

The two women plopped down on the sofa, side by side, and exhaled in unison. The sounds of people walking by down on the street drifted up through the window, a distant but constant buzz.

"Think we could find an apartment with a garden?" Georgette asked, letting her head slump onto the Nymph's shoulder. "Or a patio? We should really get you more plants. You've just had the one since we left Boston."

"Another plant or two and a sunny window is enough," Mei-Xing said, resting her cheek against the top of Georgette's head. "We need to find a space you can make into your own—a place that will help your power consolidate like a nest around you and make you stronger. Something like that would be good security against Hazel."

"Yeah," Georgette said lazily. "A patio would be nice, though."

"A place of power with a patio not too far from Nocturne," Mei-Xing summarized.

"Perfect." Still leaning against her friend, Georgette slid her phone out of her bag and held it up for them both to see. "Let's chill here and look up apartments for rent."

Mei-Xing nodded, feeling her fears melt away. After months of continuous uncertainty, it was a joy to simply sit with her friend and make plans for the future. There would be worries and challenges ahead, no doubt—but for the time being, she was content to fantasize about the good life.

Epilogue

Senji gripped the railing of the fifth-floor balcony, gazing through the sliding glass door into the corner apartment at the two humans struggling to maneuver a sofa through the apartment door.

"Babe," grunted Neil, his voice muffled by the glass balcony door, "can't you just, y'know, magic this thing inside?"

From hundreds of feet above, San Jose stretched from horizon to horizon under her feet. Vaguely, she sensed the living chosen.

"Transportation spells are super draining," Georgette panted. "I'm already using magic to make it lighter."

As their deaths grew close, each signal grew louder and more frequent, guiding her to the target.

"Seriously? It's heavier than this? What the hell's it made of, concrete?"

Eyes closed, she floated, drifted, listening to her radar.

Mei-Xing slid open the glass door. Next to the tall marijuana plant on the balcony, she placed a pot of dirt, held her hand above it, and gestured. A tiny green seedling wormed its way up from the depths.

Another ping intruded into her mind—distant but fast. It wasn't one of her chosen —not a chosen at all—but she had homed in on this signal long ago.

Glancing around, Senji saw four other pots with young plants stretching toward the sky. "Expanding your garden?" he asked Mei-Xing in croaks and clicks.

Never before, however, had she heard it so rapid.

"Yes," Mei-Xing said. "This balcony is not the patio we hoped for, but it's very nice."

Senji.

He quickly refocused his attention. Through Delia's eyes, he saw the entire city at their feet. *I thought our schedule was clear for the day.*

.

It's time.

A sense of gravitas and expectation filled him, the feeling of a long-awaited destiny finally about to be fulfilled. He had not felt the like since he aimed his plane at Delia's ship and entered his final dive. *Will we get there in time?*

*We will, I promise. Tell the
witch. Have her give us ten
minutes before dampening our
power.* She paused, feeling
his heart race. *Are you ready?*

Her care centered him, and
joy rose in his chest. *I have
been ready for a lifetime.*

"*Sofu?*"

The voice was kind, full of love and concern. Nestled in the
pillowy folds of his adjustable bed, the old man stirred and
opened his eyes. He looked first at the middle-aged woman in
pink scrubs who was checking the continually beeping machines
next to him; then his gaze drifted to the source of the voice.

After squinting through cloudy pupils, he lifted one trembling hand—the skin was so wizened that every vein showed—
and gingerly reached out for the young woman in the doorway.

Smiling, she came forward and tenderly wrapped his hand in
both of hers.

"Where?" the old man rasped. He coughed, then licked his
dry lips. "Where . . . are . . . the children?"

"My girls are at school, *Sofu*, remember? They were here to
see you yesterday."

After a moment's pause, the old man nodded his gray head.
"Yes," he said, "of course. And your father? Where is my son?"

"My husband is driving him." She gave his fingers a gentle squeeze. "They will be here any minute."

The old man's eyes slid shut, as if holding them open required great effort. Ragged coughs suddenly racked his skeletal frame.

Wearing an expression of aching concern, the young woman touched her grandfather's cheek. "Can't you give him something?" she asked the nurse. "It sounds so painful."

"I've done all I can," was the placid reply. "It won't be long now."

Tears formed in the young woman's eyes, but she made no move to wipe them away. Instead, she held on to her grandfather's hand and listened to his fragile breaths. Outside the window, a large black bird perched on the sill and watched, waiting.

Following a chime on her phone, the granddaughter left the room, promising that she would be back in a moment. The nurse continued to monitor her patient.

With a muffled groan, the old man rolled his head toward the window. For a moment, he only stared. Then, slowly, his cloudy eyes filled with light.

"*Oniisan!*" he rasped.

The nurse glanced up. Her patient's gaze was fixed on a spot near the window. She glanced around the room, shrugged, and returned to her notes.

"She's probably heard elderly patients cry out like this dozens of times," Delia said. With Georgette draining their power, her armor had been replaced by her old uniform. She crossed the room to the living woman's side and waved a hand in front of her unseeing eyes. "God knows I heard plenty of wounded men cry out for their mamas."

"*Oniisan!*" the old man said again, reaching out with one hand.

"It's okay, Keiji," Senji, now in human form, said. He leaned closer to the old man but did not take his hand. "I've come to see you."

"You're here," Keiji said. He scanned his older brother from head to foot. "So young!"

"I never got the chance to grow old." Senji smirked playfully at his brother. "We aren't all as lucky as you, old man."

Keiji chuckled but then began to cough. The nurse moved to his side, a glass of water in her hand. After helping him to drink, she tried to take his vitals, but he waved her away.

"My brother Senji is visiting me," he said, pointing to the spirit she couldn't see. "He died in World War II."

"I see," the nurse said indulgently.

"He's wearing his flight uniform. I kept a photograph of him on my wall all my life."

"*Hmm.*"

"Go on," Keiji wheezed, gesturing her away. "Let us talk."

"Okay," she said, smiling professionally. "Don't strain yourself."

"*Oniisan,*" he said, looking at Senji again, "I have pain."

"I know," Senji said.

"Will my time come soon?"

"Yes."

He sighed deeply, seemingly glad. "Will it hurt?"

"No."

"That's good. I've had enough pain." He looked around, eyes straining. "Where are our parents? Our brothers? Didn't they come with you?"

421

"I'm on a different path than the rest of our family," Senji said.

"And me?" Keiji asked. "What path will I take?"

"You will follow them." Senji smiled, a little sadly. "I'm just here to see you off."

Keiji's granddaughter reentered the room, her husband and father on her heels. The old man acknowledged them but quickly returned his attention to Senji.

"My family," he explained.

"You're fortunate to have them," Senji said as the nurse calmly explained to the young woman that her grandfather was losing touch with reality, talking to dead relatives. "And they've been fortunate to have you." He took a step back to make room for the nephew he'd never met. "Spend your last minutes with them, Keiji," he said, moving to the corner next to Delia. "We will have time afterward."

The minutes passed in a tearful stride. Before long, Keiji's pulse slowed to a crawl, his breath grew shallow, and his eyes closed for the last time. The nurse donned a stethoscope, listened to his chest, and felt for his pulse. When she confirmed that he was gone, his granddaughter collapsed, sobbing, in her husband's arms. Her father, Keiji's son, leaned over the body with his head in his hands. The nurse quietly left, allowing the family space to grieve.

A great black shadow leaked into the room, unseen by the grieving family. Reaching a dark appendage past the mourners, it lifted a colorful, ethereal fog out of Keiji's body. The small cloud quickly formed into a human shape—that of a man.

From within the shadow's depths emerged a long, curved

blade. The black entity raised it, poised to slice at the thin, ephemeral cord that connected the spirit to its flesh. As the blade swung down, a silver flash cut between the dead man and the shadow. Still in her Navy nurse uniform, Delia stood next to Keiji's grandson-in-law, her sword holding the sickle at bay.

"Not yet," she said to the black shape.

The shadow shuddered and a whine so soft that it was barely audible over the wild sobs of Keiji's granddaughter escaped its depths. It raised its weapon a second time; again, Delia deflected it.

"Not yet," she repeated, her voice firm.

The shadow shrieked. The sound had no effect on the dead man's loved ones, but it set Delia's teeth on edge. Rippling, the shadow lunged at her. She dodged but it grazed her cheek, sending an icy burn through her.

She gripped her weapon. "All right," she said, a grin spreading over her face. "Come on, then." She launched herself over the deathbed and—bellowing a battle cry, her sword held aloft—dove at the thing.

Keiji's soul watched the ensuing battle with a nervous look on his face.

"Keiji."

The spirit turned—and, seeing Senji again, smiled. As he jumped into his brother's embrace, his image shifted, suddenly becoming young.

Senji closed his eyes, elated. The sight of his brother's boyish face and the strength of his hug sparked a million memories. For just a moment, he felt like a young man again—freshly home

Alison Levy

from the war, greeted by the family who loved him. That honey-kissed feeling lit up his soul, making him ache for all that he had lost. It had been three-quarters of a century since his last contact with Keiji. And this would be the last time.

Keiji stepped back and looked his brother in the eye. "*Oni-isan*," he said, his voice bright and effortless, "the pain is gone."

"Death came for you," Senji explained, nodding at the black-ness.

"*Shinigami*," Keiji said, his eyes on the shadow. "Incredible."

"It will lead you onward soon."

"Where?"

"Where all must go."

A powerful yell cut the air, startling Keiji. Senji turned to see Delia slicing through the liquid blackness, severing a piece from the whole. It trembled in the air, quivering like gelatin, and then broke into droplets that rained sideways to reunite with the rest.

The shadow stopped, stiffened, and shot like an arrow toward Keiji. The ghost gasped, but before he could move out of its path Delia was already springing between them, forcing the shadow to veer aside.

"Who is this woman?" Keiji asked, watching Delia with amazement. "Is she a nurse or a soldier?"

"Both and neither. She's my partner. She's here to give us time." Senji placed his hands on his brother's shoulders. "The greatest gift I could hope for." Choking on the lump in his throat, he smiled. "I have missed more than seventy years of your life. Tell me everything."

The fathomless black eventually evaded Delia and sliced the silver cord that connected Keiji's soul to his body. The shadow then began to fade into oblivion, taking his spirit with it.

The brothers stood half a step apart, holding each other's gaze, as death separated them for the second time.

Senji continued staring long after Keiji was gone. The loss clawed at every fiber of his being, but he welcomed the sensation. It was the first time since his death that he'd had something to lose.

Delia moved slowly to his side. "Hell of a fight," she said wearily, her sword still in her hand. "Actually hurts where it touched me. I'm sorry I couldn't hold it off longer."

"You did very well," Senji said, his voice wistful.

"Was it enough?"

"It was enough." He tore his eyes from the last spot where his brother had stood and smiled at her. "Thank you."

"You're welcome." After thrusting the point of her sword into the floor, leaving it standing at attention, she tugged at her disheveled uniform. "It'll be your turn to do battle next."

Senji gripped the hilt of her weapon and pulled it free. For a moment, he stared at his reflection in the blade, his eyes drinking in the sight of his long-absent human features. Then he tested the weight of the sword in his hand.

"I need practice," he said. "The only weapons I've wielded in decades are my talons and beak. How much time do we have?"

"Well," Delia said, "my little sister was always a feisty one. She's a great-grandma five times over and she still complains that people around her walk too slowly." Delia listened to her internal radar—the faint, steady ping that was her baby sister, now a spritely old lady. "I'd say there's a year or two left in her."

"A year or two to have human hands," he mused, swinging the sword in sweeping arcs until the blade sang. "That's worth risking Valhalla's wrath. If," he added, "the witch agrees to maintain the *Hathiya* that long." He handed the sword back to Delia.

"I saw the look on her face when she saw her mother." She sheathed the sword. "If we tried to break the bond now, I think she would beg us to stay."

Senji looked down at his branded ankle and nodded. "We made a good bargain, Delia."

"Yes," she replied. "Will you feel the same if Valhalla comes for us?"

"Yes," he answered at once. "This was worth any price. And I will be sure to give you the same opportunity."

She smiled at him, and he beamed back. He held out his hand to her and she seized it.

Armored once again, she clutched the hilt of her sword.	
	A raven once again, he perched on her shoulder.
"*Ganbatte kudasai*, Senji."	
	"*Lâche pas la patate*, Delia."
Together, they took flight.	Together, they took flight.

Acknowledgments

Thank you to my husband, Matt. Your love and support helped me grow a spine.

Thank you to my son, Eric. I'm doing my best to break the cycle so I can watch you grow up strong and happy.

Thank you to Eileen McFalls, Barbara Levin, and the Women Writers of the Triad critique group. I continue to grow as a writer because of their time and effort.

Thank you to the staff of SparkPress for polishing this book into its final form.

Thank you.

About the Author

Alison Levy lives in Greensboro, North Carolina, with her husband, son, and variety of pets. When she's not writing or doing mom things, she crochets, gardens, and walks her collies.

SELECTED TITLES FROM SPARKPRESS

SparkPress is an independent boutique publisher delivering high-quality, entertaining, and engaging content that enhances readers' lives, with a special focus on female-driven work. www.gosparkpress.com

Caley Cross and the Hadeon Drop, J. S. Rosen, $16.95, 978-1-68463-053-0. When thirteen-year-old Caley Cross, an orphan with a dark power, is guided by a jumpsuit-wearing mole into another world—Erinath—she finds a place deeply rooted in nature where the people have animal-like powers and she is a Crown Princess—but she soon learns that the most powerful evil being in *any* world is waiting for her there.

Wendy Darling: Volume 1, Stars, Colleen Oakes. $17, 978-1-94071-6-96-4. Loved by two men—a steady and handsome bookseller's son from London, and Peter Pan, a dashing and dangerous charmer—Wendy realizes that Neverland, like her heart, is a wild place, teeming with dark secrets and dangerous obsessions.

Above the Star: The 8th Island Trilogy, Book 1, Alexis Chute. $16.95, 978-1-943006-56-4. *Above the Star* is an epic fantasy adventure experienced through the eyes of three unlikely heroes transported to a new world: senior citizen Archie; his daughter-in-law, Tessa; and his fourteen-year-old granddaughter, Ella. In this otherworldly realm, all interests are at war, all love is unrequited, and everyone is left to unravel the truth of who they really are.

The Thorn Queen: A Novel, Elise Holland. $16.95, 978-1-943006-79-3. Twelve-year-old Meylyne longs to impress her brilliant, sorceress mother—but when she accidentally breaks one of Glendoch's First Rules, she accomplishes the opposite of that. Forced to flee, the only way she may return home is with a cure for Glendoch's diseased prince.

Red Sun: The Legends of Orkney, Book 1, Alane Adams. $17, 978-1-940716-24-4. After learning that his mom is a witch and his missing father is a true Son of Odin, 12-year-old Sam Baron must travel through a stonefire to the magical realm of Orkney on a quest to find his missing friends and stop an ancient curse.

The Goddess Twins: A Novel, Yodassa Williams. $16.95, 978-1-68463-032-5. Days before their eighteenth birthday, Arden and Aurora's mother goes missing and they discover they belong to a family of Caribbean deities. Can these goddess twins uncover their evil grandfather's plot in time to save their mother, themselves, and the free world?